Praise for the novels of Delores Fossen

"This is a feel good, heartwarming story of love, family and happy endings for all."
—*Harlequin Junkie* on *Christmas at Colts Creek*

"An entertaining and satisfying read...that I can highly recommend."
—*Books & Spoons* on *Wild Nights in Texas*

"The plot delivers just the right amount of emotional punch and happily ever after."
—*Publishers Weekly* on *Lone Star Christmas*

"Delores Fossen takes you on a wild Texas ride with a hot cowboy."
—B.J. Daniels, *New York Times* bestselling author

"Clear off space on your keeper shelf, Fossen has arrived."
—Lori Wilde, *New York Times* bestselling author

"This is classic Delores Fossen and a great read."
—*Harlequin Junkie* on *His Brand of Justice*

"This book is a great start to the series. Looks like there's plenty of good reading ahead."
—*Harlequin Junkie* on *Tangled Up in Texas*

"An amazing, breathtaking and vastly entertaining family saga, filled with twists and unexpected turns. Cowboy fiction at its best."
—*Books & Spoons* on *The Last Rodeo*

To see the complete list of titles available from
Delores Fossen, please visit deloresfossen.com.

DELORES FOSSEN

TWILIGHT AT WILD SPRINGS

CANARY STREET PRESS

**CANARY
STREET
PRESS™**

Recycling programs
for this product may
not exist in your area.

ISBN-13: 978-1-335-50688-7

Twilight at Wild Springs
Copyright © 2023 by Delores Fossen

Tempted at Thoroughbred Lake
First published in 2023. This edition published in 2023.

Copyright © 2023 by Delores Fossen

For questions and comments about the quality of this book, please contact us at CustomerService@Harlequin.com.

Canary Street Press
22 Adelaide St. West, 41st Floor
Toronto, Ontario M5H 4E3, Canada
CanaryStPress.com

Printed and bound in Barcelona, Spain by CPI Black Print

CONTENTS

TWILIGHT
AT
WILD SPRINGS

CHAPTER ONE

LILY PARKMAN HIT the brakes when she turned into her driveway and spotted Sherlock Holmes and the *Hunger Games'* Katniss Everdeen in her front yard. Well, they were people dressed like those characters, anyway.

And Sherlock and Katniss weren't alone.

There were at least two dozen other people milling around the yard as if such milling around in that particular area was perfectly normal. It wasn't.

"What the heck?" Lily muttered, automatically going with the milder profanity that she'd trained herself to use because her fourteen-year-old daughter, Hayden, was seated right next to her in the truck. But there were some much harsher curse words going through Lily's head.

Some mountain-sized questions, too.

Despite the clothes and getups, Lily recognized every single one of the folks doing the milling around. Not hard to do since she'd lived her entire life in Last Ride, Texas, and knew all the residents. However, to the best of her knowledge, many of these folks had never paid a visit to her Wild Springs Ranch.

"What's going on?" Hayden asked.

Lily thumbed back through her memory to recall if today was her birthday and if this was some sort of surprise party. An unwanted one. But her birthday was months off. Ditto for Hayden's. And months off, too, for her ranch foreman, Jonas Buchanan, and his stepson, Eli, who lived on the ranch grounds just a quarter of a mile from her own house.

Nope. No birthdays. No anniversaries. So, either she'd won the lottery, unknowingly become a celebrity or... Lily stopped and mentally thumbed back through another date.

Since it was the first of August and just past 7:00 p.m., this crowd could have something to do with the Last Ride Society—aka a group of her Parkman kin who had way too much time on their hands, more time than she did, anyway. But many of her kin would say the Last Ride Society was the ultimate tribute to their ancestor and town founder, Hezzie Parkman.

Lily knew the spiel as well as the faces of those in her yard and on her porch. Hezzie had formed the Last Ride Society before her death in 1950 as a way for her descendants to preserve the area's history. The woman hoped to accomplish that by having a quarterly drawing so that a Parkman would then in turn draw the name of a local tombstone to research. Research that required the Parkman who'd drawn the name to dig into the deceased person's history, take a photo of the tombstone and write a report for all the town to read.

The date fit for the Last Ride Society meeting since the quarterly drawing was done on the first of the months of February, May, August and November. The timing fit, too, since the drawing was usually done around 6:00 p.m. So, maybe her guests were all there to tell her that she was this quarter's drawer and to give her the name of the drawee since Lily hadn't attended the meeting.

Her stomach tightened.

Oh, heck. She hoped she hadn't drawn Maddie Buchanan's name. The woman had been married to Jonas and had died two years earlier from cancer. He was still grieving for her, and researching Maddie would only take jabs at that grief.

At least the name couldn't be one that would jab at her own grief. Griff Buchanan. He'd died years ago and had not only been Jonas's brother, but he'd also been the love of Lily's life.

Well, maybe he had been.

Since Griff had died when they were teenagers, maybe that love would have faded by now. Still, Lily wouldn't have to take that particular trip down memory lane because her own twin sister, Nola, had drawn Griff's name a year ago, and those jabs of grief had had some time to fade.

Lily took her foot off the brake and inched closer to the house. The sound of her approaching truck obviously got the attention of, well, everyone since they all stopped milling around and turned in her direction. Some of them cheered, and others came rushing toward her.

Crap.

This couldn't be good. Now that she'd gotten a better look at the expressions of her visitors, Lily could see the downright giddiness coming off them in gleeful waves. She saw something else, too. Glancing in her rearview mirror, she spotted her sisters, Nola and Lorelei, pull up in Lorelei's car. They came to a stop behind her and proceeded to barrel out. Yes, barrel. They were obviously in a hurry.

Alarmed they were there, Lily got out as well and turned toward them, ignoring the shouts of welcome and congrats from the others. "Is everything okay?" Lily couldn't ask her sisters fast enough. "Are the kids all right?"

It was a reasonable question since Nola had a three-month-old son and Lorelei had a nearly two-year-old daughter, but her sisters just seemed puzzled that she'd gone there with her response. *Welcome to the club.* Lily felt like a poster child for puzzlement right now.

And she got another gut punch of concern.

Even though Lorelei and Nola were heading toward her and the crowd of visitors were converging on her from behind, Lily glanced at her phone that she'd silenced while Hayden and she had been doing some errands and having an early dinner in nearby San Antonio. She goggled at the sheer number of texts and calls she'd missed. They probably equaled the number of visitors she had right now, but none was from her mother, Evangeline. So, all was probably well with her.

"It's Hezzie," Nola said, causing Lily's attention to snap to her twin sister.

Before she could grasp the unlikelihood of what she was doing, Lily glanced around as if expecting to see her great-great-great grandmother's ghost since the woman had been dead for over seventy years.

"Hezzie," someone in the crowd verified while others kept doling out congratulations to Lily.

And Lily got it then.

"I'm the drawer, and Hezzie's the drawee," Lily grumbled, trying to wrap her mind around that.

Many verbally confirmed it, and some patted her on the back. Others did little bouncy dances around the grass. Katniss, aka Frankie Parkman, the owner of the town's costume shop and tat salon, shouted, "I volunteer as tribute."

That got some laughs, and the president of the Last Ride Society, Alma Parkman, stepped through the crowd to reach Lily. She took hold of Lily's hand and gave it a few enthusiastic pumps and pats.

"Congratulations, congratulations, congratulations," Alma gushed. The woman was in her eighties, but clearly had a lot of energy since she was bobbling around in glee as well.

Lily couldn't muster up the matching enthusiasm or glee, but she did have some questions. "In the past seventy-odd years of the Last Ride Society, no one has ever drawn Hezzie's name?"

"Nope," Alma confirmed. "Her name was one of the first in the drawing bowl, and over the decades, hundreds of names have been added. Now you'll get to do the highest honor a Parkman can have by researching her."

Others joined in on that *highest honor*, and one of the Sherlocks, Derwin Parkman, threaded his way to her. "Of course, the Sherlock's Snoops will help you in any way we can."

This was a little out of the realm of the Sherlock's Snoops, a club formed to investigate mysteries. Lily suspected there were no mysteries left in Hezzie's life, but she gave a polite thanks to Derwin anyway.

"I'm sure you'll do Hezzie proud," Alma went on, and while she slid her arm around Lily's waist, she turned to the others. "Now, why don't y'all head home so Lily here can get started? I need to go over the research rules with her so she can dive right into doing the report."

That brought on some mumbled groans from those who clearly wanted to stretch out this moment a little or a lot longer, but the crowd started moseying toward their vehicles. Alma waved at each one, smiled and kept waving and smiling until they'd all driven away. Then the woman released a long, weary breath, and both her smile and enthusiasm went south.

"Let me get the research packet from my car, and then we'll have a little chat," Alma muttered on a sigh and headed toward her vintage VW that she'd had painted to resemble a turtle.

The sudden change in the woman's mood baffled Lily, but she supposed this might be a situation of catching the biggest fish in the proverbial pond. Everything else after this would be a small haul, and some Parkmans might lose interest in the drawings.

"Oh, there's Eli riding one of the new mares," Hayden said, and her daughter immediately headed in the direction of the pasture where Eli was astride an Andalusian horse that Lily knew had been delivered to the ranch earlier that day.

"A lot of people will bug the crap out of you about drawing Hezzie's name," Nola remarked, speaking what Lily knew was the God's honest truth. As Nola was prone to do. "That's why Lorelei and I came right over."

"We'll try to run some interference for you so you don't have a constant flood of people showing up to ask you about the research," Lorelei added.

"I appreciate that," Lily told them.

And she did. That was the God's honest truth, too, and since both her sisters had gone through this, they had some experience in research pitfalls of the Last Ride Society. Still, Lorelei and Nola had busy lives, what with their babies and businesses. Nola was a glass artist, and Lorelei owned the shop that sold Nola's pieces and other glass art.

"But don't worry if you don't have the time," Lily added. "I suspect I won't have much to do since Hezzie's life is probably an open book…"

Her words trailed off. So did her attention on the subject of Hezzie. Her sisters' attention shifted as well, and the reason for that was the hot, hunky guy who walked out of the barn.

Jonas.

He'd stripped off his shirt, baring a muscled chest that was toned, tanned and perfect for being bared. Mercy, the man could give hot cowboy cover models an inferiority complex with that body and the rest of the package that went with it. The midnight black hair, sizzling green eyes and a face that had to be a benchmark for "hot guy" faces.

"So can't believe you haven't tapped that," Nola muttered.

Lily automatically frowned. "So can't believe you'd think I'd *tap* my ranch foreman. A man who works for me and lives just a stone's throw away."

But since Lily wasn't blind and had normal urges, she had fantasized about such things. Then again, probably every woman in Last Ride had had some smutty fantasies about Jonas. About his brothers, too, who had those same dreamy looks and bodies.

"You're lusting over your own brother-in-law," Lily pointed out to her sisters.

"Looking at, not lusting," Lorelei automatically corrected in her usual prim voice. The rest of her was prim, too, with her blond hair tumbling perfectly over the shoulders of her perfectly fitted turquoise-colored top. "I'm allowed to look."

Nola made a grunting sound of agreement. No primness for her. Her long blond hair was scooped in a disordered ponytail, with just as many strands falling out as there were gathered up. No makeup and, judging from her stained jeans and old Roper boots with burnt specks, she'd been blowing her glass art right before she'd made this visit.

"Besides, Wyatt will benefit from any lustful urges I get from gawking at a hot guy," Nola added.

Wyatt, Nola's husband and the love of her life. In their

case, that particular label was actually true since they'd started their romance way back in high school, and after some bumps and hitches, some of which had been plenty serious, their relationship had continued and led to marriage.

Lily cleared her throat, looking for a change of subject. A change of mindset, too, since she didn't want to be mentally stripping off any more of Jonas's clothes. "Where are Stellie and Charlie?" Stellie was Lorelei's daughter, and Charlie was Nola's son.

"With Dax and Wyatt," Nola answered.

Dax and Wyatt Buchanan were not only Jonas's brothers, but they were also married to Lily's siblings, which made this sort of a *Seven Brides for Seven Brothers* deal. Minus Jonas and her, of course, since they'd never ever hooked up in any kind of way. Probably never would, either, because while Jonas was hands-off for Lily, she was no doubt hands-off for him, too, because she had been his kid brother's girlfriend.

"Dax is having a daughter-daddy playdate with Stellie," Lorelei said, keeping her gaze on Jonas as he made his way toward them.

Nola groaned softly when Jonas pulled on his shirt, covering those amazing abs and six-pack. "Well, since Alma got rid of your visitors, I guess our services aren't needed right now."

"Yes, but call us if things get too wild," Lorelei added. She brushed a kiss on Lily's cheek. Nola gave Lily a light punch on the arm, and her sisters headed back to Lorelei's car.

Alma was parked right next to them, and the woman appeared to be looking through file folders in a box. *Appeared to be*, Lily noted. But Alma also kept glancing back at her in a way that made Lily think she was waiting for everyone else to leave so they could talk alone. Maybe Alma intended to emphasize to Lily just how important this research would be.

"You okay?" Jonas asked Lily when he stepped up beside her.

Lily nodded, and because she was still doing some lusting, she didn't look up at him. Best not to make eye contact until she was certain she'd temporarily squashed those smutty thoughts about him.

"I got Hezzie's name in the Last Ride Society drawing," Lily explained.

"Yeah, I heard. I was checking fences in the east pasture when I got a call from Larry, whose wife was at the meeting. I rode back because I thought you might need help getting rid of the folks coming here. Then I saw you had it all under control."

Larry Davidson, one of the horse trainers, who was married to Lily's distant cousin, Ellie, and yes, Ellie would have definitely been at the drawing and probably would have come with the crowd of well-wishers if she hadn't had to get back to their twin toddlers.

"When I first got the call from Larry," Jonas went on, "I thought he was going to tell me that you'd drawn Maddie's name."

Lily made a quick sound of agreement. "I thought the same thing when I spotted the crowd." She didn't add they'd dodged a bullet by it not being Maddie because she had a bad feeling in the pit of her stomach there might be a bullet of a different kind headed her way.

"I think it would have been hard on Eli to have Maddie's life dissected," Jonas added.

"Yes," she verified. Because such dissecting would have brought up her death.

"What's Alma doing?" he asked, tipping his head to the woman. Since only Alma's overalls-clad butt and legs were showing, Jonas no doubt recognized her from her car.

"Getting some research stuff on Hezzie." Lily didn't add that Alma was also acting weird. Then again, Alma had begun her stand-up comic career at a point in her life when most people would have been winding down, so weird was usually Alma's default behavior.

"Alma, you need help carrying that?" Jonas called out to her.

"Nope. It's not heavy. I'm just making sure it's all here before I give it to Lily." Alma glanced back at them and kept aiming those glances at her while she continued to thumb through the box. It seemed to Lily, though, that Alma was stalling more than verifying the box's contents.

Since Jonas was studying Alma, too, Lily expected him to remark on her odder-than-usual behavior. But he didn't. "Once Alma's gone, we need to talk," Jonas said, keeping his voice low. "I found something in the mailbox."

Now Lily had to risk that eye contact when she turned toward him. "What?"

Her mind started doing more whirling with speculation. Some kind of prank maybe, like poop? After all, she had a teenage daughter and Jonas had a teenage stepson, so one of their kids' *friends* could have thought that was a fun way to pass the last week of summer break.

Jonas didn't answer because Alma chose that exact moment to drag the box from her back seat and head toward them. Despite Alma's assurance that it wasn't heavy, Jonas hurried to help her with it.

"Thanks bunches," Alma said. "If you want to go ahead and set it on Lily's porch, that'd be great."

Of course, Jonas didn't refuse, but Lily saw the suspicion on his face and was sure it was on hers as well. Alma clearly had something she wanted to tell Lily in private.

As Nola and Lorelei had done, Alma watched Jonas as he took the box from her and walked toward the porch. The woman shook her head.

"Not sure how you can get work done when you've got a view like that," Alma remarked.

The *view* was Jonas's butt, which she knew was just as prime as the rest of him. The fit of his jeans verified that.

Alma fanned herself, and then, as if snapping herself out of a lust-induced trance, she cleared her throat and swiveled back to Lily. Her expression went into the "total serious" mode.

"Full disclosure," Alma said after an extremely windy sigh. "Every quarter before the drawing, I make sure to shove Hezzie's name all the way to the bottom of the bowl."

Because of all the speculation Lily had already done over Alma's oddball mood, that didn't come as a surprise. "Because now that Hezzie's name has been drawn, you think people might lose interest in the Last Ride Society."

Alma blinked as if that thought had never occurred to her. Then her forehead bunched up. "No, I put Hezzie's name at the bottom of the bowl because I never wanted it to be drawn. *Never ever*," she emphasized.

Now Lily had to shake her head. "I don't understand."

"I know, but I'm about to explain it to you." Alma gave another of those windy sighs. "Girl, we got to be very, very careful about this big-assed can of worms you're about to open."

CHAPTER TWO

JONAS SET THE box of file folders and letters on the porch and looked back at Alma and Lily. Judging from their expressions, they were in the throes of a serious conversation. One that Alma's body language suggested she wanted to stay just between them. So, Jonas headed to his office in the main barn.

When he'd taken the job as Lily's ranch manager eight years ago, she'd suggested converting one of the rooms in her sprawling three-story Victorian house into an office for him, but Jonas had instead chosen to create one in the barn. He hadn't wanted to mix business with Lily's living space. He'd learned with Lily that it was best to establish personal boundaries and keep them.

Not always easy to do.

But so far, so good. There'd been times during the past two years when the grief over Maddie's death had been chewing him to bits, and it would have been so easy to turn to the comforting shoulder that Lily would have no doubt offered. However, comforting shoulders often came with an enormous price tag that he was pretty sure neither Lily nor he wanted to pay.

Couldn't pay.

Jonas didn't care much for the mushy-sounding term *soulmate*, but that was what Maddie had been. And it was what Lily had been for his brother Griff. It didn't matter that Lily had gotten involved with Cam Dalton and had his child. That had likely only happened because Griff died from suicide when Lily and he were nineteen, and Lily had sought out that comforting shoulder from her pal Cam.

If Jonas needed proof about that high price tag for such comfort, he only had to look at Lily. She'd gotten involved with Cam, had his daughter and then Cam had abandoned both of them when Hayden had been just a baby. It'd no doubt given Lily a heartbreak on top of the heartbreak of losing Griff.

Jonas knew way too much about heartbreaks. Not just from losing Maddie. It was the way he'd lost her.

For months before Maddie died, Jonas had noticed that she was tired all the time and that she'd been having night sweats. He had asked her to go to the doctor, but he sure as heck hadn't pushed her to make that appointment to have some tests done. And because he hadn't pushed, it had been too late by the time she'd finally sought medical attention. Jonas had ended up watching her die as the cancer spread. Eli had, too, and Jonas knew the boy was still grieving. Both of them always would.

With that sour thought doing a number on his mood, Jonas made his way through the barn, taking in the scent of the horses, the fresh hay and the leather from the saddles in the tack room.

This helped, and yeah, the location of his office suited him just fine.

Being near the horses always helped, too, and Lily and he had built something here by raising some fine Andalusians and Arabians with stellar champion bloodlines. Their breed stock had given them more than mere comfortable livings and put the Wild Springs Ranch on the proverbial map. Jonas could have done that on his own, of course, but the success had happened a whole lot faster because of Lily and him working together on this.

Thankfully, Lily had never made him feel like an employee. If she had, he would have been long gone. She'd not only given him an equal part in running the ranch, but she had also shared the profits equally with him as well. Lily had even sold him shares in the Wild Springs and allowed him to buy the land where he'd built a home for Eli and him.

Lily would have gladly given him the land and the shares. Offers she'd made multiple times, but Jonas had figured that kind of gift could put a kink in their working relationship. He hadn't wanted any kinks or dents in that, and in the end, Lily had sold him the land and 49 percent of the shares for fair market prices.

Jonas opened his office door and welcomed the cool air from the AC. This part of Texas could be hotter than hell in August, and that heat didn't ease up much just because the sun was about to set.

There was a stack of invoices on his desk just waiting for him to deal with before heading home, but Jonas had barely moved toward the desk to get started on them when he heard a sound. Sort of a moan. Since none of the ranch hands were on the schedule to be in the barn, he went back out. And heard it again along with some whispering this time.

Jonas followed the sounds to the supply room at the far back of the barn, and he threw open the door. A split second after doing that, he was so sorry he had. Because he saw something he definitely hadn't wanted to see.

Eli and Hayden in a lip-lock.

Jonas made a strangled sound of his own and cursed, which clearly got their attention because both whirled around to face him. They could have been the poster kids for guilty looks. And there was a reason for that. They might have been fourteen, but they had to know the ranch foreman wouldn't want his son kissing the boss's daughter.

Hell.

What now? Jonas couldn't even think of anything to say. Wasn't sure he could form words because he had seemingly developed a severe case of lockjaw.

"Uh, we were just talking," Eli blurted out.

It was the worst lie in the history of bad lies, but again Jonas was having trouble pointing out that he'd witnessed a kiss, not any talking.

Thank merciful heaven that both of the teenagers were fully dressed, and there'd been no tongues or groping. Well, none that Jonas had seen, but since he'd once been a teenage boy himself, he knew that kissing, tongues and groping often went hand in hand.

"Please don't tell Mom," Hayden insisted, and she was adding more of those pleading pleases when Jonas heard something else.

His name being called out. By Lily.

If Jonas had been in a laughing mood, he would have found it comical just how wide both Eli's and Hayden's eyes got. But he sure as hell wasn't laughing. Wouldn't be tattling to Lily, either. Not today, anyway. He already had to talk to her about what he'd found in the mailbox, and that would likely concern her enough without adding their kissing teenagers to the mix.

"Don't do this again," Jonas warned them, and he stepped back to intercept Lily before she came this way looking for him.

It didn't take Jonas long to spot her since Lily was, indeed, heading his way, and he also noticed her troubled expression.

"Is everything okay?" they asked in unison. So, obviously he had an unsettled look on his face as well.

"You go first," he insisted.

Jonas motioned for her to head into his office with him so they'd have some privacy for this chat. Also, this would give their kids a chance to sneak out the back of the barn, and maybe Lily would never be the wiser about the kissing. He added another *maybe* that Hayden and Eli would actually take his "no kissing" order to heart and never touch lips again.

"I think Hezzie had some skeletons in her closet," Lily told him once she was inside his office and had shut the door.

Well, that would explain why Alma had joined in on the "troubled look" club. "Literally?"

Lily shrugged. "Alma didn't get into specifics, but I don't think it's as serious as a dead body. Alma just said I might uncover stuff about Hezzie that wouldn't be flattering."

In the grand scheme of things, that didn't sound like much of a deal, but then, he wasn't a Parkman. The Parkmans had built their family legacies on Hezzie and the woman's accomplishments. On the surface, those accomplishments were pretty darn impressive since Hezzie had not only founded Last Ride, but she'd personally run three different businesses. Successful businesses that had allowed her to leave a boatload of money to her descendants.

Some of that money had made its way to Lily in the form of a trust fund that had then allowed her to buy the ranch, so Jonas was appreciative that Hezzie was in Lily's gene pool.

"That was in the box Alma gave you? Info about those possible skeletons?" he clarified.

"Nope. Apparently, what's in there is what everyone believes to be the facts about Hezzie. According to Alma, some of it is, indeed, facts, or rather *true-ish*, she said, and she wants me to stick to the true-ish that everyone has accepted as gospel."

Jonas was still seeing a lot of trouble in Lily's expression. "Will you?"

She gave another shrug. "Maybe, but it does bug me that Alma wants to keep a dead woman's secrets. I've also got enough curiosity to try to find out what those secrets are." But she stopped and waved that off. "Probably best, though, not to rock any boats."

Jonas went with his own idiom. "That'd be the path of least resistance."

And it would mesh more with the way Lily lived her life. She wasn't a boat rocker—not in her personal life, anyway. Maybe because she'd had her boat rocked too many times when Griff and she had been together.

"I'll think about the research on Hezzie tomorrow." She paused and dragged in a long breath. "Now, tell me what you found in the mailbox."

Jonas knew she hadn't forgotten about that, and he hoped Lily was doing a whole lot of steeling up because she just might need it.

"There was a single sheet of paper, no envelope," Jonas explained.

Which meant the note-leaver or someone on the leaver's behalf had actually been to the ranch. Lily didn't have security cameras on the Wild Springs. Not enough crime in or around Last Ride to justify that. But it was possible one of the hands had seen someone drop it off, and Jonas would ask around about that.

He took the note from his center desk drawer and handed it to her. It wouldn't take long for her to read it since it was only two sentences, but he figured the handful of words could possibly pack a punch.

"'It's time you hear the truth,'" Lily read aloud. "'Call me. Love, Dad.'" Beneath the *Dad*, there was a phone number with a Texas area code.

"It wasn't addressed to anyone," Jonas added, "and I don't ever recall anyone leaving a note in the mailbox for one of the ranch hands—"

"I'm pretty sure it's for Hayden," Lily muttered.

He noticed that her grip tightened on the note. Her breathing kicked up, too. And that was possible confirmation of something that Jonas had suspected for a long time. Still, he didn't spell out his suspicions. That Cam Dalton wasn't Hayden's bio dad.

Griff possibly was.

And that meant Hayden could be his niece.

Of course, that was just a suspicion. Lily's reaction might be because she hadn't expected to hear from her ex after all this time. Since Cam had essentially deserted Hayden and her, this kind of contact likely wouldn't be welcome.

"Well, crap," Lily finally said, and as if the bones in her legs had suddenly dissolved, she sank down onto the floor, landing on her butt with her back anchored against his desk.

Jonas went to the small fridge behind his desk, took out two beers—the only alcohol he had in his office—and he joined her on the floor. She immediately opened the bottle he handed to her and took a huge gulp.

"Crap," she repeated, going for another gulp.

Obviously, she hadn't steeled herself up as much as needed, but Jonas still didn't try to soothe her. That was because he doubted soothing was possible right now. He also didn't pepper her with questions since she was clearly still trying to process what this could mean.

"I haven't heard a peep from Cam in years," Lily finally muttered after more sips of her beer. She paused. "Why wouldn't he have just come to the house…?" But she stopped. "Because he wouldn't have been sure of the welcome he'd get."

Jonas made a sound of agreement, and after a few dragging moments, Lily looked at him. And looked. She seemed to be trying to examine his expression to suss out what he knew or didn't know. Apparently, she sussed out that he was aware of Hayden's possible paternity, because she groaned.

"Before Griff died, did he tell you I was pregnant?" she came out and asked.

"No. Griff and I weren't doing a lot of talking back then." And that was a guilt that had stayed with Jonas even after fifteen years. If he'd been there for his brother, then Griff might not have ended his life.

"But you guessed," Lily said. "Because you're not surprised." She stopped, her eyes widening before she turned to him. "Is it because you think Hayden looks like Griff?"

"No," he repeated. "She's the spitting image of you and your sisters." But he could understand her worry. If he'd seen a resemblance, then maybe others had, too.

Including Hayden.

And that confirmed something else for Jonas. That Hayden was not only his niece, but that she didn't know Griff was her father. The girl believed Cam was, and now Cam intended to spill the truth. The question was, why now?

"You must think I'm a horrible person," she muttered.

"No. I think you were a grieving, desperate person."
Now he paused. "Did Griff know you were pregnant?"

She nodded. "I told him the day he died. He said I deserved someone better than him." Lily moaned and shook her head. "At the time, I didn't think there was anyone better than Griff. He wasn't perfect," she quickly added. "But I loved him. I loved him so much."

Jonas had never doubted that. "He loved you, too." He didn't add that it was maybe out of love that Griff had done what he had by ending his life. His brother had just gotten a horrible diagnosis of ALS and hadn't wanted to be a burden on anyone.

Especially Lily and the child she was carrying.

"I didn't tell my sisters or my mom I was pregnant," Lily went on. "But I told Cam. Or rather he guessed when he came looking for me right after Griff died, and he found me puking on the side of the road. Morning sickness," she tacked on to that. "I'd pulled off the road when I realized my stomach wasn't going to cooperate with the crackers I'd just eaten."

Griff, Cam and Lily had all been friends. Besties, as some would call it. But Jonas had always suspected that Cam tolerated being Lily's bestie because he'd believed he couldn't be anything more to her. Griff's death had opened a door to what Cam really wanted.

"Cam offered to marry me then and there," she went on. "I refused and kept refusing for a week, and then I was just too exhausted to say no. He was giving me a chance to avoid some gossip while offering me comfort. God, I needed comfort." Her voice trembled, and he saw her swipe away a tear.

Hell. That got to him, and he reached for her, but she

shook her head. "If you hug me right now, I'll break. And I can't break. I need to get my butt in gear and figure out how to handle this."

Jonas considered that a moment. "Whose idea was it to let everyone believe Cam was Hayden's father?"

"Cam's," she readily answered. "Obviously, though, he's changed his mind about that." She paused. "Maybe Cam's met someone he wants to marry, and he intends to tell that person the truth. Of course, that would mean Hayden learning the truth as well."

"Had you ever planned on telling Hayden?" he asked.

"Yes." Again, that was a fast answer. "While Cam was still around, he insisted on Hayden never knowing, but after he left, I'd intended to tell her when she was old enough." She grimaced at that last part. *"When she was old enough,"* Lily repeated. "That kept getting pushed further and further into the future."

No need for Jonas to spell out that the future was right here, right now. Also no need for him to predict how Hayden would deal with this. With teenagers, you just never knew. But Jonas doubted Hayden would be thrilled to learn she was the daughter of a man who'd been as troubled as Griff. Even after all the years, folks talked about Griff's bad boy, reckless reputation.

"Other than Cam and us, who else knows about Hayden being Griff's child?" he asked.

"Only Nola. I told her about a year ago. Or rather she guessed." Lily paused. "Hayden doesn't even ask about Cam anymore. She hasn't mentioned him in years." She groaned softly. "Does Eli ever mention his bio dad?"

Jonas shook his head. "Maddie was always up-front with Eli about his father not wanting to be a dad. His loss, my gain," Jonas insisted. He hesitated a moment. "If you want some emotional support, I can be there when or after you talk to Hayden."

She looked at him, dredging up a smile that she in no way felt, and she patted his hand. "Thanks. I might take you up on that during the aftermath."

Still hanging on to the beer, Lily got to her feet, and she took another look at the note that had just thrown her life into chaos.

"I'll deal with making the call to Cam tomorrow," she muttered, stuffing the note in her jeans pocket and heading for the office door. "First, though, I have to figure out a way to tell Hayden that her mother is a big fat liar."

CHAPTER THREE

As SHE WALKED from the barn and back to her house, Lily wanted to curl into a ball and cry her eyes out. But the only thing that would accomplish would be to give her a stuffy nose, splotchy face and perhaps muscle cramps from the balling up. It wouldn't fix anything. And things definitely needed some fixing.

Thanks to the Texas-sized mistake she'd made nearly fifteen years ago.

It was impossible for her to justify that mistake of lying to everyone about the father of her child. Impossible, too, for her to forgive herself. Her only excuse was that she'd been so overcome with grief from losing Griff that she hadn't had a grasp on just how much the lie would snowball.

And linger.

She had no one else to blame for that. Especially not Cam. Yes, he'd begged her to marry him, to let him be a father to another man's child, but he'd been young like her. Just nineteen. Stupidity was part of the teenage package. So, she wouldn't toss any blame at him for pressing her to marry him or for leaving Hayden and her just a year later when he realized he couldn't handle being a husband or a daddy.

The truth was—and wasn't it ironic that she was dwelling on the truth tonight?—if Cam hadn't left her, she would have left him. Never Hayden, though. She loved her daughter with every piece of herself that was capable of loving, but it hadn't taken Lily long to realize that Cam couldn't replace Griff. No one could. So, at the tender age of twenty and despite having an infant to raise, Lily had decided that if she couldn't have Griff, then she was better off going solo.

That decision to become a single parent hadn't been a mistake. She'd thrived. So had Hayden. However, she was now going to have to pay for that big-assed mistake she'd made by not telling her daughter the truth.

Squaring her shoulders and trying to put on a normal face, Lily went inside the house through the kitchen, where she thought she might find Hayden. But nope. Nor was she in the living room. Lily used the temporary reprieve to thread her way through the house to the trio of rooms off the side hall. The master bedroom, Hayden's room and Lily's office.

Lily tapped on Hayden's door while she did more shoulder squaring and such, but there was no response. Since there was still a sliver of light left from the setting sun, it was possible Hayden was with Eli and the new horses. If so, she'd be in soon, and that would give Lily a little more time to steady herself. Or time to make her nerves even more frazzled. She was betting option number two would win out in this particular emotional battle.

It's time you hear the truth. Call me. Love, Dad.

Yes, that was a surefire way to frazzle nerves all right, and because those nerves were zinging right at the surface, Lily decided she could use a hot bath. She went into her bedroom and had already caught onto the bottom of her shirt to shuck it off on the way to the adjoining bathroom, but a garbled scream left her mouth when she saw the face.

A man's face squished against the screen.

Still making those garbled sounds, Lily ran across the room, snatching up the baseball bat she kept under her bed, and she turned, ready to swing.

"It's me," the squished-face man said, lifting his hands in the air.

Lily still didn't recognize him until he stepped back, and then she cursed. Not G-rated mommy profanity, either. It was the real deal that might have made a sailor or two blush.

"Derwin Parkman," she spit out, going to the window. Lily didn't put down the bat, even though her seventy-something-year-old cousin wasn't a threat. But he'd scared the heck out of her.

"What the hell are you doing out there?" she snarled.

Derwin was still wearing his Sherlock Holmes garb, and he motioned for her to open the window. She did but then didn't wait for him to respond before she threw a couple more questions at him.

"Why didn't you go to the front door and ring the bell?" Lily demanded. "Better yet, why didn't you just go home like everybody else?" This time her voice was more of a snap than a snarl. She so wasn't in the mood for Derwin, his Snoops, or anything else, for that matter.

Derwin didn't say anything until she had the window open, and even then he leaned in until his mouth was against the screen. "I need to talk to you," he whispered, "and I didn't want anyone to see me. You've got to pinkie swear that I was never here."

Lily felt herself scowl. Considering the man had been here earlier when she'd arrived home, anyone in that crowd on her lawn and porch would have known Derwin had been to the ranch. So, what had changed for him in the past forty-five minutes or so?

"I'm not really a pinkie-swear kind of person," Lily answered. "Just tell me why you're here, and then I can lecture you about hanging around outside a woman's bedroom window. How'd you even know it was my bedroom, anyway?" She waved that off, but Derwin answered regardless.

He tipped his head to the nightstand. "The picture of Hayden and you when she was a baby. Plus, the decor is kind of plain for a teenager or a guest room."

Lily felt another frown come on, but she refrained from glancing around to determine what this Sherlock Holmes–wannabe would consider plain. "Why are you here?" she pressed.

Derwin lifted his little finger, maybe hoping she'd go for the pinkie swear after all, but Lily just continued to scowl at him and made a whirling motion with her index finger for him to get on with the reason for this strange visit.

"It's, uh, about Hezzie," Derwin finally said. "I saw the box of files on your front porch, and I know those are the things Alma gave you." He paused and stared at her. With his face behind the screen, he looked like a cartoon Sherlock avatar on a messed-up computer screen. "Well, what's in that box is, uh, lies."

That got her attention, mainly because Alma had made it seem as if she was the only one who knew the truth about Hezzie. Whatever the truth actually was. But if Alma could dig up some unsavory things about their ancestor, then so could someone else. Someone like Derwin, who made a habit of digging into anything and everything he considered a mystery.

Lily didn't invite the man in because she didn't want him there when Hayden came in. However, she did toss the bat on the bed and tried to ease up on scowling. "All right, what's the deal with Hezzie?"

He shook his head and actually glanced around as if to check if anyone was eavesdropping. "It's complicated and, uh, delicate."

She so wanted to roll her eyes. "Hezzie's been dead for over seventy years. I don't think she'll care what comes to light about her."

"Oh, she'll care about this all right," Derwin argued. "So will some of her kin, because they won't want to think of Hezzie as anything other than a proper woman passing along proper Parkman DNA to them."

Lily wasn't sure DNA had anything to do with the kind of people Hezzie's heirs had become, but she had heard stories of some folks doing genealogy and then getting upset to learn they were related to outlaws and such.

"You didn't hear this from me, but before Hezzie settled here and founded Last Ride, she—" Derwin stopped and ducked down out of sight. "Someone's coming," he whispered.

Lily didn't hear anything, but she followed Derwin's gaze toward the back of the house. It was possibly Hayden, but she expected Derwin to at least finish the rather intriguing revelation he'd started or to tell her that they'd talk soon.

The man didn't do either of those things.

He just took off running toward the road, and when Lily pressed her own face against the screen so she could better peer out, she could see Derwin's car that he'd left out on the road. He hightailed it out of there as if a pissed-off T. rex were after him.

Lily turned back to see what Derwin had been trying to avoid, and she made another of those garbled sounds of surprise when she came face-to-face with Jonas. He was glowering and hiked his thumb toward Derwin, who was now speeding away.

"I saw a man wearing a weird hat outside your window, so I came running because I thought you had a Peeping Tom," Jonas explained. "Was that Derwin Parkman?"

She nodded and tried to steady her heart that was now thumping hard. "He apparently wanted to dish up some dirt on Hezzie, but he got spooked when he heard someone coming. He can run fast for a guy his age."

Jonas's forehead bunched up as if he were trying to make sense of why an elderly man dressed like Sherlock would deem it necessary to communicate with her through her bedroom window.

"What dirt?" he wanted to know.

Lily had to shrug. "He didn't get a chance to tell me specifics, but he insisted whatever's in the box that Alma gave me will be lies. Right before he ran off, he said, and I quote, *before Hezzie settled here, she—*"

She definitely hadn't wanted Derwin to hang around, but Lily so wished he'd been able to finish that particular fill in the blank because it was causing some interesting scenarios to pop into her head.

Jonas sighed, shook his head. "You want me to have a talk with him and tell him to stay away from your bedroom window?"

"Thanks, but no thanks. I hate to admit this, but he piqued my interest. I guess I always figured Hezzie was a straitlaced...or maybe a *plain decor*...kind of person."

And that caused her to frown. Because she was apparently now a "plain decor" person, but once upon a time she'd certainly done some scandalous things. Like lie to her daughter and everyone else in Last Ride for the past fourteen years.

"Are you okay?" Jonas asked, drawing her attention back to him.

One look at his handsome face and she could see he was troubled. "Been better. How about you? Is something else going on I should know about? Because you seem worried."

Her stomach tightened when he didn't jump to assure her that all was well, that there was nothing in that "should know about" category. She would have pressed for him to spill, but like Derwin, Jonas shifted his gaze to the back of the house.

"It's Hayden," he relayed. "She's heading to the back porch."

Talk about tightening her stomach even more. It was showtime. She wouldn't get that hot bath to settle her nerves after all, but that would have been asking a lot anyway from a mere bath.

"If you need to talk afterward, let me know," Jonas muttered.

He headed away from her window. Not running, and he didn't go in the direction Hayden would be approaching. Jonas went toward the front of the house, where he no doubt intended to circle around and make his way either back to his office or home.

Gathering the strength that she was certain she'd need, Lily forced herself to get moving as well. She walked out of her bedroom and went to the back door to wait for Hayden. She didn't have to wait long. It was only a couple of seconds before Hayden came rushing in, and she practically skidded to a halt when she spotted Lily.

"Oh, I thought you'd be diving into the research on Hezzie," Hayden remarked.

Lily noted the tightness in her daughter's voice. Actually, the tightness everywhere. Something was wrong.

No, no, no.

Had Cam already gotten in touch with her? Did Hayden know the truth?

Lily tried to interpret what all that tension was about, but if Hayden did know, she wasn't hurling eye daggers at her. Nor did she appear to be in shock.

"I'll start the research soon," Lily said, still keeping her attention pinned to Hayden. "Did, uh, anything happen?" she asked at the same moment that Hayden said, "Have you talked to Mr. Buchanan?"

By Mr. Buchanan, she meant Jonas, and that snagged Lily's attention, too. It was possible Hayden had overheard Jonas and her talking in his office. But if so, why wasn't she just blurting out what she'd heard?

Lily decided how best to approach this and went with a safe option in case there hadn't been any eavesdropping in Jonas's office after all. "Derwin Parkman came by again to pester me about the research, and when Jonas saw him, he came to the house to nudge Derwin into leaving."

That was close enough to the truth, anyway.

"Oh," Hayden repeated. She looked and sounded way too relieved. "Good for Mr. Buchanan."

Yes, her daughter was way too relieved, which meant something was, indeed, wrong. Since this could be about Cam after all, Lily just decided to confess her wrongs to Hayden here and now.

But Hayden didn't give her the chance.

"I'm so tired," Hayden blurted out. "I'm going to take a bath and do the online forms for school. Some of the teachers want to know about hobbies and junk. Get-to-know-you stuff.

Good night, Mom," she added. Within a blink, she'd kissed Lily on her cheek and hurried to her room.

Lily considered going after her, but it was obvious Hayden wasn't in a chatty mood. Maybe what was wrong with her had nothing to do with Cam or learning the truth. School was starting in a week, and Hayden could be apprehensive about that. Heck, since she was a teenager, the list of apprehension-causing things was likely pretty long.

After dumping out the rest of the beer Jonas had given her, Lily poured herself a glass of wine before she went back to her own bedroom, where she shut both the door and the window. She even closed the curtains in case Derwin decided to make a return visit.

"Hayden, I need to tell you about a huge mistake I made," Lily muttered, and she gave that line a few more practice tries before she stopped. Just stopped. And cursed herself. She needed to try to start making things right, and the best way to begin that was to call Cam and see if he wanted them to tell Hayden the truth together.

She fished out the note from her pocket with her left hand and tugged her phone from her back pocket as well. Lily pressed in the number before she could chicken out and start practicing again.

"Hello?" the man said, answering on the first ring.

Lily frowned because she'd thought she would instantly recognize Cam's voice. She didn't. "Cam?" she asked.

"Uh, no," he said without even a moment of hesitation. "Sorry, but you have the wrong number."

Her frown deepened, and she checked what she'd dialed. "I don't think I do." She repeated the number on the note to him.

This time he did pause. "Who is this?"

If this was Cam, he'd obviously not been prepared for

a quick follow-up to his note. "It's Lily," she said and then added "Lily Parkman" when he still didn't respond.

Well, heck. Cam had obviously written down the wrong number.

"Look," she continued, "this note with the number was in my mailbox—"

"Lily Parkman," the man interrupted. "You own the ranch where Jonas Buchanan works."

Now she was the one who paused. "Yes. Who are you?"

The snail-crawling silence came before he cleared his throat. "I'm Wade Bentley."

Lily repeated the name a couple of times to see if it rang any bells. It didn't.

"You don't know who I am," he concluded a moment later.

"No," she verified, and if she hadn't been so confused, the relief might have washed over her that Cam wasn't about to rush in and blurt out all her sins.

"I'm Eli's father," he said.

The shock came. Mercy, did it. And yes, definitely no relief. The note had been meant for Eli, not Hayden. It took her more than a moment to let that sink in, and then Lily looked again at the message.

It's time you hear the truth. Call me. Love, Dad.

"It's time Eli knows the truth," she stated, trying not to make it sound like some kind of protective accusation. But heaven help her, she was suddenly feeling a whole lot protective of the boy.

"So, you read the note," he muttered. "I didn't have Eli's number or email and thought he and I should talk before I spring a visit on him."

"A visit to tell him the truth," Lily spelled out, and this time the accusation came through loud and clear.

Bentley's next pause was even longer. "Yes," he finally verified.

"You didn't even put Eli's name on the note," Lily added. "How were you even sure he'd get it?"

"Really?" Bentley said. "I left off his name? Huh. Didn't mean to do that. Then again, Eli's probably the only one on the ranch who'd get a note like that from his dad left in the mailbox."

No, not the only one. And Lily had just assumed the worst. But this *worst* was for Jonas.

"Please give Eli the note and have him call me. He needs to hear what I have to say."

And with that ominous-sounding comment, the man ended the call.

CHAPTER FOUR

STANDING AT HIS kitchen sink, Jonas ate the rest of his bacon and toast while he loaded the dishwasher—his day for the particular chore since Eli and he alternated doing such things. Because it hadn't been Eli's duty day, the boy hadn't spent more than a minute in the kitchen. After Eli had gotten up, he'd slapped together a breakfast sandwich and headed out, saying he wanted to look in on the new horses. That was possibly the truth.

Possibly.

But Jonas also figured it was his son's way of avoiding any more talk about the kissing that Jonas had walked in on the day before. Jonas couldn't blame the kid. It wasn't exactly a comfortable subject, but eventually they'd have to talk about it so Jonas could try to make sure it didn't get out of hand.

While Jonas continued to load the dishes and eat, he read through the emails on his phone. He didn't usually multitask his way through breakfast, but he'd wanted to hurry so he could go to the main house and check on Lily. He was betting she hadn't gotten much sleep after telling Hayden about the note left from Cam.

If she'd told Hayden, that was.

She wouldn't have chickened out. No, not Lily. But it was possible the timing hadn't worked for her to do a tell-all. If the confession had happened, though, if Hayden now knew that Griff and not Cam was her father, then Jonas wanted to be able to lend whatever support was needed.

Once Hayden had started to come to terms with the truth of her DNA, it was possible she'd have questions about Griff. Hard questions about the person he was and how he'd died. Lily would no doubt be able to answer those, but Hayden might want some input from someone other than the woman who hadn't been forthcoming with her about her father.

Depending on the level of Hayden's anger—and Jonas was betting there'd be plenty of it—she might be more willing to talk things over with him rather than her mother. That would hurt Lily, no way around it, but Lily would also want any comfort he might be able to give to her daughter.

Jonas topped off the coffee in his mug with plans to finish most of it on the short walk from his house to Lily's. After all, Lily and Hayden weren't the only ones who probably hadn't gotten much sleep. Jonas had spent a good chunk of the night tossing and turning and worrying about his boss and his niece.

He chugged some of the coffee, headed out the front door. And he immediately came to a stop. Lily was there, sitting on the top porch step with her back resting against the handrail post. She, too, was downing some coffee that was no doubt sorely needed, because the moment she looked at him, he saw the fatigue and worry in her Parkman blue eyes.

Sighing, Jonas met her gaze. "How bad is it?" he asked, and his mind was already spinning with the possibilities. A teenager's emotions were often in the "full throttle" mode, so it was possible that Hayden hadn't taken the news well at all.

Lily matched his sigh and patted the spot next to her. "You should probably sit down for this."

Hell. "Did Hayden run away?" he asked, going with one of those possibilities. "Do I need to go looking for her?"

Lily still didn't answer. She merely patted the porch again and kept her attention nailed to him while he sank down.

"The note wasn't for Hayden," she said. "It was for Eli."

Jonas was certain he blinked, and his mind went blank for a moment as he tried to process that. Then it hit him. Hit him hard, not like a gut punch but a lead-footed kick right in the balls.

"Shit," Jonas managed to say, though it did take him a couple of seconds just to drag some air into his lungs so he could speak.

"Yes," Lily agreed. She took his hand, clamping it into hers. "I called the number on the note last night. I expected Cam to answer, but it was this guy named Wade Bentley."

Jonas didn't have enough breath to repeat the guy's name aloud, but it meant nothing to him. He'd certainly never heard Maddie mention him by name. Then again, Maddie had never told him who Eli's bio father was.

"Wade Bentley claimed that Eli is his son," Lily finished, and she squeezed his hand even harder. "Is he?"

Jonas had to shake his head. "Maybe," he settled for saying.

But he immediately had to mentally amend that. Even though Maddie had never said who'd gotten her pregnant, she'd had a child. So, there was a bio father out there, and this guy must have believed he was the one. And that was when the words in the message flashed through his head.

It's time you hear the truth. Call me. Love, Dad.

"Shit," Jonas repeated, and rather than risk spilling hot

coffee on his crotch, he set his cup aside, eased his other hand from Lily's so he could scrub them over his face. And he released the loud groan that was piling up in his chest.

"I'm so sorry," Lily muttered.

That wasn't just lip service. In a way, Lily and he were family, and had Griff been alive, she would have no doubt been his sister-in-law. Still, Jonas figured her empathy went deeper than that. Once Hayden learned the truth about her dad, it could tear Lily and her apart. The same could happen to Jonas if this guy was truly Eli's father.

Jonas let out another of those groans, and then he tried to shove away some of the emotion so he could think this through. Best to start by getting as many facts as possible. Including the big fact. What the hell did this man want?

"Tell me about the conversation you had with this guy," Jonas insisted. "Why did he leave the note in the mailbox?"

"We didn't talk long," Lily readily explained. "And he said he left the note because he thought Eli and he should talk before he visited him."

That was another kick to the balls. A visit. Hell. Of course the man would want that, but Jonas wasn't sure how either Eli or he would handle it.

"Bentley finished the conversation by telling me to give Eli the note," Lily explained. She reached in her jeans pocket, extracted said note and handed it to him. "He insisted that Eli needed to hear what he had to say."

Jonas did some more repeating of *shit* and *hell*. The man wouldn't be satisfied with just a conversation and a visit. No, there was the whole "it's time you knew the truth" part that he'd written in the damn note.

A truth that would probably smear the hell out of Maddie. And since Maddie was dead, she wouldn't be able to defend herself.

But Jonas sure as hell could do that.

"The few times Maddie mentioned the birth father to me, she said they were better off without him," Jonas stated. "That tells me he's a son of a bitch. Or at least he was fourteen-plus years ago."

It twisted at his gut even more to think that the SOB could have changed. Changed enough to be worthy of Eli hearing him out and forgiving him for not being a part of his life. Because if Eli bought into that, then he would also have to buy into that so-called "truth" that could hurt Maddie from beyond the grave.

Could hurt Jonas, too.

Except it would be a hell of a lot more than hurt. It would be the worst kind of heart crushing. It would feel as if he could lose the only part of Maddie that he had left. Added to that, it felt as if he'd be letting Maddie down since he'd made a deathbed promise to her to take care of the son they'd raised together.

"I googled this guy," Lily added a moment later.

Jonas whipped his gaze to her, and he was hoping he saw something in her eyes or expression to indicate this Wade Bentley was a lying sack of shit that Jonas would need to keep far, far away from Eli. But Jonas saw just the opposite.

"Wade Bentley is a doctor. A pediatrician," she explained. "He has a practice in San Antonio."

San Antonio was only a half hour's drive from Last Ride. Too damn close. Then again, any place on the planet suddenly felt too close. Then there was his profession. Jonas had been hoping the guy would be less than stellar. And maybe he was. But if Bentley had a medical practice, then he was likely doing something right. Now, anyway. That didn't account for how he'd been with Maddie and how badly he'd treated her to make her want to cut him out of their life.

"He's thirty-eight," Lily went on, obviously recalling the details of what she'd learned since she wasn't reading from notes. "Same age as you. No criminal record that I could find, but I asked Azzie to take a look."

Good, because if there was something to find, Deputy Azzie Parkman would find it.

"Is he married?" Jonas asked. Because that could play into this as well if his spouse either wanted or didn't want him to start giving a damn about the son he'd fathered.

Lily shook her head. "Divorced. For about ten years now, and he was involved with a few women since then. He has a couple of social media pages, and he currently doesn't seem to have a partner or significant other. No other kids either."

That could explain why the man suddenly wanted to see Eli. Bentley might be searching for something missing in his life. Then again, Jonas didn't have a partner or significant other either, and he wasn't looking to make any changes.

At the exact moment that thought went through his head, Lily looked up at him, and their gazes collided. She obviously wasn't prepared for the intense eye contact. Obviously wasn't prepared for the kick of…well, whatever the hell it was…because she had a "deer caught in the headlights" moment before she shut off the intensity and glanced away.

Jonas couldn't quite force himself to tear his gaze from her. Which made him stupid. Because he wasn't so vague about the *whatever the hell* it was he was feeling. He'd just gotten a slam of lust. It was natural since Lily was an attractive woman.

But it was also wrong.

Very, very wrong.

They had too great of a working relationship to dick around with lust. Lust could burn out in a flash and mess up everything. Heck, even if it was more than a flash, that was still bad, too, because it could screw up everything.

"I resemble Griff," he heard himself say.

In hindsight, he should have clamped something over his mouth to stop himself from blurting that out. Because there was no way he should be offering up reasons why Lily might be feeling her own bout of lust for him.

Her expression went slack, and because she looked up at him again, Jonas was able to see her processing what he said. Lily definitely didn't offer up a confirming nod or mutter anything about him just having spoken the gospel truth. Just the opposite. At first, she just looked confused, and then the shock came.

"You think I see Griff when I look at you?" she asked, her voice sputtering a little. "Because I don't."

Jonas was pretty sure Lily had a hindsight moment, too, because she looked as if she suddenly wanted to borrow a clamp for her own mouth. However, beneath the regret over her confession, there was something else.

That blasted heat.

No. This shouldn't be happening. Correction—it couldn't happen. And it was probably just a knee-jerk kind of reaction to the heart-to-heart chats they'd been having because of that note.

"Yoo-hoo!" someone called out.

Jonas was beyond thankful for the interruption. So thankful he would have welcomed a rabid gorilla clomping across the pasture. But this was no critter. It was Azzie, and she was making a beeline toward them.

"Am I interrupting anything?" Azzie asked. She eyed them in a way only a cop or a seasoned kindergarten teacher could have managed.

"No," Jonas and Lily said in unison. They'd also issued the denial darn fast, which, of course, made it seem like a lie.

It wasn't, Jonas assured himself.

Azzie hadn't interrupted anything that Lily and he weren't about to douse. Jonas was reasonably sure that Lily didn't want to screw up their status quo any more than he did.

"Jonas and I were just talking about Wade Bentley," Lily tacked on to her denial.

Still giving them a skeptical once-over, Azzie nodded and hiked her thumb in the direction of Lily's house. "I stopped by there first, but when nobody answered my knock, I headed this way."

Lily frowned and glanced toward the barns. "Hayden must have gone out for an early ride," she muttered.

There was no real worry in Lily's tone, just some surprise that her teenage daughter would be up this early since it was barely eight in the morning. But there was some real worry inside Jonas. Hell, yeah, there was. Because he recalled the way Eli had lit out of the house, and now Jonas had to wonder if all that hurrying was because he'd planned to hook up with Hayden.

He definitely had to have that talk with Eli.

For now, though, Jonas put his attention on Azzie. After all, it was early for her, too, to be making a visit.

"Is Wade Bentley the one who left the note in the mailbox?" Jonas came out and asked.

"That'd be my guess," Azzie said somewhat cryptically,

"but he went about things in a candy-ass sort of way, if you want my opinion."

Jonas did, indeed, want Azzie's no-nonsense opinion, especially when it involved slamming a man Jonas didn't mind slamming. That might be petty, but at the moment he wasn't feeling very gracious toward the man who was trying to push his way into Eli's life.

"After you called me last night," Azzie went on, directing her comments to Lily now, "I did a background check on Dr. Bentley. The man has a whole bunch of speeding tickets and parking violations."

Jonas silently groaned. That wasn't the kind of dirt he'd been looking for. "That's it?" Jonas asked.

"That's plenty," Azzie assured him with a crisp nod. "Folks who make a habit of breaking the law often have habits of doing other unlawful things."

Maybe. But it was also possible the doctor had a lead foot and a penchant for parking in the wrong place. Hardly infractions that would cause Jonas to try to block him from communicating with Eli.

"So, how is he candy-assed?" Lily asked.

"Because he didn't do his own bidding, that's why," Azzie readily answered. "This morning, the candy-ass doc had a private investigator call the police station to inquire about the two of you." She pointed first to Jonas and then to Lily. "He demanded any and all information, and when I asked him who wanted to know and who he was working for, he refused to answer. Well, we all know the candy-ass hired him."

Probably, because Jonas couldn't think of anyone else who might be digging for dirt on them. But Jonas could have pointed out that Lily had been the one to call Azzie and ask about Bentley. Jonas hadn't been the one to do that. Of course, at the time Lily had called Azzie, Jonas hadn't had a clue about the man and the firestorm he might possibly bring.

Jonas clung to that *possibly*. What exactly had Lily relayed to him about what Bentley had actually said? Something along the lines of give Eli the note and have him call because he needed to hear what the man had to say. Jonas had latched on to the notion that Bentley would slam Maddie for the choices she'd made, but maybe Bentley just wanted to explain himself. Or rather try to do that. Heck, the man might even own up to the fact that he would have been a crappy father. Ironic about the "crappy" part since Bentley had become a pediatrician.

"I figure the doc wants to see what kind of folks Eli's around," Azzie went on, yanking Jonas's attention back to her. "Maybe to give himself some peace of mind." She lifted her shoulder. "Or maybe because he's actually a candy-ass who'll duck and cover if he hears something he thinks he can't handle. Things like Eli is plenty happy here, and nobody oughta screw around with that."

Jonas appreciated Azzie's take on things. And Eli was happy. Well, happy-ish, anyway, since he was still grieving for his mother while going through the hormone hell of being a teenager. Still, Eli was loved, wanted and safe. That had to count for something in Bentley's eyes.

"Is there any actual proof the candy-ass is Eli's sperm-donor dad?" Azzie asked.

The question threw Jonas because he hadn't gone there. Not yet, anyway. Maddie had never named Eli's father, and while she hadn't been the sort to have a string of lovers, that didn't mean there was only one father possibility. Added to that, Bentley could have had a relationship with Maddie before she'd even met Eli's bio dad.

Mentally spelling that out had some of the tightness easing up in his chest. It wasn't a fix. Not by a long shot. But it gave him a better perspective as to how the conversation should go with Bentley. One thing was for certain: Eli wouldn't be talking to the man until Jonas was sure it was safe. And warranted. No need for the meeting to happen if Bentley didn't have any biological claim on Eli.

"I talked this over with the sheriff, of course," Azzie went on a moment later, "and we're not gonna say anything about either of you to the PI or the candy-ass. If one of them pesters you, all you have to do is call the station and somebody will be out to help you handle it."

Both Lily and he muttered a thanks. Jonas didn't think there'd be a need for police intervention, but it didn't surprise him that the offer had been made. Sheriff Matt Corbin and he were friends, and Matt had a kid of his own. He knew how much Eli meant to Jonas. And what he meant was, well, everything. That didn't mean there weren't other things in Jonas's life, but Eli was the most important part of it.

Azzie shifted both her body and her eyes back to Lily. "Anyone messing with you over the Hezzie research?"

Lily sighed. "I put my phone in the sleep mode before I went to bed, and I woke up to eleven texts. Mainly from Derwin," she tacked on to that. She paused a moment, studying Azzie. "If you know about the dirt or whatever there is on Hezzie, I wish you'd tell me."

Azzie shook her head. "It's not mine to tell. If it comes out, it comes out, but you won't be hearing it from me." And with that cryptic response, Azzie added a muttered goodbye and walked away.

"Crap," Lily said after dragging in a long breath.

Jonas could feel for her and this particular Pandora's box–

deal, but at the moment, he was dealing with a situation that could result in a whole lot of trouble. He looked at the number that Bentley had written on the note and took out his phone.

"You're calling him?" Lily asked.

"I am," he verified, and since it was best just to dive straight in, Jonas pressed in the number and went ahead and put the call on speaker since he was certain Lily would want to hear what the man had to say.

Considering how early it was, Jonas thought the call might go to voice mail so he could leave a message. But no. The man answered.

"Eli?" he immediately said.

"No, this is Jonas Buchanan. You're Dr. Wade Bentley?"

"I am." He paused. A long time. "I was hoping to speak to Eli today."

Jonas nearly went with some poetic snark about hope being a thing with feathers, but snark might fuel a fire that should stay cool. At least for the moment, anyway.

"How sure are you that you fathered Eli?" Jonas came out and asked.

Another pause, followed by a sigh. "I'm sure. Do you want me to get into the timing of when I had sex with Maddie?"

Okay, so there was definitely some snark there. "Yeah, I do, but the timing report can wait a little while. First, I'm going to need DNA results that prove what you're saying is true."

"Not a problem," Bentley said without hesitation.

Jonas wanted the hesitation. Hell, he wanted anything that would get this man out of the picture.

"I can bring a DNA test kit to the ranch," Bentley offered. "I could be there with it in two hours."

Jonas didn't even have to think about his answer. "No.

You can drop off your DNA sample at the Last Ride police station. I'll do the same with Eli's." Though he would need to figure out the best way to get that. "Once we have the results, we'll go from there."

"The results will be a match," Bentley insisted. "I'm Eli's father."

"To be determined," Jonas insisted right back.

"And what happens when it's determined?" Bentley continued. "Will you try to stonewall me?"

Again, that was to be determined. Even if the DNA was a match, Jonas needed to make sure it was safe for Eli to be around this man.

"What exactly do you want from Eli, from me?" Jonas pressed.

"Easy answer." Again, the man didn't hesitate. "Mr. Buchanan, I want my son, and I have every intention of getting him."

CHAPTER FIVE

IN THE DREAM that Lily knew was a dream, Jonas re-created his shirtless walk from the barn. Muscles rippling, his hot gaze fixed with hers, he strode toward her.

He'd hosed down, and the water was dripping from his black hair, sliding down his face. Down his neck. Down his chest. And what a chest it was, because those muscles of his were still rippling. The water was still sliding, too, and some arrowed its way down into his jeans. Jeans that framed his incredible butt to go along with his incredible face.

She stood there, watching him. Wanting him. Possibly drooling. And since this was a dream, she intended to have him.

Jonas apparently intended to do some having, too, because when he reached her, he hooked his arm around her waist and yanked her to him. His mouth came to hers, claiming and taking, just as any good dream kiss should do. But this was far better than good. It caused her to climax.

He chuckled, kissed her again, and with the snap of his clever fingers, they were naked, and Lily felt the cool breeze brush over her bare butt. Her own hand brushed over Jonas's, and then she had to latch on hard when he lifted her. She wrapped her legs around him, and he thrust into her with his erection. It filled her and apparently fulfilled her, too, because she had another climax.

"Why is this happening now?" she murmured with her mouth against his.

"Because you had three glasses of wine before bed," he drawled in that sexy voice that was just as effective as, well, sex. Lily felt the third climax ripple through her.

"But it can't actually happen," she managed to say.

"Sweet Lily, anything can happen in a dream." And that sounded like a wonderful promise that she needed him to keep.

Obviously, holding her and having upright sex wasn't a challenge for the hot-bodied Jonas, because he continued those thrusts, continued to make her climax again and again.

"Have you gone deaf?" someone asked, interrupting the flow of those amazing ripples in the center of her body.

In the dream that Lily knew was a dream, she also knew the question she'd just heard was the real deal. And it was her daughter's voice.

Lily's eyes flew open, and she saw Hayden looming over her. "I knocked on the door a whole bunch of times," Hayden said, "but you didn't answer. Are you sick? Because you're usually up by now."

Those were way too many words for her lust-clouded mind, but Lily forced herself to focus. She groaned, though, when she checked the time. It was nine o'clock, a good two hours past when she usually woke up.

"Is something wrong?" Lily managed to say.

"No." There was plenty of suspicion in Hayden's eyes, but hopefully the girl couldn't read minds, because the Jonas effect was still lingering in Lily's mind and body. "I just wanted to let you know I was heading out. Dara and her mom are here to pick me up. They're waiting out front."

Again, it took Lily a few seconds to wipe away enough

haze to know why Hayden was telling her this. Dara McCann and Hayden were friends, and Dara's stepmom, Millie, was going to drive them into San Antonio to do some school clothes shopping.

Lily had volunteered to go with Hayden but hadn't been overly disappointed when Hayden had insisted it wasn't necessary, that they could do a separate trip if she didn't find any outfits she liked.

"After we shop, we're coming back to Last Ride so we can have lunch at O'Riley's," Hayden added.

"Well, have fun," Lily muttered. "Call me if you need me."

Hayden nodded, and even though she turned away, she stopped at the door and looked at Lily. "Are you keeping something from me? Like some big secret, I mean?"

Lily could have sworn her heart skipped a couple of beats. She opened her mouth, to say what exactly, she didn't know, because with Dara and Millie waiting out front, now wasn't the time to confess all.

"Why do you ask?" Lily finally got out.

Hayden lifted her shoulder. "Because the way you moaned out Mr. Buchanan's first name in your dream, I figured you were keeping something about him from me."

"No, nothing," Lily muttered. "There's nothing going on between Jonas and me."

But after the dream, Lily wasn't sure how to make sure the "nothing going on" stayed that way.

FULLY EXPECTING TO be yelled at, Lily stepped into the workshop. And yep, the yelling commenced.

"Close the door," her twin sister, Nola, shouted. "You're letting the heat out."

It was Nola's customary greeting when anyone dared

enter her workshop when she was blowing glass, and despite the industrial fans chugging away, there was, indeed, heat to be let out.

Loads and loads of heat.

The furnace that Nola was using to melt and shape her glass art was hotter than a dozen Texas summers, and within seconds after stepping in—and yes, closing the door—Lily could feel the sweat popping out on her body. Very soon, she'd be drenched and might also have to deal with Nola's wrath if the interruption screwed up the execution of whatever vision of art she had in her head. Still, Lily would endure the potential heatstroke, the equally potential sibling wrath and deodorant failure because she wanted to see her sister.

No. She *needed* to see her. Nola sometimes wasn't the voice of reason, but she always, always had Lily's back. And vice versa. Nola wouldn't judge her for what she'd done, not too much, anyway, and she could give Lily the push to do what she already knew she needed to do.

Tell Hayden the truth about her father.

With that reminder throbbing in her head, something it'd been doing for two days now, Lily watched as Nola blew into the pipe she'd just pulled from the glory hole of the furnace. Nola's motions were like a dance. Blow, turn. Repeat. Letting the fiery heat, the movements and her breath create whatever it was supposed to become.

The glob of glass was a mix of aquamarine and emerald, and Lily watched as it took shape. Nola kept at it until it was a fluid column. And then a cresting, crashing wave from some exotic sea. To Lily, it was perfect, but Nola continued to tweak it several more minutes before she must have finally deemed it finished. She hacked it from the blowing tube and hauled it to an annealing oven so it could do a slow cooldown to prevent it from cracking.

"It's beautiful," Lily remarked.

"Thanks." Nola picked up a thermos of water and drank deep. She poured some over her sweat-drenched head. "It's for Mom to put in an auction for a fundraiser."

Lily didn't know about this specific fundraiser, but their mother, Evangeline, was always raising money for various causes, and any piece from Nola would bring in loads of money.

"Do you have a name for the piece?" Lily asked. "It's, uh, very sensual."

Nola guzzled more water, and while she eyed Lily, she used a remote to turn on the AC. "Sensual," Nola repeated. "Funny you should ask about the name, because the piece is sort of like an internal mirror. What you see is what you're feeling. So, I suppose I should call it Lily's Lust."

Lily gave an exaggerated laugh, and it was maybe the lack of humor in it that caused Nola to back down from poking more fun.

"Did Jonas get back the results from the DNA tests?" Nola asked.

It was a question Lily had expected because she'd told Nola and Lorelei all about Wade Bentley. Jonas had likely told his brothers as well, but since the news hadn't hit the gossip mill, that meant everyone who knew was keeping the news to themselves. And that was a good thing.

Lily shook her head. "He sent in the test kits yesterday, so it could be two or three days before the results come back."

If it wasn't a match, if Bentley wasn't Eli's father, then it would all end there. Eli wouldn't even have to know about the gut punch this had given the man who'd raised him.

But if it was a match…well, that would be an even worse gut punch for Jonas because Bentley had made it clear that he wanted *his son*.

"Eli still doesn't know," Lily explained. "Jonas used Eli's toothbrush to send in with the DNA test."

Nola went to a fridge, took out a bottle of water and brought it back to Lily. She did all of that while continuing to study Lily. Trying to suss out what this visit was all about. Nola and she didn't have a twin ESP, but they were usually on the same page.

"You finally had sex with Jonas," Nola threw out there. "That's why you're thinking of sensual things."

"No." Lily stretched that out a few syllables, and her denial was the truth. Mostly. "Only dream sex," Lily finally admitted when Nola gave her a raised eyebrow and flat stare.

Nola smiled. "Was it good?"

It'd been amazing, complete with multiple orgasms, but Lily had no intention of fueling this particular fantasy. "I'm not having sex with Jonas."

"Not yet," Nola concluded. "But there's heat. Deny it and your nose will fall off from the lie," she quickly added.

Lily rolled her eyes at Nola's use of the old childhood threat from their grandmother. Even though her nose wouldn't fall off, Lily thought the denial would stick in her throat, so she didn't even attempt it.

"There's heat," Lily confirmed. "The same kind of heat I'd feel for any hot guy."

Okay, that was a lie. There were plenty of hot guys in Last Ride, but she darn sure wasn't having dream sex with any of them. Wasn't exactly lusting for them, either, though she could appreciate some innocent ogling if the opportunity arose.

"Jonas thinks he reminds me of Griff," Lily stated.

And that was all she needed to say for Nola to get the big picture on that. Jonas believed the heat stirring inside her was because he stirred memories of old heat between Griff and her. There were memories of that old attraction. Plenty of memories of Griff, too, but it sure as heck hadn't been Griff doling out those multiple orgasms in her dream. Nope. It'd been a bare-butted Jonas who'd been darn good in the sack.

Lily didn't want the lingering fire from the dream sex. Didn't want to imagine what it would be like to experience the real deal. No. She wanted to put a lid on these urgings so she could deal with the reason she'd come for this talk with Nola.

Since the AC hadn't cooled things down nearly enough, Lily motioned for Nola to follow her so they were standing directly in front of one of the fans. It would mean speaking louder because the fans were noisy, but it would dry up some of the sweat that had soaked through her clothes.

"When Jonas found the note in the mailbox two days ago," Lily started, "I thought it was from Cam."

She waited, giving Nola a chance to recall the note that Lily had told her all about. No way would Nola forget the part about the note saying it was time to hear the truth. And she clearly hadn't, because she went straight to Lily and pulled her into a hug.

"That must have given you the jolt from hell," Nola muttered.

"It did. A jolt, and the realization that I should have told Hayden the truth a long time ago."

Dang it. She had to blink back some tears, not over her daughter learning the truth about her mother lying.

But because this could cause a permanent rift between Hayden and her.

Nola sighed, tightened the hug for a couple more seconds and then pulled back. "How do you plan on telling Hayden? Or is that why you're here, to brainstorm ideas with me?"

"No, I'm mainly here for the hug," Lily admitted.

Nola gave her another one. This one was long and very much needed. "If you want to brainstorm, I'm up for it," Nola said.

When she eased back from her sister, Lily didn't take Nola up on the offer. She knew what she had to do. She just had to get it done.

"I plan on going to the cemetery to get a picture of Hezzie's tombstone for the Last Ride Society research, but after that I'm stopping by the police station to ask Azzie if she can get a phone number for Cam so I can call him," Lily explained.

That was the start of the game plan she'd come up with after wrestling with the problem for the past two days. Heck, since Hayden had been born.

"Cam," Nola repeated, the disapproval slathering the man's name. "How long has it been since you've spoken to that worthless turd who ran out on you?"

Lily had much less venom for her ex because she put the blame for their failed relationship squarely on her own shoulders.

"Thirteen years," Lily answered. Cam had left when Hayden had been just a baby, and he hadn't contacted Lily since. Then again, she hadn't attempted to contact him, either, before now. "I want to give him a heads-up in case Hayden manages to get in touch with him after I tell her that he's not her father."

Lily was seriously hoping Hayden wouldn't do that, but it was possible Hayden would be so upset with her that she'd want answers from Cam. Heck, maybe even Jonas or his brothers once the girl learned they were her uncles.

Nola patted her arm. "You want me there when you call Cam?"

Lily appreciated the offer, but she shook her head. "He might not even take my call, but I want to at least leave him a message." If Azzie managed to get his number, that was. Thirteen years was a long time, and it was possible he'd moved out of state.

She hugged Nola, murmured a thanks for the TLC that she'd known Nola would readily give, and Lily turned toward the door. However, it opened before she even reached it.

"Yeah, I know. Shut the door," Jonas said as he walked in. "I'm letting out the heat."

Nola grinned. "Nope. You're in luck. I'm already done with the piece." She motioned toward the annealing oven as she went toward it. "Want a peek at it? I'm calling it Dream Sex."

Lily narrowed her eyes at Nola and hoped Jonas didn't make any kind of connection to her. However, her hope went south because Lily didn't manage to get her eyes unnarrowed before Jonas looked at her. He no doubt— *no doubt*—saw the visual scolding she was giving Nola. Which meant he likely connected the dots and came up with a reason for the scolding.

He didn't say anything, but his gaze did linger on Lily, making her wonder if he was trying to figure out if there was anything he could say to get out of this embarrassing snake pit that Nola had set up for them. Lily was certain there was nothing he could say.

But she was wrong.

"I was at the hardware store ordering some supplies when I got a call from Larry," Jonas explained, keeping his voice low, probably so Nola wouldn't hear, but her sister was already on the other side of the workshop to give them the privacy that Nola suspected Jonas wanted. "He said he spotted a guy in a suit knocking on the front door of your house. It was Marty Cantor, the PI that Bentley hired."

Her stomach tightened. "What did he want? Why was he there?"

"He was looking for me, and he told Larry he just needed to pass along a message from his employer. I called the idiot employer and let him know to keep his lackeys off the ranch. Bentley said he merely wanted to know if there was any way to expedite the DNA tests because he was eager to get the results that he's positive will prove Eli is his son."

There was no *merely* in any of this. "Bentley's trying to strong-arm you."

Jonas made a sound of agreement. "Neither Hayden nor Eli saw the guy because they weren't home," he explained. "In fact, I saw Hayden when I was driving by O'Riley's café."

"She went on a shopping trip for school clothes, so she hasn't been home all morning," Lily explained. Then she paused. "We should have Larry talk to the other ranch hands and let them know to keep an eye out in case the PI returns."

"I'll do that." Jonas gave a weary sigh. "And I'll need to go ahead and tell Eli what's going on. If Bentley or the PI sees him, I don't want them springing the news on him."

Even though Lily knew that telling Eli would be hard, it was the right thing to do. "If I can help, let me know," she said, and she meant it. "Once you've told Eli, I'll explain everything to Hayden, too." She could work that in before she told Hayden the truth about Cam.

Jonas nodded, and their gazes connected again. He looked as if he wanted to say something to her, but then he seemed to change his mind when he glanced back at the annealing oven where Nola had said the Dream Sex piece was.

"I'll let you know once I've told Eli," Jonas assured her, and he headed out, leaving Lily feeling down and in want of another hug.

Not from Nola this time but from Jonas.

Since that was a temptation best left alone, she didn't go after him. Besides, she had her own personal mess to mop up.

"Thanks," Lily called out to Nola. "Not thanks for the Dream Sex remark but for hearing me out."

"Anytime," Nola assured her and came back across the workshop to give her a sisterly punch on the arm. It was the equivalent of a "good luck" and "let me know if you need help" all rolled into one.

Instead of heading to the police station, Lily fired off a quick text to Azzie while she walked back to her truck, and she asked Azzie if she could locate any contact info for Cam. There were plenty of gossips in Last Ride, but Azzie wasn't one of them, so her deputy cousin would keep the request to herself. Azzie gave her an almost immediate reply that she'd get right on that, leaving Lily to get right on the next thing she had on her to-do list.

She started the drive to the Parkman Cemetery.

It shouldn't take long for her to get a photo of Hezzie's tombstone. A step that seemed like overkill, considering there were already so many photographs of her ancestor's final resting place. Still, the research notes had insisted it be a recent photo, and since the research itself might turn out to be an "it's complicated" mess, taking a picture could be the easiest part of this process.

Lily recalled that in high school she'd actually done a report on her great-great-great grandmother, and she wondered if her own mother had that stashed away somewhere. Of course, there would be nothing scandalous in it. Maybe it would even be filled with lies, but it could end up saving her some time, especially since Hezzie's public life had been pretty much an open book.

According to the accepted spiel about Hezzie that Lily had put in her high school report, when the woman had been a young widow and the mother of three boys, she had started the town of Last Ride by building a church, a grocery store and a guesthouse—in that order—on what would become Main Street. Along with raising her sons, Hezzie had personally run all three for years before marrying her second husband, a rich rancher who'd ponied up the money so Hezzie could have more businesses built. That had added, added and added to what would become his wife's legacy. After he'd died, Hezzie's third and last husband had added even more.

Even if there did turn out to be a lot of dirt on Hezzie, Lily figured that wouldn't diminish the woman's accomplishments. Not in her eyes, anyway. But she could sort of understand folks wanting to keep the proverbial halo on an ancestor that the town revered.

Lily was still a good half mile from where Hezzie was buried when she spotted another cemetery, and as if her foot had developed a mind of its own, she hit the brakes and looked out at the field of tombstones.

One of them was Griff's.

She'd personally never seen it. Hadn't wanted to see it. Not when the grief had been fresh and raw. Later, when the grief had faded, then there had been so much anger. Too much for her to want to see Griff's final resting place, but she apparently wanted to see it now because her hands developed minds of their own, too. Lily turned onto the road that led to the graves.

She didn't have time for this, Lily reminded herself, and there was nothing she could gain from coming here. Still, she stopped, and braving the scorching heat, she got out to make her way to a trio of oaks in the corner of the cemetery. A year earlier when Nola had drawn Griff's name at the Last Ride Society meeting, Hayden had gone with Nola to get photos of the tombstone, and she had seen enough of them to know the general location.

Lily found it right away.

It was one of the smaller headstones in the cemetery, probably because it had been all Jonas and his brothers could afford at the time. Still, it was simple and tasteful and had the heart-touching script above Griff's name.

Beloved Brother.

She'd seen that in the photos, too, and it had given her a gut punch of emotion. Much as it was doing now. There was still some grief. Some answers. And plenty of questions, including why Griff had ended his life the way he had.

There was also the question of the ring.

It was a simple gold band on top of the tombstone, and it seemed to catch every available ray of sunshine so it was glinting and sparkling. Perhaps it was a wedding band, but it'd been etched inside with little hearts, so it was possible that it'd been meant for non-marriage purposes. It'd been too small for Griff's hands. The size was more suited for a woman.

There'd been a lot of speculation from folks as to what it was and why it was there, and Lily knew that most people believed she'd been the one to put it there. She hadn't. But the talk still lingered on about how in her grief-stricken state she must have put it there as a symbol that she would always be Griff's. Some pooh-poohed that since, after all, she had married Cam, but those who persisted on the theory of her being the ring donor believed she'd married Cam on the rebound.

Which was true.

On the rebound, grieving, scared and pregnant with a dead man's child.

All of those things were true, but still Lily hadn't been the one to put the ring there. And that led her to the big question of who had. Maybe it'd been left by one of Griff's former girlfriends. There'd certainly been some of those. It was also possible that it was just a sentimental gesture by someone who'd been touched by the death of someone so young.

It occurred to her that Jonas, one of his brothers or Cam might know who was responsible. The answer might also be in the box of mementos and such that Lily had packed away after Griff had broken up with her. She had tossed the items into a box, and she was pretty sure it had ended up in her attic.

Once Hayden got over the shock of learning the truth about her father, she might want to go through the box. First, though, Lily would need to have a look to make sure there was nothing disturbing. Or just plain embarrassing, since Griff had had a habit of taking pictures of her when she was half dressed. Or selfies of when they'd been kissing. There wouldn't be any nude shots, thank goodness, but Hayden probably wouldn't want to see her parents in a lusty teenage lip-lock.

"I'm still mad at you," Lily blurted out, her gaze sliding over Griff's name. And his death date. He'd died too damn young. "Then again, you were probably pretty pissed off at life when you got the diagnosis of ALS. If I'd known about it, I would have been pissed off right along with you."

She would have also been crushed. Devastated. But that would have only made her try to hold on harder to Griff. Which could have possibly played into him ending his life. He might have been trying to spare her. No chance of him doing that, though. She'd loved him, so sparing hadn't been an option. A part of her had gone straight into the grave with him. Then again, an even better part of him, Hayden, had gotten her through the darkest of days following his death.

"I'm going to tell Hayden you're her father," Lily went on. "I suspect she'll be pissed off, too. Not with you. You'll be the hero in all of this, but I'll be the 'liar, liar, pants on fire' mother."

As if confirming that, a blue jay let out a jarring squawk and jetted past her. Probably not a message from Griff, but it sort of felt like one.

She'd always been puzzled with people going to graves to talk to the dead, but she could now see the appeal of it. With the name right there in front of her, it brought the memories and feelings into the front of her mind, too. Added to that, the lost loved one couldn't argue or condemn anything that was being said.

"Since I'm here pouring out my heart," Lily went on, "I should probably tell you I have the hots for your brother. For Jonas," she clarified, in case Griff had actually somehow managed to tap into this conversation and wanted to know which of his three siblings she meant. "I'm not going to act on it because, hey, can't risk messing up a good thing." She paused and flushed when she remembered what had happened earlier. "But I had dream sex with him."

Shrieking, the blasted blue jay dived down at her, swooping so close to her face that she felt the air from his wings. That felt a little creepy and she truly didn't want to get into the details of the dream sex or the fact that Hayden had apparently heard her moaning out Jonas's name.

Figuring she'd had enough heart-to-heart with a man who was long gone, she turned. And did some shrieking of her own. Because there was a man peering around one of the trees.

"Don't hit me," he insisted.

But Lily had already gone into fight mode and had started to swing her purse at him to bash him in the face. Right before she made contact with said face, the sound of the voice sank in.

"Derwin," she snarled.

He made a "who else" sound, which she supposed he had a right to make since there probably wouldn't have been many old men wearing deerstalker hats following her around. And it was obvious he was following her since he was right here.

"What the heck do you want?" Lily snapped, and then everything inside her went still. "Did you hear what I was going on about?"

His hesitation told her that he had. Crap. The president of Sherlock's Snoops now knew she'd had dream sex with Jonas. This called for drastic action.

Putting on a seriously mean face, Lily stalked closer and aimed her index finger at him. "If you tell anyone what you just heard, I'll knee you in the balls, understand?" It wasn't exactly an empty threat. She wouldn't knee him, but she would curse him and call him every bad name in the proverbial book.

This time, he gave a quick nod. "And I'm sorry I interrupted your chat with Griff. I've been looking to have a private talk with you, and when I saw your truck, I decided to come up and wait for you."

"You waited within hearing distance," she pointed out.

He gave another nod, and she thought she saw some genuine regret that he'd overheard what he had. Derwin also made a furtive glance around as if to make sure no one else would be capable of hearing what they said.

"There's a blue jay squawking around, but I doubt it'll develop power of speech to repeat anything it hears," she said, and yes, there was still plenty of venom in her voice. "Now, what the heck do you want?" Lily repeated.

He stepped out from behind the tree. "It's about Hezzie."

She groaned. Of course it was. That was supposedly the reason he'd lurked outside her bedroom window.

"All right, spill it," she insisted. "No waffling, no whining about pinkie swears and such. Tell me what's so hellfired bad about Hezzie that you're convinced no one should ever know about."

Derwin didn't waffle. Didn't whine. He looked her straight in the eyes as he started spilling some very grimy dirt.

CHAPTER SIX

JONAS WENT ON the hunt for Eli. He hadn't wanted to text the boy because then he didn't know what to say. He definitely didn't want to message something like I have something to tell you or it's important we talk. Heck, even a simple where are you? might cause Eli to get alarmed, especially if the boy thought Jonas was checking to make sure he wasn't with Hayden.

Which Eli just might be.

It'd been about an hour since Jonas had seen Hayden at O'Riley's, so it was possible the girl had come back to the ranch and was with Eli. If so, they weren't at either of the houses, because Jonas had checked. First at his own house, which had been empty. No one answered the door at Lily's, either, which meant she was likely still off on her quest to get Cam's contact info and take a photo of Hezzie's tombstone.

Jonas headed to the main barn next, recalling that was where he'd found Eli and Hayden kissing two days ago. That "discovery" seemed a lifetime ago, and during those forty-eight hours, his own life had changed on a dime. And all because of that note Bentley had left in the mailbox.

It was possible—God, he hoped it was possible—that all of this mess with Bentley would come to nothing, that the man wouldn't have any kind of biological connection to Eli. If that happened, then Jonas still wouldn't be celebrating, though, because Lily's life was about to do its own "turn on a dime" thing, too, once she told Hayden the truth about Griff.

Jonas had barely made it to the barn door when he heard a vehicle pull into the driveway. His first thought was this would be the PI, and it surprised him just how much he wanted to confront the asshole for the attempted browbeating. But it wasn't the PI. It was his brothers, Wyatt and Dax.

Hell.

He loved his brothers, but a joint visit meant there was trouble. In this case, his trouble, no doubt, and the pair was there to either lend him moral support over the crap that was happening, or they were there to bust his balls for not already having come clean with Eli. Either way, Jonas was certain there'd be plenty of advice and commiserations doled out. Well, their own brand of commiserations, anyway, considering he was their big brother.

Wyatt was behind the wheel, and instead of parking in front of Lily's house, he pulled his truck to the parking area at the side of the barn where there was already a line of vehicles. It was an area they not only used for the tractors and other ranch equipment, but the hands parked there as well.

Neither Dax nor Wyatt asked if Jonas had a minute to talk because this wasn't an optional social call. "I was looking for Eli to tell him about Wade Bentley," Jonas said while they all made their way toward his office. "I'll spill everything, including the fact there are DNA samples on the way to the lab for testing."

"Good," Wyatt stated. "Because shit's about to hit the fan. A little while ago, a guy named Marty Cantor came to my ranch."

"He came to my place, too," Dax piped in, speaking

over Jonas's "under the breath" profanity. "When he asked about you, I told him to get lost."

"Same here," Wyatt chimed in. "Except I added some of those curse words you just used. After he left, I called Matt, but he said other than refusing to let the guy onto our properties, we can't actually run him out of town."

Yeah, when Jonas had talked to Sheriff Matt Corbin, he had told him pretty much the same thing.

"This PI has taken a room at the inn," Dax continued as they went into Jonas's office. "I haven't heard any gossip about Wade Bentley being there, too."

Jonas made a quick sound of agreement, and he was certain if Bentley had checked into the town's inn, he would have heard about it. Folks might not know who Bentley was, or rather they might not know that the man was claiming to be Eli's father, but there would have still been talk about a stranger staying in town. Talk like that would have made it back to either Lily or one of the ranch hands, who would in turn have relayed it to Jonas.

"Bentley's convinced he's Eli's bio dad?" Dax came out and asked.

"That's what he claims," Jonas said. "He also wants Eli to know what he says is the *truth*." He put some emphasis on that last word. "Whatever the hell he thinks the truth is, anyway. I figure he'll try to dump the blame on Maddie for him not being in Eli's life."

Neither Wyatt nor Dax argued with that. Blame and accusations with Bentley painting himself in the best light possible.

"The problem is I can't find a sinister motive for the man to seek out Eli after all this time," Jonas went on. "The guy's a doctor, and on the surface there doesn't seem to be loan sharks or such after him so he'd need Maddie's life insurance money that I socked away for Eli."

Though the money was something Jonas intended to investigate. There was a quarter of a million plus interest in a trust fund for Eli, and someone with computer hacking skills might have learned the money was in the boy's name.

"Bentley might need a kidney or bone marrow that he has to get from a blood relative," Dax threw out there.

Jonas frowned, but yeah, he'd already gone there in a general sort of way. Heck, he'd tried to come up with any and all reasons. "If he's sick or dying, I can't find anything about it," Jonas explained. "But this could be a 'make your peace before dying' kind of situation."

That theory would work if Bentley hadn't added the need for Eli to know the *truth* into this. And that brought Jonas back to his concern about Bentley trying to smear Maddie in some way.

"You want us there when you tell Eli?" Wyatt asked.

Jonas shook his head. "Best to do it solo." Then he shifted his attention to Dax. "But Eli might call you about it." That was because Eli and Dax had gotten close over the years. Maybe because Dax was seven years younger than Jonas, and Eli possibly looked at Dax as more of an older brother than an uncle.

"I'll be there for him," Dax assured Jonas. "For you, too. Are you all right?"

"I'm fine," Jonas answered fast.

He wasn't even sure if that was the truth, but when it came to his brothers, Jonas never wanted them to worry about him. After their parents had died in a boating accident when they'd been kids, Jonas had taken over more of a father role. Especially when they'd ended up in the care of a mean-as-a-snake cousin, Maude Muldoon, who hadn't done a whole lot of *caring*.

Dax and Wyatt exchanged a glance, letting Jonas know his *I'm fine* hadn't worked. They were worried.

"You're not going to lose Eli," Dax tried to assure him. "You've raised the kid, and he's yours."

If only. Yeah, he'd done the raising, and unlike Maude, Jonas had, indeed, done some caring. He couldn't have loved Eli more even if he had been his own blood kin. But he could lose him, and that was a fear that tore him from the inside out. He had to hope that all these years with Eli had created an unbreakable bond, but it was possible that Bentley wouldn't give up fighting for the son he seemingly hadn't cared squat about until now.

"Now, what's this about the Dream Sex glass piece that Nola made?" Wyatt asked, breaking the silence.

Jonas would have been happy about a change in subject. But not that particular one. "What about it?" Jonas snarled. And as he'd expected, the poking fun soon followed.

Wyatt grinned. "Nola said she was thinking of Lily and you when she made it."

Jonas didn't grin. No way did he want to be teased about dream sex with his boss. Especially since his stupid body was having thoughts about real sex with her.

"I'm not hooking up with Lily," Jonas spelled out for them just as Lily called out his name.

"Jonas, you're not going to believe the sex stuff—" She stopped when she threw open the door and spotted Wyatt and Dax. Both of his idiot brothers grinned in an "I told you so" kind of way that made Jonas want to punch them. "Oh, sorry."

Lily's face went red, and it looked as if she wanted the ground to swallow her up, but before that, before she'd blurted out the sex-stuff comment, he'd seen the surprise and maybe the excitement in her eyes. Excitement that he was sure wasn't meant for him since there'd been no sex stuff between them.

"I didn't know you were here," Lily muttered, obviously directing that comment to his brothers.

"Hi," Dax greeted her, oozing his usual charm. "We were just leaving."

Dax gave Wyatt a nudge with his elbow, and they hurried out after Dax murmured to Jonas to call if he needed them. The quick exit was no doubt because his brothers believed Lily and he had a personal aspect—sex—to discuss. They didn't.

"Is this about the Dream Sex glass piece that Nola made?" Jonas came out and asked her.

Judging from the way she blinked, the answer to that was no. She confirmed the no by shaking her head. "It's about Hezzie." Then she hiked her thumb in the direction of the door that his brothers had left open. "I'm sorry about interrupting your visit with Dax and Wyatt. Is everything okay?"

"Okay enough," he settled for saying. "I was about to find Eli and tell him about his bio father. Wait," he tacked on to that when she turned as if to leave. "What's this about Hezzie?"

She opened her mouth, then closed it as if she'd changed her mind. "The short version. According to Derwin Parkman, Hezzie was sort of a sex queen. She made, uh, porn."

Jonas was sure he did some heavy blinking, too. Along with looking totally stunned. Whatever he'd been expecting Lily to say, that hadn't been anywhere on his radar. Despite his mind being on other things, Jonas would have asked a question or two about Hezzie, but she motioned toward the door again.

"I'll just go so you can find Eli," she said. "Later, we can talk, and you can maybe fill me in on how he took the news."

"And you can fill me in on Hezzie," he countered. "Porn?"

She blushed, nodded and turned toward the door. "Let me know how it goes when you tell Eli."

Jonas didn't have time to respond to that because Eli stepped into view, and it was obvious from the boy's bunched-up forehead that he'd heard at least part of Lily's and his conversation. Jonas wasn't sure what topic he least wanted to discuss with Eli—the porn or what he needed to tell him.

"Am I in trouble?" Eli asked.

Lily glanced back at Jonas, obviously leaving this one for him to answer, and she patted the boy's arm before she headed out. Jonas gathered the breath that he was certain he'd need and motioned for Eli to come in.

"No, you're not in trouble," Jonas assured him, and once Eli was in the office, he shut the door. Word of this would get around soon enough, but Jonas didn't want any of the hands overhearing the private conversation he needed to have with Eli.

"Are you going to talk to me about kissing Hayden?" Eli asked.

It was tempting to press for an update on that, but Jonas didn't want to cloud the waters, especially with something that might end up sounding like a lecture. "This is about your birth father."

That was all Jonas said because he wanted to give Eli some time to let that sink in. And to see if Bentley or his pestering PI had already gotten the info to the boy. They clearly hadn't, because Jonas saw the shock register in Eli's eyes.

"Is he dead?" Eli asked after several moments.

Jonas hadn't expected Eli to make that leap, but maybe that was what he believed so it would justify why the man hadn't attempted to contact him before now.

"No," Jonas said but had to do an immediate backtrack. "A man claiming to be your father is trying to get in touch with you. Two days ago, he left a note in the mailbox for you in case you wanted to contact him."

Eli stared at him, and some confusion replaced the shock. *"Claiming to be,"* he repeated. "You don't think he is?"

Jonas refrained from saying he didn't want Bentley to be the bio dad because that would only do more water-muddying. This wasn't about him, about his feelings over what this would do to the boy he loved and had raised. This was about Eli.

"I don't know," Jonas settled for saying. "Your mom didn't tell me your father's name, so I'm having your DNA compared to his so we'll know for sure."

Eli went quiet again, and the thoughts and questions were no doubt firing through his head, so Jonas didn't push. Didn't offer up anything else, like how he'd gotten Eli's DNA and why he hadn't volunteered all of this when the note was found. No way did Jonas want to mention that Lily and he had originally thought the note was for Hayden.

"So, if the DNA is a match, he's my dad," Eli muttered.

The boy hadn't meant the words to cut like a knife, but they did. Mercy, did they. Because Jonas didn't want to share that *dad* title with anyone. But that was a selfishness that wouldn't do Eli any good.

"Yes," Jonas confirmed. "We might have the results in

a day or two. I was going to wait until then to tell you, but I didn't want you to hear it from anyone else."

Eli's gaze fired to his. "You mean anyone like Hayden or her mom. Do they know?"

"Lily does." And apparently he was going to have to touch on the mix-up after all. "At first, I didn't know who the note was for, so I showed it to her."

Eli groaned, and he sank down in the chair next to Jonas's desk. Jonas didn't think the boy's reaction was because Lily knew but rather because all of this was hitting him. Even after all this time, Eli likely hadn't shoved his bio dad completely out of his mind, but he also probably hadn't expected the guy to try to contact him.

"Mom always said he didn't want to be a dad," Eli muttered.

Yeah, she had, and Jonas was hoping that was the truth. Hoping that there wasn't some big bad truth out there about Maddie that would end up crushing Eli.

"What's his name?" Eli wanted to know.

Jonas went to the fridge and got them bottles of water. He had a long drink of his before he answered. "Wade Bentley." Again, he didn't volunteer anything else. He wanted Eli to hear all of this at his own pace.

Eli repeated the man's name a couple of times, the way a person did as if trying to recall if he'd ever heard it. When the boy shook his head, Jonas figured he hadn't.

"So, why does he want to see me?" Eli said after a long silence.

That was the million-dollar question, and Jonas didn't know the answer. It could be something as simple as a man wanting to meet the child he'd fathered nearly a decade and a half ago. But Jonas figured something had triggered that "wanting," and he had to make sure that Eli didn't get hurt because of that trigger.

"You've met him? Do I look like him?" Eli asked.

"I haven't met him. I've only spoken with him on the phone. I've also seen some pictures of him on social media, and no, you don't look like him. You favor your mother."

That was the truth. Well, Jonas hoped it was. It was possible he hadn't wanted to see any resemblance to Eli when he'd combed over that handful of photos.

Eli opened his water and downed nearly half the bottle. "All right." He repeated that a couple of times, too. "What happens next?"

Jonas tried to keep his expression and tone calm and unruffled. Hard to do when he wasn't feeling either of those things. "We wait for the results of the DNA test. If it's a match, well, we'll go from there."

Eli locked gazes with him. "You said he wants to see me, right?"

This time, Jonas responded with just a nod.

"Do I have to wait until the DNA test, or can I call him before that?" Eli asked, standing.

It seemed that every drop of air rushed out of Jonas's lungs. Eli no longer looked shell-shocked from the news. He looked excited. Happy.

Hell.

Jonas had thought that maybe Eli's first response would be anger over why the man claiming to be his father hadn't contacted him before now. Anger because he'd never been part of Eli's life. But apparently that didn't matter to Eli, and it showed in his son's hopeful grin.

"It'd probably be best to wait until we get the DNA results," Jonas was able to say after a couple of moments. "But if it's confirmed, you can call him."

Eli's smile widened, going from merely happy to down-right giddy, and he gave Jonas a backslapping hug. "Good, because I can't wait to meet him," he gushed.

Jonas stood there, reeling, sick to his stomach because it felt as if he'd just lost his son.

CHAPTER SEVEN

LILY FIGURED SHE should just go home and wait for Jonas to tell her how Eli had handled the news that his possible bio father wanted to meet him. After all, a talk like that could go on for hours and she had plenty of work waiting for her in her office. Added to that, she should work out what she needed to say to Cam once she had his contact info from Azzie.

None of those reasons, though, caused Lily to head out of the barn.

She just kept pacing and worrying. Eli had no doubt heard her tell Jonas about Hezzie and the porn, and that definitely wasn't something she'd wanted him to overhear. Teenage boys could blab, especially when it came to anything related to sex, and even though Lily hadn't gone into details with Jonas about Hezzie's adventures in the sex world, Eli could no doubt fill in the blanks.

Lily wanted to… Well, she wasn't sure what she wanted to say to Eli and Jonas about what the boy had overheard, but at a minimum, she owed Jonas an apology. Probably owed him more of those details, too, since he'd wanted to know Hezzie's deep dark secrets. Even if those sexual secrets were probably things she shouldn't be talking about with Jonas. With the heat simmering between them, she should probably keep her conversations bland with him.

Frustrated with herself, the pacing and the worrying,

Lily finally headed out of the barn, and she took out her phone to text Azzie again to see if she'd had any luck with Cam's number. She hadn't even managed to look at the screen, though, before she practically ran right into Hayden.

Apparently, she didn't know what to say to her daughter, either, because she garbled out a few sounds that were similar to those that Hayden muttered. They'd obviously given each other a start.

"Uh," they said in unison, and Lily fluttered her fingers toward the house, indicating that was where she was heading, while, also in unison, Hayden tipped her head to the barn.

"I'm looking for Eli," Hayden added. "We're going for a ride."

Lily went with another "Uh," while she tried to figure out what to say. Or rather what not to say. "Eli's with Jonas in his office. Best not to interrupt them."

Hayden's head snapped toward her, and the girl's gaze collided with Lily's. "Is Eli in trouble?"

Lily opened her mouth to give a quick no, but then she closed it and rethought her response. Strange that *trouble* had been what Eli had asked about as well when he'd first gone into Jonas's office. Even stranger that Hayden looked guilty of something. Exactly what, Lily didn't know, but she mentally went through the last couple of days. There'd been plenty happening, what with the Last Ride Society drawing, Wade Bentley's note and Lily planning to tell Hayden the truth about her father.

But Lily zoomed in on the rides that Hayden and Eli had been taking.

Lots and lots of rides.

Lily could have brushed that off as the excitement of trying out the new horses, but paired with that guilt that was practically oozing from Hayden, it was a combination that told Lily something was wrong. Maybe Eli had somehow learned about Bentley two days ago and had been talking it over with Hayden.

"Anything you want to tell me about Eli?" Lily came out and asked.

Hayden huffed and rolled her eyes. Both were proof that there was, indeed, something the girl was keeping from her. If so, maybe this was a sign for her just to go ahead and tell Hayden the truth.

"Did Mr. Buchanan tell you?" Hayden used that teen tone that was equivalent to a "huff and eye roll" combo.

Lily settled for making a noncommittal sound and a mother's stare. Best to just wait for Hayden to fill in the blanks on this. She didn't want to spill anything about Bentley that Hayden might not already know, but it was puzzling that her daughter would word her question that way. *Did Mr. Buchanan tell you?* indicated that Jonas had been the one who'd spilled something, and if he had, Jonas would have likely mentioned it. Then again, they hadn't exactly had a chance to finish their conversation before Eli had come in.

"Eli and I kissed, all right." Hayden threw her hands up in the air, and her tone went from pissy to defiant. "It's no big deal, but I guess Mr. Buchanan thought it was or he wouldn't have gone to you about it."

Lily kept up the mother's stare, but that was because it was about the only form of response she could manage. Seconds later, she got a "What?"

The question was obviously enough to get Hayden to continue. "It was just a kiss, that's all. I like Eli, and he likes me. There's nothing wrong with us kissing."

Now Lily managed to lift her index finger in a "wait a second" gesture. She needed that second to let all of this sink in. "You kissed Eli, and Jonas saw it?"

"Eli and I kissed each other," Hayden corrected, adding another huff. "There's nothing wrong with it," she repeated.

"I beg to differ." Lily forced her mouth and mind to get working. "Eli's father and I work together, and this could create an awkward situation." Awkward and troubling since Lily hadn't known Hayden even had an interest in boys. Great day, did that mean she needed to have *the talk* with her?

"Eli and I like each other," Hayden emphasized, and she seemed to think that would ensure there were no problems with her kissing a boy who lived right next to her. A boy she had been raised with and saw daily.

Because Lily could recall her own mother's objections to her seeing Griff, she throttled back on both the mom stare and her tone. "I'm worried about you developing feelings for Eli. If things don't work out between you, then it could be very uncomfortable for you two to be around each other."

Of course, a bigger fear was that things did work out. That the kissing could lead to other things. Like sex. Oh, yes. She definitely needed to have the talk with Hayden.

"Eli and I aren't like his dad and you," Hayden insisted, causing Lily to frown.

"What do you mean by that?" Lily asked.

Hayden's huff indicated the answer was obvious. "You and his dad have a thing for each other. Everybody knows you do."

Lily shook her head, dumbfounded at the *everybody*. Oh, mercy. Was that true? Were folks eyeing Jonas and her as if they were a sexual powder keg about to blow?

"But you're too scared to do anything about Mr. Buchanan and won't go for it," Hayden went on, "because it might mess things up. Well, Eli and I aren't scared, and even if it doesn't work out between us, it won't mess up anything."

Oh, from the mouths of babes. A babe who'd clearly never had to live with a broken heart while being around the heartbreaker. Lily would have tried to explain that in a way that didn't include her own experiences with Griff and their turbulent relationship, but she didn't get a chance. The barn door opened, and Jonas came out.

Jonas stopped as if he'd slammed on brakes attached to his feet, and he gave them both a wary glance. "Is, uh, everything okay?"

He probably thought she'd just told Hayden about Cam not being her father, so to cut off that confession at the pass, Lily went with, "Hayden just told me about Eli and her kissing."

Of course, that brought on more huffing and eye rolling from Hayden. "It's no big deal. We like each other," she said, as if that fixed everything in this potentially explosive situation. "Can I go now and find him?"

Lily looked at Jonas, and while he didn't nod, she judged from that troubled look in his eyes that he'd told Eli about Bentley. If so, Eli might need a friend right about now. Even a friend with kissing benefits. And Lily hoped that was the only "benefits" Eli was getting from her daughter.

"Yes," Lily finally said, and she'd barely gotten out the word when Hayden took off, practically sprinting away.

"I'm sorry," Jonas muttered, scrubbing his hand over his face. "I didn't tell you about the kissing because I was hoping it was a one-off."

"I'm not sure what it is," she admitted and wanted to

do some face scrubbing, too. There was a lot going on in their lives right now, and she didn't especially want to add a teenage romance to the mix. She also had no intention of mentioning what Hayden had said about everyone knowing Jonas and she had a thing for each other.

"I'll talk with Eli again about it," Jonas said.

Lily didn't refuse his offer. In fact, she welcomed it. "I'll have another chat with Hayden, too, though she doesn't see the dangers in fooling around so close to home."

Even though she hadn't intended to do it, her gaze met Jonas's. Oh, yes. He knew the dangers, too. Dangers that seemed to be growing by leaps and bounds, and all because of their gazes connecting. And holding. And because his gaze seemed to pull her closer and closer to him.

Lily thought of the amazing dream sex, and she couldn't stop the sensations that were tugging away at parts of her body. Tuggings that urged her to do the very thing she'd just cautioned her daughter about. Well, she'd cautioned Hayden about kissing, anyway. She hoped her daughter wasn't having hot dream sex with Eli.

Thankfully, the tugging and such ended when she yanked herself back to reality and remembered that Jonas had just spilled to Eli about Bentley.

"How did Eli take the news?" she asked.

He didn't jump to answer that, and Lily didn't think his hesitation was because he was having to yank himself back. No. He was troubled, which meant the chat hadn't gone well. If so, then it was a good thing that Hayden was going after the boy. She might be able to soothe him in a non-kissing kind of way.

"Eli wants to see Bentley," Jonas finally said. "In fact, he's excited about meeting him."

"Oh," she managed and then tacked on a "Well, crap."

Jonas made a sound of agreement and then groaned. "If Bentley is his father and he's actually a good guy, then it's only right for Eli to meet him. To get to know him," he added in a mumble.

There was no need for Jonas to spell out what might happen if Eli did get to know the man. And if Eli began to think of him as his father. Because that could lead to Eli wanting to be with Bentley.

"I'm sorry," Lily said, because she didn't know what else to say.

Raising kids was hard. Losing them, though, would be soul crushing, and since Lily was facing a potential soul crushing if Hayden rebelled when she learned the truth, she could definitely feel for what Jonas was going through.

"We should distract ourselves by talking about porn," she threw out there.

In hindsight, she should have chosen a different subject, what with the heat between them and all. It seemed to work, though. Jonas still looked troubled, but he also looked interested in a guy sort of way.

"Porn in general or do you mean Hezzie?" he asked.

"Hezzie porn," she verified. "I have no idea if it's true, but Derwin tracked me down at the cemetery and gave me an earful, all with the caveat that I should know what I might find if I dig deep into Hezzie's life."

Lily was still mulling over Derwin's motive for that earful of info. She wasn't sure if he'd been afraid she would stumble onto anything shocking and blab about it. So, maybe he'd wanted to provide her with the shocking stuff so she'd have time to absorb it and then choose to keep it hush-hush. Then again, he would just want her to spill it and let the Parkman descendants know their true roots.

"Derwin said that in the early 1890s, when Hezzie was

barely twenty, she became a photographer. One who spe-
cialized in nude shots, not the artsy kind, either. Her market
was mainly women interested in, um, sexual titillation."

Again, this wasn't something she should be discussing
with Jonas, who often provided her with plenty of titillation.
But at least for the moment he didn't seem to be thinking
about Eli and Bentley.

"What kind of pictures?" Jonas wanted to know.

Lily had to shrug. "Derwin just said naked guys." And
she had to admit that she, too, had been intrigued by her
ancestor's choice of profession.

Jonas's forehead bunched up. "How the heck did Derwin learn about all of this?"

"From Marie Parkman, who owned the antique shop
when she was alive. Derwin's known about it for nearly
forty years now, and he's kept it secret all this time."

The shop, Once Upon a Time, sold an odd collection of
just about everything, but Lily had never seen the current
owner, Millie McCann, display any naked photos, especially photos taken by their mutual ancestor, Hezzie. It was
possible Millie didn't even know about this.

"Marie apparently acquired some of the photos through
an estate sale about ten years after Hezzie died in the
1950s," Lily went on, "and she asked Derwin to help her
investigate it since one of the pictures was of Hezzie's first
husband, Horace Parkman."

"She photographed her husband," he muttered. "Maybe
like the forerunner to sex recordings people make on their
phones?"

That gave Lily a jolt of fresh heat. And curiosity. "Yes,"
she agreed.

She opened her mouth to ask if he'd ever made a sex
video but stopped herself in the nick of time. She didn't

need the images of a naked Jonas frolicking in her head, especially since she was still dealing with the "dream sex" footage.

"No," Jonas answered anyway. Either he'd read her mind, or her body was sending off heat from that jolt. The corner of his mouth lifted into a near smile that could have melted chrome.

Oh, man. She so needed to close the lid on these fires that Jonas was lighting. *I'm his boss*, she mentally repeated. It would have been a far more effective mantra had she not been imagining him naked.

"Anyway," Lily went on, forcing her mind off the raging lust, "Hezzie's photographs became really popular, especially with some buyers in New Orleans, and Hezzie ended up making a ton of money. It's how she was able to start Last Ride."

That didn't mesh with the currently held belief that Hezzie had used her money she'd inherited from her late husband to buy the land and start building. Lily had never heard a whisper of talk about Horace being a nude model. Then again, maybe he hadn't been, since it was possible that Derwin had gotten it all wrong.

"So, how many people know about the way Hezzie supposedly earned her fortune?" Jonas asked.

Lily had to shake her head. "If Derwin knows, then I suspect at least half of his club members do, too." She couldn't imagine the Sherlock's Snoops not sharing tasty tidbits like that with their like-minded friends. "Also, Alma is clearly aware of something that she wants to stay hush-hush." And again, Lily couldn't see Alma keeping stuff like that to herself.

"So, what are you going to do with this info?" he asked.

Again, she had to shake her head. "I think that decision

will stay in the 'to be determined' category for a while."
She took out her phone. "I did get a picture of Hezzie's
tombstone, so I've checked the easy thing off my to-do
list."

She showed him the photo, then paused. Lily looked up
at him. Felt more of the blasted heat. And did something
she was pretty darn sure would turn it to ice.

"I went by Griff's grave," she said. "My first time there."
She waited, and yes, the heat cooled. This time when Jonas
looked at her, he had that expression. The "you'll always
be Griff's girl" one.

And in a way he was right.

But she wasn't a girl now. She was a woman.

"I saw the ring that everyone gossips about," she went
on. "Any idea who put it there?"

Jonas took a moment before he answered. "No. Wyatt
and Dax don't know, either. We always assumed you'd
been the one to leave it."

"No," she quickly assured him.

She might have gotten into some more speculation about
that, but Lily heard Larry call out her name. She looked
over her shoulder to see the ranch hand making a beeline toward them, and Larry was sporting a concerned
expression.

"Did you leave the front door of your house open?"
Larry asked.

Lily frowned because she was certain she hadn't. She'd
come and gone through the back door when she'd made
the trip to see Nola and to the cemeteries. Maybe Hayden
had left it open, though, when she'd come back from shopping and lunch. She didn't usually lock up, but she made
a mental note to start doing that. She'd need to mention it
to Hayden, too.

But there was another possibility.

Had Bentley's PI tried to sneak in and find something that would help his boss speed up the process of confirming that Eli was Bentley's son? Or was this about the Hezzie research? There were a lot of people in Last Ride who might be worried about the stuff she could be uncovering about the woman.

"Also, this was lying on the porch," Larry said, handing her a folded piece of paper.

Lily's stomach dropped when she saw what it was. Another blasted note. Great. The last one had certainly messed with their lives and their heads, and she figured this one would try to do the same. Still, she took it from Larry, and Lily unfolded it so that Jonas and she would both be able to see it. One look at it, and Lily knew it was, indeed, another round of attempted messing.

"'You know what you need to do,'" she muttered aloud when she read it. "'So, quit stalling and do it.'"

CHAPTER EIGHT

STANDING AT THE window in Lily's kitchen, Jonas tried to keep a lid on his anger. Hard to do, though, because the note left on her porch had pissed him off. A bad kind of pissing off that made him want to kick something.

Preferably Bentley's ass.

But since he preferred not to end up in jail, he'd opted for trying to call Bentley to tell him to back the hell off. When Bentley hadn't answered, Jonas had made another call to Sheriff Matt Corbin, who was now on his way out to the ranch to talk with Lily and him.

"You want a beer?" Lily asked.

She was in the process of hauling food from the fridge. Lots of food. Cut-up veggies, grapes, whipped cream and a cheesecake. Apparently, this was how she intended to deal with the anger over having Bentley or his PI leave what was basically a whiny threat.

Jonas didn't mind the threat or the whine as much as he did the fact that the person who'd left that note had had to trespass to leave it on her porch. Lily had to feel a violation of sorts over that, and judging from the occasional mom profanity she was mumbling, she wasn't happy about that.

Thankfully, nothing had seemed out of place or missing in the house—they'd both made a search while he'd called Matt. Then again, in a house this size, someone could have taken something and they might not know.

Jonas declined her offer of the beer but took one of the cans of Coke she'd gotten from the fridge. Best not to have the smell of alcohol on his breath when he talked to a cop. Yes, Matt was his friend, but he was still the sheriff, and he was coming here on official business on his way to his own ranch that was only a couple of miles from the Wild Springs.

Lily went into the pantry and came out with a large jar of peanut butter and some crackers. She dragged out two plates and some silverware next, and while she settled into one of the chairs, she smeared some of the peanut butter not onto a cracker but rather a celery stick.

"I missed lunch," Lily muttered through the bites.

No surprise there. It'd been lunchtime when he'd run into her at Nola's, and she'd likely left to go to the cemetery shortly thereafter. Then there'd been the "interruptions" of Derwin's revelation and the note that Larry had found.

"Help yourself," she added, motioning to the stash.

He started to decline that, too, because he'd had lunch, but he munched on one of the crackers while he drank the Coke.

"Unless Bentley confesses to having left the note," Lily said as she crunched, "I doubt Matt will be able to charge him with anything."

Yeah, Jonas had already gone there because either Bentley or his PI might have been smart enough to wear gloves and not leave any evidence behind. Still, a warning from the cops might get the SOBs to back off.

Well, if it was the note-leaving SOBs, that was.

"What was Derwin's stance on the info he told you about Hezzie?" Jonas asked. "Is he in favor or against the truth coming out about her?"

She paused, obviously considering that with a *hmm*ing

sound. "He didn't spell it out, but I got the impression he wants everyone to know. He just doesn't want to be the messenger of such news. And you're thinking that he might have left that note to spur me into spilling it."

"It's possible. The note could have also come from someone else who knows Hezzie's secret and wants it revealed." Jonas mentally sighed. "And maybe I'm just grasping at straws because it pisses me off to think of Bentley pushing like this. It's the kind of crap that a sneaky kid would…"

His words trailed off as he saw his own kid. And Lily's. Eli and Hayden were both on horseback, and they were riding across the pasture toward the barn. They were smiling at each other. Not a friendly, "isn't this a pretty day" kind of smile, either. This looked like goo-goo eyes to him.

Lily must have noticed him not finishing his sentence, because with the rest of the celery stick in hand, she went to the window, standing side by side with him as they looked out. This time, Jonas's sigh wasn't an internal one. Neither was Lily's.

"Crap," she muttered. "I was hoping this would burn itself out before it even got started."

He was pretty sure she was talking about their kids and not the heat that was between them, but Lily did send a glance his way. A glance that Jonas was able to catch because he was doing some glances at her as well.

"There's not any especially good scenarios for this," she added, watching as Eli maneuvered close enough to Hayden to reach out and give her arm a playful poke. "If things escalate, as teen romances so often do, then we'll have to watch them like hawks to make sure they don't do something we're not ready for them to do."

Jonas nearly smiled at the way she'd worded that. Nearly.

Because, yeah, he didn't want teenage sex anywhere on their radar.

"And after the escalation," Lily went on, "there's the likelihood of crash and burn. Then we'd have to deal with that."

Jonas couldn't agree more. It was hard enough to handle teenagers when they weren't moping from a breakup. That made him think of Lily and Griff. They had been only a year older than Hayden and Eli when they'd started dating. No way did Jonas intend to ask when they'd had sex—

"Griff and I were sixteen," she said, as if she'd read his mind. "But I wasn't his first."

This seemed a good time to stay silent, because Jonas had known about Griff's first. It'd happened when he was fifteen, and it had prompted Jonas to give Griff the talk about safe sex and condoms.

Jonas muttered some profanity because it was obviously a chat he needed to have with Eli. Despite all the other stuff going on, this wasn't something Jonas wanted to fall through the cracks. No way did he want Eli to have sex at such a young age, but he also didn't want the boy to have to deal with a teen pregnancy.

The sound of an approaching vehicle had Jonas tearing his gaze from the window, but not before he saw Eli give Hayden another of those nudges. Oh, yeah. He had to have that talk. For now, though, Lily and he set their snacks aside and went to the front door. When Lily opened it, they saw that Matt was already out of his truck and was making his way to the porch. He was carrying a small satchel.

Matt was tall with a lanky build, and he looked just as much a cowboy as a cop in his jeans, Stetson and boots. He was darn good at both since he owned the Stallion Ridge

Ranch and had been a cop since his early twenties, first in Amarillo and now here in Last Ride.

"You okay?" Matt asked before he even reached them.

Both Lily and Jonas nodded, and after giving Matt a friendly hug, she motioned for him to follow her into the living room. She immediately picked up the note that she'd left on the coffee table.

"That's what was left on my porch," she explained.

Matt took gloves and an evidence bag from the satchel, and he didn't take the note from her until he'd put on the gloves. "I can send this to the lab, but I should let you know that it'll be a low priority for them. It could take months to hear anything back."

Months. Hell. "Could I pay to have it analyzed in a private lab?" Jonas asked.

"You could, but it would be hard for me to use the results to file any charges. If there are any actual charges to file, that is. Bentley or his PI could claim there aren't any no-trespassing signs posted and that they were merely dropping off the note."

"A note that seems threatening," Lily pointed out.

Matt nodded, read it and nodded again. "And when Jonas called me, he said your front door was open?"

"I texted Hayden and asked if she'd left it open, but she said she didn't. Neither did I," Lily added. "But nothing in the house looks as if anyone has rifled through it or anything."

Matt nodded, muttered a "that's good," and he slipped the note into the evidence bag. "I'll compare this one to the other that was left in your mailbox, but did you notice if the handwriting is the same?"

"It could be," Lily said, sitting on the sofa and motioning for Matt to take the chair. "It's hard to tell, though, because it's block lettering. We're sure that Bentley left the one in the mailbox. He admitted to that. Not sure if he'll fess up to this, though, because it feels like a threat."

"Yeah," Jonas agreed. He sat next to Lily and faced Matt, who dropped down in the chair across from them. "And if either he or his PI did come into the house, he's probably not going to admit that."

Matt made a sound of agreement. "I'm guessing none of your ranch hands saw anyone come to the house?"

"No," Jonas answered. "I'd asked them to keep an eye out for visitors, just in case the PI returned, but if someone parked up the road and walked here, the hands might not have noticed."

Matt glanced up from the note that he'd still been studying, and his eyes were all cop now. "That's happened before? Someone parking elsewhere and walking here?"

Lily didn't come out and wince, but she looked as if that was what she wanted to do. "Derwin did that the night of the Last Ride Society drawing."

Matt gave her a puzzled look. "Derwin Parkman?"

Lily nodded. "He said he didn't want anyone to know he'd come here to talk to me but that he needed to tell me some things about Hezzie. He got spooked, though, when he saw Jonas and ran off."

Matt stayed quiet for a while, obviously processing that, and Lily was no doubt doing some processing, too, as to how much to tell Matt about what she'd learned about her ancestor, just in case it played into this.

"You think Derwin could have left the note and gone into your house?" Matt pressed.

No quick nod for Lily this time. "No. There would have been no reason for him to do that. Earlier today, he found me at the cemetery and spilled what he'd wanted to tell me.

I think if he'd left the note here at the house before finding me, he would have let me know."

Matt stared at her for a moment. "I'm guessing Derwin told you about Hezzie Parkman's, um, checkered history?"

Now it was Jonas's turn to stare. He'd lived in Last Ride most of his life and had never caught a whiff of Hezzie not being the prim-and-proper founder of the town. Obviously, Derwin, Alma and Matt had caught more than mere whiffs.

Lily let out a long breath that she'd obviously been holding. "Yes, he told me. You knew?"

Matt lifted his shoulder. "Someone—best not to say who—came to me shortly after I took the job as sheriff and informed me that the town was built on Hezzie's tainted money. This person thought I should know but also said if I blabbed that a lot of people would be very upset. Not just with learning about Hezzie but with me, the messenger."

"Yes," Lily repeated, but it was more of a confirmation this time. It was more of her acknowledging that Matt and she were in the same boat. "So, you know about Hezzie photographing naked guys," she added in a mutter.

Matt blinked. Shook his head. "No." He stretched out the word. "I was told that Hezzie used to dress as a man, smoke, drink and play poker in the saloons. According to the source, she was really good at stud poker, and on one particularly good night, she won the saloon where she was playing. The Silver Slipper in San Antonio," Matt provided.

Jonas looked at Lily to see if Derwin had mentioned anything like that. Judging from her expression, the answer to that was nope.

"Anyway, my source said Hezzie then sold the saloon and used the money to start Last Ride," Matt continued, then paused. "I have no proof whatsoever about the poker playing or the Silver Slipper, though there are records that such a place actually existed. What about you? Any proof that Hezzie was actually into nude photography?"

"None whatsoever. I suspect if Derwin had had actual proof, like one of the photographs, then he would have shown it to me to confirm what he was saying."

Jonas had to agree with that. Then again, Derwin was old-school in some ways, so maybe he wouldn't have thought it fitting to show such a photo to a woman.

Lily sank back against the sofa cushion and seemed to relax a little. "So, two totally different stories about Hezzie. It's possible neither is true and that the standard accepted facts about her are, indeed, facts."

Jonas totally got the reason for Lily's hopeful tone and more relaxed body language. If the stories weren't true, she wouldn't have to be the messenger for what plenty of people wouldn't want her to tell. It would make these next weeks of research much easier.

"Well," Matt said, standing and motioning toward the evidence bag, "I'll check into this and see what I can find out. I'll also have a chat with Wade Bentley and the PI. Like I said, I probably won't be able to file any charges against them, but I'll see what they have to say." His gaze came to Jonas's. "If I press too hard, though, Bentley might just go ahead and try to find a way to tell Eli."

Yeah, Jonas had already gone there. "Eli knows about him." So, it wouldn't be a shock to the boy, but Jonas wasn't ready for the two to meet just yet. Not until he was certain Bentley was on the up-and-up.

"Is there any chance Bentley or his PI could tamper with the DNA kits that were sent to the lab?" Jonas asked Matt.

Matt's eyebrow lifted a fraction. "Is there any reason why he'd do something like that? I mean, if he's not Eli's biological father, then is there a reason he'd want Eli to believe he was?"

"I don't know," Jonas admitted. "I just have a bad feeling about all of this. And no, it's not because I'm jealous of Eli's so-called father surfacing."

Matt didn't question what Bentley's motives would be for lying about the paternity, but as a cop, he knew that many things were driven by money. Or revenge. If Bentley was twisted and hurt by Maddie's breakup with him, he might want to try to use her son to get back at her. And yes, that was reaching, since Maddie was dead and her relationship with Eli's father had ended nearly fifteen years ago.

"Eli inherited Maddie's life insurance money," Jonas added. "And there's the ranch. Wild Springs is successful. Profitable. Bentley might think I'd be willing to pay him off."

Judging from the sound of surprise Lily made, that was something that hadn't occurred to her yet. "If it's that, if that's the reason Bentley is sniffing around here, then you can arrest him, right?" she asked Matt.

Matt nodded. "It could be hard to prove, though, so it's best if there's a witness to any conversations either of you have with Bentley or the PI. You can't record him, not without telling him first, and they likely wouldn't say anything incriminating if they knew it could come back to bite them." He shifted his attention to Jonas. "Is Bentley listed as the father on Eli's birth certificate?"

"No." Jonas didn't have to check to verify that. He had Eli's birth certificate in the lockbox in his office. "Maddie left the father blank because Bentley had told her that he didn't want anything to do with the child."

"Good," Matt said, "because if his name was on it, then

Bentley could try to use it to force you into letting him see Eli."

That caused Jonas's chest to tighten, and he had to wonder what other tactics Bentley might use to get to Eli. Whatever those tactics were, whatever motive Bentley had, Jonas's first priority was to protect Eli.

"I'll let you know if I find anything," Matt assured him, and he headed toward the door.

Lily let him out. Then locked up, causing Jonas to curse, which in turned caused her to look up at him. "Oh, no. You're not going to shoulder any blame for my needing to lock up, something I wasn't so diligent about before Bentley."

Jonas was about to point out that if he didn't live on the grounds, Bentley wouldn't have come here. He wouldn't have left that note in the mailbox. But Lily just verbally rolled right over him.

"Besides, I'm not locking up solely because of Bentley. There's the Hezzie factor, and after what we just heard from Matt, I think it's clear that there are stories floating around about Hezzie. Stories that some people want to stay hushed and others want revealed. Fanatics on both sides might try to get in here to see what I've researched, and the revealers might leave a note like that."

He wanted to argue with her since this did feel like his responsibility, but her phone dinged with a text, interrupting whatever he might have said.

"It's Azzie," Lily muttered after she took out her phone and glanced at the screen. "She got Cam's number for me."

Jonas figured Lily would take some time to steady herself or wait until she was alone to call her ex. She didn't. Gathering her breath, Lily tapped the number and put the call on speaker.

"Best to do it now," she muttered, "before something else comes up to delay me calling him."

Considering how chaotic things had been, he agreed, but he hadn't expected her to want him to listen in on this call. Maybe this was her way, though, of making sure she went through with it.

There were three rings that seemed to last an hour before the call went to voice mail. Jonas had known Cam, of course, since he'd been Griff's best friend, and despite all the years that'd passed, he recognized Cam's voice when it began to pour through the room.

"You've reached Cam Dalton," he said. "Can't take your call right now, so leave me a message."

Lily cleared her throat. "This is Lily. Lily Parkman," she added, though Jonas was pretty sure Cam would remember his ex-wife. "We need to talk, so when you get a chance, please call me back. It's about Hayden," she tacked on after a hesitation.

She ended the call but continued to stare at her phone, and the longer she stared, the deeper her frown became.

"I'm not usually this much of a coward," she muttered.

"Not a coward," he assured her and hated that she was having to go through this. "It's been a rough day."

She made a sound of agreement and finally slipped her phone back into her jeans pocket. "Definitely no picnic. For you, either," she said, looking up at him.

Yeah, but he hadn't coupled the "no picnic" portion of the day with visiting Griff's grave. If he had, it wouldn't have been the ordeal that it likely had been for Lily. But Jonas had to rethink that. Maybe a visit wouldn't be so comfortable. Not solely because seeing the tombstone would remind him of Griff's untimely death. No.

It'd be because of this fresh heat zinging between Lily and him.

The heat felt like, well, cheating or something. Like he was betraying Griff, and that was why he wouldn't act on it. Why he had to figure out how to make things the way they had been between Lily and him before this chaos had thrown them together. Before the note in the mailbox, there'd only been a little heat. The kind he could ignore.

He stopped again. Did some more rethinking. And realized it was a sad day in a man's life when he started BS-ing himself.

There'd been heat between Lily and him for years now, and he'd never been able to ignore it. He'd just been better at keeping some distance between them so the heat didn't get a chance to flame up and burn their asses.

Lily looked up at him the exact moment he looked down. Now, this should have been a signal for him to come up with an excuse, any excuse, to get the hell out of there.

He didn't.

"Screw it," she muttered, and coming up on her toes, she brushed her mouth over his.

For a little bitty kiss that hardly qualified as a kiss, it definitely had a bite to it. A bite she must have felt, too, because she jumped back from him as if she'd just gotten scalded.

"I'm sorry," she said. "We work together, and I'm your boss. I shouldn't have done that."

Well, he wasn't going to call human resources and complain. But, proving that the kiss had left him stupid, he went closer and did a quick touch of his mouth to hers. Not a tit for tat, exactly, but because he'd wanted to see if a second little bitty kiss could pack as much heat as the other one.

It did.

Heat that felt as if it had, indeed, burned his ass. And other parts of him, too.

"I'm sorry," he said, repeating her apology, and Jonas shoved aside both heat and stupidity and headed out the door.

CHAPTER NINE

LILY READ THROUGH the monthly business report that Jonas had emailed her. Yes, emailed. Normally, it was something he handed to her in person, but he'd opted for the non-personal delivery with this one.

And that made her want to hit herself over the head with her laptop.

Three days ago, she'd kissed him, and he'd shocked the heck out of her by kissing her back. Talk about playing with fire, running with scissors and doing every other dangerous thing possible. Jonas and she had had a wonderful working relationship. A wonderful friendship, too. Other than her sisters, Jonas was her best friend, and she'd blown it, and all for a couple of seconds of pleasure.

Okay, it'd been more than a couple of seconds.

The kisses had been quickies, but the immense pleasure from them was still giving her a buzz. Not good. Because pleasure was obviously addictive, and her body was clamoring for more, more, more. If Jonas's body was doing the same, and she thought maybe it was, then it made sense for him to avoid her. Even when they were both going through their own mountain-sized trouble.

Cam still hadn't returned her call, so she had the looming worry of telling Hayden about her father. Lily had given herself a deadline, and if she hadn't heard from Cam by the end of the day, she intended to go ahead and tell her daughter the truth. Then deal with the inevitable fallout.

So, yes, mountain-sized trouble.

Since Jonas had kept her updated with texts, Lily knew that Bentley and his PI had denied leaving a note on her porch or going into her house. Even when Matt had let them know he'd be sending the note to the lab and interviewing ranch hands to see if any of them had spotted the men at the ranch, both Bentley and his henchman had claimed innocence. That basically tied Matt's law enforcement hands, and he'd only been able to give them a warning to stay away from the ranch, Jonas and Eli.

So far, the men had heeded Matt's "stay away" warning, but Bentley was still pestering Matt to get the DNA test expedited. However, since the results were due back any day now, they'd all know soon enough. That soon enough would likely be too soon for Jonas. But she reconsidered that. Maybe he was in the same mindset as she was and just wanted to get the truth out in the open so they could deal with it.

"I'm heading to the barn for a ride," Hayden called out to her a split second before she appeared in the doorway. "I'll be with Eli, so does that mean you'll lecture me about it first?" She didn't add an actual eye roll, but there was an implied one.

"Do you need a lecture?" Lily countered.

Hayden clearly hadn't expected that response and gave an actual eye roll. "No, and I don't want you to give me another talk." She put the last word in air quotes.

Lily had, indeed, done the talk with her two nights ago. The entire spiel about waiting for sex until you were in love, which Lily had emphasized probably wouldn't happen until Hayden was much older. Lily had dwelled on safe sex, all sorts of nasty diseases and unwanted pregnancies. It definitely hadn't been a "sunshine and roses" kind of chat, but Lily thought she'd gotten her point across. And that point was Hayden shouldn't be going past second base with Eli or any other boy for at least another year or two.

Or twelve.

"How's Eli doing?" Lily asked. "How's he handling the news about his possible dad resurfacing?"

Hayden's face brightened a little. "He's pumped about it. I mean, all this time he thought the guy wanted nothing to do with him, and now that he does, Eli can't wait to meet him."

Lily felt for Jonas. Not only because it must feel as if he were losing his son but because Jonas was worried about whether or not Bentley was on the up-and-up.

"See you," Hayden added, and she headed off for that ride that Lily hoped stayed only a ride. And maybe a friendly ear if it turned out that Eli needed to talk to her about what was happening.

Lily jolted a little when her phone rang and automatically began to steel herself up, something she'd been doing since she'd left that voice mail for Cam. Not Cam but it was a familiar name on her screen.

Alma Parkman.

Since Alma was no doubt calling about the Last Ride Society drawing, Lily had to do some steeling up of a different kind. "Good afternoon, Alma," she greeted her.

"Afternoon to you, too. I know it hasn't even been a week yet since the drawing, but I'm checking to see how the research is going."

Lily didn't have to debate whether or not she would spill what she'd learned from Derwin and Matt in the five days since she had drawn Hezzie's name. She wouldn't. That was because she hadn't verified any of it and didn't want to start any gossip with what could turn out to be tall tales.

"I got the photo of Hezzie's tombstone," Lily told the woman, "but that's about it." She glanced at the box Alma had left her. It was in the exact spot where she'd put it a week ago. "I'd planned to start looking through the info you gave me tonight."

Not a lie. Lily was planning to do that if work or something else didn't get in the way. She needed to talk to Hayden. And Jonas. She needed to try to undo the damage caused by those kisses. And while she was at it, Lily also should figure out a way to make herself immune to the man who'd doled out that kiss.

"I know you told me the contents of the box wasn't the actual story of Hezzie's life," Lily went on, "but I'll still go through it and see what's there." Would see, too, if there was any hint whatsoever of the things Matt and Derwin had told her.

Alma didn't respond. In fact, the woman stayed quiet for so long that Lily thought the call had been disconnected. "Alma?" she finally prompted.

The woman's sigh sounded strong enough to blow out candles on a cake. "I'm here. Let me just lay this out there and you can think on it. I'm sure if you start digging into Hezzie's life that you'll hear things. People talk. People take little kernels and turn them into cornfields."

Lily couldn't argue with that and wondered if the nude pictures, poker playing and saloon were cornfields. "Yes," she said as another prompt since Alma had stopped talking again.

"All right, this is me spelling it out since I'd rather you hear it from me. When I'm done, I'm hoping like a broke preacher passing the collection plate that you'll keep it to yourself and write your research report in a manner that's fitting to our ancestor and town founder."

In other words, you want me to lie. That was the first thought that popped into Lily's head, but thankfully it didn't pop out of her mouth. No need to get snarky with Alma when this was likely gnawing away at her. Alma was a pillar of the community, giving her time and money to make Last Ride a better place. If Hezzie's reputation was smeared, that smear would also be on the town she loved.

Still, Lily had to wonder if folks shouldn't know the truth. Or if the truth would surface with or without a research report. She was definitely on the fence as to what to do about it, but one thing was for certain: she wouldn't include anything in the research that she hadn't verified.

Alma gave another of those gusty sighs. "All right, here goes. Hezzie had a business of supplying a certain kind of books to a certain kind of people."

Lily waited for more, but that was apparently it. "Books?" Lily finally asked.

"Ones with a lot of sex and stuff in them. Pictures, too. Hezzie got them from somebody in New Orleans and became a distributor of sorts. There was apparently a market for that sort of thing. There's more," Alma quickly tacked on to that. "Hezzie wasn't actually married to her first husband, Horace Parkman. They just shacked up, and she took his name after she had their first son."

This time it was Lily who didn't speak, but she was certainly mulling that over. The sex books could have been connected to what Derwin told her about Hezzie photographing naked men, but neither he nor Matt had mentioned the marriage deal.

"Now, I know you're judging Hezzie," Alma said. "Other folks will, too—"

"No," Lily interrupted. "I'm not judging her. I suspect women like her had limited career choices back in the late 1800s, and maybe it wasn't easy to actually get married. I mean, if you lived in the sticks, it could have been hard to get a marriage license or find someone to perform the ceremony."

"I'm glad you feel that way." But there was no relief in Alma's voice. "Full disclosure, though—Hezzie's grand-daddy was a minister who could have gotten them married in no time flat. Hezzie was just apparently what we'd call headstrong and set out to earn her own fortune with or without the benefits of wedding vows. Of course, that means many of Hezzie's descendants spring from her first-born that some say was born on the wrong side of the sheets."

Yes, and that might bother some people. Obviously, not Lily, though, since that tacky term could be used on her own daughter.

"I just want you to think long and hard about anything you write in your report," Alma went on. "Think long and hard, too, about who you talk to about this. Even carefully worded questions can lead to gossip."

True, and they could also lead to the truth getting out. Oh, yeah, she had some thinking to do.

"Is there any proof of, well, anything you've said in the box of stuff you brought over?" Lily asked.

"None, and there's nothing about it in the research library. I check any and everything that goes in there to make sure it doesn't smear Hezzie's name."

Lily could see Alma being diligent about that sort of thing, and it ruled out the woman for having left the note on her porch. Judging from everything Alma had just said, there was no way she wanted the truth out about Hezzie.

"I'm not going to censor whatever you decide to write," Alma added. "But I just want you to think hard about the poop storm it'd cause if anything I've told you got out."

Definitely, and that poop storm would be significantly worse if she added the details of what she'd gotten from Derwin and Matt.

"I will think hard about it," Lily assured her, and after Alma gave a sound of satisfaction, they ended the call.

Lily sat there a moment, staring at the box and wondering if and how she could get to the truth about Hezzie. She couldn't ask anyone in town because Alma was right about the gossip, but there might be something on the internet. Maybe something in the old records, too, that would prove or disprove Alma's claim of the timing of Hezzie's marriage and Hezzie's ownership of the Silver Slipper.

Going with that, Lily went to a search engine and typed in the name of the saloon. And got way too many hits. She added *Texas* and fared somewhat better, but there were still a lot of sites with those three words. Lily began to scan through those to see if any of them had a connection to Hezzie or the likely time period for the poker game.

When her phone rang again, she didn't pull her attention from the laptop. Lily answered it without looking at the screen because she figured it was Alma calling back with a tidbit she'd forgotten to mention.

"Lily," the man said.

Cam.

And with just his mere mention of her name, she got yanked back into the past. Both a good and bad yank. There were memory flashes of the three of them. Griff, Cam and her. Flashes, too, of the aftermath that'd followed Griff's death.

"Sorry I'm just now getting back to you," Cam added.

"I've been away on my honeymoon, and Elsa and I made a pact not to check our phones when we were in the islands."

She didn't know this Elsa or what islands he meant, but then, she hadn't kept up with his life. "Congrats on the marriage," she felt compelled to say.

Compelled because she was in the neutral zone when it came to her feelings for Cam. No love, no hate, only the regret that she'd dragged him into her messy life after she'd lost Griff.

"Anyway, how the heck are you?" Cam asked, and he sounded way too cheerful for the conversation she was about to have with him. "I heard somewhere you're a rancher now."

Ah, small talk. Not what she wanted, and it definitely wasn't settling her nerves that'd popped right to the surface. Still, she didn't want to be rude by cutting him off and diving into what she had to tell him.

"Yes, I am a rancher," Lily verified. "I bought the Wild Springs and raise Andalusians and Arabians."

"Wow, the old Sandiford place. Good for you. You always did like the horses."

"Yes," she muttered. She started to ask him what he was doing these days, but those unsettled nerves were shouting at her.

"Look, Lily," Cam continued before she could blurt out anything. "For years now I've wanted to tell you how sorry I am about how things ended up working out with us. We were so young. So stupid," he added with a chuckle. "But I hate the way I left things between us."

"Yes," she repeated and just went with it before he could cause her to stall again. "I'm going to tell Hayden that you're not her father, that Griff is. I wanted you to know in case she tries to get in touch with you."

Silence. No small talk, no verbal reaction of any kind, for a string of really long moments.

"Why?" Cam finally asked, and the cheeriness was finally gone from his tone.

For a simple one-word question, it was a doozy because it encompassed a lot of possibilities. For instance, he could be asking why she wanted to tell Hayden now. Why was it important that Hayden know since Griff was dead? What had happened to make her come to the decision to reveal the secret she'd kept all these years?

Lily didn't want to get into her trigger being the note in her mailbox. Especially since that had been for Eli and not Hayden. Still, it had given her the mental shake she'd needed.

"Is this about Griff's ALS diagnosis?" Cam added.

Lily went still because that was one question she hadn't added to the possibilities of that *why?* "You knew about that?"

"Yeah. Are you worried that Hayden might have inherited it from Griff?"

She had been worried. Terrified, actually, when Nola had uncovered the ALS diagnosis when she'd been researching Griff's name for the Last Ride Society.

Lily didn't ask Cam how he'd known about the ALS. It was possible Griff had told him. Equally possible he'd heard about it from someone in Last Ride since the news had created a lot of gossip when Nola had written it out in her research report.

"I talked with Griff's doctor, and while he wouldn't share any medical info with me, he did with Jonas," Lily explained. "Griff didn't have what's called familial ALS, so he wouldn't have passed it on to Hayden."

"Well, that's good," Cam said. "So, if it's not medical, why tell her after all this time?"

"Because she should know the truth. I should have told her long before now."

Cam didn't jump to argue with her. "She's a teenager, so she might not take the news well."

"Probably not," she muttered.

"Look, if you're telling Hayden because you're worried about her coming to me and learning the truth, don't be. I won't tell her. And Elsa and I aren't planning on having kids, so it's not as if I'd have to explain to them about a child who isn't their biological half sibling."

She didn't ask if his wife knew the truth. No need since Cam had obviously written them out of his life when he'd left and never gotten in touch with them.

"Hayden has biological family," Lily spelled out for him. "Three uncles who live right here in Last Ride, including the uncle, Jonas, she's been raised around most of her life. She should know that." And now that she was spelling out the reason, Lily was even more disgusted with herself for not doing this sooner.

"Look, I'm a psychologist now," Cam continued a moment later, "and I can give you some pointers as to how to talk to her. Also, if she wants to talk to me afterward, then give her my number." He paused. "Jonas knows the truth?"

"He does." She nearly added more, that Jonas and she were friends. Close friends. But the reminder of those kisses that weren't actually kisses had her holding back.

"Good," Cam concluded. "Then maybe Jonas can help you tell her. He always did strike me as levelheaded."

She got yet another jolt of heat from the memories of those kisses. And who was she kidding? They were actual kisses. The quality of a kiss wasn't determined by length but rather intensity and pleasure, and there'd been a whole lot of those two things.

"You still there?" Cam asked.

That yanked her back from her "kiss grading" daydream, and Lily made a sound to indicate she was. "Well, I just wanted to give you a heads-up," she said, wrapping up the call.

But Cam obviously had other ideas about the wrapping up. "I was wrong to have pressed you to marry me," he admitted. "Wrong to make you promise not to tell anyone that I wasn't the father of the baby you were carrying. I was so much in love with you, Lily." He gave a dry laugh. "I mean, head over heels in love with you, and that blinded me to the reality that you were never going to get over Griff. *Never*," he emphasized. "Griff was your one and only."

Lily frowned, and her frown was partly because a few seconds earlier, she'd been rating Jonas's kissing skill set. But it made her wonder if Jonas thought the same thing, that Griff had been her one and only. If so, that would give him yet another reason to make sure their lips never met in another kiss.

"I should have just been a good friend to you after Griff died," Cam went on, "and not pressed you for anything else."

Yes, but she went through the reminder again that Cam and she had both been so young and grief-stricken over losing Griff.

"This isn't only on you, Cam," Lily said. "Marrying you was one of the biggest mistakes of my life."

Lily heard the gasp, and for a moment, she thought it'd come from Cam, that he'd been shocked to hear her spell it out like that.

But it wasn't Cam.

Lily's gaze flew to the doorway where she saw the movement. Where she saw her daughter. And she realized that the gasp had come from Hayden.

She quickly replayed what she'd just said to Cam, and she groaned. "I didn't mean it like that," she told Hayden, the words rushing out as she got to her feet.

But Lily was talking to the air because Hayden had already turned and was running away.

CHAPTER TEN

JONAS HAD JUST made it onto the back porch of Lily's house when the door flew open and nearly smacked him in the face. He dodged it, barely, but then Hayden bolted out and slammed right into him, her head hitting his chest so hard that it knocked the breath out of him.

Despite the gasping and wheezing he was doing, Jonas wrapped his arms around her, and since they were off-balance, he tried to keep them from landing on their butts. The girl had been running and obviously hadn't been watching where she was going.

She was also crying.

One look at those tears sliding down her cheeks, and Jonas did some mental cursing. Lily had likely told Hayden the truth. A truth that she clearly hadn't taken that well.

"Hayden?" Lily called out.

Jonas was still fighting for breath, so he didn't respond. Neither did Hayden. Well, the girl didn't respond to her mother, anyway.

"I don't want to see her," Hayden insisted with more of those tears falling. "Keep her away from me because I don't want to hear anything she has to say."

Yeah, he'd deduced that from the way she'd been blindly running and trying to get out of the house. But Jonas held on to her, mainly because they were both still unsteady and because he didn't want Hayden to escape until he'd tried to get her to stay put and talk to her mother.

A very frantic mother.

Like Hayden's tears, one look at Lily's face, and he had no trouble seeing the panic that was etched there. Some relief came when she spotted Hayden and him, but she practically skidded to a stop and then took a few cautious steps toward them.

"Hayden," Lily said, her voice tight and reflecting a tangle of nerves. "I didn't mean—"

"I don't want to see you," Hayden repeated. "I don't want to see anyone right now." And with that, she tore herself out of Jonas's arms and leaped off the porch steps. She broke into a run toward the barn the moment her feet landed on the ground.

"Hayden?" Lily called out again. She hurried onto the porch as if prepared to go after the girl, but then she stopped. And cursed. A whole bunch of cursing, some of it generic, but most of it was aimed at herself.

"You told her about Cam," Jonas concluded, and this was where he wanted to do some nongeneric cursing at himself. Because he didn't pull Lily into his arms and try to give her a comforting hug.

He could blame the kiss for that, which meant he could blame himself. He'd violated way too many rules when he'd lost his mind and kissed her. And now they were both paying for it, since Lily wasn't getting the TLC that she could have clearly used, and he was beating himself up to hell and back for screwing up.

"No," Lily said, and now she began to cry. Not loud hiccuping sobs but soft quiet tears that pooled in her eyes. "Hayden overheard me talking to Cam. She overheard me say that marrying him was one of the biggest mistakes of my life."

Oh. Jonas had no trouble following that through to the blanks that Hayden had filled in. The girl believed if the marriage was a mistake, then so was she.

"And now Hayden thinks…" Lily started, but then her words trailed off, and she stared at the barn where Hayden had no doubt ducked inside. She lifted her teary eyes to meet his. "I know this is a huge favor, but could you go after her and try to make her understand that I wasn't talking about her? You heard what she said, and she won't be in the mood to listen to anything I say right now." .

Since he had a teenage son, Jonas couldn't agree more. Hayden was upset. Specifically, she was upset with her mom, and it was going to take a little while for Hayden to cool down enough to listen to reason. Or in this case, listen to the truth.

"It's not huge," Jonas assured her, not wanting Lily to feel as if she owed him a big favor in return. This was something that friends did for friends.

Friends.

And that was why he resisted another round of urges to hug her. Instead, he gave her what he hoped was a reassuring look, a quick squeeze of her hand.

"I'll find her and try to talk to her," Jonas added, "but when I'm done, it might be a good time to go ahead and tell her that Cam isn't her father. That way, she'll better understand why you said what you did."

Lily nodded, but her expression was filled with more of that panic and dread. She might believe the truth would already add fuel to her daughter's anger. And it might. But he thought once Hayden had the big picture that the healing could finally begin.

Jonas made his way off the porch, stepping back out into the blistering heat of the summer sun, and he went to the barn. He hadn't expected to find a sobbing Hayden sitting on the floor, and he was right. She was nowhere in sight, so he started looking for her.

As expected, Hayden wasn't in his office. He wouldn't be her first choice of someone's shoulder to cry on, but Eli would be. After Jonas did a search of the barn, he went through the back and into the corral. And there she was. Sobbing and with her face buried on Eli's shoulder.

They were sitting on the ground with their backs against the barn and thankfully in the meager shade of the over-hanging roof. It was still unmercifully hot, but Jonas figured if he convinced Hayden to talk to him, he wouldn't be able to get her to agree to go inside with him—where she might think Lily was waiting to ambush her with the dreaded talk Hayden didn't want to hear.

"I don't want to see her," Hayden snapped when she looked at him.

Jonas just nodded and made eye contact with Eli. Judging from the look in the boy's eyes, Eli was well aware that he was out of his depth here. Probably because he hadn't had any experience comforting a teenage girl. Neither had Jonas, but since he had three younger brothers that he'd helped raise, he'd been through some ugly bouts of temper and hurt.

"Don't try to make Hayden go to her mom," Eli pleaded with him.

"I won't," Jonas assured him, "but I would like to talk to Hayden." He waited for the girl's gaze to come to his.

"She sent you after me to bring me back to the house," Hayden flung out there.

Jonas stayed put, shook his head. "Your mom asked me

to check on you. I won't take you back to the house unless that's what you want."

After all, Hayden wasn't a toddler in the throes of a tantrum. She was in pain and needed to hear what might help ease some of that pain. If Jonas just blurted out that Hayden had misunderstood Lily, the girl likely wouldn't accept it. Nope. First, he had to try to do some soothing.

"I'm not leaving her," Eli insisted.

Jonas nodded and actually approved. It would have been easier for Eli to hand a crying girl off to him, but the boy was going to stick this out. Which meant if Eli didn't already know what had upset Hayden, he soon would.

Jonas walked closer, sinking down on the ground on the other side of Hayden and wishing he could do this in the AC. When you were fourteen, you obviously didn't feel the sweatbox heat the way he did. Still, Jonas didn't want to try to coax Hayden elsewhere when she was barely holding it together.

"Don't try to defend her," Hayden muttered. "I heard what she said."

"Yes, but I have to defend her because what you heard wasn't what she meant." And with that opening, he stepped onto boggy ground. "What your mom said was in the heat of the moment, and she didn't mean it the way it obviously sounded to you. She meant she should have just had you without being married, since Cam was too young to make that kind of commitment to her."

"He left me, too," Hayden snapped.

Oh, yeah. Boggy ground, indeed. "Because he was young and didn't know how to handle being a father or a husband. But that doesn't mean your mom believes you were a mistake. She doesn't. She loves you, and it's cut her to the bone that you were hurt by what you overheard."

There. That was about the best he could do without going into anything else that had played into Cam's decision to leave. For instance, he'd left because his wife wasn't in love with him, and the child she'd given birth to wasn't his.

The silence settled between them, blending with the sounds of the horses that were cropping grass in the nearby pasture. Silence that shattered, though, when Eli's phone buzzed.

"It's the coach, calling about football practice," he said, looking at the screen. Then the boy's gaze drifted to Hayden. She'd quit crying, but she still looked plenty unsteady. "I can talk to him later," Eli decided.

"No, go ahead and take the call," Hayden insisted. "You've been worrying about if you'd get to start the first game or if you'd be coming off the bench."

Jonas had known about the upcoming football game. It was scheduled for the first week of school. But Jonas hadn't known that Eli was worried about whether or not he'd start on the junior varsity team. Well, hell. That was what he got for focusing on Bentley, the damn DNA test and beating himself up about this unwanted attraction to Lily.

Eli had a quick debate as to what to do, and he finally stepped away to take the call. He didn't go far, though, and he kept his attention on Hayden.

"Did my dad leave me because Mom was in love with your brother?" Hayden came out and asked.

Oh, man. The girl could go for the jugular, and she must have taken Jonas's hesitation as a cue for her to continue.

"I know about your brother, about Griff," Hayden added, causing Jonas's heart to skip a beat or two.

"Oh?" he settled for saying.

"Yeah, I helped Aunt Nola with the research she did on

him for the Last Ride Society deal. I even took some pictures of his tombstone." She pulled out her phone, scrolled through the photos and pulled up one. It was a good shot of not just the headstone but the ring lying on top of it. "He was Mom's boyfriend before he died, and I've heard people say that my dad, Griff and Mom were best friends."

"They were," Jonas verified. "His death hit your mom hard."

Hell, it'd hit all of them hard. Still did. And it made him wonder if Hayden had heard anything else about Griff. Like maybe rumors that Griff was actually her father.

"So, is that why Dad left?" Hayden pressed. "Because he was still so torn up about losing his best friend?"

Again, Jonas had to consider his answer. "That must have played into it." And since Hayden seemed to be waiting for more, Jonas added, "I'm four years older than your mom, dad and Griff. I know that doesn't sound like a big age gap, but it was when we were all younger. Unfortunately, I didn't know a lot of what was going on in their lives."

He sure as heck hadn't known about Griff's ALS and the depression that'd gone along with it. He hadn't known that Lily had been pregnant with Griff's child, either. If he had...

Jonas mentally stopped and wondered what would have happened had Lily come to him back then after she'd lost Griff. He would have definitely stepped up to help Lily. Not with the pressure of marriage and paternity secrets the way Cam had done, but he would have helped her raise Hayden.

And if he had, who knew where they would have been now.

That thought didn't help with the heat between them. No. Because in that alternate "what if" world, Lily and he would have likely ended up together. Maybe that would have happened in part because of the guilt Jonas felt over Griff's death, but the guilt had nothing to do with the fact Lily and he were attracted to each other. Attracted despite the obstacles standing in their way.

Eli finished his call, and he was smiling a little when he made his way back to them. "I'm starting," he announced, and that was apparently what Hayden needed to pull her out of her low mood.

The girl practically sprang off the ground and went to Eli to hug him. It was such a natural response that Jonas figured they'd hugged a lot. Since he didn't want to think about that, or about the kissing that was no doubt going on between them, Jonas got up, too. Not as easily as Hayden had done, but he stood and went to them.

"Congrats," he told Eli. "I'm proud of you. Can't wait to be watching you from the front row of the bleachers."

With his grin widening, Eli hugged him, too, and it was a surefire treatment for pulling Jonas out of his own low mood. Jonas hadn't been a football star like Wyatt, but he'd been in the starting lineup for Last Ride High, and while he hadn't urged Eli to play because of the potential injuries, he was glad his son had found something he was apparently good at and loved.

"You okay?" Eli asked Hayden. "You want to go for that ride now?"

"I do," she assured him but then looked at Jonas and added, "Thanks for trying to cheer me up."

"Anytime, but you should talk to your mom. I know she's worried and very sorry for what she said."

Hayden made a noncommittal sound to indicate she wasn't totally convinced of that, lifted her shoulder in an equally noncommittal shrug. "Tell her I'll talk to her soon," she finally said and then hurried off with Eli to get in that ride.

A ride that Jonas was hoping would be just that and not some sneaking off somewhere so they could make out.

Since Lily was no doubt waiting on pins and needles, Jonas headed toward her house. He figured she'd be waiting for him on the back porch, but instead she was in the side yard. And she wasn't alone, and Jonas groaned when he saw her two visitors. Not Bentley and the PI, thank merciful heaven, but Charlene and Marlene Parkman, which he wouldn't be thanking anyone or anything for.

The sisters were in their late sixties now and were retired schoolteachers. Jonas had had Charlene for geometry and Marlene for English. Even though they were identical twins, it was easy to tell them apart because they dressed as different as night and day. Charlene wore prim suits and heels and Marlene wore clothes more suited for tending horses on the ranch.

Both women had been here the night of the society drawing—the only time Jonas ever remembered them coming to the ranch—but apparently they'd felt the need for a return visit. And their timing was just plain awful since Lily still had to be reeling from her encounter with her daughter.

Charlene and Marlene looked in his direction, the women dipping down their heads to eye him over the tops of what he assumed were reading glasses, since they were both holding some papers, and that was where their attention had been focused when he'd first spotted them.

Marlene grinned and winked at him, clearly flirting. Charlene frowned and her mouth tightened, clearly not flirting.

"Jonas," Marlene greeted him. "How the devil are you?"

He supplied his standard answer of "Good" since it wouldn't require any follow-up from him. He definitely didn't want to mention anything about Bentley surfacing. Or that Lily had just been through an ordeal, but he looked at her to see how she was handling the unexpected visitors.

Not well.

While Lily wasn't in the throes of crying, her eyes were red, and judging from the way her gaze latched on to his, she wanted to get rid of the sisters so she could find out how his chat had gone with Hayden.

Jonas hiked his thumb to the barn, and while his message was meant for the sisters, he settled his attention on Lily. "Two of the hands have the stomach flu," he lied. "Lots of vomiting, and it must be spreading like wildfire, because others are complaining about not feeling good."

The ploy worked. Well, for Charlene it did. She gasped as if he'd just announced an outbreak of the bubonic plague and backed away from him.

"That stuff's going around," Marlene commented. No backing away for her.

"We should be going," Charlene insisted, practically shoving the papers she'd been holding into Lily's hands. "Just read through that and give plenty of thought and heart searching to what you decide to write."

Marlene rolled her eyes and shoved her papers into Lily's already-filled hands. "Yeah, just read through that and give plenty of thought and heart searching to spilling the truth. Bullshit doesn't quit stinking just because it's covered up with a fresh cabbage leaf."

And with that puzzling observation on life, the sisters turned and walked back toward their car.

"How's Hayden?" Lily asked the moment the women were out of earshot.

Jonas dragged in a long breath, wishing he could give Lily better news. "I think she's still upset, but she stopped crying and talked to me. I tried to make her understand that what she overheard didn't have anything to do with her but rather your too-young marriage to her too-young father."

Lily nodded, but the worry stayed on her face. Since he didn't want heatstroke added to her slate of worries, he took hold of her arm and started walking with her to the house.

"How long did you have to put up with Marlene and Charlene?" he asked.

She sighed. "They drove up within a minute after you went into the barn, and I made the mistake of looking around the side of the house. They saw me before I could duck in and avoid them." She sighed again when she looked down at the papers. "They're on opposite sides of the fence when it comes to the report I'll be doing on Hezzie."

"Yeah, I gathered that from what they said. Charlene wants you to go the status quo route, and Marlene wants you to blab about Hezzie's secrets." He paused as they went up the porch steps. "Did Marlene get into what those secrets were, and did they mesh with anything you learned from Derwin, Matt or Alma?"

"According to Marlene, Hezzie was an actress, and not in the modern sense of the word, either, but more of a glorified saloon girl who did cancan dances and such."

So, another story that was causing all stories about Hezzie to be suspect.

"Is Marlene the one who left the note on the porch?" he asked.

Lily's head whipped up, and her eyes widened before she muttered some profanity. "I didn't even think to ask her."

"Of course you didn't. That's because you had other, more important things on your mind." He opened the back door and led her into the kitchen. "FYI, there's no stomach flu, just in case you didn't pick up on that I was trying to get rid of the sisters."

She nodded, made a sound of acknowledgment. "I'm glad you got rid of them. I can't deal with Hezzie stuff today." Lily dropped the papers onto the kitchen island and looked up at him. "Does Hayden hate me?"

"No." He didn't believe something like this could cause a child to actually hate a loving parent. Temporarily hate, yes, but not the real deal that would outlast a day or two. "She's just hurt, and she said she'll talk to you later. I'm not sure how much later," he tacked on to that when he saw the hope practically overflow from her eyes. "She's riding with Eli right now."

Because Lily was a mom, one who knew about her daughter kissing his son, she raised her eyebrow. "I've had the talk with him. Eli knows it's best not to dive into anything too serious."

And because Jonas was a parent, who knew that a teen-ager didn't always think before they dived, he could only hope that the fact it was daylight and that Hayden was coming down from a bad hurt would stop them from doing anything more than kissing. Jonas had given up on figur-ing out a way to make that stop.

"All right," Lily muttered, as if steeling herself up. "Ad-vice time. I'll text Nola and ask her opinion, but I want yours, too. Should I wait until Hayden's not so hurt and pissed off at me before I tell her about Griff?"

It was a tough question, and Jonas had no idea what the right answer was. "It could take her a while to recover from a double blow. But it also might better help her understand why you said what you did."

"Marrying you was one of the biggest mistakes of my

life," she muttered, repeating what she'd told Cam. "Yes, the truth might make that easier for Hayden. But the rest…" Lily stopped, shook her head and groaned. "I can't imagine what this will do to her."

Oh, he figured she could imagine it all right, because Lily was going through her own version of hell on this one. It was one of those moments when friends would have normally given a friend a hug. But with those kisses, Lily and he had changed things. Not to friends with benefits.

More like friends with baggage.

The really heavy kind of baggage that could wear you down. Or make you snap. If Jonas thought a romance could screw up things for Eli and Hayden, then it would screw up things times a million for Lily and him.

"I'll go out to the barn and pasture in about an hour," Lily said, checking the time. "If Hayden will talk to me, I'll go ahead and tell her. Will you be around in case, well, in case she goes running from me?"

"I'll be here," Jonas assured her.

He saw that exhausted fear in her eyes, and there was nothing short of paralysis that would have stopped him from pulling her into his arms. Common sense be damned. He had to try to make this easier for her.

Jonas reached for her and managed to get one arm around her when his phone rang. "Answer it," Lily immediately said. "It might be Hayden."

He didn't believe the girl would call him, but since it was possible, Jonas put the hug he'd planned on hold and took out his phone. He frowned, though, when he saw the number.

"It's Bentley," he snarled.

Because he preferred to go through with comforting Lily, Jonas considered not answering it, just letting it go to voice mail so he could listen to whatever this jerk had to say. But Jonas wanted to press a little to see if he could get Bentley to admit that he or his PI had left the note on Lily's porch.

"Yeah?" Jonas greeted him. It was slightly friendlier than the "what the hell do you want?" response he'd considered.

"Jonas," Bentley said, as if they were old friends, and there was way too much cheeriness in his voice.

That cheeriness put Jonas on instant alert, along with making every muscle in his body tighten. He didn't tell the jerk that he didn't approve of him using his given name. Jonas just stayed quiet and tried to steel himself up for whatever the heck the man was about to say.

"It's a match," Bentley announced, the cheeriness going up to a sickening level of glee. "The DNA test," he added, as if Jonas hadn't known exactly what he'd been talking about. "A match," he repeated. "I have the proof now that Eli is my son."

CHAPTER ELEVEN

EVEN THOUGH JONAS hadn't put the call on speaker, Lily knew what Bentley had just said. Or rather what Bentley was continuing to say. Lily couldn't make out Bentley's exact words, but she was close enough to Jonas to hear the buzz of the man droning on and on.

Jonas sure as heck wasn't droning. His shoulders dropped, and he squeezed his eyes shut a moment. It must have felt as if he'd just had an avalanche fall on him.

"No," Jonas said to Bentley. "I'll be the one to tell him, and you won't come here until Eli knows." And he ended the call, obviously not wanting to hear any argument that Bentley might have had against Jonas taking that on.

"I'm so sorry," Lily immediately said, and she did what Jonas had been about to do before he'd gotten the call.

She pulled him into her arms.

Yes, it was risky, but this wasn't about the heat of attraction. This was about comforting a friend who needed it. Mercy, did he need it. She could practically feel the hurt and worry coming off him in thick, hot waves.

"I need to verify if Bentley is telling the truth," Jonas muttered.

She pulled back, meeting his eyes, and she tried to tamp down the hope that the man was lying. Hope that could give Jonas a temporary lift but then send him crashing if Bentley wasn't lying through his teeth.

"When I sent in the test kits to the lab, they gave me a contact number," he explained as he searched through his phone. "But the instructions said I'd be sent an email with the report of the..." He trailed off, his fingers hovering over his email inbox that he'd just accessed. "It's here. The report is here. It came in ten minutes ago."

Jonas didn't keep hovering, something she might have been tempted to do. He opened the email, then the report that'd been attached to it. Apparently, the lab had given the results in an "easy to understand" way, because it didn't take long for the muscles in his face to go tight again.

"It's a match," he said, his voice barely louder than a whisper. Then he groaned, and it seemed to Lily that he wanted to crush his phone and those test results.

This was devastating news, no way around that, but she forced herself to think. To try to find any loopholes or flaws that would make this all go away. She quickly latched on to something.

"How did Bentley get the results?" she asked.

"I gave him the name of the lab, so it's possible he contacted them. Since he's a doctor, maybe he pulled some strings to get the results." He paused a heartbeat. "I'll need to have the samples retested. At another lab this time."

"Yes," she agreed, and while his mood didn't do any brightening, she figured it would help him to have a plan of action.

"But Bentley isn't going to wait on a retest," Jonas concluded a moment later. "If I block him from seeing Eli, he'll likely get pissed off and take the lab results to a judge to get some kind of court order."

A judge would probably be on Bentley's side in this, too. After all, they hadn't been able to find anything sinister in

Bentley's background that would prevent him from seeing the child he'd fathered.

Fathered.

The word made her want to puke. Mentally puke, anyway. Because it was one of those words, like *mothered*, that meant squat if it didn't have the love and commitment behind it. Bentley might have contributed the DNA that'd started Eli's life, but that didn't make him a father.

"It'll take another lab at least a couple of days to redo the test," Jonas said, and it seemed as if he was talking to himself now, trying to work out the best way to approach this. "Bentley will want to see Eli or at least talk to him before then, but I'm going to try to put him off for a while."

Lily wasn't sure how Jonas planned to accomplish that, especially since Bentley seemed more than eager to have a meeting with Eli, but she watched as Jonas composed a text to Matt, filling him in on what he wanted done. He asked Matt to arrange to have the DNA samples tested at another lab.

"It'll be faster having Matt do it," Jonas explained to her.

He got an almost immediate response from Matt confirming that. Matt assured Jonas he'd get right on it.

"I'm sending another text to Bentley," Jonas added, already typing it. "I'm informing him that the results are going for a retest and telling him—not asking—to put off contacting Eli until tomorrow. That way, Eli will have a chance to process what he's about to hear."

She watched as Jonas finished and then fired off the text, and then he slipped his phone back in his pocket. Her heart was breaking for him.

"I'm sorry," she repeated. "And I know that's not much, but I wish it were more. A whole lot more. I wish I could give you something that would fix this so that everyone wins."

Now he looked at her, and while she didn't think his attention was solely on her but rather the task he had to do of telling Eli, Jonas managed a slight smile.

"Thank you for that," he said. "You're a good friend, Lily."

Normally, that would have made her smile, too, but there seemed to be an unspoken *and* at the end of that last part. *You're a good friend, and I want to keep it that way.*

She totally got that. She needed to keep his friendship, too, but she was beginning to wonder if they could just try a fling. Maybe a fling with rules that would spell out if things didn't work out between them, that their friendship would still remain strong. And, of course, that was the lust talking. Lust that Jonas would likely be able to cure just fine with some great sex.

Instead of an *and*, though, Lily had a *but* at the end of her own thought. And that *but* was a doozy. The cure for lust could rip their lives apart at the seams. It could change everything between them forever, and they already had enough changes on their proverbial plates to add another side dish.

"I'm not putting this off," Jonas said, yanking her attention back to the immediate side dish. "I'm going to tell Eli now." He looked down at her again. "Since Hayden will be with him, you could maybe see if she's cooled down enough to talk to you."

Lily jumped right on that offer. Not only because she wanted to see her daughter but because she could be in the same general vicinity of Jonas in case he needed a shoulder after he'd told Eli.

It felt a little like a "dead man walking ordeal" as Jonas

and she made their way out of the house and toward the barn. But once they spotted their kids—and Eli was still Jonas's kid, as far as she was concerned—it felt like an ordeal of a different sort. That was because she saw Eli and Hayden riding, and they were close and clearly flirting as they'd done on their previous ride. Both were smiling. Smiles that might wane considerably once the parents arrived on scene. Hayden might not want to see her, and Eli could be shaken if this visit didn't go as well as he thought it would.

Eli muttered something to Hayden when he saw them, and Hayden spared the adults a glance before Eli and she rode toward them.

"I'm not ready to see you yet," Hayden insisted, aiming that at Lily as she dismounted.

"She's not here to talk to you," Jonas said before Lily could think of how to respond. "She's here for moral support because of something I have to tell Eli."

That got the boy's attention all right, and he volleyed some glances at both of them before he got out of the saddle. Taking the horse by the reins, Eli led him to the watering trough and looked at Jonas.

"I'm having the DNA tests redone to make sure they're accurate," Jonas stated, "but the initial results are you're a match to Wade Bentley."

Eli just stood there, silent as the tomb and staring at Jonas with eyes that gave away zilch of what he was feeling. Then again, it was possible the boy didn't know how he felt. It wasn't every day that someone learned the identity of their birth father.

"Why are you having the retest done?" Hayden asked. "It's a match, right? I mean, the DNA test says it is?"

Jonas took a breath. "The DNA test says it's a match,"

he stated, and it didn't surprise Lily that he left it at that. It wouldn't be wise for Jonas to get into his concerns about Bentley because it would sound like some kind of accusation. One with nothing to back it up.

"Wade Bentley is your dad," Hayden muttered, giving Eli's arm a nudge.

Eli's head bobbed in a nod. A silent one.

"I'm arranging for him to see you tomorrow," Jonas added. "If you still want to see him, that is."

"Tomorrow?" Eli repeated, and his gaze connected with Jonas. "Yeah, I still want to see him."

Eli not only sounded eager about that, but, well, happy. The corner of the boy's mouth lifted into a smile. One that immediately faded a bit. "I want to ask him why he hasn't tried to see me before now. He probably has a good reason," he added in a mutter.

Lily was sure Jonas was wondering about that reason. Wondering, too, what Bentley's intentions were. She certainly was, and she truly hoped the man wasn't up to something bad.

"If I can't see him until tomorrow, can I call him now?" Eli asked Jonas a moment later. "I really want to talk to him, to find out what he's like."

That must have felt like a physical blow to Jonas, but she had to hand it to him—he stayed steady and nodded. He took out his phone, scrolled through the contacts and texted the number to Eli's phone.

"Mind if I wait around while you talk to him?" Jonas suggested.

Eli didn't jump to say yes, and the boy's hesitation must have felt like another blow to Jonas. But Lily couldn't blame him for wanting to hear what Bentley might say since Eli's mental well-being was at stake here.

"Uh, sure," Eli finally agreed.

Since that agreement was only half-hearted, Lily figured that was her cue to bow out. The call was likely going to be awkward enough for Eli, and he didn't need his girlfriend's mom/dad's boss listening in.

"I've got some things I need to do," Lily said, and she looked at Hayden to see if she planned to leave with her. Apparently not, because Hayden stayed right by Eli's side.

While she heard Eli pressing the number to make the call, Lily went back through the barn and toward the house. She hadn't lied about having something to do. There was always ranch work, and she'd let some of it slide, what with the twisty turns her life had taken.

She groaned when she heard a vehicle turn into the driveway and hoped it wasn't Bentley or anyone there to dish anything else on Hezzie. Her head was throbbing and she wasn't sure she could handle any more dirt or monkey wrenches. Thankfully, though, it was Nola.

When her sister parked the car, she got out and hauled something from the back seat. At first Lily thought it was Charlie, Nola's little boy, but it was the large glass piece that Nola had jokingly named Dream Sex. Nola hoisted it into her arms as if it were a giant watermelon.

"I made another one for Mom's fundraiser. I figured you wouldn't want this one auctioned off since it's sort of a personal piece for you, so consider it a gift," Nola joked, and she was grinning as she walked toward Lily. "You can maybe keep it in your bedroom as sort of a talisman to bring on future dreams—"

Nola stopped, and her grin vanished, though probably because Lily hadn't been able to keep the worry off her face. "What's wrong? Is it Hayden? Did she run away or something when you told her about Griff?"

Lily lifted her hand to stop any other speculation and tipped her head to the barn. "The DNA test came back, and Wade Bentley is Eli's bio father, and Eli is on the phone to Bentley right now."

"Oh," Nola said, sounding and looking relieved. Then not so relieved when she obviously realized what this would be doing to Jonas.

Yes, it would be eating away at him like acid.

Instead of continuing this conversation in the heat, Lily started toward the house, hoping she'd be able to talk her sister out of gifting her anything that would remind her of Jonas and her having sex.

"Jonas wants a retest on the DNA samples," Lily went on as they walked toward the back porch. "But I'm guessing it, too, will be a match."

"He wants a retest because he thinks it's a false positive?" Nola asked.

"Or he's grasping at straws and trying to hang on to the son he loves." Lily sighed and opened the door. "Bentley is a pushy jerk, and Jonas wants to rule out that the man has somehow tampered with the DNA results, but I can't think of why he'd do something like that. Or how."

Nola made a sound of agreement. "You mentioned that Bentley might be after Eli's life insurance money, but if he tampered with the test to get that started, his plan would crash and burn unless he also planned to keep tampering. And that would be a long shot since Jonas probably wouldn't be using the same lab for a retest."

"He's not," Lily verified, and she went to the fridge to grab them two Cokes. "And Jonas is being careful. He's with Eli now while he's talking to Bentley. Hayden's with them, too."

Nola didn't question why Lily wasn't there with them.

Probably because she already knew the answer. Instead, her sister eased the sculpture onto the island and had some of the Coke while she studied Lily.

"So, other than the paternity things with Jonas and Eli, what else is wrong?" Nola came out and asked.

She hadn't expected to put on enough of a mask to fool Nola. Nor did she want to keep it from her. "Hayden overheard me talking to Cam and telling him that I made a mistake by marrying him."

"Ah," Nola said. "Got it. Hayden believed you were talking about her, and she ran out before you could tell her the truth. Now she's pissed at you and doesn't want to talk to you about anything."

"All of the above," Lily verified. "So, she still doesn't know about Griff, and she'll have to burn off some of her mad before I can even attempt to tell her."

"Wow." Nola had more of the Coke. "I was going to complain about Charlie puking on me this morning and that Marley had to cancel plans for us to have a mother-daughter date this weekend, but my misery pales in comparison to yours."

Marley was Nola and Wyatt's daughter they'd had when they were teenagers. Had and then given up for adoption since they hadn't been able to raise her themselves. Marley, who was now eighteen, had not only tracked down Nola and Wyatt, but she'd become a part of their lives—an important part—and Lily knew how much Nola had been looking forward to spending time with her daughter.

"Yes, this is misery all right," Lily agreed, and she glanced at the notes from Marlene and Charlene that she'd left on the kitchen island. "At least you're not a Hezzie fanatic, here to help me with the research."

"Is that what that is?" Nola asked, obviously noticing Lily gazing at the papers. She scooped them up and began to read through them, punctuating her reading with a "Wow" and an "Oh, my." When she'd finished, she looked up at Lily. "Well, I hate to burst your bubble, but I had a twofold mission coming here. To give you Dream Sex and to show you something I found about Hezzie."

Lily didn't groan about not being able to get a reprieve from Hezzie. In fact, coming from Nola, it might be a good distraction. Right now, she welcomed anything to keep her mind off what was going on in the barn.

Nola took out her phone and brought up a photo that she then passed to Lily. Not a recent picture but a grainy shot of four men standing in front of a wooden bar. Behind the bar was a mirror and a sign.

The Silver Slipper.

"Where did you get this?" Lily asked, using her fingers to enlarge the image so she could better see the details.

"One of my best customers is into genealogy, and when she heard about the Last Ride drawing and Hezzie, she did some poking around and came up with that." Nola moved closer and pointed to the heavily bearded man in the center. He was holding a large old-fashioned key.

"Look at the face and tell me who you think that is," Nola insisted.

Lily did look, and look. She was about to shake her head, but when she focused on only the visible part of the face, the part not covered by that beard, she thought she recognized the features. Not only because she'd seen many photos of her ancestor but because some of those features were on her own face.

"Hezzie," Lily muttered, and yes, she gasped. Not because this had come out of the blue but because she hadn't thought the account of Hezzie winning the saloon was true.

"There's a family story," Nola went on, "which means there aren't any facts to back it up, that the owner, a guy name Grover Patrick, lost the saloon in a poker game. According to my customer, there aren't any business records or such. They existed in the late 1800s but many were lost. Anyway, she believes this is a photo of Grover turning over the Silver Slipper key to the winner."

"To Hezzie," Lily concluded.

"Yeah, either that or it's a Parkman relative, because those are Hezzie's eyes and forehead."

Lily couldn't argue about that, and if Hezzie had, indeed, won the Silver Slipper, it likely meant she'd been good at poker. Which in turn likely meant the whole story about her dressing up as a man and frequenting saloons was true.

For some reason, that made Lily smile.

"I always thought of Hezzie as this really astute business-woman trapped in the restraints of the times she lived in," Lily muttered. "But it looks as if she was a whole lot more."

"Yep." Nola grinned, too. "Makes you wonder if she did the rest of this stuff as well." She tapped the papers. "I mean, an actress who performed in saloons might have access to a fake beard and men's clothes. She might have learned the art of poker that way, too."

Lily thought this should be celebrated. Or at least acknowledged for something other than what some would call a disastrous smear of their ancestor's reputation. Hezzie was a resourceful woman, and a far more interesting one than her sanitized bio had made her seem. And while it might be over-simplifying it and slapping on some rose-colored glasses, it was what it was. It was the life Hezzie had lived, either by choice or because she'd had limited choices.

"My customer got the photo from someone's family she

researched," Nola went on, "and is going to ask the person if it's all right if I contact her. You want to get in on that phone call or visit? Or would you rather just put Hezzie to rest here and now?"

It was tempting not to have to deal with what would essentially be an interview, but Lily felt invested now and actually wanted to get to the whole truth about the woman who'd given her this genetic legacy of features.

Lily nodded. "Of course, things around here might get… hectic," she settled for saying. "So, if I'm tied up, go ahead with talking to this person." She stopped when the back door flew open, and Hayden rushed in.

Lily's heart dropped because there were tears in her daughter's eyes. She hurried to her, to reach for Hayden, but Hayden brushed her off and went to Nola instead. Nola doled out Lily a silent apology and pulled the girl into her arms.

"It's okay, baby girl," Nola murmured to her. "What happened?"

Hayden was sobbing now. "It's Eli," she finally managed to say.

Oh, God. Had Bentley done something to upset him? Lily had to fight the urge to tear the man limb from limb and try to get to the reason her daughter was crying about Eli.

"What's wrong with Eli?" Lily asked, but Hayden didn't respond with anything but tears until Nola repeated the question.

"Eli's so happy," Hayden said, causing plenty of confusion for Lily.

Obviously, Nola was puzzled as well. "Uh, don't you want Eli to be happy?"

"Yes, but not like this. Not like this," she echoed in a

hoarse mumble. She finally lifted her tear-filled eyes and met Lily's gaze. "I can tell from the way Eli's talking that he'll want to leave the ranch and go live with his real father."

CHAPTER TWELVE

JONAS FELT AS if he had a ten-ton weight on his shoulder, and his muscles had been tight from tension for so long that he was starting to cramp up. Still, his discomfort was only a minor nuisance in the grand scheme of things.

And the grand scheme was that his life, and his heart, had just been tossed up into the air.

Of course, Eli hadn't meant to make him feel that way. No. The boy had only done what was natural. He'd had a conversation with his birth father. A pleasant conversation with lots of laughter and smiles.

The talk with Bentley had lasted well over an hour, and the only reason it'd ended was because Bentley had said he'd gotten called into work. When the man had said his goodbyes, he'd left Eli grinning and saying something that added an extra gut punch for Jonas.

"See you tomorrow," Eli had gushed to Bentley.

Tomorrow, as in about twenty-four hours from now. Jonas had to figure if a call had pleased Eli as much as this one obviously had, then a visit was going to send the boy over the moon. Eli's mood and the possibility of even more glee had troubled Jonas.

And Hayden.

Eli had been so wrapped up in his call that he hadn't seen the look on the girl's face when she'd said something about needing to go to her house. Eli had just given her an absent wave, but if he'd glanced at her, Eli would have seen the start of some tears. Those tears were the reason Jonas was now heading to Lily's while Eli was walking on air and doing his chores in the barn.

Well, one of the reasons he was going to Lily's, anyway.

He did want to check on Hayden, to make sure she was okay, but he needed to see Lily, too. Even though his brothers would be willing to listen to him, Lily was the one person he wanted to hear him out. Lily would verbally bash Bentley, would take Jonas's side when he went on and on about the bad feeling he had about Bentley. She would get it, and while talking it out with her wouldn't solve anything, Jonas was pretty sure it'd make him feel better.

This had nothing to do with kissing, he assured himself. Or sex. But when he knocked on the back door, and Lily opened it, he got an immediate reminder of lust. Once, he'd been able to look at her and not have his first thoughts about her go dirty. Apparently, those days were gone.

There were lots of dirty thoughts.

Like how it would feel to haul her against him and kiss her. A long, deep kiss that would land them straight in bed. Or on the floor. And that was exactly why it couldn't happen. They wouldn't have the guarantee of privacy, for one thing, and for another, it just wouldn't be wise to give in to this simmering heat. Even if the heat was threatening to boil over.

She looked at him, their gazes connecting, and he wished he didn't see his own need mirrored in her crystal blue eyes. But he did. And that was why he forced his attention off her. Unfortunately, it landed on yet something else that reminded him of sex.

The glass art piece on her kitchen island.

She followed his gaze to the glass, then frowned and

made a loud sigh. "Nola brought it by. For some reason, she thought I'd want to own it."

While the piece didn't actually remind him of dream sex, or any other kind of sex, for that matter, Jonas recalled that was what Nola had named it. And she'd no doubt given it that name to poke a little fun at Lily and him. Or maybe to give them a nudge so they'd do something about this heat between them. But glass, like heat, could be ignored. Hopefully.

Lily stepped back so he could come in, and he glanced around, looking to see if they were alone. They were.

"Nola left about ten minutes ago," Lily explained, "and Hayden went to her room, where she'd made it clear she doesn't want to talk to anybody."

"Is she okay?" he asked.

Lily shrugged. "Hayden came in crying and said..." She trailed off, studying his expression as if to make sure he could handle what she was about to tell him. Jonas motioned for her to continue. "She said she was worried about Eli wanting to live with Bentley."

Yeah, Jonas had seen all the signs that it was what Hayden had been thinking. He'd been thinking it, too, and it'd been hard as hell to hold that all in while his son made happy talk with Bentley.

"Any truth to Eli wanting to do that?" Lily pressed.

Now it was his turn to shrug. "The call went fine. Well, for Eli and Bentley, anyway, and they made plans for Bentley to come to the ranch for a visit tomorrow at two."

"So soon," she muttered.

Way too soon for him. Then again, a week or month would be too soon as well. "The timing took some negotiations because Eli's got football practice first thing in the morning." That was so the team could get in some time on the field before the temp soared. "And I wanted him to have lunch before he met Bentley."

Of course, now that Jonas had spelled out his reasoning for scheduling the visit twenty-four hours from now rather than immediately, it sounded a little petty and overprotective. But the bottom line was he couldn't and wouldn't stop Eli from seeing the man. That didn't mean, though, that the meeting had to take place before they'd all come to terms with it.

And he included Hayden in those terms.

The girl had clearly been upset, and this would give Eli a chance to talk to her. Maybe a chance to even soothe her fears about his leaving the ranch to go live with Bentley. God, Jonas hoped that wasn't a real possibility.

"Eli's fourteen," Jonas started, spelling out the thoughts that were racing through his head. "If he wants to live with Bentley, I won't be able to stop him."

But that didn't mean Jonas wouldn't be sick with worry. And loss. Still, if it was a decision Eli ended up making and no red flag surfaced for Bentley, then Jonas would have no choice but to let the boy go.

Sighing, Lily went closer, touched his arm and rubbed it lightly with her fingers. "When I was a kid and I'd get down, my mom would make me square-dance. Yes, square-dance," she said when he gave her a blank stare.

"I thought square-dancing was for a group of couples," he pointed out.

"Oh, it is, but my mom had this notion that it could be done solo or, better yet, me dancing with just her. I hated all the do-si-do stuff with a passion, but I swear, it worked every single time. If you think it'll help, I could put on some hoedown music and we could give it a try."

Despite his crappy mood, that made him smile a little. As she'd probably known it would do. It didn't last. His phone dinged with a text, and for one "heart leaping" moment, he thought it might be Bentley canceling. But it was Matt.

The DNA tests are being sent to another lab for retesting, the sheriff had texted. Will let you know the results as soon as I have them.

Jonas answered back with a Thanks, and he was thankful. He didn't believe, though, that the new tests would do anything but verify the fact that Bentley was Eli's biological father.

"So, do you want to give the square dance a try or talk about how bad the phone call was for you?" Lily asked.

Part of him wanted to choose the square dance. Well, attempt it, anyway. But he also wanted to spell all of this out.

"Bentley didn't say anything inappropriate," Jonas explained. "Just the opposite. He let Eli do most of the talking about riding horses and about him getting the starting position on the junior varsity football team. Even his favorite music."

"The rat bastard," she muttered, making him smile again. And groan. His groan was a lot more reflective of his mood than these smiles she was coaxing out of him. "Did Eli ask why Bentley's never been in his life?"

"No." Though Jonas had hoped that would come up, it hadn't. "I don't think Eli can see the big picture right now. He's just focusing on talking to and meeting this man who provided the sperm that made him."

"Eli's smart. Eventually, when the shine wears off, he will get the big picture, and he'll understand that Bentley stayed away by choice. That you were the one who was there for him."

Maybe. But Jonas felt the storm coming. The one that

would likely blow his world to pieces. Because whether or not Eli actually wanted to live with Bentley, the boy would probably want him to be a part of his life. Maybe a big part. Jonas could share—you couldn't have three siblings and not learn all about sharing—but mercy, it seemed as if he would have to give up a part of Maddie's son.

Her heart, she'd always called Eli.

That would be the biggest cut of all, and Jonas felt it in his soul that he was letting Maddie down.

"All right, I'm bringing out the big guns," Lily said after she stared at him a couple of seconds. During those seconds she no doubt saw that his blue mood had gone so dark that it would now qualify as indigo.

She scrolled through the music app on her phone and came up with, well, Jonas didn't know, but it was obviously a tune meant for square-dancing. When the rusty-voiced singer called out "Circle Left," Lily took hold of his hand and began pulling him into a walk around her kitchen island. She started out slow and then cranked up the speed. They nearly collided with all sorts of things, but Lily kept him moving.

Jonas was 100 percent sure this wasn't going to do squat for his mood.

Still, Lily didn't give up. When the singer called for "Allemande Left," she gripped on to his left forearm and then clamped his hand over her own arm. Again, she started moving, circling them around. And around. And around. Until they did bash into the kitchen island.

Lily laughed, and all right, it was a little infectious, and he was touching her. A bonus that shouldn't be a bonus because he should be keeping his hands off her.

When the singer called out another move, the Swing, Lily stopped running with him and moved him into a ballroom dance pose. "Your right hip to my right hip," she instructed.

But she didn't just instruct him. She took hold of his hip and pressed it to hers. Jonas felt the jolt of heat. Man, did he. And he was pretty darn sure that Lily felt it, too, but that didn't stop her from doing exactly what the move called for—swinging around in a circle.

"We're supposed to stop at one," she let him know, "but we're going to do this for a while."

A while lasted...a while. There were more injuries. More banging into cabinets. And into each other. Until soon, it wasn't just their hips that were touching. The entire fronts of their bodies landed against each other when Lily broke into a giggling fit.

Jonas had to hand it to her mother, Evangeline. The square-dancing worked. Or maybe it was Lily's laughter.

Or the fact that now her breasts were against his chest.

Yeah, that was definitely playing into this. Playing into and messing with his head. Jonas wanted to feel more of her against him. He wanted to take her mouth and taste that laugh. He wanted to taste her.

And that was what he did.

In midswing, he tightened his grip on her waist, pulling Lily against him until he got that contact he wanted, and in the same motion, he lowered his mouth to hers. Since they were still moving, he missed the first time. The kiss landed on her cheek. But Jonas got it right on the second attempt.

Mouth met mouth.

Oh, man. He got a taste of that laughter all right. A solid taste of Lily, too, and the need and heat shot straight through him.

Her laugh turned to a moan, a throaty, silky one that only added more fire to flames that were already too hot.

The emotion came. Not just from this fierce need that had been building for her, but it mixed with the emotions they were both feeling. Over the past couple of days, they'd been scraped raw. That didn't tone down or overshadow the blast of heat, though. No. Even a new ice age likely couldn't have managed that.

They jumped straight from a kiss to something that could qualify as intense foreplay. When she put her arms around him, her body moved against his, and her breasts taunted the muscles in his chest. Of course, her mouth was doing some taunting, too, because Lily wasn't a passive participant in this. The kiss was hard, hungry and already way out of hand.

Jonas tried to do something about that. He tried to rein in the heat enough so he could think straight. He failed at that. A big-assed miss on straight thinking, but he grasped on to a thin straw of restraint. Not much, but it was enough for him to succeed in tearing his mouth from hers so he could look at her.

A big mistake.

Her eyes were wide, not from concern. More like she was drinking him all in, and she was issuing a lot of non-verbal invitations that he should sure as hell decline. This was the heat "talking," and it shouldn't have the top say in this.

"You stopped," she pointed out. Her breath was gusting. Her face flushed as if she was just coming down from an orgasm.

"Yeah," he managed and should have added he'd done that because it was the right thing to do, that they shouldn't be kissing. At least not without giving more thought to something they should really be thinking about.

Consequences.

At the moment, Jonas hated the crap out of that word. He wanted to be reckless, to tell consequences they could go screw themselves. But that was his erection talking, and yes, he had one. One that was begging him to finish what he'd started. Since erections often made stupid decisions, Jonas figured he could pretty much discard any input it was trying to make.

"I should go," he finally forced himself to say.

Lily slid her gaze over his face. "Do you want to go?" she asked.

No. Both his dick and he were in perfect agreement about this, and if this had been any other woman, he might have said to hell with it and stayed.

But this was Lily.

And he couldn't mess up things with her.

"No," he said aloud, "I don't want to go."

And that was exactly why he had to do the opposite of what they both obviously wanted. Jonas turned and headed out the door.

CHAPTER THIRTEEN

LILY HADN'T REALIZED just how long the buzz from a really good kiss could last. But she knew that the kiss she'd gotten from Jonas had been particularly good, and the buzz had lasted nearly twenty-four hours. So far, it showed no signs of easing off.

Multiple showers hadn't helped. Neither had throwing herself into work, usually a surefire way to occupy her mind.

Not this time, though.

She was still sitting at her desk, squeezing her longhorn stress ball and looking at horse training schedules that she wasn't actually seeing. The thoughts and memories—especially the memories—had stayed with her, and she had known she was in trouble when earlier that morning she nearly scalded herself pouring coffee.

The scalding had happened when she'd caught a glimpse of Jonas from the kitchen window. He'd been in the corral, doing nothing in particular other than looking mouth-watering and amazing. That was when she had decided it was best not to look out any more windows for a while.

Lily had also moved the Dream Sex glass piece from the kitchen and into her bedroom closet, where she'd hidden it under a bathrobe that she never used. She hadn't wanted that kind of a visual to keep hammering home for her that real sex with Jonas was a possibility. And she wasn't sure who was more troubled by that. Jonas or her. It was probably a tie.

Neither of them wanted to rock the boat, tip the scales and any of the other clichés that could screw up their lives six ways to Sunday. But the kiss had happened anyway. She was positive of one thing, too.

It could happen again.

Jonas had walked away before any groping or anything other than kissing or square-dancing had started, but she knew it had taken a lot of effort for him to go out the door. A lot of effort for her to let him leave as well. However, she had anchored her feet in place by reminding herself that Hayden was in the house, and Hayden had been upset over the phone call she'd heard between Eli and Bentley.

More anchoring had happened when she'd recalled why Jonas had been in her house in the first place. It'd been because he'd needed a friend, one who would hear him out since he was worried about losing his son. She'd failed big-time in the friend department, and in hindsight, she shouldn't have started a dance that would put them hip to hip.

Lily's head whipped up and she put down the stress ball when she heard the footsteps outside her office. The door was open, and Hayden walked into view. Slowly. As if she hadn't made up her mind yet if she was going to stop or not. Lily decided to give her an excuse to stop.

"Is that what you're wearing for Eli's meeting with Mr. Bentley?" Lily asked. It was a far safer question than diving into other topics. Such as *are you still upset about the "mistake" comment that you overheard?* Or *do you want to get into a heart-to-heart where I reveal the identity of your real dad?*

Nope. Clothes choice was a far better way to go here.

Hayden automatically looked down at the jeans and white top she had on. She wasn't a "dress" kind of person, but the top was one of the better pieces in her wardrobe. She'd also fixed her hair and put on some makeup.

"Yeah, why?" Hayden countered. "What's wrong with it?"

"Nothing's wrong. You look very nice." And nervous. Hayden wasn't nibbling on her bottom lip, but she did keep doing quick, brief clamps of her teeth over it.

"Thanks," she muttered, clearly throttling back on her tone. "Is that what you're wearing?"

Lily looked down at her own jeans and blue shirt. She wasn't a dress person, either, but she'd made an effort. That included putting on her good boots that she was certain wouldn't have horse manure on them. Like Hayden, she'd done the "hair and makeup" deal, too. She'd even put on the tastefully classic gold hoop earrings that Lorelei had given her for Christmas.

The preparations were likely overkill, considering that this meeting was all about Eli and Bentley. Jonas, Hayden and she would be in the background, but Lily had wanted to make some effort to look her best. And no, not because of wanting to look her best because of Jonas and the lingering kiss buzz. This time she'd be the friend he needed her to be. But she also wanted to show Bentley that he wasn't dealing with people without decent clothes and resources.

Especially the resources.

Of course, the man would likely be able to figure that out just by looking at the ranch, but Lily figured it didn't hurt to drill the point home. That way, Bentley might think twice if he tried to do something low-down and dirty like taking legal action to try to get custody of the boy he'd fathered.

"Have you seen Eli today?" Lily asked, but what she actually wanted to know was if Eli still had the same rosy outlook as he had the day before during his phone call with Bentley.

"Just for a minute. He had practice, and after he got back, he came out to the corral to find me to make sure I was still planning on being at the meeting with his dad. I told him I was, and then he had to go so he could shower and eat before Mr. Bentley shows up."

Yes, Lily had done the same when Jonas had asked her to be there. And she would. The kiss they'd shared hadn't changed that. But Eli's rush to shower and eat told Lily loads about the boy's mindset.

Lily had seen when Jonas had returned to the ranch after picking up Eli from practice, and that'd been three hours before the scheduled meeting with Bentley. Most teenage boys didn't need three hours to get ready, so that likely meant Eli was making an effort, too, to present himself in the best possible way.

Hayden paused. "I really think Eli might end up leaving the ranch. Leaving Last Ride," she tacked on to that.

Even though it was possibly a big fat lie, Lily shook her head. "Eli loves Jonas and loves living here. He can still have visits with his birth father and keep his life on the ranch."

Lily prayed that was the way it played out, anyway. So that Jonas wouldn't lose his son. But there were no guarantees. And that brought her back to telling Hayden about Griff. No guarantees, either, about what her reaction would be, and if the meeting with Bentley went well, Lily would try to do a tell-all later today.

"Are you and Mr. Buchanan going to get together?" Hayden asked, snapping Lily's attention back to her daughter.

"Uh, why do you ask?" And for a horrifying moment, Lily thought maybe Hayden had seen Jonas and her kissing in the kitchen.

Hayden shrugged. "Things just seem different between you two."

Lily would have pressed for a more thorough explanation if she had not heard the sound of a vehicle approaching the house. She checked the time. It was too early for Bentley. He wasn't scheduled to arrive for another hour, but this could be another descendant of Hezzie here to dish more stuff or try to drill home that she needed to lie about the woman. On a sigh, Lily got up from her desk and headed to the front door so she could deal with it.

Lily froze, though, when she glanced out the window and saw the silver Lexus drive past her house. Bentley was behind the wheel, and he was obviously going to Jonas's place.

"That's Mr. Bentley, right?" Hayden asked, coming up behind her.

Lily nodded. She recognized the man from his social media pages, and Hayden obviously had, too. "I guess the meeting will be starting early," she muttered, and she doubted Jonas would be happy about that.

But there was another concern as well. It was possible Jonas wasn't even at home. He could be working in his office. Which meant Eli could be meeting with Bentley alone. Not good since Jonas wasn't sure yet that he could trust the man.

With Hayden right on her heels, Lily went out the door and started toward Jonas's. Since she had a clear line of sight to Jonas's house, she saw Bentley when he parked his car and got out. Not empty-handed. He had two large shopping bags squeezed together in his left hand, and the man glanced around as if assessing the place before he began walking toward the porch. He'd barely reached the first step when someone opened the front door.

Eli.

The boy was smiling and looking a little shy at the same time. Jonas was right behind him, not smiling, not looking shy. Jonas was giving Bentley a thorough once-over, and when Lily got closer, she could see that Jonas's mouth was tight. No surprise there. This was definitely a muscle-tightening situation.

Lily and Hayden reached the porch just as Bentley extended his right hand in greeting to Eli. "Hi," he said. "I'm your dad."

And there it was, what had to feel like a gauntlet to Jonas, who dragged in a deep, steadying breath and offered his own hand to Bentley once Eli and he were done with their shake.

"Jonas Buchanan," he said, not tacking on the step-dad label. Probably because it would have set his teeth on edge. She knew for a fact that Jonas had never thought of Eli as his stepson.

"This is Hayden Parkman," Eli volunteered, "and her mom, Lily."

Bentley swung his gaze in their direction, and yeah, he continued the assessment. If he objected to them being there, he didn't come out and say it, but Lily didn't see any hint of a warm welcome in the man's eyes.

Eyes that were nowhere near a genetic copy of Eli's.

In fact, Lily couldn't see a resemblance at all. Eli's hair and eyes were both brown. Like Maddie's. In contrast, Bentley's hair was blond and his eyes were blue.

The lack of resemblance was in their builds, too. Eli was tall and lanky, already at least an inch taller than Bentley, who had a beefy build. Of course, it was possible that Eli, being a teenager, would likely bulk up some and grow into a beefier physique, but for now, there was no way Bentley could look at Eli and think *that's a carbon copy of me, me, me.*

"It's good to meet you," Bentley said to Lily and Hayden. He chuckled when he made a show of glancing at his watch. "I know I'm early, but I just couldn't wait any longer to meet Eli." He shifted his free hand to take hold of Eli's shoulder. "I hope you're as happy to see me as I am to see you."

"I am," Eli assured him.

Lily attempted an "I'm happy for you" smile, but since Eli wasn't looking in her direction, she gave up on it.

Jonas didn't attempt a smile, either. Instead, he stepped back out of the doorway, a signal that everyone should come in out of the blistering heat.

"You're so big," Bentley told Eli in a "proud papa" kind of tone, and he kept his hand on Eli's shoulder as they all trickled inside. "I saw on your Facebook page that you're starting quarterback now and have your first game in a couple of days."

Eli nodded. "School starts tomorrow, and the first game is Thursday night. The junior varsity plays on Thursdays because the high school plays on Fridays."

"Just like it was when I was your age," Bentley said. "I played plenty of football myself back in the day."

"You did?" Eli asked.

"I sure did." Bentley handed him one of the bags while they made their way into the living room. "That's some stuff I got for you."

"Thanks," Eli gushed, and he started to go through it the moment they sat. Jonas and he took the love seat, with Bentley opting for the chair right next to Eli. Lily and Hayden took the sofa.

Eli pulled out a football, several dozen signed trading cards encased in plastic sleeves, a football video game and a printed paper that said it was redeemable for any Dallas Cowboys' game of the upcoming season.

Of course, all of that caused Eli to gush, too, and Bentley turned a sheepish glance to Jonas. "I got a little carried away, I know, but it's not every day a man gets to meet his son."

Lily had no idea how Jonas was supposed to respond to that, so she wasn't surprised when he stayed silent. Unlike Eli. The boy continued to remark and go on about every single thing he took from the bag.

"I know you have other hobbies," Bentley went on. "Riding horses, for instance." He glanced at Hayden, which meant Eli had likely posted pictures of Hayden and him on horseback. "And you write some poetry."

Now Eli blushed, and Jonas looked surprised. So was Lily. This was the first she was hearing of that, but apparently it wasn't news to Hayden, because she made a quick sound of agreement.

"Eli's really good at poetry," she piped in. "But he doesn't let a lot of people read it."

"Well, maybe he'll let me have a look at it someday," Bentley concluded and then looked at Jonas. "I'm sure you've read it."

Lily couldn't be certain, but she thought that maybe Bentley had seen Jonas's surprise and now wanted to take a jab at it. A sort of "just because my boy lives with you, it doesn't mean you know him."

"Dad's... He's not into poetry," Eli said.

Oh, that shift from *Dad* to *he* had to slice out a huge chunk of Jonas's heart, and it brought on a long, uncomfortable silence. One that Lily couldn't stop herself from trying to fill.

"Jonas taught Eli to ride when he was four," she volunteered. "By the time he was six, he could handle a horse better than some of the hands that Jonas hired."

That sent Bentley's gaze spearing back to Jonas. "*You* hired? I was under the impression that Lily owned the ranch."

"She does," Jonas said.

Since there was no way Lily intended to let Bentley get away with that cattiness crap, she added, "But along with being the ranch manager, Jonas is part owner, and he makes all the decisions about personnel."

That last part was mostly true, but Lily had no intentions of saying that Jonas usually discussed such matters with her before he acted.

"Well, that's good," Bentley said in a way to indicate that it wasn't good at all, and he lifted the other bag he'd brought in with him. "I thought you might want to know about your family. There are some photos of your grandparents, my parents, in there. Some are of me when I was about your age. I thought you'd want to see them."

Bentley plucked out a couple of the photos and held them up. Apparently, one was of him when he would have been about Eli's age. Lily moved in to have a closer look and had to mentally shake her head. She still didn't see a resemblance to Eli.

"Your grandparents," Bentley continued, passing Eli several photos of the couple. "Oh, and here's one of me and your mom."

That got everyone's attention, and Hayden actually got up so she could have a look from over Eli's shoulder. Lily didn't look. Not at the picture, anyway. She watched Jonas as he saw it, and her stomach dropped when she saw that it had been another emotional punch.

"Mom," Eli said, running his fingers over the picture. He was smiling. "She looks so young."

"She was. We both were." Bentley chuckled as if that were a fine joke.

Lily gave up on staying put and went over to have a look for herself. Yes, it was Maddie all right, and she was, indeed, very young with that fresh face and her long hair tumbling onto her shoulders. She was standing next to Bentley, and he had his arm around her waist.

The pose was intimate enough. So were the smiles the two were aiming at each other. Those smiles and the intimacy were no doubt the reason Bentley had wanted Eli, and Jonas, to see it. The man had probably searched high and low to find the one image that could portray him in a good light while giving Jonas a "not so subtle" reminder that Maddie had had another life before she'd met him.

A life that had created Eli.

"I don't think your mom knew it yet," Bentley went on, "but I believe she was already pregnant with you when a friend snapped that picture of us."

Lily so wanted to say something, anything, that would wipe that smug look off Bentley's face, but she forced herself to hold her tongue. It wouldn't do anyone any good if she brought up that Maddie and he hadn't stayed together, that they'd likely broken up shortly after that photo.

"Maddie never mentioned you," Jonas said.

Well, apparently he hadn't been able to hold his tongue after all. And good for him. Lily wanted to cheer, but she could also tell that Jonas wished he'd kept his mouth shut because anything he slung at Bentley would come back on Eli.

Eli looked at Jonas, then at Bentley. Little by little, his smile faded. "She didn't," he agreed.

Bentley gave a heavy sigh and squeezed his eyes shut a moment as if the pain of hearing that was just too much to bear. "I'm sorry she didn't tell you about me." He paused and waited until his gaze was locked with Eli's. "I'm sorry she kept you from knowing the truth, son. Because your mother…well, your mother told you some very big lies."

CHAPTER FOURTEEN

JONAS COULDN'T GET to his feet fast enough, and he didn't even try to stop the anger from rolling over him. He wanted the anger to fuel what he intended to make crystal clear to Bentley. No way was he going to let this piece of crap come into his home and bad-mouth Maddie.

"With me, now, Bentley," Jonas snarled through clenched teeth. *"Now,"* he repeated in a much louder voice when Bentley made a "what did I do?" huff and didn't budge.

"Dad…" Eli said, volleying glances at both Jonas and Bentley.

Jonas didn't know if that *Dad* was meant for both of them or not, but Eli must have been aware that there was about to be trouble. Ditto for Lily and Hayden, too, because they also stood, and Lily gave him a silent questioning look because she no doubt wanted to know if she could help in any way. Jonas hadn't wanted to upset any of the three of them, but he sure as hell intended to upset Bentley.

"It's okay," Jonas told Eli. "Mr. Bentley and I just need to have a little chat. You can just hang out here with Hayden and her mom for a while. Come with me," he tacked on to that for Bentley.

When the man finally moseyed himself into a standing position, Jonas hiked his thumb in the direction of the kitchen. They wouldn't talk there because there might be some yelling involved, and he preferred Eli, Hayden and Lily not to hear it. Later, though, he'd need to fill in Lily.

And Eli.

His son was going to want to know what had happened, and Jonas couldn't keep it from him. However, he might have to give the boy a sanitized version of how this all played out.

As Bentley and he walked, Jonas forced himself to remember to hang on to his temper. He couldn't punch Bentley. Even if that was what he wanted to do, oh, so much. Still, he didn't want to give the man any fuel he could use against him, and a weasel like Bentley might be purposely baiting him so he could end up filing assault charges. Maybe he'd do that to try to put a wedge between Jonas and Eli. Or it was possible this was part of a bigger plan to convince Eli to live with him.

"I was just stating facts," Bentley grumbled as he followed Jonas.

Jonas didn't respond, didn't tell the asshole that he was putting that liar label on the woman that Jonas and Eli loved. On Eli's mother. That connection was strong for Eli, Jonas had no doubts about that. And he didn't intend to let Bentley try to break it.

When they made it to the back porch, Jonas still didn't say anything until he'd closed the door. Then he snapped toward Bentley, clamped another rein on his temper and laid out a ground rule.

"I will not have you come here and upset Eli," Jonas spelled out for the man. "And that's exactly what you're doing when you call his mother a liar."

Bentley gave his head an indignant wobble that reminded Jonas of a strutting rooster. "Maddie was a liar because she never told me she was pregnant with my son.

Then she compounded the lie by telling Eli and you that I hadn't wanted to see him." He threw his hands up in the air. "How the hell was I supposed to want to see Eli when I didn't even know he existed?"

Jonas had geared up to do more snarling, to add more ground rules, but that stopped him cold. Then he had to work back through his memories.

Better off without him.

Those were Maddie's words that quickly came to mind. But had she ever come out and said that she'd told the birth father and he'd chosen not to be involved in Eli's life?

No.

At least Jonas couldn't recall her ever saying it, and that caused him to mentally curse. To mentally take a step back, too. The Maddie he'd known and loved wouldn't have been capable of not telling a man he was going to be a father. Unless…and this was a big *unless* that refueled the anger. Unless the man was an asshole who didn't deserve the father label.

Jonas was going with that.

Because he'd loved and trusted Maddie, and he sure as hell didn't trust Bentley. Of course he'd want to paint himself the victim here. It was the only way he could explain why he'd waited fourteen years to see his son.

Bentley paced across the porch a couple of times as if he was trying to walk off some of his frustration, but Jonas knew this could be an act. One meant to convince Jonas that he was the wronged party here. Jonas still wasn't buying it.

"Look, like I told Eli, Maddie and I were young when we met," Bentley explained while he continued to pace. "You saw that picture of us. We were young and in love.

Yes, in love," he emphasized, even though Jonas hadn't made a sound to refute that.

Couldn't refute it. Maddie would have been about nineteen or twenty in that photo. Because of the background check, Jonas knew that Bentley was four years older than her, so that would have made him in the twenty-three to twenty-four range. Yes, young. But Bentley hadn't been a kid.

"Because we were young," Bentley went on, "we were also immature. We argued about things, and Maddie was jealous if I even looked at another woman."

"Jealous?" Jonas's tone was flat, and he figured his expression was filled with a boatload of skepticism.

He'd been married to Maddie for nearly a decade, and Jonas hadn't found her to be argumentative. Yeah, they'd had arguments. Most couples did. But it'd been a rare occurrence for them. As for jealousy, he'd never once seen her act that way. Not that he'd ever given her reason to be. But maybe Bentley had.

"You cheated on Maddie," Jonas concluded, and he didn't keep that conclusion to himself.

"She thought I cheated on her," Bentley quickly argued. "I didn't, but she could be unreasonable about that sort of thing." He scrubbed his hand over his face. "Things were just so fiery and intense between us, and I think that intensity spilled over into all parts of our relationship."

It wasn't easy for Jonas to stand there and hear about his soulmate being hot for another man. But maybe that part was true. Maybe Maddie had truly loved Bentley and had been unable to tolerate him looking at another woman.

Maybe.

But again, this was Bentley's spin on things, and Jonas

had no intentions of buying that particular spin hook, line and sinker.

"You must know what I mean," Bentley went on. "You must have seen how hot-blooded Maddie was."

That required yet another rein on his bubbling temper, but the remark had hit hard, piercing him right through the heart. Sex with Maddie had been great. He was sure of that. And in the beginning, they hadn't been able to keep their hands off each other. That'd been when everything was fresh and new. But things had cooled some over the years. He could admit that now. Could also admit that Maddie had become the woman she was, a more "toned down" version of her younger self, because Bentley had broken her heart by cheating on her.

But the million-dollar question was, had that heartbreak caused her to withhold from Bentley the fact she was pregnant?

"Maddie walked in on me talking to a friend," Bentley continued a moment later. "Just talking, and yes, she was just a friend. Maddie took what she thought she saw the wrong way, packed her things and left." He paused, his gaze snapping to Jonas's. "She did tell you we'd been living together when she got pregnant, right?"

No, she hadn't, but then again, this went back to Maddie not telling him much of anything about her relationship with Eli's birth father.

"She didn't tell you," Bentley concluded when he must have seen signs of that on Jonas's face.

"It doesn't matter what she did or didn't tell me," Jonas fired back. "Maddie wouldn't have kept the pregnancy from a decent man who'd treated her right. Not from a man she was certain would have been a decent father."

Bentley rolled his eyes. "She would have and she did.

The proof of that is standing right in front of you." He patted his chest, obviously indicating that he was decent in both the man and father department.

And maybe he was decent-ish these days, but that didn't mean it'd been true fifteen years ago. Jonas wasn't going to lose faith in Maddie over anything Bentley had to say about her and her time with him.

"You obviously loved Maddie, and it's hard for you to see her as she was back then," Bentley continued. "But I loved her, too. I saw her for who and what she was, and I loved her anyway."

"You loved her," Jonas repeated in a mumble. He hefted on yet some more skepticism. "Then why didn't you try to track her down after she left you?"

"I did," he insisted. "Her folks were still alive then, so I went to them. She wasn't there, and they claimed they didn't know where she was. I asked her friends, and they said the same thing. By then, she must have known she was pregnant, so I suspect she was hiding out from me."

Jonas figured if he got more skeptical, he'd start drowning in it, but he was damn sure he was only hearing a part of the story. The part that would make Maddie out to be the bad guy in this. It sickened Jonas to think of what had really happened to make Maddie leave the father of her child and start a new life. Maybe the asshole had verbally abused her. Or worse, hit her.

"If Maddie was hiding out from you, then she had a good reason for it," Jonas stated, though he had to talk through clenched teeth. "And I won't stand here and let you bad-mouth her."

"She deserves bad-mouthing." Bentley threw up his hands again. "Any woman would who did what she did.

Maddie had a falling-out with me, and she decided to get back at me by not letting me see my son."

Jonas had to shake his head because that just didn't add up. "Maddie didn't change her name until she married me when Eli was two years old. If you'd truly wanted to find her, you could have. And if what you say is true, you would have discovered then that you had a son."

Bentley sighed and shook his head, and Jonas thought the weariness he was seeing was the real deal. But it could be weariness because the man had thought he was going to come in here and steamroll over Jonas to get to Eli.

"I looked for her," Bentley insisted. "But I gave up after a few months when I couldn't find her. I figured she was done with me, and that was the end of it. Trust me, I wouldn't have stopped looking for her if I'd known she was carrying my son."

Maybe. But that brought Jonas to something else he wanted Bentley to answer. "How exactly did you find out about Eli?"

"From an old friend of Maddie's, Tessa Drake. You know her?" Bentley asked him.

He nodded and thought back to the petite blonde who'd visited Maddie in Last Ride about a year or so after Jonas and Maddie had married. Tessa and Maddie had gone to high school together in San Antonio, and she'd been the only friend from the past who'd ever visited Maddie.

That caused Jonas to pause.

Maddie had always said there was no one from her past that she wanted to stay in contact with. Tessa included. But maybe Maddie had said that because she didn't want word getting back to Bentley that she'd had a child.

"About a week ago, I ran into Tessa at a party," Bentley went on, "and she remembered me from the time Maddie and I were together." He paused again and swallowed hard. "Tessa told me that Maddie had died. I was sorry to hear that. Sorry that she'd passed without us having mended things between us."

"She never mentioned any desire to mend anything between you," Jonas quickly pointed out.

"She wouldn't have," he said on a heavy sigh. "Because she was angry with me over the misunderstanding." Another pause, another sigh. "Anyway, while I was talking to Tessa, she mentioned that she felt so sorry for Maddie's son. At first, I just figured she was talking about a boy that Maddie and you had together, but when we started getting into specifics, I realized the timing lined up for Eli to be mine."

"He doesn't look like you," Jonas had to point out.

"I see some resemblance," Bentley countered, "but, yes, he favors Maddie more than me." His gaze hardened when it met Jonas's again. "That doesn't mean he's not mine. The DNA test proved it."

Jonas didn't mention that he was having the test redone. He just stayed silent with his own hard gaze in place while he waited for Bentley to continue. It didn't take long. Bentley was obviously more than willing to tell his story.

"Anyway, I did some looking around on social media and found some posts where Eli's friends were wishing him a happy birthday. I did the math and realized the obvious. That Eli is my son."

Jonas wasn't totally clueless about Eli's social media pages. He sometimes checked them to make sure the boy wasn't spilling too many personal details about himself or making connections that he shouldn't be making. So, yes, there were birthday posts, and yes, it wouldn't have taken Bentley long to see that the dates lined up for his possible paternity.

"One of Eli's friends had mentioned the Wild Springs Ranch," Bentley went on, "so I did more digging and found out about Lily Parkman owning it and you working for her."

From there, it wouldn't have been hard for him to learn that Jonas and Eli had a house on the grounds of the ranch. That would in turn have prompted Bentley to leave the message in the mailbox.

"You dug into Lily's life," Jonas stated, definitely not pleased that her privacy had been dragged into this.

Bentley didn't look the least bit apologetic about that. "Of course. My son was living here on her ranch, and I needed to see what kind of person she was since she would obviously have a lot of contact with Eli."

Jonas supposed that Bentley thought that made him sound like a good father, sort of like the checks Jonas was making of Eli's social media pages, but that wasn't the same thing. No way did Jonas want Bentley poking into Lily's life.

"Are we done here now?" Bentley asked him. "Because I'd like to get back to spending some time with my son."

"No, we aren't done yet. We need to go over the ground rules for this visit and any future ones," Jonas snarled. "And FYI, these aren't negotiable. You will not say anything bad about Maddie in front of Eli. You won't call her a liar, and you won't give him this sob story about his mom misunderstanding what she walked in on when you were *talking* with your friend."

The anger lit in Bentley's eyes. "I'm not allowed to mention that even though it's true?" he fired back.

"Not even if it might be true," Jonas verified. "That's

because I believe it's a lie meant to make yourself look a whole lot better than you are."

"I am better," Bentley spit out.

Oh, and there it was. The doctor looking down on the cowboy. Jonas did some literal "looking down" on Bentley when he took one slow, menacing step closer and stared him down.

"That better is in the 'to be determined' category," Jonas informed him. "Until I'm certain you won't harm Eli in any way, you will follow the rules."

Bentley opened his mouth, and Jonas braced himself for the man to threaten him with legal action. But he also saw the exact moment that Bentley rethought what he'd been about to say and backed down.

Jonas doubted that backing down was permanent.

No. Bentley was likely just regrouping so he could figure out the best way to approach this. And the best approach definitely wasn't insulting the man who'd been raising Eli. The man that Eli called *Dad*. Or at least that was what Eli had called him in the past. That might change, though, now that Bentley had come into his life.

"All right," Bentley finally agreed. "No saying anything bad about Maddie. But what if Eli comes out and asks why I wasn't here for him? Do you expect me to lie?"

"No," Jonas snapped. "I expect you to give him an answer suitable for a fourteen-year-old boy who loved his mother and doesn't know you from Adam. Because trust me on this—if you do bad-mouth her, you're going to alienate Eli and piss me off. Do you really want to piss me off?" he demanded. Again, his teeth were clenched.

Bentley didn't jump to agree but finally muttered a "No."

Maybe that was the truth, but Jonas wasn't under any

illusions about the man playing fair. Though Jonas hoped that was what Bentley would do. Play fair and put Eli first. And maybe Bentley would do that. Just in case he didn't, Jonas planned to keep a close eye on him.

They stayed in a staring match for a couple more seconds, long enough for Jonas to settle himself. He didn't want Eli to be upset with anything he saw in his expression, and as it was, the boy already would have questions and concerns. Jonas hoped to alleviate some of those. Maybe Bentley would, too, and if he did, it would be a solid beginning for Jonas to start trusting the man.

Jonas opened the door, and with Bentley right behind him, they returned to the living room. Eli and Hayden were going through the contents of the bags that Bentley had given him, but Lily was still on her feet, and she had her worried gaze pinned to Jonas. She didn't come out and ask if all was well, but Eli did.

"Is, uh, everything okay?" Eli stopped looking at some sports cards and slowly stood to face them. Eli studied them, hard, no doubt looking for any signs of trouble.

"It's okay," Jonas tried to assure him. "Mr. Bentley and I just had to cover a few things."

Eli didn't question what those things might be, though he had to know they were about him. Everything happening here was about him.

"Yes, it's all just fine," Bentley agreed. "Your stepdad and I just had a few things to work out." He plastered on a big smile. "Hey, what do you think about the stuff I brought you? Pretty cool, huh?" he tacked on to that before Eli even had a chance to answer.

"It is," Eli agreed while still volleying glances at them.

The silence that followed was long and thick. "I like the

game you gave Eli," Hayden volunteered. "It's something Eli and me can play together."

"Good. I was hoping it'd be fun." And with that came more silence.

Jonas didn't try to fill it, but Bentley did. "Well, do you have any questions for me?" Bentley asked. Again, though, he didn't wait for an answer. "Maybe you'd like if I told you about myself. I'm a doctor, and I live and work in San Antonio. I'm divorced."

"Do you have any other kids?" Eli asked.

The question shouldn't have surprised Jonas. Of course the boy would want to know if he had any half siblings.

Bentley shook his head. "No. You're my only one." He paused. "I want you to know I've loved you from the moment I found out you existed, and I'd like to get to know you better."

Eli looked at Jonas, causing Jonas to mentally curse. He knew what this was all about. Eli didn't want to hurt him by saying yes, but Jonas could tell that getting to know Bentley was exactly what the boy wanted to do.

Jonas gave Eli a nod, and it caused an instant reaction. Eli grinned and then shifted that grin to Bentley. "I have a horse named Cupcake. Would you like to see her?"

"I would." And Bentley seemed to release some pent-up breath.

"Is it all right if we go out to the barn and corral?" Eli asked Jonas. Again, Jonas nodded, but he was glad when Eli added, "You and Miss Parkman could come, too, if you want. Hayden, too, of course. I'd really like for Hayden to come."

Since everyone, including Lily, seemed to be standing around and surrounded by eggshells, she also glanced at him.

"That'd be nice," Lily said only after she'd gotten the nod from Jonas.

Eli brightened even more. "It's kind of hot, but we can stay in the barn when you meet Cupcake," the boy told Bentley.

Eli continued to chat about Cupcake and how much he loved riding while they all ambled out of the house and toward the barn. It was only a short trek, and they settled into two groups, with Eli, Hayden and Bentley walking ahead of Lily and him. No one seemed to be in a hurry, and that was fine with Jonas. He was hoping the fresh air and the heat would clear his head.

Lily took hold of his hand and looked at his knuckles. "No bruises," she whispered, "and I didn't see any on Bentley's face, so I'm guessing you two didn't duke it out."

"We didn't." Jonas kept his voice at a whisper, too. Not that the others would have heard Lily and him, because they were deep into a conversation that was punctuated with bouts of laughter. "But I made Bentley understand he wasn't going to be able to say anything bad about Maddie." He paused. "Was I wrong to demand that? I mean, if it's true that she lied, should Eli know that?"

She shrugged and continued walking at the same slow pace as the others, keeping Jonas and her a good fifteen feet behind them. "Eli's got a lot to deal with right now. If it's true, and I'm not at all sure it is, then you can work out how to tell him down the road. For now, I'd just let him get used to the idea that Bentley has surfaced and seemingly wants to be involved in his life."

That was good advice, and he figured the sigh she added was because she hadn't managed her own truth-telling with Hayden. Jonas was glad, though, that she'd held off on that, because it was obvious that Eli needed all the emotional support he could get right now, and Hayden was clearly giving him some of that.

"So, after your heart-to-heart with Bentley, do you trust him?" Lily asked.

"About the same, I guess." Which meant he didn't trust him much at all, and that was why Jonas took out his phone and sent off a text. "I just asked Matt to recommend a good PI that I can hire to look into Bentley's life," he explained to Lily.

"It couldn't hurt. Might give you some peace of mind."

He wasn't sure that was possible. If he learned something bad about the man, that would end up hurting Eli. If there was nothing bad to find, then it meant Jonas had no right whatsoever to keep Bentley from him.

Jonas huffed. "Part of me wonders if I'm just being a petty bastard because I'm scared spitless of losing my son."

"Feeling like a petty bastard comes with the territory of being a parent." Lily gave him a poke on the arm with her elbow. "Hey, don't make me drag out the square-dance music to cheer you up."

He could tell she regretted the words the moment they left her mouth. She blushed, squeezed her eyes shut a second and muttered, "Son of a monkey. Sorry about that."

She was no doubt remembering the kiss. Remembering, too, that remembering it just wasn't a good idea when they were trying… Well, he didn't know what the hell they were trying to do. But if they were hoping the lust would cool off, they were failing big-time at it.

"Since I've blabbed, I might as well confess all. I had to hide the Dream Sex glass piece," she went on. "Even though it's not really about it, it was sort of an 'in the face' reminder because of what Nola named it."

That made him smile a little, and it felt so good just

to do something other than snarl and be worried that his world was about to implode.

"Eventually, we should talk about that kiss," she said. Ahead of them, Eli reached the barn and opened the door. Bentley, Hayden and he went inside, but Jonas slowed his pace even more.

"Yeah. Give it some thought and then let me know just how big of an apology you want from me."

Lily slowed even more by coming to a complete stop. She looked up at him. "No apology whatsoever." She paused. "But I need you to talk me out of something I'm about to suggest."

Jonas didn't like the sound of that, but he was definitely intrigued. "Talk you out of what?"

She swallowed hard before she answered. "Becoming friends with benefits. I know, I know," she quickly tacked on to that. "It could mess everything up. Well, everything but this 'pressure cooker' heat that's been building inside me. Sex with you could fix that, I'm sure—"

It was such a bad idea. And Jonas made it even worse. He dropped a quick kiss on her mouth. In broad daylight where any of the ranch hands, Eli, Hayden or Bentley could have seen them. The kiss was proof he didn't need that sex with Lily wasn't the brightest thing to do.

But bright didn't always win out over heat.

Jonas knew that. Lily knew that. And the heat sure as hell knew it. Jonas might have gone for doubling the stupidity by kissing her again, but he heard the ranch hand Larry call out.

Jonas mentally cringed at hearing the man because it meant that Larry could have witnessed that kiss after all. Definitely not good. Something like that could undermine Lily's and his authority and could beat the hell out of morale if the hands thought the ranch manager was sleeping with the boss. Then again, maybe the hands wouldn't care.

And Jonas cringed at that thought, too.

Because it was that way of thinking that could lead to friends with benefits where there were zero guarantees that sex wouldn't play hell to havoc with Lily's and his lives.

"You got another one," Larry said. He held up an envelope as he walked toward them. "This one was on the ground next to the mailbox."

Lily groaned and looked up at him. "You don't think Bentley would have been ballsy or desperate enough to put it there, do you?"

Jonas wished he knew the answer to that and had to settle for an "I don't know why he would."

After all, Eli knew who Bentley was. Or rather who the man was claiming to be. And Bentley had gotten the face-to-face meeting with Eli, a reminder that said meeting was going on in the barn right now, and Jonas should be in there, making sure Bentley didn't violate the ground rules. That was why Jonas started toward Larry so he could hurry this up. Jonas took the envelope and handed it to Lily.

"It's probably about the Hezzie research," she muttered, the frustration written all over her face.

Jonas watched, though, as that frustration turned to something a whole lot worse after she took out the single sheet of paper. Larry picked up on it, too, because he asked, "Is everything all right, Miss Parkman?"

Lily nodded, but Jonas knew that nod was a lie. A big one. Hell. What was in that envelope that had knocked the wind out of her?

"Thanks for finding this," she said to Larry, and she stuffed the paper back into the envelope.

Lily moved away from the ranch hand, taking hold of

Jonas's arm to get him moving, too. Jonas didn't ask her any questions, curse or do any mental speculations. He just waited for her to stop outside the barn door where they had a little privacy. Emphasis on *little*.

Larry was still watching them, and the man was clearly worried about the boss lady. From inside the barn, Jonas could hear Eli telling Bentley about Cupcake's fondness for potato chips, which meant Eli, Bentley and Hayden were all within earshot. That was no doubt why Lily's profanity was whispered when she handed Jonas the envelope.

Hearing her curse, seeing that look on her face, had Jonas muttering his own profanity even before he saw what was on the sheet of paper.

Well, shit.

Spill Hezzie's secrets, and your own secret will be spilled, too had been handwritten, and beneath it the sender had printed a photo.

It was a grainy shot, probably taken from a distance and then enlarged, but Jonas had no trouble making out the image.

Specifically, the image of Lily at Griff's grave, and in the photo, Lily was touching the gold ring on the top of his brother's tombstone.

CHAPTER FIFTEEN

HAYDEN SMILED AND paced while she waited outside the locker room for Eli. She figured Eli was doing his own smiling, along with getting all kinds of congrats because of the touchdown he'd scored.

It'd been the best kind of moment. Fourth quarter, tie game, and with the clock running down, Eli had taken the ball in for a touchdown when he hadn't been able to hand it off or pass it. He'd won the game by diving into the air and landing a breath inside the end zone.

The people in the bleachers had cheered so loud for him. Especially her mom and Eli's dad and stepdad. Mr. Bentley had yelled the loudest, and he'd waved around a pom-pom deal that he'd brought to the game with him.

In that moment, everything had been sort of perfect. Eli's dads weren't looking as if they wanted to punch each other. Her mom wasn't nagging her to sit down and talk. Something Hayden most definitely didn't want to do since her mother probably wanted to go on and on about safe sex and stuff. Hayden had decided she'd rather show up at school in her underwear than go through something like that again with her mom.

Thinking of her mom, she glanced over at the parking lot and saw her and Eli's stepdad. Mr. Bentley wasn't with them. He was standing by his own chill-looking car and was no doubt waiting for Eli, too. Hayden was thankful they'd hung back, giving her the chance to be there when he finally came out of the locker room.

Whenever that would be.

She hadn't exactly timed Eli, but he'd been in there a good half hour with the coach and the rest of the team. Others were waiting for their sons, boyfriends or whatever to come out, too, and they were all chatting about the game. About Eli. About just how amazing he was.

Hayden glanced at her mom again, just to make sure she was staying put. She was. Eli's stepdad and she were still in the parking lot, and they were standing close and talking. Probably not about safe sex, she mentally joked.

But then she frowned because maybe that was exactly what they were whispering about.

That didn't tick Hayden off or anything. She liked Eli's stepdad, and she figured he had to be lonely after losing his wife and all. Her mom might be lonely, too, and that was probably why she kept wanting to have all these talks with her. If Hayden kept dodging her, then maybe her mom would get her own life and quit bugging her about not getting too serious about Eli.

Some of the people milling around the locker room cheered when the coach, Mr. Thompson, stepped from the locker room. He was smiling all right, and so were the other players who started to trickle out behind him. Hayden felt the gush of warmth when Eli finally came out.

Eli got as many cheers and slaps on the back as the coach did. Maybe more, and Hayden felt more of that warmth when she saw him glance around the well-wishers and spot her. He smiled that really cool smile that she knew was meant only for her.

During the "safe sex" talk, her mom had said stuff about love not really being love when you were fourteen, that the real love didn't happen until you were older. But Hayden figured that was BS because these things she felt for Eli had to be love.

Didn't they?

He smiled at her again, and she kind of thought the answer was yes.

Eli worked his way to her, and she wished she could kiss him right then, right there, but she didn't want his teammates to tease him about it. And they would. If they teased him too much, it might make Eli never kiss her again, and that was the last thing Hayden wanted. She didn't want to lose him.

She felt her smile widen with each step Eli took to get to her. He'd obviously showered, and his hair was still damp. His face was a little rosy, too, maybe because he was blushing some from all the praise he was getting.

"You won the game," Hayden whispered when he finally reached her. No kiss but she gave his hand a squeeze.

Eli shook his head. "I only scored six of the points, and I wouldn't have managed that without a good offensive line."

He was being modest, and that was yet something else she really liked about him. Eli was nothing like Caleb Dayton, who was by the water fountain going on and on about what he did in the game. Since Caleb was hot, he had plenty of girls listening to him, and they were hanging on his words as if he were spewing out free shopping trips.

"I'm glad you came," Eli added, giving another of those "just for her" smiles. His gaze drifted toward the parking lot, where he no doubt saw his dads and her mom. "Uh, they didn't, like, have any arguments or anything while I was playing, did they?"

"No," she quickly assured him. "They didn't really even talk to each other. Well, my mom talked to your stepdad, but neither of them said anything to your actual dad." She paused. "Is that what I should call him, your *actual dad*?"

Eli sighed, and maybe because his fathers both waved at him at the same time, he sighed again and nudged her to start walking in their direction. Like earlier in the week when his stepdad and her mom had taken their time to follow them to the barn, that was what Eli and she did now. Took their time and talked.

"I don't know what to call him," Eli admitted. "He's my dad, but if I call him that…"

He didn't finish. Didn't have to, because Hayden knew it would probably hurt his stepdad for Eli to give him the stepfather label.

"Has your mom said anything about any of this?" Eli asked her. "Because I get the feeling they're not telling me everything."

Hayden made a sound of agreement because she'd had the same thought. Her mom was keeping something secret, and that was why she'd considered just going to her and agreeing to the talk. But Hayden also had a bad feeling that what her mom would say would be something she wouldn't want to hear.

In fact, Hayden could say the same thing about Eli.

She wasn't keeping secrets from him, not really, but she was holding back on telling him something that had been bothering her since that first phone call he'd made to his dad. The call where Eli had smiled and looked happier than she'd ever seen him look.

"Are you going to leave the ranch and go live with your dad?" Hayden risked asking him.

Eli slowed his pace, but he didn't answer, and that made her feel as if someone had put something hard and heavy on her chest. A slow throb started in her head.

"I don't know," he finally said.

That didn't help her head, her chest. Or her heart. "Do you want to go live with him?" she tried again.

Eli shrugged. "I want to get to know him better. I want to spend time with him." He paused. "And I want him or somebody else to tell me the truth."

"The truth?" she repeated.

He nodded. "Because I think my mom told some lies about my dad. I think that's the reason he's never seen me. And if that's true, then...well, I think I deserve to give him a chance to be my real dad."

LILY STARED AT the threatening note that had been left for her, and she did something she'd been doing for the past three days since it had arrived. She cursed. She'd been doing a lot of that lately, and it had to stop. Ditto for the threats, and the one way to neutralize this particular threat was to tell Hayden the truth about Griff.

Hayden hadn't made that easy for her.

Heck, the girl hadn't even made it possible. Every time Lily had tried to broach the subject, Hayden had gone "grouchy teenager" on her and snapped and snarled about any and everything.

Most of the snaps and snarls had been about fairly minor stuff, being loaded down with so much homework, what with it being the beginning of the school year, having a tiff with a friend, etc., but Lily thought her daughter's biggest worry was over Eli's connection with his bio father. It was a worry for Lily, too.

Along with chatting for a long time with Bentley after the football game, Eli had exchanged texts with Bentley, and they'd arranged to have lunch together.

Without Jonas.

Lily had gotten that last bit from Jonas when they'd had one of their morning briefings over coffee. Normally, those would have been just about ranch business, but for the last couple of mornings, they'd turned into laments about their kids. And there was plenty to lament about with Bentley, Hayden's surly mood and their kids' continuing romance.

Lily hadn't fully accepted that Hayden and Eli now considered themselves boyfriend and girlfriend, but they certainly didn't show any signs of breaking up.

And that brought her back full circle to Jonas and her.

There were no signs that the heat between them was waning. Just the opposite. During one of those particularly hot moments, she'd offered him the "friends with benefits" deal, but the more she rethought that, she wasn't sure either of them could be that casual about sex.

Sure, in the beginning—if they ever got around to a beginning, that was—when the sex eased some of the tension from the heat, it might feel casual and noncommittal. And fun. But at some point after those sated moments, they would no doubt begin to think of the other feelings that went along with good sex. The intimacy. The closeness.

The need for the closeness and intimacy to grow.

And with growth came commitments and such, all the while they dealt with the ranch, their kids and anything else that life threw at them. If life hurled enough tough stuff, then the intimacy might shatter, which now brought her back to another full circle. The worry over failing with Jonas.

She'd sure as heck failed with Griff, and their on-again, off-again relationship had been proof of that. Lily could blame part of the failure on immaturity, on the then-fiery tempers both had had at the time. Who was to say, though, that once that mellowed, that the bond with Griff wouldn't have mellowed, too. So much so that it would have eventually faded.

Griff's death meant it was impossible for her to know how things would have turned out between them, and while she accepted that, it didn't mean it was something she had shoved completely out of her mind. Not because she still loved Griff. No. That love was a thing of the past. But because Griff would always be part of her life.

Proof of that came through the door.

Hayden walked in. Or rather sulked in. She had her arms folded over her chest in a textbook defensive pose, and her shoulders were hunched.

"I don't want to talk about sex, okay?" Hayden immediately snapped.

Lily hadn't planned a sex talk, but that got her attention, and she nearly blurted out *do we need to talk about sex because you're considering having it with Eli?* But she held her tongue and hoped that Hayden had snarled that only because there was nothing else left to say in the "safe sex" department.

"All right," Lily agreed, and because she'd considered how to go about this, she eased the most recent note across her desk so that Hayden could see it.

Hayden did look at it, and as she read it, her arms lowered. She picked up the note and appeared to reread or study it.

"I recognize Griff's tombstone from when I was helping Aunt Nola with the research for the Last Ride Society," Hayden muttered. She lifted her gaze to Lily's. "Why were you at his grave, and what does this mean?"

There was no need for Lily to reread it. She had memorized the words. Or rather the threat.

Spill Hezzie's secrets, and your own secret will be spilled, too.

"It's possible that Hezzie Parkman did things that some might not want others to know about," Lily told her.

"What kind of things?" Hayden asked before Lily could add anything else. Or move on to a different subject.

Lily shrugged. "I haven't been able to find proof that Hezzie did anything other than the 'straight as an arrow' stuff that's in her bio."

But the photo of the person in the saloon flashed into her mind. Still, that was only possible proof and not a sure thing.

Lily didn't want this to turn into a tell-all about Hezzie, because she didn't want this conversation to get off track. Added to that, she didn't want to say anything that Hayden might repeat and add to the rumors and stories that might be totally groundless.

Hayden made a sound that could have meant anything, and while still holding the note with the photo, she went to the window beside the desk and stood there with her back turned to Lily.

"You loved him," Hayden said. Lily couldn't see what Hayden was doing, but it appeared she was touching the photo of the tombstone. "And that's why you told Dad you should have never married him. I get that. I went back over the research Aunt Nola did, and I can figure out that the only reason you hooked up with my dad was because you were all messed up because Griff had died."

Lily went through all of that and made her own sound that could have meant anything. But Hayden had, indeed, gotten the first and last parts right. She had loved Griff, and his death was the reason she'd married Cam. That was the perfect lead-in to what she had to say, but she groaned when she didn't get the chance to say it.

First, Hayden's phone dinged with a text, and then Lily heard the footsteps. A moment later, Jonas appeared in the doorway. He opened his mouth, no doubt to launch into something, but he stopped when he spotted Hayden.

"Sorry to interrupt. I'll come back later," he immediately said.

But Hayden was already shaking her head and moving toward the door. "Not interrupting," the girl insisted, dropping the note with the photo back on Lily's desk. "I gotta go. Homework stuff," she added without even a glance back at Lily.

Jonas huffed after Hayden had walked away. "Crap," he grumbled. "Sorry about that." He stepped out of the doorway. "You want to go after her?"

Lily shook her head. If it was truly homework, then she didn't want to interfere with that. If the text had been from Eli or one of Hayden's friends, then Hayden wouldn't want her interrupting. So either way, it wouldn't set up an ideal atmosphere for having a chat with her daughter.

"I'll tell her eventually...when there's the correct alignment of the stars or some other cosmic event or divine intervention that finally works in my favor." She sighed and then glanced at Jonas's face. One look at him, and she knew something was wrong. "Is it Bentley?" she asked. "Did something happen?"

"I was going to give you an update on one of the Andalusian mares and fill you in on what I found out." But he stopped, shook his head and hiked his thumb in the direction where Hayden had disappeared. "You're sure you don't want to go after her?"

"Absolutely." Lily stood and went closer. "What about the mare, and what'd you find out?"

He gathered his breath as if this would be a lengthy explanation. "The mare with the blaze markings just went into labor, and considering the problems she had with her last delivery, I've called in the vet. She'll be here in about a half hour."

Lily didn't have to thumb through her memory to know which mare he meant. Even though they currently had close to a hundred horses on the Wild Springs, she made a point of keeping updated on each one. In this case, the mare that Eli had named Pearl was prime breed stock. Then again, all of their horses were. But Pearl was a favorite and had, indeed, had a hard time birthing her last foal.

She checked the time and made a mental note to talk to the vet, Melissa Garcia, after she arrived. The vet would no doubt go straight to the barn to examine Pearl and would be able to give Lily, and Eli, updates. Lily knew the boy would be very concerned about the mare.

"Now, what did you find out?" Lily prompted.

"A lot," Jonas replied. "Matt got back to me last night with the recommendation of a good PI, a guy named Hudson Granger. After we chatted and I told him what I wanted, he said he'd take the job and call me if he spotted any red flags on Bentley."

Lily latched right on to a big heaping of hope. And worry. Because any red flags could end up hurting Eli.

"Bentley's had three failed engagements over the years, and one of the women filed a restraining order against him for stalking," Jonas explained.

Her heart dropped. "Is Bentley dangerous?"

Jonas shrugged, but it wasn't a casual gesture. "He doesn't have a criminal record, but apparently his ex filed the restraining order when he just kept calling her and showing up at her work. She had money. Old money," he emphasized. "So did one of the other fiancées."

She tried to wrap her mind around that. Three failed relationships could be a fluke and mean nothing more than just bad luck when it came to love and such. But it felt like a whole lot more than that. More that could mean that Bentley truly didn't have Eli's best interest at heart.

"There's something else," Jonas went on. "A couple of years ago, he bought some land with the plan to build some apartments. It failed, and he lost a lot of money. Money he apparently didn't have, because he's still paying off the debt. Still paying off his student loans for medical school, too. Added to that, one of his coinvestors in the apartment deal has sued Bentley, and that litigation is still going on. Bentley is fighting it, but the PI thinks the coinvestor will eventually win and Bentley will have to pay up."

Oh, this wasn't painting a good picture of the man. "The PI found out a lot in a short time. I'm guessing he'll continue to dig to see if there's more?"

"He will." Jonas stopped, sighed. "Of course, I can't tell Eli any of this. It'll make it seem as if I'm trying to turn him against Bentley. I'm not."

"I know that," she assured him. "You're just trying to make sure Eli doesn't get hurt."

He nodded and then paused again. "Eli wants to go visit Bentley tomorrow. Without me. He says Bentley will come to the ranch to pick him up and then drop him back off after they've spent some time together."

As a parent, she knew it was very hard to trust people with your kids. Even a person who had a DNA connection, as Bentley did. That trust came even harder when there were those potential red flags.

"Are you all right with Eli doing the visit?" Lily asked.

"I have to be." But his groan confirmed that he wasn't happy about it. "I mean, I don't think Bentley will try to physically harm him, but he could say something about Maddie that'll hurt him. I plan on having a talk with him before Bentley picks him up."

She'd expected that, but Lily also knew something else. That if Maddie hadn't told the truth about Bentley not wanting a child, not wanting Eli, then learning the truth was still going to hurt Eli. Maybe even more since it had come from a mother he'd loved.

"I'm sorry," she said.

He looked at her. "I'm not square-dancing."

That made her laugh. Made her remember they had other things going on between them. Things not as important, of course, because nothing was more important than their children, but Lily doubted Jonas had developed selective amnesia about her suggestion of friends with benefits. She certainly hadn't forgotten it, either, but she had known then and she still knew now that there was a big obstacle for Jonas standing in the way of them exploring this heat between them.

Well, voluntarily exploring it, anyway.

Their bodies seemed to have a different plan of action when it came to the lust.

Lily reached in the top drawer of her desk and took out the papers that she'd just gotten from her lawyer a couple of hours earlier. She'd printed them out, not knowing when she'd be giving them to Jonas, but she decided there was no time like the present, so she handed them to him.

"Did you get another threat about Hezzie…?" he started to ask, but then his words trailed off. He muttered a single word of bad profanity when his gaze lifted to meet hers. "This is a contract to sell me one percent of the ranch."

"It is," she readily admitted. No need for her to spell out what that meant, but the 1 percent would give him a 50 percent holding of the Wild Springs. It would make them equal partners.

There was no way Jonas could have managed to give her a flatter look. It was already as flat as it could possibly get. "You're only doing this so you'll no longer be my boss."

She wasn't the least bit surprised by his resistance. "Well, duh. Of course that's why I'm doing it. Equal ground and all that, and it's sort of a formality since we share both the profits and the losses of the ranch anyway."

Nor was she the least bit surprised when he launched into an argument to support his resistance.

"You bought this ranch. It's yours," he insisted.

"I bought this ranch with my trust fund, and you're just as much responsible as I am for making it what it is today. You've been there for all the ups and downs, and when money got short, you bought shares of the ranch to keep our cash flow going. I figure that put you under some financial strain until profits started to soar."

He didn't argue that financial strain part, but Jonas must have dipped deep into his savings to buy those shares.

"I'm so thankful you stepped up to help the way you did," she went on. "So thankful for you. And this place has always been as much yours as it is mine. Your home. Your business. Your life. That's why I continued to offer you shares of the ranch even when our cash-flow problems were a thing of the past. You bought those shares because, well, because of all those other things I've already said." She ticked them off with her fingers. "Your home, business, life."

"It's fifty-one percent your home, your business, your

life." He huffed. "I don't want that to change so we can have sex. If we have sex, I want it to be because of sex and nothing else."

Oh, that shot a stream of heat right through the center of her body, but she held herself back because she knew one thing for certain. If they kissed, it wouldn't stop there. Nope. They'd passed some kind of threshold in the kissing department, and being mouth to mouth was only going to fan the flames. Still, she moved toward him and would have done some fan flaming if the doorbell hadn't rung.

Judging from the way Jonas belted out some more bad words, he had been aware that a kiss was coming. And would have welcomed it big-time. Lily would have, too, but she had no such welcome for a visitor.

"Hold that thought," Lily said, dropping a quickie of a kiss on his irresistible mouth before she headed to the door.

On the short walk, she forced herself out of her lust haze and told her brain to focus on getting rid of whoever it was so she could go back to Jonas and do things they probably shouldn't be doing. She figured the visitor was one of the hands or one of her kin there to pester her about Hezzie.

But Jonas obviously thought it could be more than that.

He went past her, and when he reached the door, he turned to face her. She wasn't sure he realized he was still holding the contract she'd given him for the share of the ranch. "It could be the person who left that threatening note," he pointed out.

That stopped Lily in her tracks. Not because she was afraid to face this person, but because a confrontation could end up in a shouting match. One that Hayden could end up hearing.

Lily gave a crisp nod to acknowledge that Jonas could be right, and when he stepped aside, she steeled herself up before she looked out the peephole. Then she frowned because she didn't recognize the young auburn-haired woman on her porch. She certainly wasn't from Last Ride. So, maybe this was about buying a horse or boarding one.

"Yes?" Lily greeted her when she opened the door.

The woman smiled at her. "Lily Parkman?" she asked.

Lily nodded. Waited for her visitor to explain who she was and why she was there. She didn't have to wait long.

"Good," the woman concluded, reaching in her enormous purse to pull out an envelope. "I'm Shayla Carson, and Hezzie Parkman was my distant cousin."

Lily groaned. "Look, if you're here to tell me what to write or not to write in my research report—"

"Oh, I'm not," she assured Lily in a pleasant but efficient tone. "I'm just the messenger here, but my grandmother, Ina May Parkman, lives in San Antonio, and she heard about the Last Ride Society drawing. She thought you'd like to have those."

Lily glanced at the envelope. "What's in here?" she asked while she began opening it.

The woman's forehead bunched up. "Uh, you should just have a look for yourself."

Intrigued and concerned, Lily pulled out the handful of pictures, and she immediately saw why Shayla hadn't been so eager to explain. In this case, a picture was, indeed, worth a thousand words.

"Uh," Lily said, repeating the sound her guest had made. She stepped back to clear a path. "You should come in so we can talk."

CHAPTER SIXTEEN

JONAS GROANED WHEN he looked down at the photos that Lily had taken from the envelope. Groaned and did some automatic goggling, too. The photos appeared to be copies of old images that had a yellow tint to them. But even with the graininess and tint, he had no trouble figuring out what he was seeing.

Men in the full Monty mode.

Not the modern take of the full Monty, either, with Chippendale buff bodies dancing and gyrating around in provocative poses. The guys in these were scrawny with less-than-impressive willies, and their expressions seemed more suited for a funeral than for "come and take me" titillation. These definitely weren't what anyone could call boudoir portraits, either, with their artsy lighting and atmosphere. These were homely guys in their birthday suits.

So, apparently, this Shayla Carson had come bearing naked pictures.

Considering what Lily had already heard about Hezzie's various career choices, Jonas was betting the woman had been the photographer. Or else Shayla believed Hezzie was, anyway.

"I brought six of them," Shayla explained. "But there are others that aren't in as good of shape as these. Of course, these are copies. My grandmother keeps the originals locked away and out of sunlight."

Lily kept her attention on the photos and almost absently shut the door after Shayla came in. Sighing, she finally looked up at the woman when they made it into the living room.

"I'm guessing you think this is Hezzie's work?" Lily asked.

Shayla reached out and turned over the top photo. There was a handwritten message on the backside. *For Ina May, on the celebration of your birthday. Affectionately yours, Hezzie.* Beneath that was the date *June 3, 1891.*

Well, there it was. He doubted there were many Hezzies around, especially women with that name who also happened to be photographers. Jonas quickly did an approximation of the math, though, and saw a big-assed discrepancy.

"If Hezzie gave this to your grandmother, she'd be over a hundred and thirty," he pointed out.

Her nod was quick, as if she was ready to explain that. "Hezzie gave the photos to my great-great grandmother whose name was also Ina May. According to the stories that the first Ina May passed along to her daughters, Hezzie and she had been close friends and had done some acting work together." She put the word *acting* in quotes. "They were also big into playing poker and were apparently quite good at it."

Lily didn't jump to say anything, and Jonas totally understood why. She was no doubt processing these copied pictures. And Lily had to be coming to the conclusion that unless the inscription on the photo was fake, then it confirmed the most risqué of the rumors about Hezzie. That she'd been what many would call the creator of smut.

"According to the stories my ancestor Ina May told, the man in the photo is Hezzie's first husband, Horace Parkman," the woman went on.

Lily groaned. "It just keeps getting better and better."

Shayla made a noncommittal sound. "Apparently, that's how Hezzie met Horace, and they ended up making a lot of money together. Ina May Senior indicated that Hezzie even had some personal photos of Horace and her together, but if those exist, they haven't come to light."

Lily looked at her again. "Have these come to light?" she questioned, tapping the photos she still held. "I mean, how many people know about these?"

"They haven't been made public, if that's what you're asking," Shayla assured her. "But many members of my family know about them. And the main reason I wanted to come here and talk to you in person is because I intend to make a lot of things public about Hezzie."

Jonas wasn't especially surprised by that. So far, the people who'd come to see Lily were divided as to whether to tell all or keep concealing things about their ancestor.

"Make things public," Lily repeated. "How?"

"I'm a blogger, mainly travel and such, but when I heard about Hezzie's name being drawn at the Last Ride Society, I thought that others would be interested in her life. Her real life," she emphasized. "She was an interesting woman, and I think it belittles her to keep her accomplishments hidden away."

Lily cleared her throat. "I probably don't need to point out that Hezzie herself didn't publicly acknowledge these particular accomplishments." She tapped the photos. "And there are a lot of people who'll be really pissed off when faced with the proof that their ancestor and idol wasn't squeaky-clean. Those same people will probably go in the deny, deny, deny mode."

Shayla's nod was quick. "I've already considered there'll be those who'll claim I'm lying. That's why I'll print the inscription on the back of the photos that Hezzie gave the first Ina May. I also have statements from family members of the accounts they've heard about Hezzie."

"Some still won't believe you," Jonas insisted.

"No, they won't." Shayla's agreement was swift. "But I also have a copy of a photo of Hezzie dressed as a man when she won the Silver Slipper saloon in a poker game. I was also able to track down the family of the original owner of the Silver Slipper, and they confirmed that their ancestor had, indeed, lost the saloon to a woman who made a habit of dressing as a man."

Jonas thought of the photo Lily had shown him of someone receiving the key to the saloon. Possibly Hezzie, and the naysayers would latch on to the *possibly* like a proverbial lifeline.

"Then there's the facial recognition I used on the naked pictures of Horace to confirm that it's, indeed, him," Shayla went on. "Combined with the inscriptions, that'll add more credence to the article that he's not only the model but that Hezzie was the photographer."

Maybe, but again, denial was a mighty powerful tool for a naysayer. But some folks wouldn't just naysay. Nope. Something like this was going to stir up an ugly mess.

"You're sure you want to do this?" Jonas asked her.

"I am." Shayla didn't seem the least bit doubtful about her decision, either. She shifted back to Lily. "I'll be stealing some of your thunder by publishing Hezzie's story before you finish your own research on her."

Lily's nod was fast as well. "Part of me wants to say 'steal away.' Steal any and all thunder you want, but you must know there'll be a backlash."

"Yes, but it'll be aimed at me and not you." She shrugged. "Backlash is another way of saying publicity, and it'll be good for the blog. In the end, it'll be good for everyone to know the truth."

The sound Lily made indicated she wasn't so sure of that *good* part. Maybe, though, the town would get to the good once the shock and anger had died down.

But Jonas immediately rethought that.

Nope. This would be a shitstorm for years to come, and he hoped Shayla was right about this stealing Lily's thunder. Because that in turn would rid her of the pressure of what would go into the research report on Hezzie. In fact, a report might not happen at all once Shayla's story came to light.

Shayla stood, tipping her head to the photos. "Those are your copies to keep if you want them. I'll understand, though, if you want to burn them. It's probably not a fun experience, looking at your naked ancestor."

"It's not," Lily assured her, and she tucked the photos back in the envelope as they headed for the door. "You plan on printing the photos with Horace's…plumbing on display for all to see?"

Shayla gave a slight smile. "His *plumbing* will be blacked out, but there'll be enough of him visible so that everyone knows they're nude shots." She paused at the front door. "I'll post the article about Hezzie tonight at eight, and I've added a disclaimer that I got none of the info for the story from anyone who currently lives in Last Ride. Hopefully, that'll stop people from believing you might have put me up to this."

"Hopefully," Lily muttered, not sounding at all optimistic that it would be the case.

And it likely wouldn't be, either. Plenty of people would want to know if Shayla had named any and all her sources. All. Which meant Lily, the Snoops and anyone else would be put under the microscope if there was even a hint they'd known about Hezzie's secret past.

"By the way, Hezzie called her photography business Secret Longings," Shayla said, opening the door. "It has a romantic ring to it, don't you think?"

Lily muttered an agreement the way a woman in shock would mutter, well, anything, and when Shayla finally left, closing the door behind her, Lily turned to him. Yep, the shock was on her face, too.

"All right," she said, repeating it a few times. "My brain is a mess right now with all kinds of thoughts whirling around, so please tell me what you think I should do to get ready for this."

At the moment, his brain was pretty muddled, too, so he decided to take drastic action. He kissed her, knowing it was the wrong action. Knowing, too, that it would feel incredibly right.

And it did.

It felt right and eased away some of the whirling thoughts about the fallout from the Hezzie article. Of course, it gave Jonas a new set of notions that only should have proved to him that kissing Lily was a mistake.

But it didn't.

In fact—and this could be the lust talking—it seemed to make things a whole lot clearer. This heat wasn't going away, and they wouldn't be able to put the lid back on this particular Pandora's box. Attempting that would mean trying to avoid each other and such, and that could be even more disastrous than just having that "friends with benefits" deal she'd offered. That said, Jonas knew one thing with absolute certainty.

As much as it pained him to stop, he tore his mouth from hers. It must have pained Lily, too, because she immediately tried to pull him back to her. Still, Jonas held his ground—or in this case, his mouth—so he could tell her what he needed to say.

"You're my friend, but sex between us can't be casual," he spelled out. "It'll have consequences."

She huffed. "And that's why you're about to say that we must stop."

"No."

Lily looked to be on the verge of another huff, but his response got her attention, so Jonas continued.

"The consequences don't necessarily have to be bad," he finished. "In fact, they could be good ones."

Again, that might be the lust talking, but Jonas could see a shiny silver lining to this. Sex could cause Lily and him to grow even closer than they already were. They could take their support and comfort of each other to a whole different level.

Heck, they could maybe even begin to love each other.

Well, they could if Lily managed to accept that he'd never be Griff. Lily would never be Maddie, either, but it was possible that they could find a different kind of love.

Wasn't it?

Jonas suddenly needed that to be true because he didn't want to keep things status quo with Lily. Not anymore. He wanted to take the ultimate risk and see where all of this took them.

Apparently, Lily must have also wanted to take some risks and such, because she slipped her hand around the back of his neck and pulled him down to her for another kiss. He could feel the hunger gnawing away inside her, could feel the heat, but she still kept things soft and easy. As if she were sliding right into him and savoring not only the fire that came with the kiss but the tenderness of it, too.

Tenderness shot the need to a whole different level inside. His body didn't especially want it. Nope, it wanted hard, fast and now. No surprise there since he was aching for her. But this slow kiss was a reminder that even when it wasn't hard, fast and now, even when it wasn't full-blown sex, he needed this from her, too.

Hell, he needed *her*.

Lily might not be pleased to know that his feelings for her were deepening into something a whole lot more. Maybe the pace of the kiss was just meant to draw out the pleasure and to keep things in the zone where kissing and such didn't mean so damn much. If so, she was failing at it, because she made a silky sound that was both pleasure and hesitation.

Jonas matched her pace, but he turned her, pressing her against the back of the door to anchor her. He also forced himself to remember that Hayden could come walking in at any minute. That meant the clothes had to stay on, but that didn't mean he couldn't touch.

So, that was what he did.

He slid his hand between them, down her neck, trailing his fingers lower and lower to her breasts. The next sound she made didn't have a whole lot of hesitation in it. Plenty of need, though, telling him that this was a particular fooling around that she liked.

Jonas kept touching, rubbing his thumb over her right nipple while he deepened the kiss just a little more. Then some more. He would have definitely made it French, but the sound of an approaching vehicle in the driveway stopped him.

Lily stopped, too, and she looked up at him. Her eyes were glazed, her face flushed, and she blinked as if coming out of a lust fog. She also cursed.

"Oh, for Pete's sake," she snarled. "This had better not be anyone else bringing me naked pictures."

Even though he was just as frustrated as Lily, Jonas had to smile. Most people didn't have the expectation of nude shots arriving at their doorstep. Then again, most people weren't researching Hezzie Parkman.

Lily sucked in two quick breaths, no doubt steadying herself and getting enough air to verbally blast whoever was unlucky enough to show up at this time. She threw open the door, and Jonas immediately spotted the tall blonde making her way to the porch.

"I'm sorry to just show up like this—" the woman started.

"I'm not interested in any dirt or dirty visuals connected to Hezzie," Lily interrupted.

The woman blinked, stopped and stared at Lily. "All right," she said, as if talking to a human powder keg that might blow up at any second. "I'm Cordelia Wainwright, and I was once engaged to Wade Bentley."

Now it was Jonas's turn to mentally stop and blink. It was certainly the day for surprises, and he wasn't sure how this one would go, but he was betting the woman was either there to defend her ex or dish up some bad stuff about him.

"Cordelia Wainwright?" Lily repeated, looking up at Jonas.

He nodded and kept his voice at a whisper, though the visitor would no doubt be able to hear him if she listened hard enough. "The PI mentioned her. She was engaged to Bentley and then filed the restraining order against him when they broke up."

That was all Lily apparently needed to get her moving out of the doorway. "Miss Wainwright, I'm Lily Parkman, and this is Jonas Buchanan."

"Yes," the woman murmured, as if she'd already known that. "Please call me Cordelia."

Lily and Jonas offered her the same informal courtesy of using their given names, and Jonas hoped that would help set the tone for this conversation. Obviously, Cordelia had some info that she believed they would want or she wouldn't have come, and Jonas very much wanted to hear what she had to say.

Cordelia stepped in, bringing the scent of her perfume with her. She wasn't what Jonas could have called a beauty, but he was betting Bentley hadn't cared about her looks nearly as much as he had her portfolio. He wasn't a good judge of the price of clothes and such, but Cordelia looked well put together with her simple taupe pants and top that looked and moved like silk. He was betting her gold earrings and necklace weren't of the costume variety, either.

"Again, I apologize for just showing up," Cordelia said as they followed the same path to the living room that they'd taken with Shayla. "When I did an internet search, I learned that you both live here at the Wild Springs Ranch, so I got the address for it and drove here. I live in Bulverde now, so it wasn't a long trip."

No, it wouldn't have been long since Bulverde was less than ten miles away. Still, it would have taken some effort, especially since Cordelia had obviously gambled that Lily and/or he would be home.

"Would you like something to drink?" Lily asked, clearly still going the courtesy route.

Cordelia waved that off but did take a seat when Lily motioned toward the sofa. "Wade called me this morning. Out of the blue," she tacked on to that. "I hadn't spoken to him in two years, not since our breakup. Well, the aftermath of our breakup, anyway. I heard you mention the restraining order, so I'm guessing you know what went on between Wade and me?" She directed that question to Jonas.

He nodded, then shrugged as Lily and he sat down across from Cordelia. "I'm aware that you were engaged to Bentley and that things must not have ended well between you."

And he left it at that, but Jonas had questions of his own and wanted to know what the hell Bentley had said to her that would make her pay this visit.

Cordelia pressed her lips together for a moment. "Wade cheated on me with someone I thought was a friend. When I found out, I immediately ended our engagement, but he continued to press for a reconciliation. When I refused, the pressing became stalking." She paused. "I will say this, though—he obeyed the restraining order, and he didn't contact me again. Not until today."

Bentley had likely obeyed because he'd had no other choice. An arrest would have affected his medical practice, might have even cost him his license. No way could he risk that.

"Why did he call you?" Jonas came out and asked.

"Because he thought you or someone connected to you would contact me," she readily admitted. "Wade told me it was just a heads-up, that he believed you'd be getting in touch with anyone from his past."

"And did he happen to say why he thought I'd be doing that?" Jonas added.

Cordelia nodded. "He thinks you're an overprotective stepfather who's jealous of the relationship he's trying to build with his son." She stopped and leveled her gaze on him. "Are you?"

"Overprotective, yes," he admitted after giving it some

thought. "But I'm not jealous of Bentley. I'm just worried that Eli will end up getting hurt by something Bentley says or does." Now it was his turn to stop for a moment. "When Bentley and you were still together, did he ever mention he might have fathered a child?"

Because if he had, then that meant Bentley had lied to them about having only recently learned about Eli.

However, Cordelia's headshake was quick and with no hesitation whatsoever. "No, and I never heard any gossip about it, either."

That still didn't mean Bentley hadn't known. It was just possible he'd kept the info about a child close to the vest. After all, it wouldn't do his reputation much good for others to learn he had a child out there somewhere.

"My parents had Wade investigated," Cordelia went on. "They're overprotective, too," she tacked on to that with a brief smile. "The report from the private investigator didn't have anything in it about Wade fathering a child. I'm guessing, though, the PI didn't try to interview Eli's mother?"

Jonas shook his head after he considered that Cordelia and Bentley's engagement would have been about five years ago, when Maddie still would have been alive. If a PI had come around asking her questions about Bentley, Maddie wouldn't have kept that to herself. She would have immediately told Jonas.

"I brought up the subject of children to him," Cordelia continued. "You know, the way you do when you start to realize that things are getting serious. Wade said he always wanted children." Her breath trembled a little now. Probably because she was having to relive memories that weren't especially good. "In hindsight, I think he said that, though, because he knew I wanted kids."

So, no mention of Eli back then, which added some credence to Bentley's insistence that Maddie hadn't told him she was pregnant. Some. Of course, it was just as possible that Bentley had chosen not to bring up something like that to his fiancée because then he'd have to get into why he'd never bothered to see the child.

"Once, I found some old pictures, and I asked him about one where he had his arm around a woman," Cordelia went on. "She was so beautiful, and I wanted to know if she was someone important to him. He said her name was Maddie. I remember that because he made a little joke of it, Baddie Maddie, Saddie Maddie, and then he said things didn't work out between them because she'd cheated on him."

Jonas muttered some profanity, but he didn't have to consider for a second if that was true. It wasn't. Maddie wasn't the cheating sort.

"Maddie is your stepson's mother?" Cordelia asked, her tone tentative.

"Yes. She died two years ago, and she wasn't bad or a cheater."

She nodded. "I believe you. I think Wade was projecting when he said she hadn't been faithful, because he hadn't been faithful to me." Cordelia paused again. "Do you know for certain that Wade is your stepson's father?"

It put a knot in his stomach to have to answer, "More certain than I want to be," but that was what Jonas did. "I'm having the DNA tests redone, but I can't think of a reason why Bentley would want to claim fatherhood of a child that isn't his. Can you?"

She sighed and suddenly looked the very definition of uncomfortable. "Wade's family didn't have a lot of money when he was growing up. They're doing okay now, but he has this need to shake off those particular roots. I believe it's why he sought me out, courted me and asked me to marry him."

He couldn't argue with any of that, and he wondered if Cordelia knew about Bentley's other rich ex-fiancée. Probably. If Bentley was fishing in the waters for a wealthy wife, then word of that would likely get around.

Jonas leaned forward, his gaze anchored to Cordelia's. "Please be honest with me. I love my son, and I don't want him harmed. Can I trust Bentley to do what's right for him?"

Cordelia didn't dodge, didn't look away. "In my opinion, no. I think you should be very careful of what Wade might try to do."

CHAPTER SEVENTEEN

LILY DIDN'T GROAN when her alarm went off at 4:00 a.m. No need to groan when she had already been awake. It was hard to sleep when her brain just insisted on reliving and reliving every single moment of the day before.

And what a day it had been.

If twenty-four hours earlier someone had told her that a heavy kissing session with Jonas would have to take up mental shelf space with so many other things, Lily wouldn't have believed it. But she sure as heck believed it now.

Hayden, who still wasn't showing any signs of communicating with her, had gotten a prominent place on that metaphorical shelf. Then there was Shayla's article about Hezzie that should have hit the proverbial fan by now. Cordelia's revelations about Bentley.

As if all of that wasn't enough, there'd been the heart-stopping fear of nearly losing Pearl in what had, as predicted, turned out to be a hard delivery. If Jonas hadn't called in the vet when he had, they might have lost both the mare and the foal, a filly who would no doubt look like a mini-me version of her mother once her now-white coat turned gray. Thankfully, both mare and filly had made it but would need to be monitored over the next couple of days.

All of that had balled into a big heap of anxiety and worry, and Lily was betting it wouldn't be ending anytime soon. By turning on the "do not disturb" function on her phone for all but Hayden, Jonas and Eli, Lily had staved off having to deal with any fallout from Shayla. But it was coming. No doubt about it. She'd have to deal with it, help Jonas work through what to do about Bentley and somehow convince her daughter to have more than a five-second conversation with her.

The opposite of easy peasy came to mind.

On a sigh, she got out of bed, and since she planned on just a quick look-see of Pearl and the foal, she didn't change out of her pj's. Ones that sported dancing cartoon tacos—a gag Christmas gift from Nola. Sadly, the pj's got far more use than the silk nightie that Lorelei had given her. Not a gag gift but perhaps a nudging reminder that Lily hadn't had a date or a lover in…way too long.

Great. Now she had that on her mental shelf. Because it was another reminder of kissing Jonas. A reminder, too, that soon the kissing was going to get out of hand and lead to sex. She was more than ready for that.

More. Than. Ready.

But she didn't want to burn off some of this heat with him only to leave Jonas having to deal with the mother lode of guilt. Maddie had been gone two years now, but she was reasonably sure that Jonas hadn't had a date or lover since then, either. That was prime foundation for a guilt trip.

Trying not to wake up Hayden, Lily tiptoed her way to the kitchen and hit the brew button for an extra-large mug of coffee. She'd need it and much more to make it through the day, so she added a couple of ice cubes to cool it down enough so she could take her first life-giving gulp. That fueled her enough to get on her work boots, and she went out the back door and toward the barn.

Even at this hour, it was at least seventy-five degrees,

but that was a welcome relief from the blazing temps that would start to soar once the sun came up. There was also a nice breeze, and despite the dull headache, Lily took her time, savoring the peace and quiet. It was times like this when she remembered why she loved the Wild Springs so much. Her own little slice of heaven.

Yes, a cliché, but for her it was true. She'd wanted this place to be her home since the first time she'd seen it. That'd been when Lily was about eight, and she'd come to the ranch with Nola and their mother, Evangeline, who was a counselor. Evangeline must have been making an emergency house call that day because she'd gone inside the sprawling Victorian to "see" the then-owner, Maybell Sandiford, and had told Nola and Lily to wait on the porch. They hadn't but had instead wandered down to the corral to see the lone horse there.

It hadn't been Lily's first trip to a ranch, but it had been the one to leave an impression. She'd wanted to tend to the horse, paint the barn and pull the weeds from around the corral fence. Even though she was a child, she had seen the possibilities. And had made them and more come true when she'd finally been able to buy the place.

She continued walking, sipping the coffee and enjoying the boost that both the caffeine and the ranch were giving her. Enjoying the sights that Mother Nature was rolling out for her.

The sky was filled with a spattering of stars, and the breeze brought the scents of the ranch right to her. The pasture grass, the horses, feed and the roses from the flower garden. It was probably a sense memory, but she thought she smelled warm saddle leather as well.

There were solar lights on the path, so Lily didn't have any trouble navigating her way to the barn, and the mo-

ment she stepped inside, she spotted another little slice
of heaven.

Jonas.

Sitting on the hay-strewn floor, he had his back against
the open gate of the stall where she knew Pearl and her
filly were. His hand was on the mare, and he'd no doubt
been giving her some reassuring strokes before he'd fallen
asleep. Or maybe he wasn't asleep. It was hard for her to
tell. That was because he had his Stetson tipped down low
over his eyes, and his long jeans-clad legs stretched out
in front of him.

He was a sight to see all right. An amazing mouthwa-
tering one that made her wish she'd taken the time to try
to look as good as he did.

And it got even better.

He must have heard her come in because he used the
thumb on his nonstroking hand to push back the brim of
his hat, and he looked at her with eyes that were too darn
incredible, considering the hour and his uncomfortable
sleeping position.

"Morning," she managed to say after she yanked herself out of her lust fantasy about getting him out of those
cowboy clothes. "How's the new mama and baby?"

"Good." He tipped his head to the open stall door, where
she had a look for herself. Yep, that good label did, indeed, seem to apply since both were getting some much-
needed rest.

"Have you been in here all night?" she asked.

"A good chunk of it. Eli was here, but I sent him to bed
at eleven and took over. I wanted to keep an eye on Pearl."

She understood why. The labor and delivery had been
brutal, but Pearl seemed to be resting now. She wasn't doing
a standing rest but rather a full lie down with her foal.

"Coffee," Jonas said, taking in a deep breath. "What would I have to do to get some of that?"

Since her mind was still on the fit of his jeans, his face and the rest of him, a really dirty thought came to mind. A thought she tried not to convey by clamping her teeth over her traitorous "threatening to smile" lips.

Lily went closer, handed him the coffee, and then she sat down next to him. "Thanks," he muttered, and he gulped down some as if it were the cure for all ills. Which it pretty much was. "Nice pajamas," he added, giving her the once-over from sleepy eyes that still managed to look incredibly sexy and inviting.

She muttered a thanks and took back the coffee when he handed it to her. "It was either these or the red silk nightie…" But she stopped and waved that off so he wouldn't think she was throwing sexual suggestions at him.

Too late.

His wicked little grin let her know that he'd already taken that suggestion and was mentally running with it. However, he didn't run long or far, and she could see him reining in the lust. She wasn't sure if she wanted him to succeed at that or not.

"I take it you couldn't sleep," he threw out there. It was an open invitation to discuss what ailed her, and in this case, there were a lot of ailments.

She nodded, had more coffee. "I was worried about Pearl and all the other stuff." Lily passed the mug back to him. It seemed intimate, sharing a predawn hit of caffeine. Then again, almost everything seemed intimate with Jonas these days, but there was the added layer of them touching since they were arm to arm.

"One good thing to come out of this hard delivery is that Eli decided to postpone his visit with Bentley," Jonas explained. "That'll give the PI that I hired more time to do some digging into Bentley's background. I let him know what Cordelia told us."

"Good." And it was, both the digging and postponed visit.

They couldn't just accept Cordelia's comments about Bentley as gospel. After all, she was Bentley's ex, so her opinion could be colored by their failed relationship. But Lily thought this was a case of where there was smoke, there was fire, and she didn't want that particular fire burning Eli.

"Any idea how Bentley reacted to Eli postponing the visit?" she asked.

Jonas smiled, but it was short-lived. "He was pissed. He didn't direct any of it at Eli," he quickly added when she snapped back her shoulders. "But Bentley called me right after Eli had texted him that he wouldn't be coming. Bentley griped to me that I'd done something to talk Eli out of seeing him. I simply informed the jerk that Eli loved the horses and wanted to be with one of them when she delivered."

She thought about that a second while she finished off the rest of the coffee. "Implying that Eli loved the horses a lot more than Bentley."

Now she smiled, and it wasn't short. Lily savored it a moment because she suspected it was true. Still, that didn't mean all future visits with Bentley were off. Well, they wouldn't be unless the PI found something that proved the man wasn't being on the up-and-up about wanting a relationship with his son.

"Eli's already named the foal," Jonas went on, smiling again. "Dewdrop."

"Good choice," Lily muttered, studying the foal's coat

that did sort of resemble that particular morning precipitation. "Eli's good at the whole naming thing." She paused, hoping she wouldn't spoil this easy mood by saying what she hoped would be comfort to Jonas. "Eli loves the horses, this ranch. *You.* Even if things pan out with Bentley and him, I can't see Eli leaving this place to go live in the city."

"Maybe," Jonas agreed.

But the worry was still in his voice and on his face. It seemed awful to hope for the PI to find out something really bad about Bentley, something that would block him ever getting custody of Eli, but that didn't stop the hope from coming. After all, Lily wanted both Eli and Jonas happy, and she believed the way for that to happen was for them to keep their home here, together.

Pearl made a soft nickering sound, causing them to look in her direction. "She's annoyed," Jonas translated. "I guess our conversation is disturbing her sleep."

Even though Lily had been around horses most of her life, she always marveled at how fast and how well Jonas could interpret the sounds they made. The times when the ranch hands hadn't heeded Jonas's warnings that one of the horses was on the verge of a bad mood and therefore the bad behavior that went along with it, they'd paid the price with a nip or a tail flick.

"Oh, well," Lily said, getting to her feet. "We're out of coffee, anyway, and I think we're both going to need it to get through the day. Let me run to the house and make some more, and then I can take over the watch from you so you can get some rest."

"Thanks, but I got in a couple of hours while Eli was in here. I'll be good to go with some caffeine hits. Also, I think Pearl's out of the woods now." Jonas stood, too, and stretched, yawned. "Just in case, though, I can turn on the camera and watch her from my office while I get some work started."

There were cameras in a couple of the stalls so that sick horses could be monitored, but it was something Jonas and she rarely used. Nothing could beat the hands-on and eyes-on attention of a horse that needed it. In this case, though, Jonas was right about Pearl being well on her way to recovering from the delivery, and since Pearl wouldn't be having mega infusions of coffee, she probably could use the sleep and snuggles with the foal.

"If you want to come to the house, I can make a big pot of coffee," she offered, "and we can go over the report on those El Paso Andalusian mares we're thinking about buying. I can turn on the camera in the stall and do the monitoring from my laptop."

Her invitation wasn't totally out there despite the hour. Jonas and she had spent many mornings, some as early as this one, dealing with a sick horse or some other ranching emergency. But it felt different this time.

Is different, she admitted to herself.

Because Jonas and she didn't have the same boss–ranch manager relationship they'd had since the last crisis. Nope. Those kisses and this heat had changed everything, and even if she wanted it—which she didn't—they wouldn't be able to undo what had already started.

"I have coffee and the report in my office," he said, scrubbing his hand over his chin that had a generous amount of stubble. "I can grab a quick shower while you read through it."

Of course, that sounded like an invitation, too, but she'd actually been in his office when he'd made use of the shower in the attached bath. Not during the actual shower but after he'd just finished. It'd been shortly after another delivery where Jonas had assisted the mare, and Lily had come in seconds after he'd showered and dressed.

Since that was BKAS—before kissing and such—she hadn't felt an overwhelming punch of lust. But she had felt some because, hey, this was Jonas, the hot cowboy, so some lust had occurred even though she hadn't known then just what a good kisser he was. Or that his mouth was as hot as the rest of him.

Nope. She hadn't had knowledge of those things. But she certainly had it now.

They worked their way to his office, and he immediately went to the coffeepot to get that started. It didn't take long for the wonderful scent to start wafting through the air.

"The report's on the desk," he said, "and I won't be long in the shower." He stopped, though, when his phone dinged, and he frowned as he read. "Kenny's sick with a fever and sore throat and won't be in today," he relayed. "He thinks it might be strep since his mom has it."

She'd held her breath, bracing for bad news, and while that wasn't good about one of the hands being sick, it wasn't the worst thing that could have happened. However, the text was a reminder of something she'd have to do.

"I'll need to turn on my phone soon and deal with the flak that Shayla's article will cause," she said, mentally adding some profanity. "Then again, maybe folks will just keep the flak aimed at Shayla."

Jonas made a sound of agreement, but when he didn't move, she looked up at him to see if something was wrong. It wasn't. Mercy, it wasn't. Something was right. Well, right-ish, anyway, in the heat department.

He went to the laptop on his desk, booted it up, and after some keystrokes, he turned the screen in her direction for her to see Pearl and the foal. They were both exactly where Jonas and she had left them and seemed to be resting peacefully.

Lily, however, wasn't feeling much peace right now.

Good grief, she should either go for broke and throw herself at Jonas or leave and regroup. A seduction, aka throwing herself at him, was probably best suited for a sexier outfit than taco pajamas. Perhaps some makeup, too, or at least brushing her hair.

"I could take a shower," he spit out like the profanity she'd just been thinking, "or I can kiss—"

He didn't finish that, though she was pretty sure she knew what he'd been about to say. That was because he finished it by kissing her. Without breaking the lock he had on her gaze, he came across the room, and when he reached her, he slipped his arm around her waist, pulling her to him. In the same motion, his mouth came to hers.

All in all, it was the best possible place it could be.

Jonas kissed her like a man on fire. Which was a good thing since she was on fire as well. Still, Lily tried to just level out enough so she could enjoy the kiss for what it was. And what it was was amazing.

Good grief, the man could kiss. This was finesse in motion, and he was applying that finesse to adjust the pressure. To adjust the angle. To go deeper until she could no longer attempt a leveling out. The only thing she could do was hold on and let him take her wherever he wanted to go.

Apparently, he wanted an anchor, because he backed her up until they were closer to the door. He shut it and pushed her against it. All without breaking the kiss. She was glad he'd thought of such a thing as privacy. It was early, but that didn't mean someone wouldn't have come walking in on them, and the thought hadn't even occurred to her. Then again, she doubted a lot of things other than

Jonas were going to occur to her. She was lost in the kiss and didn't want to find her way back.

Lily didn't just stand there. She did her own part to deepen the kiss, and she got rewarded big-time when the taste of him shot right through her. It was amazing, but thankfully she didn't have to settle for mere amazing with her mouth. She got to touch him, to slide her hand down his back and over all those muscles.

Jonas made a grunt of pleasure, so she kept touching, kept kissing, kept pressing herself closer and closer to him until they were mouth to mouth and body to body. The position was great for making out, but it had a big disadvantage. All that contact skyrocketed the heat into the stratosphere and made her want more, more, more.

He seemed to sense her need for more. Or maybe he was just reacting off his own need. Either way, he went for gold by dropping those kisses to her neck. It only took a second or two of him doing that when she realized she'd been wrong about the best possible place for his mouth being on hers. It was better on her neck.

Better, too, when he lowered his hand to her butt. Not simply for touching, she soon realized, though that ignited some new fires. The clever Jonas used his hand to align them so they were center to center, and oh, did her center approve of it. He gave her a nudge, a hard one with his erection, that nearly caused her to climax.

She held on for dear life, or for that orgasm, which seemed now to be a sure thing. When he lifted her, wrapping her legs around his waist, she went with that, too, and got an even better nudge that had her cursing, seeing stars and, yes, wanting more. The kissing, touching and nudging were awesome, they truly were, but she had to have more, and she had to have it now.

With her back braced against the door, she went after his shirt, peeling it off him and sending it flying. It wasn't the easier thing to do because of her position, but she had plenty of motivation to get her head lowered so she could run her tongue over his neck. Then his chest.

It was even more arousing to kiss than it was to touch.

Though she didn't give up on the touching. Neither did Jonas. He went after her pajama top and got it unbuttoned. Since she wasn't wearing a bra, when he pushed open the sides of her top, her bare breasts were right there, waiting for him.

He made a sound of approval and pleasure. A hot male sound that did a number on her already-heightened senses, but that was a drop in the bucket to her soaring senses when he put his mouth on her breasts.

Oh, mercy.

It'd been way too long since she'd been kissed like this. Way too long since she'd had this much pleasure spearing through her. Thankfully, though, her body knew just what to do with it. She needed to get Jonas naked so he could do a different kind of spearing. A literal one that would put him inside her.

She reached between them to go after his zipper, but then he stopped. Just stopped. His eyes had so much heat in them when he looked down at her. Heat mixed with frustration, and she couldn't figure out why. Not until he spelled it out for her, that was.

"I don't have a condom with me," he said.

Because her mind and body were whirling, that didn't get through to her brain right away. It took a couple of moments while she had to fight off hauling him back to her. But when she finally grasped the words, Lily cursed.

It hadn't been that long ago she'd had the "safe sex" talk

with her daughter. Lily had drilled home all the bad things that could happen if there was unprotected sex. Well, here she was the driller of that wisdom, and she'd come close to not heeding her own advice.

Lily's body started urging her to do all sorts of stupid things. Like running to the store to buy condoms. Or trying to calculate the risks. But thankfully her common sense would have to win this battle. She'd curse it, but she'd win.

"We can go for broke some other time," he told her, and there must have been gallons of testosterone pouring off his voice, because she had to fight not to dive back in. "This is just for now."

Because she was still cursing, both verbally and mentally, and waging that battle with her common sense, those words didn't sink in, either. That was why she was stunned when he kissed her again. A long, deep needy kind of kiss that should have been the last bit of foreplay before the full-blown stuff.

"No condom," she reminded him in a mutter.

"This will do," he assured her.

While he went back to kissing her, he slid his hand down into the waist of her pajamas. She wasn't wearing any panties, so it was an easy, short journey for his fingers to find her.

And to slip into her.

Since she was already primed and on fire, Lily couldn't stop the orgasm. It rolled through her, taking her under and then flinging her high. Until the only thing she could do was hang on and enjoy the ride.

CHAPTER EIGHTEEN

JONAS LAY ON the floor of his office with Lily snuggled in his arms as she slept. Not exactly how he'd planned to spend 6:00 a.m. on a workday, but it felt damn good to hold her like this. To be this close to her while they weren't having to deal with the crap storm that had become their lives.

He was going to have a sore back, maybe other sore parts, too, but he figured any and all ailments were worth it. He'd gone old-school with Lily, a literal "hand in the pants" deal, but it had gotten her off and given him the chance to watch her as the climax had taken her over.

A really good climax, judging from the expression on her face and the silky sounds of pleasure she'd made.

A really good climax that had made him ache for her even more.

She'd offered him more in the form of an old-school hand job, but that wouldn't have fixed this need he had for her. All right, it would have fixed it for a few minutes, but it would have only primed him for full-blown sex, and without a condom, that would have been a reckless risk for them to take. An unplanned pregnancy would have only added to the crap storm.

But he immediately rethought that.

Immediately started spinning a fantasy of Lily and him raising their kids together along with having a baby. That fantasy quickly cooled and was replaced by a blast from the past that he didn't want. It came anyway.

Maddie.

She'd tried and tried to get pregnant, to have their child, but even after countless fertility treatments, it hadn't happened. Worse, those treatments may have masked the symptoms of the cancer, giving it a chance to take hold and grow until it had been too late to try to rid her of it.

That was a regret that had eaten away at him for two years. It might always do that. A guilt like that could last a lifetime, and now he was coating that guilt with the feelings he had for Lily. Not just lust. He could have justified that as a primal urge. But there were genuine deep feelings for her that went hand in hand with that heat, and whether it was logical or not, it made him feel as if he were cheating on Maddie.

Hell.

Jonas didn't want to feel this way. Didn't want this in his head. He especially didn't want Lily to be dealing with something similar. It had been a long time since she'd been with Griff, but it was possible she might go through her own guilt trip once the reality of a good orgasm sank in.

For now, though, he'd just let her sleep and hope she had sweet dreams because her body had been temporarily sated. Soon, he'd deal with his guilt about Maddie, his sore back and the fact that his left butt cheek had fallen asleep and was causing little pins and needles to poke at him.

Soon came a lot sooner than he'd planned.

"Dad?" he heard Eli call out.

Jonas cursed. Normally, his son wasn't up this early but, of course, Eli would want to check on Pearl and the foal. Even with the near sex and the accompanying guilt trip, Jonas should have remembered that.

Lily immediately woke up, jackknifing to a sitting position and nearly smacking him in the face. "Eli," she muttered, cursing and scrambling to get off the floor.

Jonas did his own version of scrambling, only not as fast because of that numb butt cheek. He finally grunted and worked to get upright, all the while bracing himself for Eli to knock on the door. Jonas had had the common sense to lock it right before Lily and he had ended up on the floor for her nap, so at least Eli wouldn't get the shock of walking in on them.

Except maybe it wouldn't be a shock at all.

Eli was fourteen, with his own testosterone to deal with, so the boy had likely seen the way that Jonas had been lusting after Lily. Still, Jonas preferred his son not to get too much of a visual of that lusting.

Lily was still wearing her taco pj's, so she was covered. No signs of what had gone on earlier. She apparently wanted to add to that particular facade, because she hurried to the coffeepot that'd been idle for nearly an hour and a half, and she poured two cups. While she was doing that, Jonas unlocked the door and then went to sit at his desk as if he'd been doing paperwork. He'd just taken his first sip of the coffee when the door opened.

"Dad?" Eli repeated, sticking in his head.

Jonas saw the boy freeze, blink, and then Eli's gaze shot from him to Lily. Specifically, to her pj's.

"A gag gift from my sister," Lily said with a chuckle that she'd probably had to work hard to muster up. She lifted her cup. "I came out to the barn to check on Pearl and her baby girl, and your dad had pity on me and made me coffee."

Eli didn't come out and accuse her of fudging the truth, but Jonas could tell from the boy's expression that he had a good idea of what had gone on. Or what he thought had gone on. Eli likely figured they'd had sex, because he flushed and backed away from the door.

"Uh, I just came by to have a look at Pearl and Dewdrop for myself," Eli managed to say. "They look good."

"They do," Jonas agreed and didn't mention that his particular assessment was already over an hour old.

Lily piped her own sound of concurrence and added, "FYI, I love the name you gave the foal."

"Thanks," Eli said, but he was the poster child for an uncomfortable situation. "Uh," he repeated, and he tipped his head to the front of the barn. "Did you know there's a whole bunch of people in your yard?"

It had been a bad time for Lily to take a sip of the coffee, because she choked on it. She sputtered out a cough and practically dropped the cup on his desk.

"People? What people?" she asked.

However, Jonas figured she had an inkling of what this was about. Shayla's article that would have hit the internet several hours ago. Instead of running out of the office, though, Lily whipped out her phone from her pocket, turned it on and then muttered a single word.

"Fudge."

She'd no doubt seen the massive amount of missed calls and texts, but she'd still been mindful enough to use mom profanity instead of the real deal.

"How many people are in the yard?" Jonas asked Eli.

Eli shrugged. "Just a guess but maybe a dozen. I texted Hayden to ask her what was going on. I woke her up, and she went to the window to look out. She said it was probably about the research her mom was doing on Hezzie Parkman." He shifted his attention back to Lily. "Hayden wanted to know if she should answer the door."

"No." Lily couldn't seem to say that fast enough, and her

fingers practically flew when she wrote a text. No doubt to Hayden to tell her to stay in the house.

Lily glanced down at her pajamas, no doubt wishing she was dressed in real clothes for this confrontation, but she stood no chance of sneaking into the back of her house without someone seeing her.

"I have spare jeans and shirts," Jonas offered, motioning toward the small closet. "But it might cause even more speculation if you come out of the barn wearing my clothes."

Of course, there was no *might* to it. Speculation and outright conclusions would happen, and it'd be even worse for Lily if she took the proverbial walk of shame in his clothes.

She took hold of the bottom of her pj's top and gave it a little snap as if to make sure it was as neat-looking as possible, and she started for the office door.

"I'll go with you," Jonas insisted, and he hoped that wasn't up for negotiation. He didn't want her to go solo to face a riled group of Last Ride's finest.

On a heavy sigh and nod, Lily walked out with Jonas right behind her. He didn't stop Eli from going with them, either, though Jonas hoped that no one out there had any naked pictures they wanted to flail around.

"Did Miss Lily do something wrong?" Eli muttered to him.

"No." Jonas couldn't say that fast enough, and he wanted Lily to hear it and the rest of what he had to say. "This isn't about anything she did. It's about some people not wanting to face the truth about their kin."

Eli stayed quiet for a few steps. "Is that meant to be about Mr. Bentley? I mean, did you say it because you think I'm not facing something?"

That stopped Jonas in his tracks, and since he definitely

wanted to have this conversation, he called out to Lily. "Hold up a sec, please."

She did, and after a glance over her shoulder at them, she stayed put. She'd no doubt realized that Eli might want a bit of privacy. Jonas also needed a moment to figure out what exactly to say. He certainly didn't want to spill anything he'd learned from Cordelia or the PI, but he needed to find out if Eli had picked up on anything bad from Bentley.

"Do you believe there's a truth you're not facing about Mr. Bentley?" Jonas settled for saying.

Eli shrugged. He shoved his hands in his pockets and kicked at a clump of hay. "Not really. It's just I know he said Mom lied. I didn't forget that. And, well, I just wondered if she did. You know, if she wasn't telling the truth about Mr. Bentley not wanting to see me when I was little."

Well, crap. There it was. If Jonas said no way had Maddie lied, then he wouldn't necessarily be telling the truth. Because maybe she had. Maybe she'd lied since that was easier than spelling out to anyone, including Eli as he'd gotten older, that his bio father was a gold-digging, bad businessman who was capable of stalking. Perhaps capable, too, of even worse things.

The flip side to his answering dilemma was that if Jonas acknowledged that Bentley truly might not have known he had a son, then that made the man seem like a suffering martyr or something. Jonas figured Bentley was a lot of things, but martyr wasn't one of them.

"I don't know what went on between your mom and Mr. Bentley," Jonas admitted. "He was out of her life before your mom and I even met. And I think it must have hurt her to talk about him, because whenever the subject would come up, she'd just shut down."

In hindsight, that reaction could have been guilt since

she hadn't told Bentley the truth, but screw hindsight. Jonas was siding with Maddie.

"I do know this," Jonas went on. "Your mother wouldn't have intentionally done anything to hurt you. She did the best she possibly could for you."

Eli shrugged again, and it was obvious he wasn't ready to jump on the "siding with Maddie" bandwagon. However, he also wasn't doing any hip-hip hooraying for Bentley, either.

"Did something happen with Mr. Bentley that's making you uncomfortable?" Jonas pressed.

"No." Eli's answer was quick, but it was followed by another long pause. "No, not uncomfortable. It's just I know he wants me to be his son. I mean, the kind of son who lives with him and stuff. Sometimes, it feels like he wants me to make up for Mom not telling the truth."

That tightened Jonas's jaw and pretty much the rest of him, too. "You have nothing to make up for. *Nothing*," Jonas emphasized. "And don't let Bentley or anyone else put that notion in your head, understand?"

Eli nodded, but Jonas could tell he'd in no way convinced the boy of…anything. Shit. He hated to see his son twisted up like this.

He put his arm around Eli, who was obviously experiencing his own bout of tight muscles, and Eli tolerated a brief hug before he said, "Please don't say anything to Mr. Bentley about this. He's my dad, and I don't want to mess up anything with him."

And with that heart-crushing comment, Eli moved away from Jonas and started for the barn door.

That was Lily's cue to get moving as well, but she volleyed some glances back at Jonas, silently asking if he was okay. He wasn't. He'd just had the rug pulled from beneath him, but he gave Lily as much of a reassuring nod as he could manage. No need to put this on her, not now, when she was about to face a whole bunch of pissed-off people.

Jonas caught up with her as she opened the barn door because he wanted them to go out together. He heard her drag in a breath, no doubt to try to steel herself up for whatever was about to be hurled at her.

But when they stepped out and the crowd spotted them, a chorus of loud cheers went up. There was applause, and some of the people started hurrying their way.

He recognized all of them as Parkmans, and this was obviously the side of the family who approved of what Shayla had written. Either that or Lily and he had been wrong about why the visitors had come.

Derwin was leading the pack of those coming toward the barn, and one of the twins, Marlene, was right behind him.

"Someone finally did it," Derwin announced. He paused, though, when his gaze traveled over her pajamas.

"We were with a mare," Lily explained, leaving it at that.

Derwin seemed to accept the partial truth. Maybe because he had something more important to go on about. "Someone finally told the truth about Hezzie." He was waving some papers, probably Shayla's article that he'd printed out.

That was when Jonas noticed that not everyone was in a celebratory mood. Two of the people were hanging back. Alma and the other twin, Charlene. With their faces as somber as graves and their arms folded over their chests, it was obvious they believed it was a bad thing that the truth had come out.

"Congrats, Lily," Marlene gushed.

But Lily immediately shook her head. "I had nothing to do with that blog post."

That stopped the cheering people in their tracks. "But you encouraged Miss Carson to do it," Derwin insisted.

Lily gave another headshake. "Absolutely not. She paid me a visit yesterday to tell me she'd already written the story and planned to put it online."

That clearly took some of the wind out of Derwin's celebratory sails, but Marlene only shrugged. "The truth's the truth no matter where it comes from."

"It is," Derwin agreed. He glanced at the papers he was holding. "No one can dispute now what Hezzie did. It's all out in the open, and people are just gonna have to deal with it."

He thrust the article toward them, and Jonas saw that Shayla had, indeed, gone with including some of the nudes of Horace, blacking out only his genitals and nothing else. Shayla had also included the photo of Hezzie winning the Silver Slipper and another that she hadn't shown Lily and him. It was a young Hezzie in a cancan costume. If the rumors were true, this would have been from Hezzie's acting days.

Shayla had been thorough and even included snippets of a report from a facial recognition expert who had verified that it was in fact Hezzie and her beloved in the pictures.

Lily studied the article for a couple of moments and then looked at the group of her kin. "Many people are going to be upset by this, so I don't think this is something you'll want to rub in anyone's faces." She tipped her head to Alma and Charlene, and Lily no doubt knew they were only a small spattering of those who'd be upset.

"They'll just have to accept it," Derwin repeated.

"Maybe, but it's best to give everyone some time to let all of this sink in."

Obviously, Derwin didn't agree with that. "But you'll include all of this in the report you write for the Last Ride Society," he said. "I mean, so it'll be part of the official record."

"I'm not sure what I'll write." She tapped the photos. "But I probably won't be including anything like this since people of all ages are allowed to read the reports."

Derwin had already opened his mouth, but that got him closing it. "Oh, well," he muttered. "At least the article will be available to all those who want to read the truth about Hezzie. This doesn't diminish what she did. Just the opposite. It proves how resourceful Hezzie truly was."

Yeah, and a whole bunch of Hezzie's kin were never going to buy that. They'd be pissed, and some of that anger would still likely land on Lily.

"Lily hasn't gotten much sleep," Jonas threw out there, and he added his own yawn for good measure.

The group thankfully got the message, and while they muttered, gushed and went on about the article, they turned and headed back toward their vehicles. Even Alma and Charlene joined in the exit, after they shook their heads and aimed disapproving looks at the rest. Lily and he included.

"Thanks," Lily told him.

Her sigh was loaded with the fatigue he saw on her face. She didn't start toward her house, though, until most of her visitors had already begun to drive away. She'd barely made it a step when the back door flew open, and Hayden came running out. Hayden was also wearing pj's, ones with shorts and a loose top. She was barefoot, too, so she'd obviously just gotten out of bed.

One look at the girl, and Jonas knew something was seriously wrong.

Eli had no trouble picking up on the "seriously wrong," either, because he took off running toward Hayden. Lily and Jonas were right behind him, but when Eli tried to gather Hayden into his arms, the girl moved away from him and aimed her intense eyes at Lily.

"Is it true?" Hayden asked, thrusting out a piece of paper.

Hell. It was another of those handwritten notes.

"Is what true?" Lily took the note from her.

"That," the girl said, her voice trembling. "It was taped to the outside of my window, and I saw it when I got up. Is it true?"

Hayden wasn't crying. Too many other emotions for that. But Jonas thought the girl was ready to burst into tears. After she tore into her mother, that was.

Jonas moved to Lily's side, and he heard the sound that came from deep within her throat. Part gasp, part groan. She handed the note to Jonas and then looked Hayden straight in the eyes.

"Yes, it's true," Lily said. Her voice was plenty unsteady, too. "Cam Dalton isn't your father."

CHAPTER NINETEEN

LILY COULD FEEL her heart sinking until she thought it might have dropped all the way to the ground. It always crushed her when her child was hurting, but what she saw on Hayden's face was beyond hurt.

It was betrayal.

And Lily was the cause of it.

Of course, she should have already told Hayden the truth. It should have happened years ago. She hadn't done that, and now her daughter was paying the price.

"You need to know that your mother is a liar," the note said. "Cam Dalton is not your father."

For only a handful of words, the note certainly packed a wallop. One that Lily knew had opened an emotional can of worms for Hayden. Tears shimmered in Hayden's eyes, but they didn't fall, and every muscle in her face had gone slack.

"Is Griff Buchanan my father?" Hayden asked, not a demand.

Lily would have preferred that it had been a demand. Would have preferred a major temper tantrum complete with shouting and condemnation of the mother who'd betrayed her. But no, Hayden's hurt was tamping down the fury.

For now, anyway.

But the anger would come. Lily was sure of that.

"Yes, Griff is your father," Lily said once she was able to speak. "I found out I was pregnant with you right before he died."

Lily glanced around to see if they had any privacy whatsoever for this conversation. They didn't. She spotted one of the hands driving up, and several of their visitors were in their vehicles but still might be able to hear if voices got louder. Which they might. At the moment, Lily didn't care squat about her own privacy, but she thought maybe Hayden would care if gossip started about her and the fact that she was Griff's daughter.

"Why don't we go inside and talk?" Lily suggested.

Hayden didn't budge. She just continued to stare at Lily with those hurt-filled eyes. "Then why did you lie and let me believe Cam was my father?"

Lily sighed, gearing up to finish this outside after all, but Eli gently took hold of Hayden's arm. "Let's go inside." He leaned in and whispered something to her, and that seemed to do the trick. Hayden turned and let Eli lead her toward the house.

Even though Lily had been worried about Hayden's "heating up" relationship with Eli, she was so thankful that Hayden had him right now. Thankful for Jonas as well when he slipped his arm around her waist. Not a tight grip. Just enough to let her know he was there for her.

"Once we're inside, I'll see if Eli and I can slip out so Hayden and you can talk in private," Jonas muttered to her.

But Lily shook her head. "You already know the whole story, and Eli will hear it soon enough." Because Lily figured there was no way Hayden would keep any of this from him.

Not that there was much more of that *any* for Hayden to learn.

The bottom line was Lily had lied, and Hayden had found out the worst way possible about the lie. Part of Lily wanted to throttle the person who'd put that note on Hayden's window. It had probably been someone irked enough at the Hezzie revelation that they'd wanted to get back at her.

That slowed Lily's steps, though.

Because who would have known about Griff being Hayden's father?

Lily looked up at Jonas, but he answered before she could even ask the question. "I don't know who would have done this," he said, glancing down at the note she still had in her hand. "But, trust me, I will find out. I'll take that note to Matt so he can have it checked for prints. Then I'll talk to every single person who was here at the house this morning until I pinpoint the coward who'd use your daughter to get back at you."

She muttered a thanks, though Lily intended to do some questioning of those visitors as well, but there was another layer to this puzzle. "Who would have known Griff was her father?" she whispered to Jonas as they reached the porch.

He shook his head. "Our families know, but none of them would have done this. And Cam, of course."

Lily couldn't agree with that fast enough about the families. She was 99 percent sure Cam wouldn't have, either, but just in case he'd had some kind of meltdown that'd left him with a serious mean streak, she sent a quick text to him, asking if he'd left a note for Hayden. She also gave him a heads-up that Hayden might be contacting him.

While she waited for his reply, Lily hit Jonas with another question. "You said you hadn't heard any gossip about it?" she pressed, recalling their earlier conversation when she'd come clean to him about Griff.

Another shake of his head, followed by a shrug. "It's possible the person who left the note just guessed. Your relationship with Griff was common knowledge. Ditto for your quick marriage to Cam."

True, and someone could have put the pieces together so he or she could then do this horrible thing of hurting a child. Oh, yes. Lily would find out who was responsible. First, though, she had to try to make sure her daughter was all right.

With his arm still around her, Eli and Hayden went into the kitchen first, and Eli had already managed to get Hayden to sit on a stool at the kitchen island by the time Jonas and Lily walked in. Even though the note was the equivalent of a thousand-pound elephant in the room, Lily put it on the island so they could all see it.

"Do you want me to just start?" Lily asked after she made eye contact with Hayden. "Or do you have a specific question you want answered first?"

Hayden stared at her a long time. Slow snail-crawling moments where the fear and tension skyrocketed inside Lily.

"Why?" Hayden finally said.

As questions went, it was a good one, an all-encompassing one, and Lily didn't intend to dodge any part of it. No sugar-coating, either. It was truth time.

Since her throat felt as if she had no moisture left in her mouth, Lily poured herself a glass of water while she got started. "Griff and I started dating in high school, and we had a lot of breakups and makeups. We became lovers when we were seventeen. I loved him," she emphasized.

She hadn't done the emphasis to let Hayden know that should be the example she followed when she decided to have sex. Lily just wanted Hayden to understand that she'd been conceived in both heat and love.

"I know with all my heart that Griff loved me, too," Lily went on.

She didn't look at Jonas when she said that. This was hard enough to say without seeing his face and remembering that she had seriously deep feelings for him, too. Maybe even love. And here she was, spilling everything about her and his brother.

"So, you loved each other, and you got pregnant," Hayden summarized, and there was anger in her voice now. So much anger, and Lily let it bash against her like a fierce wave.

"Yes," Lily verified. "Griff and I had had one of our break-ups when I realized I was pregnant. I went to him and told him." And now she had to pause and take a deep breath. Mercy, why did this hurt so much after all this time? "I didn't know that Griff had just gotten some hard news of his own, that he had an incurable disease, ALS."

"I know that," Hayden snapped. "I helped Aunt Nola with the research, remember?"

No way could Lily forget that. It had brought so much of the old hurt and memories to the surface. Not just for her but for all of Griff's family. Jonas especially since as the big brother he'd always thought he should have been able to help Griff more.

"I think Griff responded to the pregnancy the way he did because he'd just gotten that ALS diagnosis," Lily continued. "He told me to find someone better than him, and shortly thereafter, he died."

Hayden stared at her. No eye rolls or huffs, but Lily could tell that explanation wasn't doing anything to ease the anger building inside Hayden.

"I was devastated when Griff died," she added. "So was Cam. We were all best friends."

Now Hayden huffed. "So, Dad...*Cam*," she corrected, "married you because you were friends, and you made him tell the lie that I was his."

Lily wondered if she should just take the brunt of the blame and let Cam be the good guy in this. But it was time for the lies to end.

She needed another drink of water and a couple of long breaths before she continued. "Cam offered to marry me, and he insisted we tell everyone, including you, that he was the father. I don't know why he wanted it that way. Maybe because he thought his family would help us out more if they thought the baby was his. Maybe he just didn't want the questions of why he was marrying his best friend's girl and raising the child they'd made together."

Hayden huffed again. "And you just jumped at the chance to cover up that you got pregnant without being married, the very thing you lectured me about when we had that stupid 'safe sex' talk."

Even with everything else going on, Lily noticed that Eli blushed and suddenly looked as if he wanted to be anywhere but there. However, Lily had no intentions of turning this into a discussion about sex.

"No," Lily assured Hayden. "I didn't jump to cover up I was pregnant with you. I thought about it as much as I could think about something, considering I was an emotional mess. Cam continued to press me to marry him, and I finally said yes."

Hayden got up from the stool. "I'm surprised you didn't just get rid of me."

Oh, that stung, like a million slaps to the face. "I would

have never done that. Never. I loved you from the moment I found out I was carrying you."

Hayden's huff let Lily know she didn't quite buy that. But then, why should she believe it when Lily had lied to her about her father?

"I loved you from the moment I learned I was pregnant," Lily repeated, hoping if she said it enough that Hayden might hear it and believe it. "But I was wrong to marry Cam. I think he made the offer because he was hurting, too, and he thought raising you was something Griff might want him to do."

"But he couldn't do it," Hayden fired back the second Lily finished the last word of her sentence. "He couldn't be a father to me."

She threw up her hands, and Lily got another soul crushing when she saw what no doubt would be the first of Hayden's tears slide down her cheek. Lily wanted to pull her into her arms and try to make this better, and it sickened her to know there was nothing, absolutely nothing, she could do to fix this.

"Do you have any idea how it made me feel when Cam wasn't around?" Hayden asked, but she didn't wait for Lily to respond. "It made me feel abandoned and worthless. Unlovable. Because I thought something must be wrong with me for my dad to leave me like that."

Oh, God.

Lily's fingers were trembling when she pressed them to her mouth to try to silence the sob. She failed. The sound came, and it caused Jonas's arm to tighten around her. She so wanted to lean on him, but she couldn't. Not yet, anyway.

"I'm sorry you felt that way," Lily managed to say, knowing it wasn't nearly enough. A drop in the bucket that could in no way heal what had to have been years of Hayden believing she had been the reason Cam left. "Cam was young, and he just couldn't handle being married to me. He left because of me, not you."

That was almost the truth, anyway. Marriage to her had been the biggest reason he'd left and hadn't come back. The baby, Griff's baby, had been just added stress.

"He left," Hayden emphasized, "and you let me believe he was my father. The father who'd run out on us."

Lily nodded. "I was wrong, but at the time I thought that was better than you learning your real father had ended his life." Ended it after learning about the pregnancy. But Lily had no intentions of spelling out that reminder.

Hayden's eyes were hard and filled with tears, and she pinned them to Lily. "Yes, you were wrong. So wrong." And with that, the girl turned and ran out of the kitchen.

Lily didn't go after her. It tore at her heart, but she knew she had to give the girl some time and then hope and pray that they could eventually mend things between them. However, the thought popped into her head before she could stave it off.

That there might not be a fix for this.

That she might have lost her daughter.

"Please check on her," Lily told Eli.

The boy seemed to be waiting to hear just that, because he practically sprinted out of there. Lily still didn't move. Couldn't. But thankfully Jonas could. On a heavy sigh, he turned her, pulling her into his arms and against him.

Lily buried her face on his shoulder and let the tears come.

JONAS FELT POWERLESS to help Lily get through this. Powerless and hurting right along with her. He could only hope that Eli was faring better with Hayden and that his son would somehow magically get the girl to understand her mother's side of this.

Of course, Lily would say her "side" was a mistake. One she'd been making for years. And now she was paying the price for it.

He didn't try to tell her that this would all work out, because then he'd have to admit to her that it might not. Things like this could cause a fracture that never healed, and it didn't help that Hayden was already filled with the angst that came with being a teenager. He knew that first-hand because he'd seen it happen with Griff. Their parents had died when Griff was just a kid, and he'd never gotten over it. Griff had carried that pain and anger with him until he died. He sure as hell didn't want that for Hayden.

Jonas hadn't checked the time when all of this had blown up, but he figured he'd been holding Lily for nearly a half hour when her phone dinged. She whipped it from her pocket, no doubt hoping it was some kind of response from Hayden.

"Cam," she muttered when she checked the screen. She read the text and shook her head. "He said he didn't leave a message for Hayden."

Jonas hadn't thought for a second that Cam had done this. Basically, Cam had written himself out of Hayden's life when she'd been a baby, and there was no reason for him to hurt the girl by telling her this way.

No.

And Jonas believed this particular hurt had been intentional.

That meant they were looking at someone trying to get back at Lily, and he'd vowed to find that person, and he would. Once he had things under control here—well, as under control as they could be—he'd take the note to the sheriff and go from there to find this sick SOB.

There was the sound of approaching footsteps at the same moment that Lily got another text. "From Nola," she relayed to him. "She's on her way over." Lily showed him the screen, and he saw the line of question marks that followed Nola's text.

Jonas didn't have time to comment on that because Hayden and Eli came into the kitchen, and Hayden was carrying a suitcase. Hell. Not a good sign. That was when Jonas put one and one together and figured the girl had called Nola to come and get her.

"I'm staying with Aunt Nola for a while," Hayden insisted. Her eyes were red from crying, but her chin was high in a defiant pose. "She wants to talk to you, to make sure it's all right, but I told her this was my decision, not yours."

And there it was. The hurt put into words. Hurt that he knew had to slice right through Lily.

Lily nodded. "I'd rather you stay here at your home. But I understand if you feel the need to get away."

"Of course I feel the *need*." Hayden spit out that last word. "I can't stay here after what you did. I'm going to walk to Eli's house with him, and Aunt Nola said she can pick me up there after she talks to you."

Lily didn't try to stop her, probably because she knew it would only cause a scene. With Hayden seething with anger, the girl was clearly spoiling for a fight. A fight that would only make things worse.

Jonas made eye contact with Eli to see how he was handling this. It was a lot to put on his shoulders, but Eli gave him a nod that Jonas hoped was a reassurance, and he watched as Eli and Hayden headed out the back door.

Lily didn't start crying again, and she didn't fall into his arms. Instead, he could see her wiping her eyes and clearly making an effort to steel herself up. No doubt so she could face her sister. Nola wouldn't judge and would offer all kinds of comfort, but Lily probably didn't want to dump too much on her because she'd be counting on Nola to try to soothe Hayden.

Jonas heard the car approaching the house and decided that Nola had made good time getting there. However, when Lily and he went to the front to look out the window, Jonas saw that it wasn't Nola.

It was Bentley.

Shit. None of them needed this now.

Since the man appeared to be heading to Jonas's house, Jonas stepped out on the front porch to flag him down. Not in a friendly wave sort of way, either. Scowling, Jonas jabbed his finger at Bentley and then pointed for him to stop in front of Lily's. Bentley did, but he clearly hadn't missed Jonas's pissed-off gesture.

Jonas came off the porch and glanced back toward his place, where he could see Hayden and Eli. They were huddled together with Eli's arm around her, and they must not have heard Bentley's car because they didn't look back.

"You will not stop me from seeing my son," Bentley snarled the moment he stepped from his car.

Jonas muttered another "Shit," this time aloud. He definitely didn't want to deal with this moron now, not when Lily might be on the verge of falling apart. She had come out on the porch, but Jonas didn't want her to have to handle anything else. Especially not a visit from a man who clearly didn't have his facts straight.

"I didn't stop you from seeing Eli," Jonas fired back.

"Eli canceled his visit with you because he wanted to be here with one of the horses."

Bentley actually rolled his eyes. "That was your doing. *Had to be.* You convinced him not to see me."

Jonas didn't mutter any more profanity. It wasn't worth the breath. However, he did go down the steps so he could face Bentley head-on. "Believe what you will, but I didn't even know Eli had canceled his visit with you until he'd told me. He's a responsible kid and is very attached to the horses."

"You—" Bentley started, aiming his index finger at Jonas.

"I'm not finished," Jonas interrupted. "You don't have the right to come here unannounced. I'll play nice, to a point, if Eli wants to continue to see you, but you won't come here unless you're invited, understand?"

Oh, Bentley didn't care for that. If his eyes narrowed any more than they already were, he wouldn't be able to see. He opened his mouth, no doubt to return verbal fire, but then his gaze fired to Lily.

"What are you doing?" Bentley demanded.

Jonas looked back to see that she was filming this with her phone. "Since you're not an invited guest, I'm recording someone who's trespassing."

Well, his eyes did narrow some more, and he ground out some really nasty curse words under his breath. He stormed away. Not leaving. But pacing. Probably so he could try to put a choke hold on his temper.

"Your PI has been digging into my life," Bentley finally said when he stopped and looked at Jonas. "Didn't you think I'd get word that he'd been questioning my friends?"

"I expected you to find out about it," Jonas informed him. "I'd expect my friends to come and tell me if a PI was asking about me." He shrugged. "My life's pretty much an open book, though. No secrets. Nothing I'd want to keep hidden. Can you say the same?" he asked Bentley.

That brought on more cursing. "I'm not perfect. I've made mistakes. And one of the biggest mistakes was not trying to find Maddie after she broke up with me. I figured it was just a good riddance, but if I'd thought for one second she was carrying my baby, I would have found her. Even if she no longer wanted me, I would have been a big part of my son's life."

Jonas answered with just one word. "Maybe."

Another shot of anger fired through Bentley, causing his eyes to narrow. "You want to put a wedge between Eli and me because you want to keep him for yourself."

Jonas nearly went old-school with a *duh*. "I raised Eli, and I love him as if he were my own. Of course I want to keep him."

Bentley brought out the index finger again. "You raised him only because Maddie lied through her teeth and kept him from me."

"Maybe," Jonas repeated.

This time, the anger bubbled up in Bentley so fast that Jonas wondered if the man could literally explode. But he didn't unleash that rage on Jonas. Nope. Bentley looked at a "still recording" Lily.

"A piece of advice," Bentley said in a sappy sweet voice that no one would ever mistake as genuine. "Quit siding with your boyfriend here and try to talk some sense into him. I'm Eli's father, and I will get my son. The sooner the two of you grasp that with your tiny hick brains, the better."

Now Jonas had to worry if *he* might explode. He could tolerate the asshole going after him but not Lily.

"Of course I'm siding with him," Lily said before Jonas could speak. "Jonas is my friend. I want what's best for

Eli and him. And as for my tiny hick brain, well, golly gee shucks, I guess I need to clear out the hay from my head or something. Perhaps you could try clearing the bullshit out of yours?"

Despite the fresh flare of temper, Bentley smirked at her. Actually smirked. "Don't think two can't play the PI game," he said like a threat. "Jonas here might claim not to have any skeletons in his closet, and maybe that's true, but you had a messy life screwing around with his kid brother." He shifted his smirk to Jonas. "Does it bother you to get your brother's leftovers, that when she's with you, she's thinking about him?"

Jonas felt the leash snap on his temper, and Bentley seemed to have realized he'd just gone too far, because he turned and started running back to his car. Jonas was right on his heels.

"Don't do it, Jonas," Lily called out to him.

He heard her but didn't stop. He was going after the asshole and would make him pay for that. However, before Jonas could reach the car, Lily stepped in front of him.

"Look at me," she insisted. "He baited you. He wants you to kick his butt so he can then use it against you."

Even though Jonas heard what she said, Lily still had to hold him back. Bentley, proving he wasn't an idiot along with being an asshole, started his car, threw it into Reverse and got out of there. Fast.

"Bentley came here to start trouble," Lily added, her voice surprisingly calm. She took hold of his chin and forced eye contact. "Don't give him trouble. And don't you dare make me put on square-dance music."

The light comment didn't work, not with the anger still knifing through him. Nothing would work. Or so he thought.

But then Lily kissed him. Not a deep foreplay kind of

kiss, but a gentle, soothing one. Jonas immediately started to feel himself level out. With the leveling came some straight thinking, and that thinking led him to go over what the hell had just happened.

"What Bentley said…" Jonas muttered, trying to work it through.

She shushed him. "I don't think about Griff when I'm with you, and I doubt you consider me leftovers. I hope you don't, anyway."

"I don't." And even though he was still going through the conversation with Bentley, Jonas took the time to look at her.

To kiss her.

To hopefully reassure her that Bentley's jab had been a big-assed lie.

But maybe there was more to what the man had said. "Go back to that part when Bentley was talking about skeletons in closets. He said something about you having had a messy life…and I'm quoting here…*screwing around with his kid brother*." He paused a heartbeat. "Bentley had you investigated and found out about you and Griff."

She shrugged. "Anyone around Last Ride back then would have known I was with Griff." Lily stopped, and the color drained from her face. "Oh, God," she murmured.

Yeah. Oh, God. Because it had just occurred to Lily that Bentley had likely been the one who'd ripped her world apart by leaving that note for Hayden.

CHAPTER TWENTY

LILY CAME OUT of the barn reeking of horse manure. Her muscles were tight and throbbing. So was her head from all the crying, and she'd failed big-time at trying to work off this vibrating, intense ache in her chest. Still, the stalls were all mucked out now, a chore one of the hands or Eli usually dealt with, but she'd volunteered to do it with the hopes of it helping to get her mind off Hayden.

Yep, a big-time failure.

Something she should have known from the start. Nothing was going to get her mind off Hayden. Nothing but maybe a whole bunch of time was going to make Hayden come back home to her, and that *maybe* was huge. Lily couldn't accept that Hayden would never forgive her. Her heart couldn't take that.

It had only been six hours since she'd watched Hayden drive away with Nola, and Nola had texted her three times already to let her know that Hayden was settling into the guest room and that Nola would try to talk to her as soon as possible. Of course, ASAP for Hayden might be weeks from now. Or never.

No, her heart couldn't take that.

Nola had also assured Lily that she'd make sure Hayden got to school on Monday and that she'd step up to help if the girl had any homework stuff to deal with. It was a lot to put on Nola's shoulders since she had Charlie and her glasswork, but since Hayden had insisted on leaving, Lily was glad the girl had gone to Nola, Lily's identical twin. Maybe just seeing Nola would remind her of Lily.

And hopefully it would be a good kind of reminder.

Making her way back to her house, Lily checked her phone for updates. A hang in there from Nola. There were also texts from her mother and Lorelei, both offering to come over—again. Lily had declined their offers, insisting that she needed some alone time. The truth was she just didn't want to rehash the biggest mistake of her life that could have cost Lily her child.

There were no updates from Jonas, which was a little troubling since he'd left nearly three hours earlier to go into town so he could give the sheriff the note someone had taped to Hayden's window. The note from Bentley.

Well, maybe.

Lily didn't know whether to hope it was from him or if it was from a pro-traditional Hezzie supporter. If it was Bentley, though, it would add to those red flags that had already surfaced. That could possibly help Jonas determine whether or not Bentley was scummier than they'd already suspected. However, she wasn't sure how Jonas would be able to use that to try to keep Bentley at a safe distance from Eli.

Eli was another weight on Lily's shoulders. She wasn't sure how he was faring now that Hayden wasn't at the ranch, but she was hoping the boy was in contact with Hayden. He would be seeing her at school for sure, but Lily figured if anyone could get Hayden to open up, it'd be Eli.

It was possible, though, that Eli wouldn't be on Lily's "side." Her lie might have soured him against her, but she prayed not. She didn't want to lose both of the kids that she loved.

She left her crap-coated boots on the back porch and made a beeline toward her bedroom and the shower. Even though her muscles could have used the heat and the pressure from the spewing water, Lily didn't linger. She didn't especially want a lax body or a clear head, because that would no doubt just lead to her being able to think clearer. That would lead to worry.

And more crying.

Instead, she planned on getting the tax paperwork ready for her accountant. That would be a frustrating experience that would hopefully occupy her mind enough that she could make it through the day.

She'd just stepped from the shower when she heard the ding from a text, and Lily nearly slipped trying to get to her phone. Not Hayden as she'd hoped, but it was from Jonas.

"'Heard the shower running. I'm in the hall outside your bedroom,'" she read aloud.

Even though he didn't say anything about urgency, Lily figured he must have something important to tell her or he wouldn't have waited. Or he would have just spelled it out in the text. She was glad he hadn't done that. He'd been her rock for the past couple of days—heck, for years now—and she wanted to see him.

Hurrying, she didn't even dry off. Lily yanked on the terry cloth robe that had once been white but was now a dingy yellow, but this wasn't about making a fashion statement with Jonas. Besides, he'd seen her worse just hours earlier when she'd been wearing her taco pj's and sobbing in her kitchen.

Lily practically skidded to a stop when she saw Jonas in the doorway. Not standing but rather sitting on the floor with his back against the jamb. He looked tired, frustrated and worried. Definitely not a good mix.

Feeling that "not a good mix" herself, she dragged in some air and tried to armor herself. Since that seemed to sap what energy she had, Lily just went ahead and dropped down on the floor across from him. His legs were out-stretched, but Jonas adjusted so that she'd be able to prop her back against her side of the doorjamb. It put them leg to thigh and gave her a good look at his face.

Heck.

"How bad is it?" she asked.

"It could be worse," he said in a tone that silently added that he didn't want to get into anything worse than they were already dealing with. "I gave the note to Matt, and he's sending it to a backlogged lab that probably won't get to it before Hayden's old enough to vote."

Lily consoled herself with a reminder that the delay didn't matter because whoever had put it there wouldn't likely have been stupid enough to leave their prints on it.

"While I was in Matt's office, we contacted every single person who was in your yard this morning," Jonas went on, "and no one admitted to leaving a note. No one admitted to seeing anyone put the note or anything else on Hayden's window. And no one recalls seeing Bentley or anyone else they didn't recognize."

While that was a kicker of a disappointment, Lily had another reminder. Not a consolation one this time but more of an explanation. It had still been early morning when the crowd had been there, so it would have been easy enough for someone—Bentley—to sneak to that side of the house.

"The lab got in touch with Matt," Jonas told her. "They pushed through the second DNA test, and it's a match. Bentley is Eli's biological father."

Another kicker, but since Jonas didn't seem surprised,

it was obviously the results he'd been expecting. Or rather dreading.

"I also got an update from the PI I hired," Jonas continued, still not sounding the least bit hopeful. "He hasn't been able to find anyone who remembers Bentley mentioning that he'd gotten his girlfriend pregnant. A few had vague memories of Maddie, but all claim that Bentley never said anything about her having his child."

Too bad about that because if the PI had found someone who could confirm that Bentley had known about Eli before this past month, it would have been proof that the man was a liar. Which, of course, was a reminder of her own lie she'd told Hayden for years, and her stomach got another hard punch from the regret.

"Nola's been texting me to let me know Hayden is okay," Lily told him.

Jonas didn't jump in to try to assure her that was good, but when his gaze met hers again, Lily braced herself for whatever he was about to add to the pile of already-miserable news.

"Hayden broke up with Eli," he finally said.

That got her sitting up straighter. "When? Why?"

He shook his head, a weary kind of movement followed by an equally weary long breath. "I don't know the reason. Eli just told me they'd talked on the phone and that she'd broken up with him. I couldn't get much out of him after he spilled that. He went into the silent, brooding mode."

Well, crap. Of course Eli had. That was the default mode for many teenagers, but she knew Eli had to be miserable. While this wasn't a broken marriage or even a broken adult relationship, this would feel terrible for him. Probably for Hayden, too.

"Hayden must have broken up with him because of me," Lily muttered, cursing the thought. "Maybe because she was so upset that she lashed out at Eli." She stopped, groaned and did more cursing. "So, you don't know how Eli's handling it."

Another shake of his head. "No, but he called Bentley. I know that because Bentley called me to ask why the hell his son was so upset and why wasn't I doing a better job of watching after him."

This time a *well, crap* just wouldn't cover the anger and frustration Lily felt over Jonas being dragged into this. She didn't bother to tell him none of this was his fault, that he was doing a stellar job of parenting Eli. The words were useless. And unnecessary because Jonas already knew her position on this. When it came to pretty much anything, Jonas was doing the right thing.

The misery rolled through her, clenching her muscles and clawing at her heart. She could tell from Jonas's face that he was right there with her.

"I did ask Bentley if he'd left the note," Jonas added. "He denied it."

She didn't add the snarky "big surprise" comment that sprang to mind. Now wasn't the time for snark. Or "square-dancing" threats. Instead, Lily crawled to him, leaned in and kissed his cheek. It wasn't really all that platonic since it was Jonas, but she hoped it came off as a small gesture of comfort.

Without looking at her and while making another of those sighs, he slipped his arm around her, easing her closer and then brushing a kiss on the top of her head. Definitely a gesture of comfort, which she needed and appreciated.

She picked up the rhythm of his breathing and let the warmth of his arm settle around her. This wasn't exactly a romantic situation with both of them hurting and sitting on the floor, but again, it didn't fall into the platonic zone, either. And that was why the warmth soon turned to a tingle of heat.

The heat poked at her, reminding her that she was sitting next to a very hot guy who'd kissed the living daylights out of her and could certainly manage to do that again. Kiss her, touch her and do so many other things to make her feel good. But the timing sucked for that.

Didn't it?

It did, she assured herself. The timing was bad for both of them, but the heat must have been taking some jabs at Jonas, too, because he turned his head and looked at her. They weren't exactly eye to eye, but it was close enough to put them nearly mouth to mouth.

"Bad idea?" he asked.

"Probably," she admitted.

But Lily was tired of the old argument of sex ruining things between them. She was tired of feeling this heaviness in heart. Tired of lusting after Jonas when nothing she could say or do was showing any signs of cooling that lust.

And that was why she kissed him.

Jonas helped with that, because he started toward her just as she started toward him. Their mouths met, pressure to sweet pressure, and it sparked a firestorm of sensations that thankfully had nothing to do with the heavy state of her heart. This was primal. This was hot.

This was exactly what she needed.

Apparently, Jonas needed the same thing, too, because a husky sound of pleasure tore from his throat. Oh, there was still some reluctance. She could feel that. Maybe because he was trying to fight to remember why this could have some really bad consequences. But he must have lost that fight, because the next sound he made was rougher.

Needier. And it filled her with all sorts of dirty thoughts as to what this incredible man could do to her.

There was no hesitation in his next kiss. It was deep, hungry and sexual, tapping into her senses. His scent, a mix of the outdoors and saddle leather. His touch, soft but demanding. His taste, a blend of everything meant to make her want more and more.

Jonas had no trouble with giving her that more.

Of course he didn't. Because this was Jonas.

He used his clever mouth on her neck, and in the same motion, he hauled her onto his lap. Where everything stopped. Jonas froze, and he pulled back to meet her gaze.

"You're naked under this robe," he said, his voice strained. But it was an erotic kind of strained, as if the news of her near nudity could push him over some edge.

Lily nodded. "I just got out of the shower. Be thankful for that, or my stench would have put you off."

Jonas groaned and pressed his forehead to hers. "Lily, nothing could put me off you."

He'd not said that with a whole bunch of glee. Just the opposite, and she understood that he would have preferred things not to be this way. They were both people who preferred plans, clear thinking, logic. A need this strong threw plans, thinking and logic out the window.

"We'll be off-balanced together," she murmured.

He lifted his head, holding her eyes with his for several long moments. Moments where she thought he'd change his mind and move her off his lap. He didn't, thank goodness. Jonas kissed her again. And again. And again.

The heat inside her started the slow climb again, spreading and building until it slipped through her. Until the need for him became a throbbing ache. Lily wrapped her arms around him, moving until their centers met. In her case, it was easy to find his center because she was butt naked and his erection was straining against the zipper of his jeans.

Her center greatly appreciated the hard pressure, and while the kiss raged on, she kept pressing, revving up the pleasure. Until she remembered something.

"Condom," she managed to say.

Lily didn't want a hand job. She wanted Jonas, and it nearly sent her into a panic that this would lead to anything less than good old-fashioned sex.

Jonas reached in his back pocket, tugging out his wallet, and she nearly wept for joy when he pulled out the condom. Instead of weeping, though, she took hold of his face with both her hands and gave him a hard, hungry kiss to let him know just how pleased she was to see that gold foil packet.

Jonas took her hard, hungry kiss and gave her one of his own while he lowered her until her back was on the floor. Lily made a whimpering sound of protest because it meant she was no longer against his erection, but she soon realized what Jonas had in mind. He rolled them into the room so he could kick the door shut. Smart thinking. Yes, they had the house to themselves, but that didn't mean Eli or someone in her family wouldn't come walking in.

The thoughts of visitors flew out of her mind when Jonas rolled, too, and landed on top of her. She got that delicious pressure again when he fitted his body to hers, and he sent her soaring when he added some kisses and touches to that pressure.

Jonas reached between them, yanking open her robe, and she got the fresh slam of heat when her breasts rubbed against his chest. That slam was a drop in the bucket, though, compared to the one she got when he maneuvered lower and used his mouth, and tongue, on her nipples.

The heat changed to fire, and it slammed into her so

hard that all she could think of was Jonas and the immense pleasure he was giving her.

He gave her more.

So much more. Because he just kept exploring her body with a trail of kisses that went lower and lower until he reached her center, where the ache was so intense she had to fight not to climax. She wanted to let go. Mercy, did she. But she didn't want to go on this particular journey without Jonas.

Lily took hold of his shoulders to drag him back up so she could undress him. Jonas helped. And hindered. Because he kept kissing her while she was trying to shuck off his T-shirt. By the time she sent the shirt flying, Lily was more than starved for him, but there was no way she could resist getting a taste of all those muscles she'd ogled for years. She put her mouth to his chest and just savored the taste of him.

Jonas groaned, a mix of pleasure and torture. Something she definitely understood. He *tolerated* the kissing. The touching, too, when she began to fumble to undo his belt. His groan deepened, though, when she managed to get him unzipped and got her hand in his boxers.

So many words came to mind when she wrapped her hand around his erection. *Pay dirt. Prize. Treasure.*
Jonas.

She touched and touched and touched, sliding her thumb over the tip of his erection until Jonas made one of those hoarse strangled sounds to let her know he'd reached his threshold. He moved off her so he could get rid of his jeans, boots and boxers, all of which gave Lily an amazing view of his amazing body.

Part of her wanted to savor that view for a while, especially since she'd daydreamed about him way too often.

But that part of her didn't get its way. Not when Jonas got on that condom and rolled back on top of her.

Lily didn't see any hesitation in his eyes. Didn't feel it anywhere in his body. Just the opposite. He took hold of her hands, pinning them to the floor, and while he captured her gaze, he slid into her.

The pleasure came. And came. Not a slow ripple. Not this. This was all fire and primal need. Too much need for it to last. Still, Lily fought to hang on to the sensations that were racking her body.

She freed her hands so she could slide them over his back. So she could feel those muscles, and he pushed into her with those long, deep strokes. She touched and took until she could take no more. Lily gave up the fight and let Jonas give her the one thing the heat demanded.

Release.

She gathered Jonas into her arms while he followed her.

CHAPTER TWENTY-ONE

JONAS TRIED NOT to think too much about what had just happened. His slack, sated body helped with that. It was hard to think when he felt as if some of the weight of the world had just slid off him.

Good sex could do that. Good sex with Lily could apparently notch up that effect big-time, because he was feeling a whole lot of satisfaction and contentment right now. It wouldn't last, of course. Good sex was also like a greedy SOB who would want more. For now, though, this was enough, and Jonas held on to the moments, savoring every one of them.

Beneath him, Lily's breath was gusting, and her face was flushed in that post-arousal way that was a "kick to the gut" sexy. Her hair was tousled around her face. That amazing face that meshed with her equally amazing body that he could feel still quivering from the orgasm. Hell, he was probably doing some quivering, too, and he tried to hold on to that as well.

"Wow," she murmured in the same tone as someone who'd just achieved nirvana. "Just wow."

Her experience had obviously been as mind-blowing as his had been, and that pleased him. It'd been a while since either of them had had sex, so it was good to know their skill set in that particular area hadn't gotten too rusty.

"Wow," he repeated while he located her mouth and kissed her.

Since he figured his weight had to be crushing her, he rolled off her and heard the sound of her protest. She protested even more when he got up.

"I need to make a pit stop in the bathroom, but I'll be right back," Jonas assured her. Maybe even back for round two of amazing sex since he had a second condom in his wallet.

Jonas stepped into the bathroom that still had that damp feeling from Lily's recent shower, but underneath the soap, he caught her scent, too. A scent that went straight to his groin. Oh, yeah. He could do round two.

The question, though, was, should he?

Maybe he needed to back off and give her some time to process what'd happened. He refused to believe that she'd been thinking about Griff while they'd been in the throes of sex, but it was possible she was thinking of his brother now.

And with that, his own blasted thoughts came.

Of Maddie. Of what they had together.

His brain and body both knew Maddie was gone. Just as his brain and body knew that he cared deeply for Lily. Maybe even more than *deeply*. He was falling in love with her, and somehow he had to mesh that with the fact that neither of them would simply stop having thoughts about the partners they'd once loved.

Griff and Maddie were parts of Lily's and his pasts. Always would be. So, the trick would be to somehow hang on to that old love while not feeling guilty about the new love that was taking root right now.

Jonas figured Lily and he would need a miracle for that.

That didn't exactly give him a "jump for joy" feeling,

and it didn't help that the sated feeling was melting away and leaving him with a clear mind that he didn't especially want. He definitely didn't want Lily to see regret of any kind on his face, so he steeled himself up when he went back into the bedroom.

She was still on the floor but had put back on the robe and was sitting up with her back resting against the foot of the bed. She immediately looked up, spearing his gaze with hers, and they cursed at the same time.

"You're feeling guilty," she said.

Those were words she could have taken right out of his own mouth, because he was pretty sure he saw said guilt on her face.

He shook his head. "Just trying to work out some things in my mind."

Lily studied him as if trying to decide if that was true, and then she released a long breath. "Same here. And FYI, I don't have any regrets. Not about the sex. I'm just worried that's what you're feeling."

Jonas didn't repeat that bit about working out some things in his mind, but he was dead certain of something. That he didn't have any regrets, either. That was part of the problem. It shouldn't have been so easy for him to push the past aside and want Lily this much.

He found his boxers, tugging them on, and he smiled when Lily groaned. "I was really enjoying that peep show. We'll have to try naked square-dancing sometime."

That deepened his smile and stirred his dick. Of course, his dick was usually interested in anything Lily said or did. Jonas went to her and sat down beside her so they were shoulder to shoulder.

"This might be the post-sex talking, but here's a suggestion," she said. "Let's not overthink this or try to figure out where this is going." She looked at him. "Let's just… keep going."

She lowered her gaze to his mouth, and in another of those sexy moves, she ran her tongue over her bottom lip.

Yes, it probably was the post-sex talking, but Jonas liked what both Lily and it were saying. *Keep going* meant more sex. More pleasure. More time with Lily in his arms. Right now, Jonas thought that was the best deal he could have.

He leaned in to kiss her, to maybe get that second round started, but the sound of the doorbell stopped him. Lily and he cursed in unison. However, neither of them moved. They sat there, their gazes still connected, the fresh lust lighting up her eyes while they hoped whoever it was at the door would just go away.

That didn't happen.

The doorbell rang again, and the sound clearly yanked Lily out of her lust trance. "It could be Eli or Hayden," she said, which yanked him back to reality as well.

Hayden probably wouldn't have rung the bell, but Eli would have, and the possibility of that was enough to get Jonas off the floor. He scooped up his clothes to get dressed while Lily ran into her closet. While he was pulling on his boots, she came back into the room as she was still shimmying into some jeans.

She'd put on a blue top that was nearly the same color as her eyes, but she hadn't pulled it all the way down. It was caught on the cup of a lacy white bra that would have snared his attention had the doorbell not rung again. This time, it was followed by an impatient-sounding knock.

Lily rushed to the bedroom door but then whirled back around to face him. "Do I look as if we've just had sex?"

Yeah, she did. Her mouth was slightly swollen from their hard kisses, and she still had that rosy flush on her cheek. Added to that, she had bedroom hair. But Jonas kept all of that to himself, hoping that it truly was Eli; the boy wouldn't notice or care what they'd been doing.

"You look fine," Jonas assured her, and that was enough to get her nodding and scurrying out of the bedroom.

Jonas was right behind her, and he felt a world of disappointment when Lily threw open the door. Not Eli or Hayden but rather Alma Parkman. He wasn't sure whose groan was louder, but Jonas thought Lily had beaten him in that particular vocal department.

"Sorry to bother you," Alma said, not sounding all that sorry.

The woman's mouth was slightly swollen, too, but Jonas soon saw the reason for that wasn't hard kisses. It was because Alma was chewing on her bottom lip with her teeth.

"You're here about the Hezzie article," Lily concluded.

Alma nodded. "Can I come in so we can talk?" Her attention finally landed on Jonas as if she had noticed him for the first time. "It's all right if you hear what I have to say. I figure you know what's going on."

Jonas wasn't sure what the woman meant by that last part, and he went with Lily's advice of not overthinking it. So what if Alma had guessed Lily and he were close enough to have had sex? So what if she spread the gossip of that near and wide? In the grand scheme of things, it just didn't seem to matter.

"Don't worry about offering me tea or such," Alma went on when Lily stepped out of the doorway and motioned for Alma to come in. "I know I'm interrupting you at a bad time…"

The woman's words trailed off, and that was when Jonas noticed that Lily still hadn't fully pulled down her top. Alma was getting an eyeful of that lacy bra, and if the woman hadn't already connected the dots about Lily and him having had sex, Alma had no doubt connected them now.

Lily huffed when she followed Alma's gaze, and she yanked down her top. "Let's talk in the kitchen. I want a Coke."

They headed that direction, and when he saw that Lily's top was hiked up in the back as well, he eased it down for her. Alma didn't give him a knowing look—or a look of any kind, for that matter—which told him she was focused on her task. A task that almost certainly involved doing some kind of damage control for her iconic ancestor.

"You saw Shayla's blog post?" Lily asked, taking out three cans of Coke from the fridge.

Lily popped the top on hers and drank as if her throat was parched. Which it possibly was. Jonas's definitely was, and he had his own long drink from his can.

"I saw it," Alma confirmed. She didn't have a drink, but that was probably because her mouth was too tight to consume anything. "It shouldn't have been written."

"Shayla said she verified the things she wrote, that it was the truth," Lily pointed out.

"Yes, but the truth doesn't always have to be announced from the highest hill, now does it?" Alma quickly countered. There was plenty of bitterness in her voice now. "Take Jonas and you, for instance. No need for some busybody like Shayla to spill all for greedy gossips to serve you two up as if you were a tasty Thanksgiving dinner. Turkey, peas, Lily and Jonas."

It was true that he didn't want Lily and him to be *served up* that way, but gossip was inevitable in a small town. He was betting Alma knew all about Bentley being Eli's biological father and Hayden staying with Nola. Heck, the woman possibly knew the reason Hayden had left the ranch.

And that led him to another thought.

"Did you leave a note on Hayden's window?" he came out and asked Alma, and he watched her carefully for any signs she might lie.

Alma frowned and just looked puzzled. "What kind of note?"

"A bad one," Lily provided when Jonas motioned for her to be the one to respond to that.

Some of Alma's anger morphed into concern. "You mean like a threat?"

"In a way," Lily said. "Did you leave the note?"

"No." Alma's shoulders went back. "I wouldn't drag a little girl into this mess. This is between the adult Parkmans." She paused and looked at Jonas. "Is this why the sheriff asked if I'd seen anybody near any of the windows of Lily's house?"

Jonas nodded. "It is, and no one, including you, admitted to seeing anyone."

"Because I didn't," Alma insisted, shifting back to Lily. "Does that note have something to do with the reason Hayden went to your sister's house?"

Bingo. He'd been right about word of that already getting out.

"It does," Lily verified.

That caused Alma to shake her head and groan. "I'm sorry. That girl isn't to blame for anything this blabbering Shayla did." She paused again, her attention fastened on Lily. "People are upset, and anger makes some do stupid mistakes. If you want, I can ask around and find out who left the note."

"The sheriff is handling it," Lily said, probably because

she didn't want Alma playing amateur sleuth. "But if you hear anything about the note, I'd appreciate you telling him."

Alma gave a quick nod and then gathered her breath. "I will. In the meantime, I have a favor to ask you. It's a biggie, so hear me out before you start thinking of why you can't do what I'm asking. When you write your report on Hezzie, I want you to leave out anything that woman put in her so-called article."

Since Lily didn't show an ounce of surprise, she'd no doubt known this request was coming. Lily didn't voice a reminder that the truth was out there, and there was no way to suppress it.

"People will forget soon enough what they've read on the internet," Alma went on, "and pretty soon, they'll start to question if it's even true. They might start to wonder why that woman wanted such stuff to be told in the first place."

"You think Shayla wrote the article to get back at someone?" Lily asked when Alma didn't elaborate.

Alma lifted her shoulder but there was nothing dismissive about the gesture. "Maybe not get back at anyone specific but the whole lot of us Parkmans. Some people just want to see poop tossed on good people, and I don't believe that poop should be in a report that is in the Last Ride Society Library."

Lily's sigh was long. "But if I leave out what Shayla wrote, then the report about Hezzie won't be the truth."

"The truth is often overrated," Alma declared like gospel.

Jonas wasn't so sure of that at all, and judging from the way Lily's forehead bunched up, neither was she.

"Just give it some thought," Alma went on. "Consider

the people who'll be reading your report long after we're all gone. Consider the damage that could be done not just to Hezzie's legacy but to the town of Last Ride. We could become a laughingstock and not the 'family friendly' place where people want to live and visit."

Lily had opened her mouth, but then she closed it when Alma added that last part. A couple of moments crawled by before she sighed again.

"I'll think about it," Lily finally agreed.

Alma patted her hand on the kitchen island as if it were pseudo applause. "Thank you," the woman murmured.

Jonas caught a glimpse of Alma's expression before she headed for the door. The president of the Last Ride Society was looking plenty victorious. Not Lily, though. She looked as if this was one more straw added to her back, and when she propped her elbows on the kitchen island and buried her face in her hands, Jonas did some sighing of his own and went to her.

"You've got over two months to decide what to put or not put in that report," he reminded her, gathering her into his arms. "My advice is to put it aside for now."

She made a weak sound of agreement, followed by a groan, and she buried her face against his shoulder. Jonas figured he'd stand there holding her for as long as she needed, but he'd barely gotten started with the TLC when his phone rang. Jonas couldn't ignore it, what with the situation of their kids and possible ranch business to handle, but he hoped it was something that would allow him to get back to holding Lily.

He cursed, though, when he saw the name on the screen. "It's Bentley," he relayed to her. He hit Answer and put it on speaker.

"Still trying to convince the sheriff that I left a note

for your boss's kid?" Bentley asked, obviously going with a taunt.

Huffing, Lily moved away from him and headed out of the kitchen. Maybe because she'd had enough crap today and didn't want to deal with Bentley. Jonas couldn't blame her, but it stung some that she hadn't wanted to hang in there for him.

"The sheriff is still interviewing people and showing them your photo to see if anyone noticed you around Lily's house this morning," Jonas answered, not going for a taunt but a little badass. "If you left the note, you'll be arrested."

Bentley dismissed that with a snort that reminded Jonas of a jackass. Then again, plenty about Bentley reminded him of that particular animal, though it probably was an insult to jackasses in general.

"I won't be arrested because I've done nothing wrong," Bentley insisted. "And before you go on and on with your idle threats, I wanted you to know I'll be over soon to pick up Eli. He called me and asked if we could go to dinner tonight."

Oh, that hurt, a full "punch in the gut" kind of hurt, and Jonas had to take a second to stomp down the way-too-many emotions that were threatening to bubble up inside. Emotions he didn't want Bentley to hear because he might use Jonas's reaction in some way to win some bonus points with Eli.

"Just make sure you don't keep Eli out too late because he might have homework," Jonas managed to say.

"Oh, I thought he'd already told you. No homework, and he's looking for a little distraction since Hayden broke up with him."

Hell. That didn't sound good, and Jonas was having to do more of that emotional stomping down when Lily came back in the kitchen. She dropped some papers and a pen on the counter. Jonas immediately recognized what it was. A contract for the bill of sale for that 1 percent of the Wild Springs Ranch. The 1 percent that would make them equal partners.

Jonas understood her exit then. Bentley had said "your boss's kid" in that jackass way of his, and it had prompted her to do something about ridding herself of the boss label. He was tempted to sign the damn papers just so Bentley wouldn't be able to use that particular insult again, but no way would he make a decision like this out of anger.

He eased the papers back across the island toward her and got the expected reaction. An eye roll and a huff. She slid the papers back, and again, he pushed them toward her. By the fourth time, they were smiling. So, not quite as effective as square-dancing, but Lily had managed to lighten his mood some.

It didn't last.

The smiling bubble burst when Bentley's voice continued to pour through the phone.

"One more thing," Bentley said with enough smugness for a dozen assholes. "I just talked to my lawyer, and I think it's time."

"Time for what?" Jonas snarled.

"Time for me to be a real parent to my son," Bentley happily provided. "I've rented a house in Last Ride so Eli won't have to transfer to a new school, and I'll commute into work. Oh, I'll be filing for custody of Eli first thing in the morning."

CHAPTER TWENTY-TWO

LILY FIGURED SHE was violating a whole bunch of rules by leaving a man's bed to go to his brother's grave, but that was what she was doing.

Well, sort of.

It'd been nearly twenty-four hours since she'd been with Jonas, and that encounter hadn't happened in his bedroom but rather hers. But they had, indeed, had sex.

Amazing sex.

So amazing that Lily had to wonder if Jonas was capable of anything less than giving her first-class orgasms. Hopefully not. She didn't want less. But she also didn't want to keep feeling as if a giant ball of guilt had settled into her stomach and just wouldn't let go. Guilt for what she'd done to Hayden. That was at the very top of her worry ladder. However, there was also the guilt of what she might end up doing to Jonas if things didn't work out between them.

Jonas had his own worries, too, what with Bentley threatening to file for custody of Eli. Lily had no idea if the man would actually follow through on that, but Jonas had an ace in the hole if Bentley went that route. Eli loved living at the ranch, and she just couldn't see him ditching that to live with a man he hardly knew. Even if that man was his bio father.

Still, the possibility of losing his son had to be gnawing away at Jonas, and that was why she'd given both of them some space. Aka thinking time. She'd used some of her time to make plans to come and have a heart-to-heart chat with Griff.

Of course, this particular heart-to-heart would be very one-sided, and Lily wasn't sure what she was hoping to get out of it. Heck, she didn't even know what to say. But for reasons she might never understand, the last visit to his grave had made her feel a little better. She was hoping for that. Hoping, too, that if she spoke the right words and if those words sank into her head, her heart wouldn't be aching for her daughter and breaking for a man she didn't want to hurt.

Lily trudged up the hill toward Griff's grave, thankful again that it was in a cluster of shade trees. She needed this chat, but she didn't want to risk heatstroke while trying to make her life right.

While she walked, she glanced around, looking for any signs of another vehicle parked nearby. There wasn't one, which meant someone like Derwin wasn't going to jump out from behind the tree and scare the daylights out of her. It'd be just Griff and her, and she could tell him something she'd never gotten to tell him.

Goodbye.

"Well, here I am again," Lily said, stopping in front of the tombstone. "The love of your too-short life."

She paused and started to question whether or not that was true, but she knew that it was. Griff and she had had some serious ups and downs, but she had no doubts whatsoever that their love had been the real deal.

"I wanted to let you know that I told Hayden you were her dad," Lily went on. A gust of wind sent the overhead leaves and branches rattling, and it sounded a little like mocking applause. "She's pissed off as she has a right to be since I should have told her years ago."

Lily had to pause again. More than a pause. A full-fledged stop because her throat had clogged up, and a new round of tears pooled in her eyes.

"Hayden hates me, Griff," she finally managed to say. "I might have lost her for good, and I have no idea how to fix it."

She couldn't add any more about that. It just made the cuts in her heart too deep to think that it could be true. Instead, Lily cleared her throat, blinked back the tears and shifted the subject to something else she'd wanted to confess to Griff.

"I had sex with Jonas," Lily laid out there. "I'll spare you the details, but it was great, and I'm hoping it'll happen again." She swallowed hard. This soul-baring stuff was hard on the throat because it kept tightening. "I'm falling in love with him. With Jonas," she clarified, and then she put the whole sentence together. "I'm falling in love with Jonas."

She'd said it, and it was the truth. Falling for him didn't fix squat. In fact, it could make things a whole lot worse, but it didn't make sense to lie while standing in front of a grave having a heart-to-heart with her dead ex.

"I'm scared," Lily continued. "Scared of loving again. And I'm especially scared because what I felt for you was a drop in the bucket compared to what I feel for him."

There it was. The words that spiked fear and worry straight through her. She'd loved Griff, and her heart had been crushed when he had died, but losing Jonas could tear that same heart into tiny little pieces.

And she could lose him.

Even though they'd worked together for years, nothing

was a given in their relationship. If he lost custody of Eli, he might leave the ranch. Might leave her. Then she'd have the double crushing of having lost both her daughter and the man she loved.

Yes, loved.

Apparently, the *falling* was over and done, and she'd dived heart-first into being in love with him. The revelation caused Lily to curse, and then she gasped when the sound jolted through her. Not some cosmic reaction from Griff but rather the ringing of her phone. She yanked it from her pocket and saw Cam's name on the screen. She nearly hit Decline but then remembered this call could be about Hayden.

"Did Hayden get in touch with you?" Lily immediately asked him.

Cam wasn't so immediate in his response. Maybe because her desperate, frantic tone had alarmed him to temporary silence. "No, I'm calling because you sent me a text, remember?"

With everything else going on, Lily actually had forgotten about texting Cam to let him know that Hayden might be contacting him. "Hayden found out that Griff is her father."

Cam made an *ah* sound. "Judging from your tone, I'm guessing that didn't go well."

That was the understatement of all understatements. "She's staying with Nola and won't talk to me."

"Sorry to hear that." And his sympathy sounded genuine. "Put the blame on me. Tell her I'm the reason you kept it secret."

"*I'm* the reason I kept it secret." Lily wanted to make sure that was crystal clear because it was something she knew all the way to the marrow. "I didn't want to deal with the hard questions of telling her about a father who died the way Griff did. I didn't want to deal with my own feelings about the way he died."

"But you've dealt with them now?" Cam asked after a long pause.

She paused, too. Assessed and didn't go with the *more or less* response that first jumped to mind. "Yes, I've dealt with the feelings." The grief, the anger, the abandonment. "I'm finally ready to move on. About time, huh? I mean, it's only been fifteen years."

Cam's silence dragged on so long that Lily thought maybe he'd disconnected. "I'm glad," he said. "You'd never be able to find love again unless you let go."

"You would know," she admitted. "I didn't give you much of myself when we were married because I was still giving it all to Griff and then Hayden."

Cam could have chimed in with a quick agreement, but he didn't. "I'm glad you've come to terms with it," he repeated. "And I hope Hayden and you find the same kind of happiness I've found. I am happy, Lily," he emphasized. "It took me fifteen years to let go, too. Of Griff. Of you. But when I finally did, I found a love that had been under my nose practically the whole time. I wish the same for you."

That healed a piece or two of her heart, and she realized she'd needed this from Cam. A peaceful, final goodbye. It was ironic that she'd gotten it while at Griff's grave, where she'd just given him a peaceful, final goodbye.

"Thank you," she murmured. "Have a good life, Cam," Lily added.

She ended the call, and while clutching the phone to her chest, she stared at Griff's tombstone and let the tears come. Only a few had managed to slide down her cheeks, though, when she heard another sound. Not her phone but some movement from behind one of the trees.

Cursing, Lily whirled around. "Derwin Parkman, I'm going to—"

Her tirade stalled, though, when Hayden stepped out. They stood there, both seemingly frozen, staring at each other. Lily wanted to take hold of her and give her the hardest, longest "mama bear" hug she could manage, but Hayden was sending off a "stay back" vibe with her hands crammed into the pockets of her jeans and the wary look in her eyes.

Lily mentally spun back through the conversations she'd had with both Griff and Cam, and she cringed. "How much did you hear?" she asked Hayden.

"All of it," Hayden admitted.

Great. All of it meant she'd heard the part about Lily having had sex with Jonas. Apparently, her daughter was aware of her love life after all.

"I've been here awhile," Hayden added. "I asked Aunt Nola to drop me off and come back and get me in an hour." She lifted a small canister of pepper spray. "She was worried about me being here alone and insisted I bring this. I suspect she's parked somewhere and watching us through the binoculars I saw her put in her car before we started the drive here."

Lily glanced around, and even though she hadn't spotted it earlier, she finally did see her sister's car. Not on the main road or the cemetery parking lot but rather an old ranch trail lined with trees. Good. She was glad Nola was keeping an eye on Hayden, and while Last Ride was a safe place, it still wasn't a good idea for a teenage girl to be alone in a cemetery.

"I read the research report Aunt Nola did on him,"

Hayden said, tipping her head to Griff's tombstone. "On *Dad*," she amended. "I thought it would be like reading about Uncle Wyatt when he was young, but it wasn't."

"No," Lily softly agreed. "Griff and Wyatt were identical twins like Nola and me, but they were as different as, well, Nola and me."

Hayden's whispered "Yes" was barely audible.

"Griff...your dad was more of a bad boy," Lily went on. "Things between us were often wild and intense. A heady adrenaline high for a teenager." And she hoped Hayden didn't go searching out highs like that.

"You regret being with him?" Hayden asked, not with snark. No, not a trace of that. It was a genuine question that seemed to be weighing on her heart.

Lily was quick with her reassurance. "The only thing I'd change about being with him was the way he died. I certainly don't regret having you. Just the opposite." She hesitated to add the rest, but what the heck. Lily went for broke. "You were then and are now the best thing that's happened to me. I love you, and I always will. I'm just so deeply sorry that I didn't tell you sooner that Griff was your father."

She thought maybe that would earn her a huff or an eye roll from Hayden. It didn't. Hayden kept her attention fixed on Griff's tombstone. "Do you think he would have loved me had he gotten the chance?"

Lily didn't need to give that any thought. She went with her favorite way to answer. "Absolutely."

Hayden's head finally lifted. "You're not just saying that because you think it's something I want to hear?"

Again, this was an easy answer. "No. Griff was capable of so much love, and it's why I loved him. He just didn't want to be a burden to anyone because of his illness."

Hayden stayed quiet a moment and then nodded, causing some of the tightness to ease up in Lily's chest. She wanted her daughter to feel wanted and cherished. Because she was, and Griff would have gotten in on that if he could have.

"I hate he died," Hayden said, the emotion clogging her voice. "I hate I never got the chance to know him."

Oh, that gave Lily another heart stomping, and she was about to go to her and try to hug her, but Hayden continued.

"It helps seeing Uncle Wyatt," Hayden added. "I mean, I know they weren't a lot alike, but I can look at Uncle Wyatt's face and see that's how my dad would look. It helps," she repeated.

Lily had never considered that, but she understood how it could comfort her daughter. Sort of a living reminder that most people in Hayden's situation never had.

The moments crawled by, and Hayden moved closer to the tombstone. However, she lifted her gaze to meet Lily's. "I heard what you said about falling in love with Jonas."

Now Lily did groan because, yep, it was a reminder that Hayden also knew she'd had sex with Jonas. "I'm in love with him," Lily admitted. No sense backpedaling now, and besides, the truth was the truth. No more lies.

"Is it weird since you loved his brother first?" Hayden asked.

"A little weird," she admitted. "Jonas was always around when Griff and I were dating. The big brother. Really more of a parent to Griff and Wyatt since they didn't have a good home life. I didn't really look at Jonas because I was so fixed on Griff."

"But you're looking at him now," Hayden commented.

"I am." More truth time. "I'm scared because it could mess things up if it doesn't work out between us. Added

. to that, both Jonas and I have a lot of other things going on right now."

"Things," Hayden repeated. "The Last Ride Society stuff. And he's worrying about Eli, and you're worrying about me."

Lily had never made a sound of agreement so fast. "I'm terrified that I've lost you."

Hayden certainly didn't give her a fast denial. Or any other response, for that matter. Her daughter moved even closer to Griff's tombstone and touched her fingers to the gold ring.

"So, did you leave this here?" Hayden asked.

"No, it wasn't me." And Lily tried not to be disappointed that Hayden hadn't given her some kind of hope that their relationship could be repaired. "Your dad had other girlfriends. Not when he was with me, but when we were on-again, off-again. One of them maybe left it as a symbol of love."

"But it's a symbol of marriage," Hayden pointed out. "Maybe Dad proposed to one of them and then broke things off when he got back with you."

"Maybe." It was as good of an explanation as any, though Lily thought if Griff had gotten serious enough with someone else to propose marriage, then she would have heard about it.

Lily was still mulling that over when Hayden moved away from the tombstone and headed straight toward her. Before Lily could even catch her breath, or think, Hayden had pulled her into a hug. A warm, hard "daughter bear" embrace.

It was the most amazing thing Lily had ever felt.

Fighting tears, fighting for breath and trying not to jump for joy, Lily wrapped her arms around her daughter and hugged her right back. She wasn't sure how long they stood there. Time didn't matter, but Lily figured if Nola was watching all of this, then her twin was doing some jumping for joy for both of them.

And the joy just kept rolling in.

"I want to come back home," Hayden muttered.

"Oh, I want you back home," Lily assured her as fast as she could. She pulled back only so she could look Hayden in the eyes. "I'm so sorry for not telling you the truth about your dad."

"I know." A moment later and with her face and voice coated with emotion, she repeated it. "After I read the research report on Dad, I figured out why you'd lied. You thought you were protecting me."

"Yes." Lily had to speak through her own emotion-coated throat. "But now I know you're strong enough to handle the truth."

"I am," Hayden assured her.

The hug continued several more moments. Precious moments that Lily would treasure forever. Then Hayden eased back again to meet her eyes.

"I guess you know I broke up with Eli," she volunteered.

Lily nodded, kissed Hayden's cheek. "Are you okay?"

Hayden nodded as well but tamped it down with a shrug. "We're still friends. I guess we are. I mean, we still text and talk, and I don't think he's too mad at me."

Lily knew this was shaky ground, and she didn't want to pry too much. However, she also wanted Hayden to know she was very interested in any and all aspects of her life. "Do you think you'll get back together with him?"

"No." Hayden's forehead bunched up. "I had a good time kissing him, but the kisses messed up things. Before the kissing, we used to talk about all kinds of stuff. He'd ask me about girls at school that he liked. He'd help me with algebra homework. I'd help him with biology because he sucked at it. All of that stopped, and it felt like I couldn't talk to him about anything but the kissing."

Out of the mouths of babes, and it highlighted one of Lily's big fears when it came to Jonas. Falling in love with her best friend could mean losing that friendship that was more valuable to her than anything other than Hayden.

"Anyway, I know Eli's still dealing with the breakup," Hayden went on, "and that might be why he's going to move in with his real dad."

Lily had already opened her mouth to issue some kind of reassurance that Eli would be okay, but that stopped her. "What?"

Hayden blinked. "You didn't know he was moving in with Mr. Bentley?"

"No." And she quickly tacked on a question to that. "Does Jonas know?"

Another shrug from Hayden, and the girl checked the time on her phone. "Maybe. When Aunt Nola dropped me off here, Eli texted to say he was going to have the talk with his stepdad, so Mr. Jonas should be getting the news right about now."

CHAPTER TWENTY-THREE

JONAS SAW ELI step into the doorway of his office, and one look at the boy's face and he knew there was trouble. Hell. If Bentley had called Eli to pester him about this custody crap, then Jonas was going to have a word with the asshole.

"What's wrong?" Jonas asked.

Eli's shoulders stayed slumped as he came into the office and shut the door behind him. Definitely not a good sign because, to the best of his memory, Jonas never recalled Eli wanting a private conversation.

"Everything's wrong," Eli muttered. Along with the low shoulders, Eli was looking at anything but him. The boy seemed particularly enthralled by Jonas's plain black mouse pad.

Everything. Well, crap. That meant Bentley, Hayden and anything else that might be going on at school. Jonas didn't push the boy to start filling him in. He just waited him out and hoped he could handle whatever it was Eli was about to tell him.

"I quit football," Eli finally said. "There's too much going on in my head to make it work."

Jonas bit back a groan, barely. Eli loved football, and quitting let Jonas know just how bad and how hard everything else was hitting him.

"I'm sorry," Jonas told him. He didn't bother adding that Eli could always play next year. He remembered what it was like to be fourteen, and *next year* might as well be a century from now.

Eli didn't acknowledge what Jonas said. "Hayden told me she didn't see us getting back together, that she misses me as a friend."

Ouch. That had to have been a hard sting. But then he looked at Eli's face, what he could see of it, anyway, with his chin dipped down like that, and Jonas had to wonder if Hayden was the main cause of all that pain. Or if this was more about Bentley. Since Jonas was pretty sure that was at the core, he just went with it.

"You've talked to Mr. Bentley?" Jonas asked. He still couldn't refer to the man as Eli's father.

Eli nodded. "He rented a house right next to the school. He's going to stay here in Last Ride and then drive into San Antonio three times a week for his job."

So, Bentley had moved fast. Too fast. Jonas wished like hell he had a pause button to put on this until he at least had a clean report back from the PI. His deepest worry, though, was there wouldn't be a clean report, that there would be something in Bentley's past or present that could end up hurting Eli. Jonas would endure any hurt imaginable if he could protect his son.

"Dad wants me to move in with him," Eli went on. "So we can spend more time together."

And so that Bentley could get Eli away from Jonas. Well, maybe that was his motive. But Jonas forced himself to push aside all the bile he felt for the man and tried to see this for what it might be. Giving Bentley the benefit of the doubt, maybe he did just want to be with his son. Jonas certainly did, so he couldn't totally fault the man for wanting the same thing.

"I'm going to do it," Eli added a couple of heartbeats

later. "I'm going to stay with him for a while to see how it works out."

All the air vanished. None was in his lungs or the room. Maybe not a drop of it anywhere on the planet.

"Say something," Eli insisted.

Jonas was trying. Man, was he, but he needed air to speak, and that took a huge effort along with a couple of seconds. "I want you to be happy." And the rest of what he had to say was going to cost him big-time. "I'd rather that happiness be here with me at the ranch, but I understand if you want to be with your father."

Eli smiled and rushed toward him to give him a hug. "Thanks. I wasn't sure you'd understand."

Oh, he understood all right, but that didn't make it hurt any less.

Eli quit smiling when he pulled back and finally met Jonas's gaze. "Dad said he's going to file for custody of me, that he was working out the best way to go about that with you."

Because his throat snapped shut, Jonas went with a nod. Bentley and he weren't exactly working out anything, but it wouldn't do Eli any good if Jonas bad-mouthed the man who'd fathered him. Besides, in the end, even with this hurt washing over him, Jonas would do what was best for the son he'd raised and loved.

"I'd better go," Eli said, glancing at the time. "I've already packed, and Dad's coming to get me. You want to say hello to him or something, or would it be okay if we just left?"

"It's okay," he managed to say.

Jonas hugged him again, knowing that while it wouldn't be okay, there wasn't a damn thing he could do about it. Bentley was holding all the right cards here, and he would

almost certainly go through with filing for custody. Jonas
would become the stepdad who got visitations. If he was
lucky. It was possible that Eli would create a new life with
his dad and leave him and the ranch behind.

Jonas held on to Eli a few more moments, and he tried to
put on the bravest face he could manage when Eli gushed
out a giddy-sounding goodbye and hurried out the door.
He listened to the sound of Eli's echoing footsteps until
his son was gone.

He wasn't sure how long he stood there, but Jonas finally forced himself to move. He'd go home and… No,
he'd go to Lily because she was the one person who would
understand just how bad this hurt.

The moment Jonas stepped out of the barn, he spotted
Lily, but she wasn't alone. Hayden was with her, and the
girl was carrying a cardboard box. Lily hurried ahead of
her daughter and took hold of his arm.

"We saw Eli leave," Lily blurted out. "Are you all right?"

"No," he murmured. No way could he put on a face
for her, but he'd try for Hayden since the girl was looking darn happy.

"I'm back with Mom," Hayden announced, "and she
gave me this box of my dad's old stuff. I thought maybe
you'd like to look at it, too."

Jonas wasn't sure he could take the emotional punch
of dealing with Griff's memories, but no way did he want
Lily to have to face this alone. At least Hayden was home,
and that would maybe cushion anything that would be in
the box.

"Why don't you come to the house with us, and we can
go through the things?" Lily suggested, keeping her eyes
on him and studying every inch of his face. "Someone's

picking up Hayden for her study group in about a half hour, so we probably won't have time to go through all of it."

Lily had no doubt added that last part to let him know that this particular torture wouldn't last long, and then he'd be able to tell her, well, everything. Not that he would need to spell it out, but he knew Lily would listen to every word.

She linked her fingers with his as they made their way to the house, and Jonas shouldn't have been surprised that such a little gesture could pack such a wallop in the comforting department. Then again, this was Lily, and she could soothe him when nothing else worked.

"There's a watch in here," Hayden said, peering into the box. "It looks really old."

"It is," Jonas verified. "It belonged to our dad, and it was the one thing Griff wanted after our folks died."

"What'd you want?" Hayden asked, glancing at him from over her shoulder.

"My mom's St. Christopher pendant." He'd given it to Maddie, and because she'd worn it every day of their life together, Jonas had had it buried with her.

"Your mom and dad would have been my grandparents, right?" Hayden went on.

"Yeah, and I have some old photo albums of them, if you'd like to go through them."

"I would," she said, and with her enthusiasm practically radiating off her, Jonas figured she didn't have a problem with being Griff's daughter.

It wouldn't always be this rosy for her, though. Eventually, Hayden would have to deal with the full impact of Griff's death, but for now, he was glad his brother's daughter was okay with her particular gene pool.

They went into the kitchen, with Lily getting Cokes for all of them while Hayden set the box on the island. She pulled out the watch first and put it on, and Jonas got a flash of a memory of Griff wearing it. And smiling. Not a bad image to have of his little brother.

Hayden began to take out pictures, none of which was a surprise to Jonas because he'd taken some of them. Shots of Griff, Wyatt and Dax at various ages. Other photos of Griff and Lily hamming it up for the camera.

"Fun times," Jonas said, touching one of the solo shots of Griff.

"You loved him a lot," Hayden said.

Jonas looked up and saw she, too, was studying him, so he nodded. "Like a brother and a son." Even after all this time, the grief was still there. The hurt over losing Griff, and now he was losing Eli.

Outside the house, someone honked a horn at the same moment Hayden's phone dinged with a text. "Amber's mom is early," she said, glancing at the message. "Gotta go." She brushed a quick kiss on Lily's cheek, waved goodbye to Jonas and grabbed her backpack as she hurried off.

"Sorry about that," Lily said, tipping her head to the box. "I didn't figure you'd be in the mood for it."

"No," he agreed, "but it's good to see Hayden so happy."

She made her own sound of agreement and looked up at him. "It's not good to see you so miserable. I'm betting you didn't try to talk Eli into staying."

"I didn't." He groaned and scrubbed his hand over his face. "He was so damn happy, Lily."

Sighing, Lily went to him and pulled him into her arms. "I'm sorry."

He knew it wasn't lip service, and he welcomed both the words and the hug. But this wasn't fair to Lily. "I'm dumping gloom and doom all over your daughter's homecoming. How'd it come about, anyway?"

"Hayden overheard me talking at Griff's grave. I was crying and pouring out my heart." She stopped and went a little stiff. Maybe because she didn't want to spill the things she'd said to Griff.

Fair enough. It was possible Jonas wouldn't want to hear them. In fact, right now he wasn't sure he could take Lily jumping on the "blast from the past" train and going over how much she'd loved Griff.

She looked up at him and touched his cheek, his hair. "I'm guessing you're not up for a spirited round of square-dancing."

He cursed himself for not being able to conjure up even a small smile, and that was obviously an answer she got right away.

"Okay. I don't blame you, but maybe some naked photos will help," she added.

No, they wouldn't, but Jonas hated that she'd gotten his attention and shifted his mind to sex. "Naked photos of you?" Then he got a bad thought, that maybe there were pictures of her that Griff had taken.

"Nope. These are pictures that Hezzie apparently took of naked men. One of my Parkman cousins that I don't even know emailed them to me. One of the models has a little ball tied around his willy."

He stared at her to see if she was making that up. She wasn't.

"And another guy was lying bare-butted on a fuzzy rug while he sucked a baby bottle," she added.

Now, she was making that up. He saw the glint in her eyes that proved it.

"Seriously, the photos might make you smile," she went on. "Well, smile in a cringing sort of way because you'll be amazed that someone with such a tiny willy would be able to tie a dangling ball from it. And you'll ask yourself, as I did, why? Was it erotic for Victorian women to ogle such things, especially when the guy had two natural balls bulging behind the fake one?"

He just stared at her, vowing not to laugh because he figured in the long run that would just make him feel like shit.

"I could try tying a ball to your willy to see what all the fuss is about," she suggested. "Unlike the guy in the picture, you'd have plenty of inches for me to work with."

Hell, he smiled, and while it lifted him up a little, he still wasn't in a fit mood to be around anyone. He should just go home and let the worry and pain take over.

Jonas brushed a kiss on the top of her head. "I'll see you later." He didn't make it one step to the door, though, before she took his hand again.

"Stay, please. *Please*," she repeated, giving his hand a squeeze. "Come on. I want to show you something. No, not a willy ball," Lily joked. "But it's possibly something that'll make you say bad words."

Jonas was already mentally saying enough bad words, and he didn't want to add more. Still, he didn't dig in his heels when Lily started leading him out of the kitchen and toward her bedroom.

The very bedroom where they'd had sex.

He wanted to believe this ache in his head would temporarily rid him of the lust he had for Lily. It didn't. The lust was still there, simmering and flickering enough to make him hope that she was about to kiss him and pull him to the floor for round two.

However, Lily didn't go into her bedroom. She stopped in the hall outside her office and motioned inside to the huge stack of papers on her desk. Jonas hadn't considered work as a fix for his mood, but maybe Lily had.

"What is that?" he asked. He knew every aspect of the ranch's business, and there weren't any invoices, contracts, prospective purchases that would generate that much paper.

"It's sixty copies for the sale of the one percent of the ranch that you've been refusing to buy." Her tone made it seem as if there was nothing out of the ordinary about that tall stack. "I was going to tape them all over the barn. Sort of like wallpaper so you'd have reminders of what you'd have if you just signed one of the copies."

Jonas sighed. "You're doing this to try to cheer me up."

"No, I'm doing this because it's the right thing for us to be co-owners of the ranch we've been running together for years." She turned, faced him. "I'd figured to use sex to cheer you up."

And there it was again. That slam of lust. Lust with the really bad timing since he still intended to go back to his place and wallow in his misery.

Lily clearly had different plans.

She picked up the longhorn stress ball from her desk and gave it a few testing squeezes while eyeing his crotch. She had a glimmer in her eyes. A heat that told him he wasn't getting out of this room with his jeans on.

"You're not tying that to my dick," he warned her, though he was pretty sure if she got him hot enough—and Lily was capable of *hot enough*—that he'd be up for anything. Literally.

"No," she assured him, "but it'd be good for other things."

She gave the ball a harder squeeze and walked toward him. Correction—she sauntered. When she reached him, she hooked her hand around his neck and eyed his mouth as if she were about to kiss him into a puddle of lust.

"I think ball tying is overrated," she said, and her voice

was all silk and sex. "So yesterday when it comes to titil-lation and foreplay."

She slipped her hand between them, rubbing that damn ball over the front of his jeans. His dick stirred, of course. It was brainless and not connected to his shitty mood, and the brainless wonder gave him a reminder of how much better Lily's hand would feel on him if his jeans and boxers were off.

Oh, yeah. This had the potential to escalate big-time.

"Bottle sucking, too, is passé," she went on in that siren's voice. The kind of siren that could make a man so crazy he'd crash ships into rocks and such.

She kept sliding that ball over him. Every inch. Long, slow strokes.

"Now, there is another picture of a woman doing this to a guy." Pressing her breasts against his chest, she slid lower and lower until her mouth was on the spot where the ball had just been.

Hell. Jonas could feel her hot breath on him, and his eyes rolled back in his head when she flicked her tongue over the denim.

"There's a picture of a woman giving a BJ?" he man-aged to ask.

"She's doing something with her mouth in that general vicinity." Lily dropped the stress ball on the floor so she could use her hands to undo his belt. "But it's hard to tell what's going on because the ball is still tied to his willy, and it blocks out the money shot."

Jonas wasn't getting fired up by the thought of such an image. No. He was getting fired up at the thought of Lily—

Hell. She got him unzipped and went after the front of his boxers with her mouth. Then her tongue.

Jonas cursed the thin layer of fabric between him and her

mouth. He cursed what she was doing because he wanted to be inside her. He wanted that more than a BJ, more than a hand job from a ball. More than his next breath.

Still cursing any and everything, he went down to his knees with her. In the same motion, he took hold of Lily and kissed her as if there were no grief, no tomorrow. She could do that to him. Give him these scalding moments of pleasure while clearing his mind.

And he'd take it.

He'd take her.

The kiss was hard and rough. Too rough. But Lily didn't seem to mind. In fact, she added some roughness of her own when she started the war to get off his clothes. In this particular war, the top priority seemed to be getting naked, because she battled with his shirt before getting his jeans down his hips.

Now, now, now.

That was the mantra that started to pound in his head as they kissed, bit, touched and stripped. The second they had off most of their clothes, she put him on his back and straddled him. She still had that "sexy siren" deal going on and would have taken him right inside her if the last shred of Jonas's common sense hadn't kicked in.

"Condom," he reminded her. "Wallet."

That sent them both on more frantic moving around to locate his wallet and get out the condom. Each moment that took, the lust just kept getting hotter and hotter, the need stronger and stronger.

Lily did something about that lust and need once he had on the condom, because she straddled him again and dropped down so that he pushed inside her.

For just a moment, everything went still. Even the raging need seemed to hit the pause button so it gave him a chance just to savor this. To savor her. Lily, *his Lily*, loomed above him, her blond hair tumbling around her face. Her eyes fixed on him as if he were capable of giving her a thousand orgasms at once. At the moment, Jonas felt as if he could do that, too, but for now, he'd settle for just one.

And one was what Lily gave him.

She rode him hard until he watched and felt her shatter. Until her climax took him right along with her.

CHAPTER TWENTY-FOUR

LILY LOOKED AT the paperwork that had just come through on the sale of six of the Andalusian mares. It was a good offer, which would net Jonas and her a huge return on their investment, since the mares had been born and raised here on the Wild Springs. It should have been a no-brainer for her to jot down her approval and then forward it to Jonas, but she kept looking at it while her attention drifted to the stress ball.

A stress ball that reminded her of Jonas.

Not of Jonas, her business partner and astute rancher. But of Jonas, the hot cowboy who was her lover. Well, sort of.

They'd had sex twice, once on her bedroom floor and another on the floor of her office, but that last encounter had been three days ago. Not an especially long time to go without sex, especially since her dry spell before Jonas had lasted for years. Still, Jonas was apparently like a very addictive drug. She couldn't stop thinking about him, couldn't stop wanting more of him.

But the want was the least of her problems.

At Griff's grave, she'd confessed she was in love with Jonas, and mercy, was that the truth. She knew it now with absolute certainty. She'd gone and fallen in love with him, and it wasn't going to please him. Not when he was worried sick about Eli. Not when it was possible he could actually lose custody of him.

Still squeezing the ball, Lily shifted back to the offer and considered printing it out and taking it to Jonas in person. It was an obvious ploy for her to see him. It wouldn't be for sex, though. She wanted to check on him, to see how he was. Heck, she just wanted to be with him, even if this broke with their usual work routine.

She was gearing up to hit the print function when the doorbell rang. Her heart did a little flip-flop, and she ran with the energy and enthusiasm of a teenager when she hurried to the door. She'd been so certain it was Jonas, but that was obviously wishful thinking on her part, because it wasn't.

It was Cam.

Lily watched his expression morph from a friendly greeting to some concern. She figured her own expression was morphing as well from huge expectations to, well, concern.

His gaze slid to the stress ball she was holding. "Did I catch you at a bad time?"

Now she felt herself blush because there were plenty of sexual memories tied in that little ball. "Uh, no." And she added a question of her own. "What's wrong?"

Because there had to be something on the *wrong* agenda for Cam to be here. This was not only his first visit to the ranch, but Lily also hadn't laid eyes on him in thirteen years.

Some of his friendly expression returned. "I was hoping we could talk. Is Hayden home?"

Lily shook her head. "She's at school. Why did you want to see her?"

"Well, I didn't actually come here for her. I just wanted

to make sure she wasn't around to overhear us. I'm guessing she's still pretty upset at learning I'm not her father?"

It seemed rude to say that Hayden was okay with it. More than okay. The girl was embracing the fact that she was a Buchanan and had spent a good chunk of the past three days talking to Dax, Jonas and Wyatt about Griff. First, though, Hayden had gone through everything in the box of Griff's things that Lily had given her. No nude pictures in there, thank goodness.

"Hayden's dealing," Lily settled for saying, and even though it was beyond awkward to have her ex here, she stepped back so Cam could come in.

"Good," Cam said almost absently. He studied the entry and living room when she led him there.

"Would you like something to drink?" she asked, remembering her manners. Hard to remember the little things, though, when she just wanted to cut to the chase and find out why he was there.

Cam obviously wasn't in a "cut to the chase" frame of mind, because he took the time to look at the pictures on the mantel, then at the rust-colored Turkish rug, then at the huge glass vases on the coffee table.

"Nola's work," she provided, sitting in one of the chairs.

"I thought so. Elsa is a huge fan and has a couple of pieces."

Elsa, his wife. She was about to gear up to dole out a congrats, but Cam finally quit browsing and sank down on the sofa across from her.

"I've never been happier," he said. "I'm talking 'over the moon' kind of happy."

"All right," she muttered. Had he really come here to gloat? If so, Lily felt a streak of snark coming on.

"Because I'm so happy," he went on, "I wanted to make

some amends in my life. Sort of a couple of steps in a twelve-step program." For some stupid reason, he chuckled, though Lily couldn't see a drop of humor in it. "I want to right some old wrongs."

Ah, she got it then. He was here to apologize. Rather than just say she had forgiven him for walking out on her, she just sat quietly and waited for him to continue.

"I should have never asked you to marry me," he went on. "Of course, you know that because I've already told you."

"It was a mistake," she agreed. "Old water, old bridge."

"Not quite." No smile this time, and that happy vibe was gone when he reached in his pocket and pulled out something.

She saw the glint of gold when Cam placed it on the coffee table. A ring. And even though she'd only seen it twice, Lily instantly recognized it as the ring that had been on the top of Griff's tombstone.

"You took it?" she said, getting to her feet. "Why would you do that?" It felt like some kind of sick violation. Stealing stuff from a grave. Taking something that had been with Griff for almost as long as he'd been dead.

Cam stood, too. Slowly. And his gaze locked with hers. "I took it because I was supposed to give it to you fifteen years ago." He paused. "It's yours, Lily. Griff got it for you."

Lily was aware she was shaking her head, but her body had gone numb. "What do you mean?"

He cleared his throat and looked as if he'd prefer to be anywhere but here. "About an hour before Griff died, he came to see me. He was down. Very down. And, no, he didn't say a word about ending his life. Nothing about the

ALS diagnosis he'd just gotten." Another pause. "But he did tell me you were pregnant with his child."

She couldn't move, but Lily could feel. Mercy, could she, and the pain and emotion rolled through her. Over her. And the memories rocketed her back to a past she'd thought she had put behind her.

"Griff took out the ring and handed it to me," Cam went on. "He said he'd planned on asking you to marry him but that he couldn't now. He said you deserved better than what he could give you."

The numbness had settled in her throat, making it hard for her to breathe. "Griff was going to propose to me?" she managed to say.

Cam nodded. "And he gave me that ring to give to you. He asked me to tell you that he wanted to marry you but just couldn't."

Oh, God. And Lily just kept mentally repeating that.

"Like I said, I didn't know what Griff was going to do," Cam continued. "I swear, I didn't, and after he died, I thought it would hurt you even more to know he'd wanted to marry you." He stopped, waved that off. "Twelve steps, amends," he muttered, and he pressed his thumb against his chest. "I didn't want you to fixate on Griff because I wanted you to marry me."

It took a while for those words to sink in. Long "snail slow" moments. But when the sinking had finished, some of the numbness slid away.

"You didn't carry out Griff's last wish of giving me that ring and telling me he wanted to marry me because you wanted me for yourself," she spelled out.

"Yes." Cam's voice cracked on that one word. "I don't expect you to forgive me, but this was just something I felt

. I had to get off my chest. I didn't want the past to interfere with my happiness with Elsa."

Since she was still holding the stress ball, she considered just throwing it at him to get him to hush. Instead, she turned and headed for the back door. "You can let yourself out," she muttered to Cam. "Goodbye."

And that wasn't a "see you later" kind of farewell. As far as she was concerned, she never wanted to see him again.

"Amends, happiness, bullshit," she spit out, making her way out of the house and to the barn.

With each step, she regretted more and more not throwing that ball at him. How dare the SOB withhold something like that. His last conversation with his best friend. A best friend who wanted Cam to give her the ring he'd bought and tell her that he wanted to marry her but couldn't.

Lily kicked a rock off the path, and she did it with far more force than required to remove what was merely a pebble.

The anger came in a fuming hot flash. Cam had no right to keep this from her. He should have carried through Griff's last wishes and done what a good friend should do.

"But, no, the butthole Cam thought of himself," she muttered, going off the path to kick some more rocks. "He wanted me and withheld the truth to get me. And then what did the butthole do? He ran out on me, that's what. I hope his happiness fries his sorry ass."

She threw open the barn door, intending to go straight to Jonas's office so she could tell him about the wrong Cam had done to Griff, to her. Jonas would listen to every word of what was essentially a betrayal. He would hold her, comfort her and...

Lily stopped and mentally filled in the blank. Jonas would hold her, comfort her and would come to the conclusion that she wanted to jump into a time machine and undo the past. That she wanted Griff to propose, wanted to marry him and wanted Griff not to have driven his car off a cliff.

Part of that—the Griff living part—was definitely something she wished she could make right. The ultimate amends. But she wasn't the same person she had been fifteen years ago. She would always love Griff in that "first love" kind of way. He would always be part of her heart.

But he wasn't her heart now.

And since she didn't have that time machine, she had to face the truth of her situation. She was in love with Jonas, and the last thing she wanted to do was hurt him by making him think her heart still belonged to his dead brother. Especially since her heart hadn't belonged to Griff in a long, long time.

She looked up when she heard the footsteps and saw Jonas. No numbness this time. But rather a bone-deep warmth that came with love.

He eyed her. Then he eyed the ball. "Are you here to cheer me up because I'm down about Eli?"

"Absolutely," she assured him.

Lily went to him, gathering him into her arms, and kissed him to back up every bit of that *absolutely*.

ELI SMILED WHEN he read the text. Just checking to make sure you're putting in your retainer at night, his stepdad had messaged.

It wasn't the words that had Eli smiling but the fact that his stepdad had messaged him with the reminder. It wasn't the first time he'd done that over the past three days since Eli had started staying at the rental house in town with his dad. His stepdad had sent a couple of messages each day, all little things like asking if Eli had everything he needed or if he needed help with his homework.

Some of the texts had been about the mare Pearl and her foal, Dewdrop, and once his stepdad had even sent a picture of them. It made Eli miss them, made him miss the ranch and his bedroom, but he was glad his stepdad wasn't pissed off at him for being here with his dad.

Eli wasn't a kid; he knew that it'd hurt his stepdad when he'd left, but it wasn't for good. He'd be back at the ranch. But his dad had just wanted them to spend some time together so they could get to know each other. That seemed fair since his dad had missed so much of Eli's life.

And his dad blamed Eli's mom for that.

That wasn't so easy for Eli to hear, but he knew adults lied. Hayden's mom was proof of that. She'd lied about Hayden's father for years, so his own mom could have done the same thing. She could have told him that his father hadn't wanted to see him so she could keep him all to herself.

Adults did that kind of thing, too.

His stepdad hadn't. He hadn't stopped Eli from going with his dad, and Eli thought maybe he could have by going to court or something. At least until his dad did a bunch of paperwork. But his stepdad had just given in, and while Eli was mostly happy about that, he sort of wished that his stepdad had pitched at least a little fit. Then again, his stepdad wasn't the kind of person who did that.

Eli scrolled back through the old texts and pulled up the photo of Pearl and Dewdrop. The little filly had already grown a lot, and he was betting she was prancing around and trying out her legs. It twisted his stomach that he was missing that, and he decided to ask his dad if it was all right if he spent part of the weekend at the ranch.

Of course, his dad had probably already made plans. He sure loved keeping them busy. They'd gone to movies together, watched TV and eaten at O'Riley's three times. His dad had dropped him off at school, gone off to work and then had been there waiting for him when school had let out. Maybe because he had been worried that Eli might leave before they'd gotten the chance to know each other.

Eli had another look at the picture of the horses and got off his bed to go to his dad's makeshift office on the other side of the rental house. He could ask him about going to the ranch and maybe tell from his face how he felt about that.

The house wasn't that big, just three bedrooms, two baths, a living room, dining room and kitchen, so it didn't take Eli but a few steps to make it down the hall to the other side of the house toward the third bedroom that his dad was using as an office. He stopped, though, when he heard his dad's voice.

"I'm working on it," his dad said, and that was when Eli realized he was talking to someone on the phone. He didn't sound happy. In fact, he'd snarled that out. "You're just going to have to wait to get your money."

Eli couldn't hear what the other person said, but his dad huffed.

"Not long," his dad said, and it was another snarl. "My son has moved in with me, and I should have access to his accounts in a day or two."

Eli froze, and his stomach went into a tight ball that made him want to puke.

"Yes, I'm sure there'll be enough money. The PI I hired found that the kid's sitting on the life insurance payout Maddie left him. A quarter of a million. That'll be enough to cover what I owe you."

Life insurance?

Eli nearly said that aloud, but he stayed quiet and kept on listening.

"I might be able to tap Lily Parkman, too," his father went on. "She's an emotional wreck right now because I messed things up with her and her kid. I played on a hunch and left a note for the kid that caused enough chaos. Miss Parkman might be willing to give me whatever I ask for to get me out of her life."

Each word only made Eli want to puke even more, and the tears started burning his eyes. He turned, went out the back door and just kept on walking.

CHAPTER TWENTY-FIVE

JONAS LAY SNUGGLED with Lily on the small sofa in his office. A spot they'd landed after having sex. Sex that she'd probably meant to cheer him up. And it had worked. For now, anyway.

His body was still humming from the climax, and with his every breath, he took in her scent. Mother Nature was helping out with the moment by adding a soft rain that he could hear pattering against the tin roof of the barn.

He knew all too well that they couldn't stay this way, cuddled up and naked. For one thing, their backs and such would start to cramp up. Thankfully, he didn't have to worry about the ranch hands interrupting them since they would have already left for the day, but Hayden would likely be getting back soon from her study group, and she might come to the barn looking for her mother.

"We have to get up," Lily grumbled, taking the words right out of his mouth.

"Yeah," he agreed.

Neither of them moved. They stayed there wound around each other like pretzels to keep from falling off the sofa.

"You first," she insisted. "Lift a hand or something, and that might jump-start us."

He managed the hand lift. No jump start, though. However, things livened up when he located her mouth and kissed her for the best post-sex kiss in the history of such things.

Since the kiss and the sex both qualified as stellar, and since this was their third time together, Jonas figured they'd have to have a talk soon. Not because he wanted one but because Lily might want to know where all of this was heading.

Hell.

He wanted to know where it was headed, too, but he also didn't want to push in any direction because these moments with her meant way too much to him. She meant way too much to him. And he didn't want to do anything to spoil it.

Lily groaned when her phone dinged with a text. Groaned again when she practically fell off the sofa while she was trying to locate her phone. She fished it out of the heap of their clothes.

"Hayden," she relayed to him. "She's on her way back and wants to order pizza."

Lily fired off a quick yes and managed to get to a standing position. Jonas did as well, and he ignored the twinges in his back and butt from the pretzel position on the sofa and headed into the bathroom.

When he came back out, he saw a familiar sight—Lily getting dressed. Playtime was apparently over, and they had to return to reality.

"You should have pizza with us," she said while she zipped up her jeans.

Since his sour mood would likely make a fast return, he started to say no, but then the phone on his desk rang. He groaned because this would be business stuff that he didn't want to have to deal with.

"Buchanan," he answered, knowing he sounded brusque and unfriendly.

"Jonas," the familiar voice said. It was Cam.

That automatically rid Jonas of some of the brusqueness, but he was plenty confused as to why Lily's ex would be calling him. She obviously didn't know Cam was the caller, because she fluttered her fingers toward the bathroom and ducked inside.

"I'm worried about Lily," Cam continued just as Lily shut the bathroom door behind her. "I mean, when I left her earlier, she was pretty upset."

Jonas hadn't known about Cam's visit, and he sure as hell hadn't known about it upsetting her. Though, looking back, there had been something a little off in her expression when she'd come into the barn. He hadn't pushed since she'd kissed him and that had led to sex.

"Anyway, I was just checking to make sure she's okay," Cam added.

"Everything's fine," Jonas assured him, and, of course, that was a lie.

Cam's breath of relief came through loud and clear. "Good, because I know she was rattled when I told her that Griff had planned on proposing to her and that the ring on his tombstone was the one he'd bought for her."

Even with his "post-sex hazed" mind, Jonas had no trouble processing that. "You put the ring there?"

"I did." Another loud breath. "I talked to Griff right before he died, and he gave me the ring. He said it was for safekeeping. I didn't know he'd planned to end his life, Jonas. I swear, I didn't know."

Welcome to the club. That not knowing was one of the biggest regrets of Jonas's life. Because had he known, he might have been able to stop Griff.

"Anyway, I figured Lily had to be upset hearing that Griff really did love her and that he wanted them to get married," Cam concluded. "I'm glad she's okay. Sorry to have bothered you, Jonas," he tacked on to that before he ended the call.

Jonas just stood there, naked, holding the phone and thinking. Hell. Had Lily come to him for comfort sex? He'd thought it was the other way around, that she had been trying to cheer him up because of Eli. But maybe this had been something totally different. Maybe she had been trying to assure herself that she could put Griff aside once and for all.

And Jonas had to wonder if she had.

She came back into the office, and she'd wrapped a towel around her midsection. She was smiling. "Want to share a quick shower?" The smile went south, though, when she no doubt noticed his expression. "Who was that on the phone? Did you get bad news?"

Jonas didn't intend to lie or withhold the truth, something she'd done since she hadn't mentioned a word about Cam's visit or the ring. "That was Cam."

"Cam?" Her eyes widened. "What did he want…?" Her voice trailed off, and she squeezed her eyes shut a moment. "He told you."

Jonas nodded. "Any reason I didn't hear it from you?"

"Damn straight there is," she quickly answered. "I didn't want you to think I was brooding over a marriage proposal that never happened."

He looked her straight in the eyes. "But you were brooding. You were upset," he amended.

She didn't deny it. Couldn't. Because he could see even more that Cam had been right about this rattling her.

"It's not what you think," Lily insisted, and that seemed to be the start of what he was certain would be an attempt to reassure him that he didn't have to worry about her, that all was well. Or rather well-ish. But his phone rang and interrupted her. Not the desk phone. This was his cell.

He shoved aside his conversation with Lily since it could be Eli calling, but it was the PI's name, Hudson Granger, on the screen. Considering that it was after what most would consider normal duty hours, he got a bad feeling about it.

"Is there a problem?" Jonas asked the moment he answered. He went ahead and put the call on speaker because Lily was obviously waiting to hear why the PI had called. Jonas also started to get dressed.

"A problem for Wade Bentley," Hudson said just as quickly. "I've found two people who verified that Bentley told them that Maddie was pregnant with his kid. This would have been shortly after Maddie left him."

So, Bentley had known, which meant he'd lied. "These two people are credible?" Jonas asked.

"They are. They're Bentley's parents."

"His parents?" Lily and Jonas questioned in unison.

"Yep. I wasn't able to talk to them sooner because they've been away on vacation. They got back today, so I interviewed them. And they had an earful to tell me about their son. Financial troubles, womanizing. They've basically disowned him."

Jonas felt as if a Mack truck had slammed into him. This was the jerk who was with Eli.

"The parents claim that they tried to convince Bentley to try to see his child," Hudson went on, "but he said he didn't want a kid in his life."

"Is Bentley dangerous?" Jonas came out and asked.

"Nothing to indicate that. Why? Have you seen any signs that he could be violent?"

"No signs, but Eli's staying with him, and Bentley pushed

damn hard to get Eli under his roof. I need to go check on him."

"I'm coming with you," Lily insisted.

Jonas wouldn't try to stop her. He might need someone to keep him in check so he didn't punch Bentley. However, if the son of a bitch had harmed one hair on Eli's head, then Jonas would kick his ass and kick it hard.

That thought barely had time to go through his mind when he saw the incoming call from the SOB himself.

"I'll call you back," Jonas told Hudson, and he switched over to take the call from Bentley. He was about to tear into the man, but Bentley spoke first.

"Is Eli with you?" Bentley demanded.

That felt like ten Mack trucks, and Jonas had to fight through the worry and anger just to be able to speak. "No. Where is he?"

"You think I'd be calling you if I knew that?" Bentley fired back. "He's not in his room, and he's not answering his phone. If he's with you, you'd better tell me."

"He's not with me." Jonas had to speak through clenched teeth. "Why would he leave? What did you do?"

"I didn't do a damn thing. I just went to check on him, and he wasn't in his room. I'm heading to my car now to start driving around to look for him."

Bentley said something else, but Jonas cut him off by ending the call so he could try to contact Eli. It went straight to voice mail, so Jonas tried a text.

You okay? he messaged.

And he waited. And waited. But there was no response.

"He could be at the house," Jonas muttered, though the ranch was a good mile from the rental house. Not a long walk but it was raining, and it was possible—no, it was likely—that Eli was upset. Upset about something that the asshole Bentley hadn't owned up to saying or doing.

Lily and he didn't bother with umbrellas. They just ran out of the barn together and hurried to his house. The porch light was on, which gave Jonas hope that the boy was there, but then he remembered that he hadn't turned it off that morning.

"Eli?" he called out when they rushed inside.

Nothing. And when Jonas looked around, he saw no signs that Eli had been there. While he continued to look, Lily called Hayden to ask her about Eli.

"She hasn't seen him," Lily relayed to Jonas, and while they raced out to his truck, she called Nola and Wyatt.

Lily kept the conversation brief, basically just asking if they'd seen Eli, and when they said they hadn't, she moved on to Dax and Lorelei. When she got a no from them, she backtracked, calling Hayden again to tell her they were going to look for Eli and that she wanted the girl to contact Eli's friends to see if they knew where he was.

Since his brothers and their spouses would no doubt join the hunt, Jonas had to pray that it wouldn't be long before one of them found Eli. And that Eli would be unharmed.

"Try to call Eli again," he told Lily while he drove toward Bentley's rental house.

Jonas knew where it was, of course, because he'd made a point of knowing where his son was staying. Too bad he hadn't gone with his gut and stopped Eli from ever leaving with Bentley.

"Sorry, still no answer," Lily said, and she left a voice mail for Eli to contact them right away, that they were worried about him.

Worried was a total understatement, but Jonas held on to the hope that Eli was okay. He had to be okay. He just had to be. Jonas had never considered something like guardian angels, but he was hoping if Eli had one, that he or she was in full gear and would keep him safe.

"You want me to call the sheriff?" she asked.

Jonas's first reaction was to say yes, but he wanted to find out what was going on before he called Matt into this. It was possible Eli had just stepped out to be with friends, but it didn't feel like something that simple. No, it was more likely that Bentley and Eli had had some kind of argument and Eli had left. And that had Jonas rethinking what he'd just told Lily.

"Yeah, call Matt," Jonas amended. "Let him know what's going on."

She made the call while Jonas drove and kept on praying that he was making a mountain out of a molehill.

The rain was coming down harder, and the sun had set by the time he made it into town. Jonas drove straight to Bentley's rental house, where he immediately spotted the man on the porch. He was talking on the phone while he paced.

"I gotta go," Bentley told whoever was on the other end of the line. "Did you find him?" he asked Jonas.

"No." And Jonas fired off a quick question of his own. "What did you say to him to make him leave?"

"Nothing. I swear, I didn't say—" He stopped and swallowed hard when he saw the fury flare in Jonas's eyes. "All right, all right," he added, as if trying to calm both Jonas and himself. "I was talking to a business associate on the phone, and if Eli overheard, he might have misunderstood what I was saying."

This time the anger wasn't a slam but more of a slow crawl that felt mean and dangerous. "And what exactly were you saying that Eli could have misunderstood?"

"Nothing," Bentley insisted. He scrubbed his hand over his face. "I just have a few financial problems, that's all. Nothing to do with Eli. Find him so I can tell him he misunderstood my conversation. I'm his father. I love him and I want him back. He belongs with me."

Oh, it took some effort, but Jonas put a leash on his temper so he could speak. "Eli belongs with someone who loves him. Him, and not his money."

Bentley barked out a sound of outrage. "Are you accusing me of trying to get my hands on Eli's money?"

Jonas took a step toward him. One slow, menacing step, and he shot Bentley a look that he hoped caused the guy to piss his pants. "Yeah, I am. I believe you want Eli so his inheritance can make your money problems go away."

"That's not true," Bentley snapped, but everything about the man said he was lying. "And I won't stand here and have you accuse me of such things. I'm a doctor, not some hick cowboy who's made a show of raising somebody else's kid. Eli is my kid, not yours. I have a right to him and what's his."

That was the wrong thing to say on so many levels, and Lily must have known Jonas was about to snap, because she moved closer to stop him. Or so Jonas thought.

"You want me to hold your keys while you punch him?" Lily asked. Her voice was calm enough, but Jonas could feel the anger coming off her.

Bentley smirked at her. Actually smirked. "Tell your whore to back off."

That did it. Jonas tossed Lily his keys, and without even shifting the momentum, he plowed his fist into Bentley's smirking face. It came at the exact moment that Bentley lifted his foot, trying to kick Jonas in the balls.

What kind of bullshit was this?

"Are you going to try to pull my hair or bite me next?" Jonas snapped.

Making the sound of a snorting, feral bull, Bentley lowered his head and charged at Jonas. He managed to ram Jonas into the porch railing just as Matt pulled to a stop in front of the house. From the corner of his eye, Jonas saw Matt bolt from the cruiser, but Jonas focused on restraining Bentley. If the clown really did manage to kick him in the balls, then Jonas might end up pulverizing him. That would force Matt to arrest him, especially since he'd been the one to throw the first punch.

"Bentley's a big-assed liar," Jonas heard Lily tell Matt. "He wants Eli's money, he caused the boy to run away and he called me a whore."

Jonas managed to get Bentley facedown on the porch as Lily finished that recap. "Did the fight start before or after Bentley called you that?" Matt asked, going up the steps toward Bentley and him.

"After," Lily verified.

Matt made a sound that conveyed he would have had the same reaction. "I'll take over from here," he told Jonas.

"He punched me!" Bentley howled.

"Yeah, and you tried to kick him in the nuts. I saw that before I stopped the cruiser." Matt hauled Bentley to his feet when Jonas moved back. Matt put the man in one of the porch chairs. "Where's Eli?"

Jonas had to shake his head. "This moron claims he doesn't know, either."

"I don't," Bentley snarled, "and I want you to arrest this cowboy hick—"

Matt cut him off with one hard cop's glare, and he turned back to Jonas. "Why don't Lily and you go look for Eli?

I'll have some deputies out doing the same. Check with his friends, the places he likes to go."

Jonas nodded, and with Lily right with him, he headed toward his truck.

"You're not going to arrest him?" Bentley growled.

"No," Jonas heard Matt say, "but depending on what happens with Eli, I might be arresting you for something. Just sit there and shut up while I call my deputies and get an EMT out here to check out your busted lip."

Bentley didn't launch into more of a bitching session. Probably because Matt could look mean enough to arrest him and throw away the key.

"Your hand is bleeding," Lily pointed out as Jonas drove away from the house. She located a tissue in the glove compartment and started dabbing at it. "But it looks a lot better than Bentley's face."

Jonas didn't care squat about his bleeding hand. Or Bentley's face, for that matter. He just needed to find Eli.

"I'll check with Hayden and see if she's had any luck with Eli's friends," Lily offered.

While she did that, Jonas drove to O'Riley's café. It was only four blocks from the rental house and was one of Eli's favorite places.

The rain was coming down harder now, not a gentle pattering, but rather full-blown that made it hard to see out the windshield. It sickened him to think that Eli was out in this, getting soaked, hurt by whatever he'd over-heard Bentley say.

O'Riley's didn't have indoor seating, and because of the rain, there were only four people, all huddling under the umbrellas that sheltered the tables. Eli wasn't one of the four.

"So far, Hayden's struck out, and Eli hasn't come back

to the ranch," Lily relayed to him. "But she suggested trying the football field."

Jonas immediately turned the truck around and headed there. Eli had quit the team, but that didn't mean he wouldn't go to a place where he'd spent a lot of time. But Jonas got another slam of dread when he reached the field and saw it empty. Still, he parked and got out so he could look around the locker room. No one was there.

"Eli?" he called out, just in case the boy was hiding behind something.

Nothing.

Jonas swiped his hand over his face, slinging off the rain, and he jumped back into his truck. That was when it hit him. That was when he knew where Eli would go.

"Maddie's grave," Jonas muttered, and that was where he headed.

The cemetery was a good half mile from Bentley's, and with the rain, it wouldn't have been an especially easy walk. Not an easy drive, either, since the country road leading there was curvy and slick. However, the moment Jonas pulled into the parking lot, the headlights allowed him to spot Eli standing right in front of his mother's tombstone.

Jonas bolted out of the truck but then remembered Lily was there, and she was no doubt worried about Eli, too.

"I'll wait here in the truck and tell Matt that we've found him," she said. "If you need me, let me know."

He rattled off a thanks and pushed aside any questions he still had about her feelings for Griff. That was an obstacle he'd have to tackle some other time. Eli was his focus now.

Jonas started off running, but he slowed when he approached the boy, and even though Eli had no doubt heard his footsteps, he didn't look back at him. Since Eli's back was to the headlights, Jonas couldn't see his face, but he was betting Eli had been crying. And that made him silently curse and wish that he'd given Bentley another punch.

"You want to talk about it?" Jonas offered.

Judging from Eli's silence, Jonas took that as a no, so he just stood there and waited while the rain soaked them both to the bone.

"Mom was right," Eli finally said. "My dad isn't a good man."

Jonas was glad to have Maddie's name *cleared*, so to speak, but mercy, it cut deep to hear all that hurt in Eli's voice. "Want to tell me what happened?"

Eli shrugged, kept his gaze pinned to Maddie's headstone. "My dad wanted my money. The money Mom left me. I was going to save it to buy a ranch of my own one day, but he was going to take it. Do you know why?"

There was a thick coating of emotion in his throat that Jonas had to clear before he could speak. "He's in debt, and I'm guessing he owes money to someone who wants it back."

Eli stayed quiet several more moments. Moments where this was no doubt chewing into him. He'd already lost his mother, and now it had to feel as if he had lost his father, too.

"The only reason my dad wanted me with him was because of the money," Eli concluded. "And he was going to try to get money from Hayden's mom, too. He's the one who left that note for Hayden to tell her about her real dad."

That made Jonas wish again that he'd punched Bentley even harder. The man had tried to rip all their lives apart and had come damn close to succeeding.

Eli finally turned and looked at Jonas. "Do I have to go back and stay with him?"

"No. I wouldn't let that happen." And in this case, the law was on their side. At fourteen, Eli was old enough to decide where he wanted to live. Bentley might try to press for visitations, but Jonas would try to block that, too. He wanted to keep the asshole far away from his son.

Yes, *his* son. Jonas's, not Bentley's.

Because that was exactly who Eli was.

Jonas put his arm around Eli, and the boy immediately dropped his head onto Jonas's shoulder. He wasn't sobbing. Maybe because Eli had already burned through the tears.

"I love you," Jonas told him. "And DNA doesn't play into just how strong and deep that love is. You're my son in every single way that matters. Understand?"

Eli nodded, and there wasn't a shred of hesitation in that nod. That was when some of the fisted anger eased up in Jonas's gut. Eli knew how much Jonas loved him. Knew that he would always be his father.

"Can we go home now?" Eli asked.

Jonas smiled and brushed a kiss on the top of Eli's head. "Yeah, let's go home."

CHAPTER TWENTY-SIX

LILY DIDN'T OWN a briefcase, so she'd put her paper stash in a plastic grocery bag that sported happy dancing fruit, and it made her wonder, what was up with that? Why had anyone thought that produce and other foods required such adornment on a bag that would at best be reused a couple of times and recycled?

She decided to chalk that up to one of the mysteries of the ages.

Over the past two days, she'd done a lot of chalking up and a lot of thinking while she'd given Jonas and Eli the space she'd thought they needed. Hayden and she had certainly needed some to get through the rest of Griff's things and for Lily to answer any questions Hayden had about her dad.

Lily didn't think there was any anger left in her daughter over the big lie. At least she hoped there wasn't. Hayden had just seemed to accept that she was a Buchanan and had giggled—yes, actually giggled—when she'd realized Nola and Lorelei were both her aunts and her aunts-in-law since they'd married Griff's brothers.

The fact that both her sisters and her daughter were Buchanans had caused Lily to do plenty more thinking since she, too, had joined the Buchanan bandwagon, again, by having sex with Jonas. But that thinking had led to something that had caused some worry. Some fear.

Because sex with Jonas might be a thing of the past.

Even though they hadn't had time to discuss it, she'd seen the questions and even some hurt when he'd learned from Cam about the ring and Griff's intention of proposing to her. She couldn't fault Jonas for his reaction because she'd had a similar one on the walk from her house to the barn. A reaction she'd clamped down when she had seen Jonas and coaxed him to the sofa in his office for sex.

Now here she was, making another trek from her house to the barn where Jonas was working in his office. She knew this because just minutes earlier he'd copied her on an email to a prospective buyer, and Jonas had told him that he'd be in his office for the next hour if he wanted to call and discuss it.

It was a school day, so neither Eli nor Hayden was in the pastures doing their favorite thing of hanging out with the horses. However, Lily had seen them both riding since Eli had returned to the ranch. Not flirting and riding the way they had during their brief romance but still riding, talking and hanging out. That was a good thing, a way of getting back to normal.

And speaking of normal, Bentley might be doing that, too. Lily didn't actually know the latest on him, but at least a dozen people had called to tell her that Bentley had moved out of the rental house, and since he hadn't shown up at the ranch, she had to guess that the man wasn't going to try to snatch Eli and force him to turn over his money.

There'd been other calls over the past two days. Lots and lots of them, but those had been Hezzie-related, and just so she could get some work done, Lily had resorted to letting all calls go to voice mail. She might or might not get around to listening to them. For now, though, she had another mission.

Jonas.

She waved a greeting to one of the hands who was in the corral with Pearl and Dewdrop, and she went inside the barn, making a beeline to Jonas's office. His door was open, and he was at his desk in the "rancher cowboy" mode. As opposed to the "regular cowboy" mode. Both were steaming hot.

He looked at her, those amazing and equally steaming eyes meeting hers, and she felt a flash of heat that could have dissolved rust. The man certainly had a way of firing her up. And keeping her on her toes. Right now, it was an equal balancing act of both because she felt the sharp pull of attraction between them, but he sure as heck wasn't rushing to her to pull her in his arms.

"Anything new on Bentley?" she asked, just to get that out of the way.

"Matt thinks the San Antonio cops are going to arrest Bentley for embezzling money from his medical practice, so I think we've seen the last of him."

"Well, that's a relief. Bentley hasn't tried to contact Eli, has he?"

Jonas shook his head. "I believe Bentley has figured out he's not getting any money out of it, so Eli's not worth his time."

That made her ache for Eli, but Jonas would help the boy get through it because Eli was his son. Love and attention fixed a whole multitude of problems, and Eli had been blessed with a darn good fixer in Jonas.

Lily went closer, setting the dancing-fruit bag on his desk and pulling out the binder. Not a fancy one but rather one sold as a school supply.

"The cover's temporary," she explained. "I'll have it bound into something more suitable for the Last Ride research library, but I was hoping you'd take a look at it before I did that."

He tore his gaze from her and took the binder. "This is the Hezzie research."

"It is. Don't worry—there are no penis-dangling ball pictures in there."

Jonas didn't smile as she'd hoped, and that made her heart feel as if it were being squeezed by a meaty fist. She doubted square-dancing was going to lighten him up, either, so she just continued with what would no doubt turn to babbling.

"I feel I reached a compromise with my warring kin. Those on the side of hiding any and all seedy things to those who want dangling-ball penis pictures," she explained as Jonas opened the binder and started to skim through it. "I wrote about all of Hezzie's accomplishments and business ventures."

"All?" His eyebrow slid up.

She nodded. "Again, no nude pictures to illustrate her photography skills, but I did include a copy of the shot of Hezzie winning the Silver Slipper saloon."

Jonas stopped on that particular photo that was near the end of the research and then he went to the last page.

"'Hezzie Parkman was an astute businesswoman who climbed out of her impoverished roots to become the founder of Last Ride. Without the money from the Silver Slipper and her photography ventures, Last Ride wouldn't exist. Maybe her marriage wouldn't have, either, since she met her husband during one of her photography sessions. As her descendants, we might not be here if Hezzie had chosen a different path.'"

After reading that last line, Jonas looked at her. "You did a good job."

She smiled because she didn't think that praise was BS.

"'We might not be here if Hezzie had chosen a different path,'" he repeated, his eyebrow lifting again. "Is that some kind of metaphor for our lives?"

Because of all the thinking she'd done, Lily had no trouble answering that. "Absolutely. You're the man you are because of Maddie, and I'm the woman I am because of Griff. If we took either one of them out of the equation, we might not be here today as co-owners of the Wild Springs Ranch."

Jonas gave her a flat look. "You're not selling or giving me one percent of the ranch so we can be equal partners."

"I know." She took out the next papers and dropped them in front of him. "I gave Eli and Hayden each a percent. Now, while I'm not a whiz at math, I think that means you and I both have forty-nine percent, which makes us… ta-da…equal partners."

He huffed. "You didn't have to do that."

"Yes, I did."

And here was the part where she was going to have to take a risk. A huge one. Because if Jonas rejected her, their friendship would go down the drain. She would lose him. Still, Lily siphoned off some of Hezzie's bravery that was hopefully in her own DNA and went for broke.

"Now when I take you to my bed," she said, her voice not quite as brave-sounding as she'd wanted, "there'll be no hints of sexual harassment in the workplace."

Still no smile, and Jonas dipped down his head while he stood. "There were never hints of harassment," he assured her.

"Well, now the possibility of it has been taken out of the picture," Lily managed to say. She tried to tamp down the panic that was rising like icky steam from her feet to her head.

Mercy, she couldn't lose Jonas, and she was ready to blurt out that they could just be friends, that she'd find a way to make that work and quit lusting after him. Of course, that last part would have been a lie. Lust was a given with Jonas. But she didn't get a chance to babble any of that, because he spoke first.

"What are you going to do with the ring Griff bought you?" he asked. He came out from behind the desk and faced her.

She gathered her breath, prayed her voice didn't fail. "I considered giving it to Hayden, but that didn't feel right. So, I put it back on the tombstone. I figure Griff would have gotten a laugh over everyone speculating about who'd put it there and why."

He nodded, and yes, there was the glimmer of a smile. A smile meant for some memory he was having about Griff, but that was okay. It was better than flat looks, raised eyebrows and such.

"You'll always love him," Jonas concluded.

She swallowed hard. "Yes, a part of me will. Just as a part of you will always love Maddie, but here's the way I see it. Chalk this up to a lot of thinking time, but I know that I have a lot more love in me to give."

And now she went for broke. She wanted it all—friendship, sex, Jonas. Love. The whole package.

"I have a lot more love to give," she repeated, "and I'd like to give it to you, Jonas, because I'm in love with you."

The glimmer of a smile didn't happen again, but she saw something in his eyes. Maybe approval.

Please, please, please let it be approval.

He walked closer, looking so good that she felt her mouth

water. Jonas reached out, hooked his finger in one of the loops on her jeans and tugged her to him. He didn't have to tug hard, because Lily was already heading in that direction.

Home.

That was the thought that flashed in her mind when she landed in his arms. This was home. The next thought was that her heart might not be able to hold all the love she felt for him. A third thought was a dirty one that made her hope that he had another condom handy.

Jonas leaned in and brushed a kiss on her mouth. It was scalding but way too brief. She wanted more and might have gone in for something longer and deeper, but he used his words to accomplish the long and deep.

"I'm in love with you, too, Lily."

Her heart ballooned, filling and flooding her with more happiness that she was certain set some kind of happiness record.

"Will you marry me and do all the things with me that married couples do?" he asked.

Her throat filled up, too. Ditto for her eyes, but the tears that watered them were just more of the happy stuff.

"You mean like sex?" she asked, nipping his bottom lip with her teeth. "Please let part of *all those things* be sex."

"Sex," he verified, giving her a sample of a real kiss. Oh, man. He was so good at that. "Maybe another baby. And growing old together. What do you say to all of that, Lily?"

Lily had just one response for that. "Absolutely."

* * * * *

Now turn the page for a bonus story,
Tempted at Thoroughbred Lake,
by USA TODAY *bestselling author Delores Fossen!*

TEMPTED
AT
THOROUGHBRED
LAKE

CHAPTER ONE

RUBY PARKMAN FIGURED she'd already exceeded her quota of curse words for the day, but she added a few more when she rushed into her house and spotted the pair of white lace panties on her living room floor.

Since these frilly undies appeared to be an extra small and incapable of covering even one of her butt cheeks, Ruby knew they belonged to her eighteen-year-old daughter, Vivian. It wasn't a good sign that they were on the floor, but Ruby was holding out hope that Vivian had dropped them there while carting her laundry to her bedroom.

Ruby headed toward Vivian's bedroom now, threading her way through the old Victorian house and to the equally mazelike hall. She stopped again, though, when she spotted more underwear. A white lace bra this time.

And the black boxer shorts next to it.

Ruby forced herself to take a deep breath, reminding herself that Vivian was an adult now. In the general sense of the word, anyway. But it was a punch to her mom gut to realize that on the other side of Vivian's bedroom door, wild sex might be going on between her "always will be my little girl" and the eighteen-year-old boyfriend of the "always will be my little girl," Seth Dayton.

Apparently, Vivian hadn't realized that Ruby would get home so soon. If she had, Vivian likely would have delayed sending the text that had caused Ruby to hurry back so she could find out what had prompted her daughter to message:

I have exciting news. Can't wait to tell you when you get home.

Ruby didn't care much for the wording of that. It was giving her a "hard punch to the gut" feeling, and over the past eighteen years, Ruby had learned that definitely wasn't a good feeling for a`mom to have.

She didn't knock at her daughter's bedroom door but instead decided to wait out Vivian and Seth, and that way she could take some time to settle her nerves. But she didn't get that nerve-settling time. Ruby had barely managed one long breath when the bedroom door flew open.

"Oh, you're already here," Vivian blurted out, her eyes wide with surprise and her voice breathy. "I wasn't expecting you so soon. I figured you'd stay after the Last Ride Society meeting. I got some texts from friends whose moms told them your name got picked, and I thought you'd hang around and talk to them about that."

No, Ruby had gotten out of the meeting fast. No way had she wanted to deal with the questions and poor pitying looks. Then again, she hadn't especially savored the notion of coming home to face, well, whatever the heck she was about to face.

Her daughter was dressed, more or less, in jeans and a top that she was still adjusting. Her cheeks were rosy. Perhaps flushed from the recent sex or because she was now aware that her mom had spotted the discarded undergarments on the floor. Items obviously tossed off during the frenzied lust journey to the bedroom.

Vivian scooped up the bra and boxers, moving them behind her back and muttering a "Sorry about that," while her cheeks went even rosier.

Ruby glanced over her daughter's shoulder and spotted Seth, who was also doing some adjustments to his jeans and shirt. He looked a little rosy colored as well.

"Sorry, Miss P," Seth said, using the abbreviated name he always called her.

Ruby considered mentioning the sex. Dismissed it. Instead, she held up her phone to show Vivian the text she'd sent, and she hoped like the devil that her daughter and eternally little girl wasn't about to say that she and Seth were now engaged. If so, it was going to have to be a really long engagement since both were heading off to college in just two weeks. With Vivian planning on becoming a veterinarian and Seth an engineer, they'd be in school for years.

"What exactly is your exciting news?" Ruby asked, speaking around the lump in her throat.

No lump in the throat for Vivian. Her daughter beamed out a huge smile, and Seth was smiling, too, when he hurried to her side.

Vivian lifted her left hand, and Ruby caught the flash of the small diamond solitaire. Then she got a flash of something else.

Oh, crap.

One Hour Earlier

RUBY PARKMAN WAITED until she left the Last Ride Society meeting and was in her car before she wadded up the little strip of paper into the size of a spitball and grumbled every curse word she knew. Some words she made up as well. Because this was certainly a curse-worthy situation.

Did the crappery of fate have it in for her?

Apparently so, because out of the hundreds—yes, hundreds—of names she could have drawn at the quarterly meeting of the Last Ride Society, she'd plucked the very one that could give her the most headaches.

And some sucky memories to boot.

When she had seen the name on the now spitball of paper, she had tried her damnedest not to react since she'd been standing in front of a room filled with her Parkman kin. After all, it was an "honor" to be the drawer at the Last Ride Society. Ruby had especially tried not to curse or do anything that would fuel more gossip.

Oh, but there'd be gossip.

Whispers, too, of poor pitiful Ruby, who was going to have her nose rubbed into the messy smear of memories that she would have to pore over and research all because of that "honor."

With her frustration growing by leaps and bounds, Ruby forced herself to focus on something else other than the drawing that had been dumped on her by the society members in her hometown of Last Ride, Texas. Instead, she got to work and drove the five blocks to the "charming" three-bedroom updated ranch house that was about to go on the market. Since she was the Realtor repping the property, she would need to put up the sign and do one final check of the interior to make sure all was well for the showings she already had scheduled.

Ruby stepped from her car, scowling at the scalding Texas heat that was at sauna-level, with an icky amount of humidity to go along with it. The heat would linger for a while, too, despite it being past six in the evening.

She had barely gotten started on placing the sign on the curb when she heard the sound of an approaching vehicle. Ruby looked up and spotted the dark blue pickup turning into the driveway. Her first thought was this was an eager potential buyer who wanted to get first dibs on the property, but then she got a closer look at the vehicle. And the driver.

Brennan Dayton.

She sighed because this was no buyer. Brennan already owned the Thoroughbred Lake Ranch, with its own charming house that'd been passed down several generations. He definitely wouldn't be looking for another place to hang his Stetson, especially anything in the "downtown" area.

Nope.

This wasn't a visit to tap into her Realtor skills but rather to talk to her about what had happened—she checked the time—twelve minutes ago.

Gossip was in the "speed dial" mode in Last Ride, and Ruby was betting plenty of that speed-dialing had been aimed at Brennan to inform him of, well, something he likely wouldn't have wanted to be informed about. Still, here he was, so he either wanted to know how she was going to handle things or to tell her that he didn't want to be a part of that handling.

Brennan stepped from his truck, and Ruby immediately got the same old jolt she always did when she looked at the man who could have won any and all hot cowboy competitions. The man had been causing that reaction in her for as long as she'd been aware of such things.

Once, he'd helped that jolt along with some serious kissing and some scalding touches, but that was more than two decades ago when they were in high school. There'd been no such recent activity.

Not on his part, anyway.

Ruby was certainly having some scalding thoughts about him right now.

Brennan was lean, tall and drop-dead gorgeous in his great-fitting jeans and snug T-shirt that somehow managed to make him look part bad boy, part rock star. He strode toward her, the wind taking a swipe at his storm black hair.

"You got here fast," Ruby remarked.

Brennan nodded, his cool blue eyes sweeping over her. "I was at the feed store. I called your office, and your assistant said you'd likely be here."

Since Last Ride was the textbook definition of a small town, all the shops and businesses were close to each other. Ditto for the various neighborhoods. Even if Brennan hadn't asked her assistant, Tammy Granger, where she was, he could have still easily found her.

"How many people called and texted you about the drawing?" Ruby came out and asked.

The breath he dragged in was long and weary. "Eleven."

She shrugged. "Considering there were about seventy people at the Last Ride Society drawing, I'm surprised there weren't more."

"I turned off my phone after the eleventh one," he informed her.

Ah, that made sense. The Last Ride Society was filled with both do-gooders and gossips. Many fell into both categories, but the gossips were especially skilled at spreading the news.

Many nonmembers considered the Last Ride Society a pain in the butt and a way for the town's first family, the Parkmans, to spend the overabundance of time they had on their hands. For Ruby, though, it definitely wasn't about gossip, do-gooding or filling time. It was about fulfilling a duty that had been drilled into her since she was old enough to understand such drillings.

The gist of this particular Parkman duty was the Last

Ride Society had been formed decades ago by the town's founder and Ruby's ancestor, Hezzie Parkman. Hezzie had wanted her descendants to preserve the area's history by having a quarterly drawing so that one Parkman descendant would then in turn draw the name of a local tombstone to research. After the research was done, a chunk of money would be donated to the researcher's town charity of choice. Ruby intended to give hers to help cover the costs of fixing up the playground at the town's park.

First, though, she had to get past the research.

And that started with getting past Brennan.

"You drew Alice's name," he said.

Obviously, it wasn't a question, and considering those eleven callers and/or texters had likely verified it, Brennan knew that she had, indeed, drawn his late wife's name.

Ruby nodded and continued to wrestle with the for-sale sign. Either this part of the ground was a chunk of limestone or else the spikes on the bottom of the sign weren't doing their job.

"Don't worry," she muttered. "I'll only write nice things about her."

Though that would be a challenge. And Ruby would then have to deal with the memories of Alice and Brennan's betrayal.

For Ruby, it'd been a double whammy.

"Only nice things," Brennan repeated in a grumble, as if that weren't just a challenge but would be impossible.

There was a huge reason for his skepticism. Nearly nineteen years ago, when Alice and she had been besties in high school, Ruby had had a serious crush on Brennan. Of course, she'd told Alice all about that crush and the three make-out sessions Ruby had managed to have with Brennan. Ruby had also droned on about how eager she was to ask him to go with her to the town's annual Valentine's Day dance.

Alice, who clearly hadn't embraced that whole bestie status, had obviously had her own crush on Brennan. Ditto for him having the hots for Alice.

And they'd acted on it.

Mercy, had they. When Alice and he had ended up at a party where there'd been some underage drinking as well, booze and hormones had led to them having sex. Alice had gotten pregnant, which, in turn, had prompted Brennan and her to dive into a hasty wedding when they were just eighteen.

Their betrayal had crushed Ruby to the bone, and she'd done her own "in turn" stuff and sought out rebound sex with Carson Dayton. Apparently, that'd been a bad year for the quality of condoms, because she, too, had gotten pregnant. Her daughter, Vivian, had been born just four months after Alice and Brennan's son, Seth.

Unlike Alice and Brennan, though, there'd been no hasty wedding for Ruby. She hadn't wanted to do any marital diving since she'd figured it would just end in divorce. Still, Carson and she had lived together for four years, but that had ended with the second wave of betrayal when he'd had an affair with Alice.

So, yes, Alice's name was mud.

It was still muddy despite the woman having died at the too-young age of thirty-two from cancer. That'd been four years ago, and even though both she and Brennan were divorced at the time, it'd been a hard blow since it meant his son, Seth, had lost his mother when he'd barely been fourteen.

Brennan gave another of those heavy sighs when she

continued to struggle with the sign. He went over and took it from her.

And touched her hand in the process.

It was just a touch, but man, oh, man, it could still pack a wallop. She sucked in her breath, taking in his scent in the process. A good scent. One that stirred even more parts of her that shouldn't be stirred.

She looked up at him, their gazes colliding, and she got another whammy of heat. Apparently, Brennan was well aware of the effect he had on her, because he muttered some of the same profanity she had after she'd drawn Alice's name.

"Seth will likely want to help you with the research," Brennan said.

That didn't cause all the heat to cool down, but it got Ruby's attention. Brennan's son would probably enjoy doing the research. Well, he would enjoy having his mother in the spotlight for a little while, anyway.

"Seth's leaving for Austin in two weeks," she pointed out. Austin wasn't far away, only about an hour's drive, but the boy would probably be busy starting his freshman year of college. Ruby expected it would be the same for her daughter, Vivian.

Brennan managed to make a shrug look plenty appealing. "Seth will want to make sure his mother is painted in the best light possible. What Alice did to you and me doesn't have anything to do with him."

Ruby heard the not-so-subtle warning in that. If at all possible, Brennan didn't want Seth hurt by anything that would come out in the research. Preventing that would take some tiptoeing skills, but if she could convince buyers this house actually lived up to the charming label, then she could candy-coat the details of a research report.

"Agreed," Ruby said, and when Brennan easily staked in the for-sale sign, she motioned for him to follow her into the house. They could continue this conversation and not risk heatstroke, a sweat bath and deodorant failure.

"I'll tell Seth," Brennan explained as she unlocked the door and they stepped inside. Thank heaven, the air-conditioning was on and working just fine. "If he hasn't heard already, that is."

Ruby turned to look at him when she heard a *but* or some kind of hesitation at the end of that.

"Are you okay with this?" he asked.

Since he was that whole "hot cowboy" deal, it took her a moment to switch gears. Brennan wasn't talking about this heat she still felt for him.

Was he?

No, she assured herself. Brennan had put in a lot of effort to keep her at arm's length. Maybe because being around her brought back bad memories of their exes cheating with each other. Maybe because he felt as if he could have done more to make sure she hadn't been screwed over in high school when Alice and he had hooked up at that party. Added to that, when she hadn't been involved in a relationship, he had been, and vice versa.

But not now.

Her body flung that little reminder at her.

The news certainly would have gotten back to her had Brennan been seeing anyone.

Their gazes connected. Held. Locked. And Ruby tingled—yes, actually tingled—when she saw what she thought might be the spark of attraction. It wasn't one-sided, either. Nope, and she got confirmation of that when Brennan cursed.

He groaned and cursed some more before he finally said, "Look, I've been thinking about you, thinking about asking you out. But you and I both know that's probably a bad idea."

The *probably* gave her a mountain of hope. "You're under the impression that when we're together, we'll only be able to think of the bad stuff that went on," she spelled out for him.

He nodded, but she thought Brennan might be searching her eyes to see if she believed there was any chance that wouldn't happen.

Ruby would have assured him with all the assurance that she could muster up that she believed they could get past the bad stuff. Heat, especially a scalding hot one, could erase memories along with common sense. She didn't get a chance to voice any of that, though, because both their phones dinged with texts.

"It's from Vivian," she muttered, silently cursing the interruption. Ruby did even more silent cursing when she read the message from her daughter that popped up on the screen.

I have exciting news. Can't wait to tell you when you get home.

"Mine's from Seth," Brennan relayed to her. "He says he has something to tell me."

Ruby got a bad feeling. Really bad. Bracing herself for the worst, she muttered a quick goodbye to Brennan and got ready to face whatever music her daughter was about to dole out.

CHAPTER TWO

BRENNAN HURRIED UP the porch steps of Ruby's house and wasn't surprised to see the door open. Like him, Ruby had hurried to get home after receiving that text from Vivian. Brennan had been heading home, too, to find out what Seth meant by something *exciting*, but then Seth had sent a second message saying he was at Ruby's with Vivian.

That upped Brennan's urgency. Hell. He hoped his son wasn't repeating history and had knocked up Vivian. Brennan darn sure wouldn't consider that news exciting. More like a "what the hell" and how was this going to affect Seth's and Vivian's plans for college? Seth would know that. Well, he'd know it if he wasn't seeing the future through rose-colored glasses.

Having a kid was an amazing thing, but it was also plenty of work. Brennan knew that firsthand. Knew, too, how much more work and harder it was when you were just eighteen. He didn't want that for his son. He wanted Seth to go to college, live a little and then settle down with those "amazing" offspring.

With the worry that "amazing" was going to come a whole lot sooner than it should, Brennan tapped on Ruby's door to let her know he was there, and then he winced when he saw the panties on the floor.

Great.

In addition to what would be news he wouldn't want

to hear, Ruby had perhaps walked in on his son and her daughter doing what kids their age did. But the timing sucked.

"Ruby?" Brennan called out when she didn't respond.

"Back here," Seth answered for her.

It was hard to tell his son's tone from just two words, but Brennan thought he heard some giddiness. Cursing that, Brennan followed the sound of the response, making his way around the "ant farm" layout of the house, and he finally spotted Ruby in the hall, standing outside a room. She wasn't speaking. Hadn't fainted, thank heaven. But she had her hand pressed to her chest, and her mouth was frozen open.

"Ruby?" Brennan repeated.

She whirled toward him, and he saw the whole "deer caught in the headlights" look. So, yeah, this was bad. Since Brennan wasn't a fan of delaying any form of bad, he just went with the obvious question.

"Is Vivian pregnant?"

Ruby didn't have time to respond, because Vivian beat her to it. Vivian laughed. Seth joined in on the laughter as if that were the dumbest question in the history of dumb questions.

The relief hit Brennan so hard that he made a strangled sound of relief, and hell, he wanted to start laughing, too. He might have done just that if he'd managed to gather enough breath. And if he hadn't seen what was on Vivian's left hand.

An engagement ring, yes.

But there was more. Another ring, a plain gold band beneath it. Seth was wearing an identical band on his left hand as well.

Brennan's first thought was that this was a joke to get

him laughing as much as the kids were. If so, he didn't consider it very funny.

"We eloped," Seth gushed.

There was no doubting the giddiness now in his voice. It didn't last long, though. Probably because his son was noting Brennan's expression. It sure as heck wasn't one of approval.

"They eloped," Ruby said, not because she thought Brennan might not have heard. Oh, no. She knew he'd heard it all right. This was the repetition a person might make when they were in shock.

"We want you to be happy for us," Vivian interjected when she no doubt realized this was not going to be cause for parental celebration and giddiness.

"We figured you'd be surprised," Seth added, "but once you get used to the idea, you'll see this is for the best."

"It's not," Ruby immediately argued, volleying her gaze between their kids. She was in Mom mode now, and Brennan stepped by her side to present a united front.

"It's not," Brennan echoed. "You're eighteen, and you're heading to college. You are heading to college," he said, making sure it wasn't a question.

"Of course, we're going to UT," Vivian said, giving the abbreviation for University of Texas. She snuggled even closer to Seth. "Instead of living in the dorms, we're getting a place together. There are plenty of apartments not too far from campus, and it'll be cheaper in the long run," she quickly added, clearly hoping that would win over the parents.

It wouldn't.

"You're eighteen," Brennan pointed out again.

"You can't say that's too young to get married, because

that's how old you were when you married Mom," Seth argued.

"Yeah, and look how bad that turned out," Brennan snapped.

Of course, he instantly regretted throwing that in Seth's face. Even if it was the truth, it wasn't something a son wanted to hear. Still, he had to say or do something to fix this.

"You could get an annulment for now," Brennan suggested. "And then you can get married after you finish college." They'd still be young, but those four years would make a big difference at avoiding a bad turnout.

"Yes, an annulment," Ruby said, jumping right on that bandwagon. "It doesn't matter about the money you'd save with sharing an apartment. The dorm would be a once-in-a-lifetime experience for both of you."

Experiences that both Ruby and he had missed because they'd become parents before they'd been legally old enough to drink.

Seth sighed and shook his head. Vivian, however, went in a different direction with her reaction. Tears filled her eyes and began to spill down her cheeks.

"We want you to be happy for us," Vivian muttered.

"We will be happy if you wait until you're old enough to get married," Ruby fired right back.

Clearly, that went nowhere whatsoever in convincing their offspring. Vivian and Seth held on tighter to each other. "We're old enough to get married now," Vivian insisted. "And we are married. We don't want to wait to be with each other." She paused, her bottom lip trembling a little. "Not after what happened to Jordy."

Brennan had been wondering if that was playing into this. Jordy was a classmate who'd had the misfortune to be diagnosed with a rare form of cancer, and after a long battle, he'd died. Both Vivian and Seth had been friends with Jordy since kindergarten, so it had hit them pretty hard. It'd hit Brennan hard, too, knowing that someone's life could turn on a dime.

Brennan sighed. "What happened to Jordy was awful," he agreed, "but you can't make life decisions based on that."

"Sure we can." Seth said that so fast that he had been clearly ready with this particular point of the argument. "We're not going to waste another minute of our lives." He paused, slid glances between Ruby and him. "And you shouldn't, either."

"Agreed," Vivian quickly added. "It's obvious you two have had a thing for each other for years, and you've stayed apart because of some old water under a very old bridge."

Apparently, Vivian's *observation* stunned Ruby as much as it did Brennan, because neither of them said anything. However, they did look at each other. One quick look that still managed to have the usual kick of heat whenever their eyes met. It was because of that heat that Brennan couldn't argue with what their kids had just said. Ruby and he had, indeed, had a thing for each other for years.

A scalding hot thing.

And there was that "old water, old bridge" stuff holding them back. That, and Ruby probably wasn't sure she wanted to hand over her heart to him again so it could get crushed. She had a right to feel that way after all the heart-crushing he'd done to her way back when.

After some long "stunned to silence" moments, Ruby finally cleared her throat and managed to speak. "What I feel or don't feel for Brennan has nothing to do with what's going on now. You two should wait before you dive into marriage."

Vivian lifted her chin in what Brennan had no trouble interpreting as a defiant gesture. "Well, we didn't wait. We've already dived in and you're both just going to have to accept it."

With that ultimatum delivered and with her chin still aimed plenty high, Vivian took hold of Seth's hand, and they headed out of the room. Seconds later, Brennan heard the front door slam. He debated going after them, but he couldn't figure out anything he could say that wouldn't just make them dig in their heels even harder. Besides, he had to take a moment to try to wrap his mind around this.

"Crap," Ruby snarled, and pressing her hands to both sides of her head, she anchored her back against the wall and slid down to sit on the floor.

Obviously, she needed to do some mind-wrapping around this as well. She didn't start muttering things like *what the heck are we going to do?* Nor did Ruby mention anything about that old attraction and hurt that Seth and Vivian had thrown in their faces. Neither did Brennan. However, he did follow suit, and on a long sigh, he sat down on the floor next to Ruby.

"This is about Jordy," Brennan restated.

Ruby made an immediate sound of agreement. "Our kids think getting married will help with that. It won't," she said without any doubts.

Brennan didn't have any doubts, either. Their kids were eighteen and needed to focus on college or getting training that would lead to jobs.

"I'm not sure we have a legal option to get the marriage annulled," he threw out there. Brennan hoped by talking this out, Ruby and he could come up with a way to undo what had been done.

She made another sound of agreement. "They're both going to school on scholarships, but we're ponying up part of the expenses. If we threaten to withhold the money, that could cause a rift we might not be able to fix."

"Yeah, I've already gone there." Gone there and dismissed it. The only thing withholding money would accomplish would be to make Seth and Vivian broke and estranged from their parents.

Groaning and shaking her head, Ruby turned and met his gaze. "This isn't easy for me to say, but we might just have to swallow this until…"

She stopped, but Brennan had no trouble filling in that particular blank. Either their kids would make the marriage work—a slim chance at their ages—or the marriage would fail, and they'd have to go through the hell and back that Ruby and he had been through when their own relationships had tanked.

"We'll have to swallow it," he muttered. Brennan paused and had a quick debate as to what to say about the other thing their kids had thrown in their faces. "They were right, though, about us having a thing for each other."

Her gaze stayed locked with his. Firmly locked. And she didn't dispute what he'd just said. She couldn't because even now, when things were nowhere near being rosy, the heat was there.

Ruby's nod was slow and hesitant, but it was still an acknowledgment of the truth. "Yes, they were right. Well, right-ish, anyway."

Brennan frowned, not caring much for the *ish* she'd tacked on to that. There was no *ish* when it came to the way Ruby caused all these stirrings inside him.

"We'd be stupid to act on an attraction now," she went on. "Not when we already have so much to deal with."

Again, no argument from him. Jumping in headfirst would be reckless, and they did have plenty to deal with. But apparently Brennan was feeling both stupid and reckless.

And that was why he leaned in and kissed Ruby.

CHAPTER THREE

EVEN THOUGH RUBY saw the kiss coming, she still froze. For a second, anyway. Then she felt the kick of heat from Brennan's mouth.

Amazing heat.

Heat that put her in a time machine and sent her zooming back to their days in high school. Oh, the man had not lost his particular skill in this area. Nope. Plenty of skill that did an immediate job of firing her up.

Ruby heard herself moan. A sound of both pleasure and need. And her body reacted. Mercy, did it. She felt the blaze turn into a wildfire, and it settled in all the wrong parts of her. One part in particular. That should have been a Texas-sized red flag since this was definitely something they shouldn't be doing.

Should they?

She had to force herself to push aside the heat and recall they were in the middle of a crisis with their kids. Added to that, there was a reason Brennan and she had stayed apart all those years. The problem was Ruby was having a tough time recalling exactly the reason she'd kept her distance from him.

Brennan made it even harder for her by sliding his hand around the back of her neck and deepening the kiss. He moaned, too, but his sounded a whole lot hotter than hers, and she could have sworn that all that extra heat went straight into the kiss.

He tasted good. Like something she hadn't had for a very long time. Like something she desperately wanted.

Like something she shouldn't be having or wanting.

It was that last thought that finally gave her the jolt of good sense to make her aware that she'd obviously gone wrong on this particular adventure. Ruby forced herself to move back. It wasn't easy. But she finally convinced her mouth to leave Brennan's. Unfortunately, eliminating the contact didn't erase the sensations Brennan and his clever mouth had caused.

"Uh," she managed to say.

Brennan looked into her eyes, and the corner of that pleasure-giving mouth lifted into a smile. "You aren't going to regret that," he insisted.

Ruby might have disputed that, *might have*, but she heard a sound that had her deciding to table any discussions about the scalding kiss Brennan and she had just shared. That was because she heard the front door open.

"It's me," Vivian called out. "I'm just here to get my things."

There was no mistaking the anger Ruby heard in her daughter's voice. No mistaking, either, Vivian's quickly approaching footsteps. Ruby managed to get to her feet. So did Brennan. But when Vivian rounded the corner of the hall, she came to a quick stop and eyed them both.

Ruby knew Brennan and she weren't sporting neon signs that they'd just kissed, but they must have looked guilty of doing just that, because Vivian smiled a little. Then she must have recalled that she was seriously pissed off at them, because the smile vanished and her eyes narrowed.

"You aren't going to stop me from getting my things," Vivian insisted.

That rid Ruby of the last of the heat from the kiss, and she sighed again. Something she was certain she'd be doing a lot in the coming days.

"No, I won't stop you," Ruby said. "But I would like for us to have a calm discussion about what you're doing."

Brennan must have taken that as his cue to leave, maybe to attempt his own discussion with his son. He turned, then stopped and locked gazes with Ruby. She was pretty sure he was having a debate as to what to say.

However, she was wrong about that.

No debate. Nope. Brennan dropped another kiss on her mouth, drawled an "I'll see you later," and he strolled out.

Ruby stood there and watched him go. Well, she watched his backside. Along with being a supreme kisser, the man had a great butt that was well showcased in his great-fitting jeans.

"Well, I'm glad my marriage has made you see the light about Brennan," Vivian declared, and she went into her room.

Ruby yanked herself out of her gawking, out of the effects of that gawking, too, and she followed Vivian into the bedroom. "I haven't seen the light," Ruby insisted. "It was just a kiss."

All right, it was two kisses and a whole boatload of feelings that went with them. Ruby decided to keep that to herself, though.

Vivian gave her the flattest look humanly possible and went to her closet to haul out her big suitcase. "I don't know why you won't just move on with your life," she said, putting the suitcase on the bed.

"I have moved on," Ruby insisted.

Hadn't she?

She had her own real estate business. Owned her house. Had no debt. And had a daughter. A defiant one who obviously sucked at packing.

Doling out another of those sighs, Ruby went closer and refolded the jeans that Vivian had tossed into the suitcase.

"You haven't moved on after Dad," Vivian continued, dragging out more clothes from her dresser drawer.

"But I have," Ruby insisted.

And on this, Ruby was certain. She'd moved on mainly because her feelings for Carson Dayton just hadn't been that deep. At times that made her sad. Other times, she was just glad she hadn't had to go through an extreme heartbreak when their relationship had ended.

Vivian rolled her eyes as only a riled teenager could. "You're too afraid to trust your heart again." The willy-nilly packing continued with her tossing panties and bras into the suitcase. "Brennan hurt you when you were my age, and you've never gotten over that." She put a pause on the willy-nilly and turned to look at Ruby. "Except that maybe you finally have. The kissing is a good start."

Well, the kiss itself was certainly good. Better than good. But Ruby wasn't sure it was the start of anything. Despite what Brennan had told her about not regretting it, that might be exactly what he was doing right now.

"I know you must hate Seth's mom for what she did," Vivian went on. "But that was the past. You need to let it go." She paused again. "Can you let it go, or will this research you're going to have to do just make it all worse again?"

That fell into the "to be determined" category, but Ruby was certain the research wasn't going to be fun.

"When you're eighteen, the hurt seems like a deeper cut," Ruby admitted.

Vivian tossed a pair of flip-flops into the suitcase and looked at her again. "It was a deep cut no matter what age," she said, sounding much older and wiser than her years. "FYI, Seth's mom was sorry for what she did."

That got Ruby's attention. "How do you know?"

With a lift of her shoulder, Vivian returned to her packing. "She talked to Seth about it right before she died. She told him she was thinking about asking you to come to see her so she could try to apologize."

Everything inside Ruby went as still as glass. She hadn't known that. Maybe didn't want to know it. But then she stopped and silently cursed. Of course she wanted to know it. Maybe it was those two kisses or the amazing fit of Brennan's jeans, but she suddenly wanted to accept that mistakes had been made, hearts had been broken and the past was the past.

"I'm sure you'll hear other things about Seth's mom when you're doing the research," Vivian continued. "But she was hurt by all the gossip of being pregnant at eighteen. She was hurt that she'd done something to lose her best friend. Added to that, she never really believed Brennan loved her. Not the forever kind of love like Seth and me have."

Ruby had been listening to all of that, but she mentally stopped on that last part. That was because she recalled just how it felt to be madly in love at eighteen. And it had been love for Brennan. Maybe that love wouldn't have been able to give them a happily-ever-after, but it'd been strong and certain.

Just as Vivian's was for Seth.

Ruby went with another sigh and took hold of her daughter's shoulders so she could look her straight in the eyes. "I love you, and while I don't approve of what Seth and you did, I will always love you."

Tears watered Vivian's eyes. "Oh, Mom." She hauled Ruby into a full bear hug. "I love you, too. I just want you to be happy. And I want you to be happy for Seth and me," she quickly tacked on to that.

Ruby wanted to say that she'd be happier if they'd waited at least a couple of years before getting married, but that would no doubt just lead to another argument that would have Vivian storming out with her messily packed suitcase.

"Look," Ruby said, "you can't expect me to be jumping for joy about this. I had dreams of being there with you when you said 'I do.' But I can be happy for you if you're happy."

"Oh, Mom," Vivian repeated.

Ruby held her close and got a flood of the wonderful memories of watching her baby girl grow. There'd been plenty of hard times, of course, but they were overshadowed by the joy Vivian had brought her. Still, she was hoping Vivian would hold off on adding that kind of "joy" to her life.

Vivian had that giddy smile again when she pulled back. Ruby preferred the giddiness to the anger, but there was something else she needed to get off her chest.

"You two are using protection, aren't you?" Ruby asked.

That earned Ruby another eye roll and a huff. "Of course. We don't want to make the same mistakes his parents and you did. Sorry," she added in a mutter, and her cheeks flushed with embarrassment.

Ruby wasn't offended in the least, and hearing this meant she could breathe a little easier. Well, breathe easier about an unplanned pregnancy, anyway. The marriage would no doubt give her a boatload of concerns.

She frowned when she heard the knock at the door, because she so wasn't in any mood to deal with a visitor, but then Vivian's phone dinged with a text, and she announced, "It's Seth. He's already packed his things and he's here to pick me up."

Vivian practically started running to the front of the house before Ruby could ask where they were going. She followed her daughter, intending to get an answer to that, when Vivian threw open the front door. Yes, it was Seth all right. But he wasn't alone. Brennan was with him.

Despite everything else going on, Ruby's heart did a little leap, and for just a second she got a reminder of what it was like to be a teenager in the throes of an attraction. Obviously, Vivian was in the throes, too, because she jumped right into Seth's arms and kissed him.

Leaving Brennan and Ruby to stare at each other.

Since it hadn't been that long since they'd done their own kissing, the memories were fresh enough to give Ruby another slam of heat. She might have sighed in a different kind of way, of a woman looking at one seriously hot guy, but the kids ended their lip-lock, and Seth turned to her in such a way that Ruby could see he had something to tell her.

"I'm going to take Vivian on a short honeymoon," Seth explained. "Nothing big or long. Just a couple of nights at a hotel on the Riverwalk."

The Riverwalk was in San Antonio, less than an hour away, so at least they wouldn't have a long drive ahead of them.

Apparently, Vivian approved of that, because she clapped her hands while dancing on her tiptoes. She kissed Seth again, and when she slid her hand to cup his chin, the glint of her new wedding rings flashed in Ruby's eyes. Talk about an "in your face" reminder that her daughter was married now.

"Seth and I have agreed to disagree on this marriage," Brennan added. "And I transferred some money to his account so Vivian and he can have some nice meals while they're in San Antonio."

Since Ruby had had the idea of doing the same, she couldn't fault Brennan for that. So, she was in the "agree to disagree" boat right along with them.

"I'll get my suitcase," Vivian gushed, and she ran back toward her room.

Ruby expected an awkward silence, and there was a couple of seconds of it, but her daughter broke speed records going to and from her bedroom. With her rolling suitcase, Vivian rushed back into the foyer, hooked her free arm around Seth and got them moving toward his truck.

"Have fun," Brennan muttered, sounding as concerned as Ruby was.

Their kids clearly had no concerns, though, because they were smiling ear to ear as they waved goodbye to go on their honeymoon. Ruby was glad she didn't have to say that last part aloud because it would have stuck in her throat. Of course, she was aware that Vivian and Seth were already lovers, but it was another thing to consider them going off for a weekend of married sex.

"Yeah," Brennan added, as if he knew exactly what she was thinking.

They stood there watching until Seth's truck was out of sight. Then the awkward silence came. It was accompanied by the heat that was steamrolling through the door. Ruby hadn't noticed the heat when she'd been focused on the kids, but she was sure as heck noticing it now.

Noticing Brennan, too.

It was impossible for her not to be aware of him because they were standing shoulder to shoulder. Touching. And with those vivid memories of their kiss just hanging in the air.

"Well, we've got some options," he said, looking down at her. "We can stand in this doorway and roast. We can go inside and get drunk. Or we can go on a date."

As options went, that was a wide range. Roasting was a definite no-no. Ditto for getting drunk. That would only lead to sex. A date might do that as well. Then again, anything and everything with Brennan might lead in that particular direction. And that was why Ruby didn't even try to fight it.

She was going on a date with the man who'd crushed her heart six ways to Sunday. And if she wasn't careful, he'd get the chance to do that again.

CHAPTER FOUR

BRENNAN FIGURED RUBY had a whole lot of doubts about this date. So did he. Not the same doubts as she did since hers almost certainly centered around not wanting to get hurt again. His were more about making sure that hurt didn't happen at all while they both tried to come to terms with the blow their kids had dealt them.

It was those things—the blow and the doubts—that had made Brennan decide to keep this date low-key. That wouldn't have happened had they gone to any of the restaurants in town, where they would have stirred up gossip and felt as if they were in a fishbowl for all to see. Instead, he was driving Ruby to his ranch, where he planned to grill them some steaks.

A grilling date like that wouldn't give the gossips any fodder. Well, not much, unless some of Ruby's neighbors had noticed her getting into his truck and driving away with him. If so, there'd be speculation that the two people who'd had the hots for each other were finally going to do something about it, but even that speculation would take a back seat to news of Seth and Vivian's elopement.

Of course, Brennan's mind was on that hasty marriage, but it was on Ruby, too. He could blame the kisses for that. Hard to block out thoughts of a woman who had been firing him up for decades. And she had, indeed, fired him up. That was something his body wasn't going to let him forget. First, though, he wanted to open up a different kind of emotion. Venting, maybe. Maybe pure "pissed off" anger. Maybe resignation. No matter which, he thought it was best to go ahead and get this marriage out in the open.

"I guess this elopement makes you and me in-laws of sorts," Brennan threw out there.

Ruby had stayed pretty much still and silent so far on this short drive, but that caused her to turn to him. "Yes. In-laws who'll have to deal with the fallout if things don't stay rosy."

There was that. The non-rosy factor. Marriage could sometimes be a hard road. The wrong road, too. Brennan figured the first would definitely apply to their kids, but the *wrong* part was still in the "to be determined" category.

"My folks got married at nineteen," he reminded her. "They're still together." That was the only example of a success he could recall off the top of his head. "Of course, I got married at eighteen, and my marriage tanked."

Ruby made a soft sound of agreement. "Ditto for my relationship. Too young. Too stupid. Too rash."

All of which might apply to Seth and Vivian. "I considered standing my ground and telling them either they got an annulment or no college funds. But considering the too-young and too-rash parts, they'd probably just leave and never speak to me again."

"Yes, and then we wouldn't be there to pick up any pieces that might need picking up." Ruby groaned, leaned her head against the window as he made the turn to Thoroughbred Lake Ranch. "Vivian and I talked while she was packing and she said something that's niggling away at me."

Brennan's attention hadn't strayed far from Ruby—again, he could thank those kisses for that—but that comment caused him to make glances at her so he could try to figure out where this was going.

"Seth told me Vivian's not pregnant," he stated, hoping like the devil that it was the truth.

"She's not. That's not what we talked about. It was about Alice." She paused, maybe to let this shift in topic sink in. As best he could recall, Ruby and he had never discussed her former bestie and his late ex. "Vivian told me that Alice had regrets about what happened back in high school."

"She did." Brennan pulled to a stop in front of the house, but he didn't turn off the engine. He just sat there, letting the memories from the past wash over him. "Alice knew what we'd done hurt you, and she regretted it. I regretted it," he added, just in case Ruby didn't know that.

In fact, it was the biggest regret of his life. When he'd been younger, he'd put the blame for his having sex with Alice on both of them being drunk, but there was no way he should have let things get that far. At that time, Ruby and he had gone on three dates, and he'd known that she had feelings for him. Hell, he'd had feelings for her, too, but he blew all that to smithereens by acting on impulse.

Ruby dragged in a long breath. "Alice's remorse changes the slant I'll take on the research for the Last Ride Society."

Brennan had put that research way back in his mind, but it was obvious that Ruby hadn't if she'd applied Alice's regret to her research plans. "Maybe that means working on the report won't be so hard for you."

"Oh, it'll still be hard, but I'm hoping I can remember some of the good times. Because there were good times."

"Yeah," he agreed. "One of those good times was us having our kids. I'm hanging on to that, hoping it'll get me past the point of wanting to throttle Seth for being so…eighteen."

Ruby smiled. Then she chuckled. He thought it was a good thing they'd moved on to something other than the shock and anger. Then again, the kisses had probably helped them cut some corners there.

Still smiling just a little, Ruby looked out the window at the pastures and the house. "It's beautiful here."

"Thanks," he muttered, and then it occurred to him that this was the first time she'd been here since he had inherited the place. He had brought her here when they'd been teenagers, but he'd made a lot of improvements since then. "It's the only place I've ever wanted to call home."

Not exactly small talk. It was the truth. He was anchored here, and he'd hoped that Seth would be, too.

Ruby made another of those sounds of agreement and shifted in the seat again to look at him. Ruby's gaze stayed locked with his for several moments. The kind of eye lock a person had when they were trying to suss out something. Brennan was right there on the same page with her, and he nearly said they probably wouldn't be working out anything tonight.

But then, once again, he remembered those two kisses.

Those had certainly seemed to work out, well, something, and that something was that this heat between them was not only still there, but it also wasn't going away anytime soon. Apparently, Ruby felt the same way, because she moved toward him just as Brennan leaned in her direction.

And the third kiss happened.

Oh, man. It was as good as the others. Better, since they weren't dealing with the initial shock of their kids' elopement. The shock had worn off, some, and that made plenty of room for the heat.

When they'd been in high school, they'd made out in his truck, too, but this was so much better. Ruby brought some experience and a whole lot of need to this kiss. She immediately deepened it while fighting to get out of her seat belt. Brennan did a battle to get out of his as well, and without the restraints holding them back, they latched on to each other.

He pulled her to him, dragging her closer. Not that he had to work too hard on that since she was doing her own share of dragging. Despite the console between them, they managed to land their upper bodies together so that her rather ample breasts pressed against his chest. His chest obviously approved of that, but with the combination of the hungry kiss, it fired up his body to the "take Ruby now" mode.

And that couldn't happen.

Even though his body was burning and his mind was cloudy, Brennan forced himself to remember where they were. Right in front of his house, and there was plenty of sunlight left that any one of his six ranch hands would be able to see them if they wandered this way. Best for his workers not to see their boss acting like a lust-filled teenager.

"We should take this inside," Brennan managed to say when Ruby and he finally broke for air.

With her breath gusting and her face flushed with arousal, Ruby eased back from him and met his gaze. He could see the debate in her eyes. Part of her no doubt wanted to dive back in. So did Brennan. Dive back in and have sex with the woman he'd been having fantasies about for years. But Ruby's thirty-six years had obviously also given her common sense.

"Wrong time, wrong place," she muttered.

"But not the wrong man," he insisted, and Brennan waited, hoping like the devil that she didn't dispute that.

With their gazes locked, she slowly shook her head. "No, not the wrong man. And maybe it's time I did something about that."

CHAPTER FIVE

SITTING IN HER home office, Ruby forced herself to finish some paperwork on the sale of a house that was scheduled for closing in two weeks. Routine paperwork, thank goodness, that didn't require a lot of brainpower. Which was good.

Because her brain was on Brennan.

The night before, they'd kissed the daylights out of each other in his truck, and she'd made a Texas-sized confession to him. That he wasn't the wrong man. She was certain that was the truth.

Well, almost certain.

And it was because of that tiny thread of doubt that she'd asked Brennan for some time to come to terms with not only leaping into a relationship with him but also with their kids' marriage. She'd made some progress with both. Yes, she still had a doubt or two about Brennan, but she figured he was a risk worth taking. As for the kids, well, they'd be back from their honeymoon tomorrow, and Ruby hoped she could sit down with them and come up with some realistic living and budget goals.

All thoughts of such goals slid right out of her mind when she got a message from Brennan. Clearly, he wasn't much of a texter, because he'd sent no actual message but rather an emoji of a dancing horse. It made her laugh, which meant he was a good texter after all. It took her a couple of moments to find one, but she sent him an emoji of a dancing duck.

Mercy, she needed this levity. Needed the contact with him even if it happened to be in an animated cartoon conversation. It was that levity that caused her to put aside the paperwork. To put aside that small shred of doubt she had about him. And to get on with proving to herself that he was, indeed, the right man.

Up for some company? she texted.

His answer came right away. Your place or mine?

That flooded her with warmth. Then heat. Yours. I'll be there soon.

Ruby didn't just dash out the door, though that was what she wanted to do. She took the time to freshen her makeup and brush her hair. What she didn't do was change into sexy underwear, but that was because she didn't own any. Unlike her daughter, she didn't make a habit of shimmying into "barely there" lace. Still, it was something she might consider if this turned into a fling with Brennan.

The word *fling* gave her a few moments of hesitation, but that didn't stop her from going to her car and heading toward the Thoroughbred Ranch. However, that word gave her something to consider on her drive. She wasn't looking for a forever deal with Brennan.

Was she?

No, she tried to assure herself since, after all, she had to guard her heart just a little. But she wouldn't mind acting on all this heat that was between them and seeing where it would take them. Of course, it would take them to bed. That was obvious. However, there might be more than just sex.

With that hopeful but somewhat scary thought, she turned onto the ranch road and watched the house come into view. The porch lights lit up the porch that wrapped around three sides of the place. A stunning view, what with the clear night sky glittering with stars and a crescent moon. But what made the view even more stunning was that Brennan was waiting in the doorway for her.

"I was afraid you'd change your mind," he said the moment she stepped from her car.

"I was afraid I might, too," Ruby admitted.

She didn't change her mind, though, about what she wanted to do, so she went up the porch steps to him, pulled him into her arms and kissed him. If she'd had any doubts whatsoever, that would have rid her of them.

"I'm glad you came." Brennan broke the kiss just long enough to say that, and then he took her mouth again.

His kiss was long, slow and deep—perfect—and Ruby might have anchored herself right there in the doorway for it to continue if the mosquitoes hadn't started buzzing around them. While keeping that kiss long, slow and deep, Brennan batted the insects away, hooked his arm around her waist, pulled her inside and kicked the door shut. He reached behind her and locked it.

Just like that, they had the privacy for this to escalate. And it did.

Ruby didn't even try to slow things down, not that she could have managed it anyway. She just let herself be swept away with the heat and need.

Brennan gave that need a huge boost when he pressed himself against her, bringing back memories of when they'd been teenagers. Making new memories, too, because he no longer had a rangy teen body. The man was built, solid muscle, a side effect from all those years of ranching. Ruby knew she was benefiting from that work because she had plenty to hang on to.

It turned out that she needed the hanging on since she thought her legs had dissolved when Brennan added some touching to the firestorm of kissing. He slid his hand between them, cupping her right breast and swiping his thumb over her nipple.

Oh, yes. No doubts whatsoever about this.

Ruby did her own share of touching, running her hands over those tight muscles in his back, but she recalled something else that had once set Brennan on fire. She kissed his neck and was rewarded when he made a low groan of pleasure.

She'd heard him make that sound before, though back then she had been well aware that she was going to have to nip the making out in the bud. Back then, Ruby had felt they hadn't been together long enough for them to have sex. Especially since he would have been her first. Now, though, all things were possible.

Brennan certainly made her aware of all things possible when he returned the favor and kissed her neck as well. He didn't stop there, thank goodness. He went lower, sliding his body against hers while he kissed her breasts through her top. Apparently, he also recalled that was a hot spot for her, and he chuckled when she made her own sound of pleasure.

Apparently, her moaning spurred him on, because he kept kissing. Kept touching. Kept building the heat higher, higher, higher.

She hadn't thought it possible, but things started to move even faster. The battle started to get naked. Ruby won when she managed to get off his shirt and was able to get her hands on all those muscles. She didn't have time, though, to savor her victory, because Brennan slid off her top and bra and then took his mouth back to her breasts.

Oh, mercy.

This was, indeed, her hot spot, and the pleasure shot through her. Ruby figured she probably would have lost her balance if Brennan hadn't scooped her up into his arms.

Along with being incredibly hot, the man could multi-task as well. He continued to kiss her as he carried her through the living room and into a hall. The kissing didn't stop, either, when he laid her on a bed. In fact, it got even better because Brennan followed, landing on top of her.

Since their high school "making out" sessions hadn't involved a bed, this was a sexual luxury of not having to navigate the seat of a truck. She could wrap her arms around him, feel the weight of him on her. And they could keep on kissing while they worked on the "getting naked" part.

Obviously, Brennan was better than she was at clothing removal. While he tormented her breasts with his mouth, he shimmied off her skirt. Then her panties. And he kissed his way down her body. Ruby got another slam of pleasure that caused the urgency to skyrocket.

"Take off your jeans," she insisted.

Brennan complied, but again he went with the multi-tasking approach. He got up, continuing to tongue kiss her stomach while he tugged off his boots, jeans. And then his boxers.

More pleasure came just from looking at him, and she might have savored that view a couple of seconds if he hadn't dropped back down on her. Naked skin to naked skin now. Added to that, he'd landed in just the right place so that his sex touched hers. The urgency became a scalding need, and she had to have him now.

"Condom," he snarled when she lifted her hips to take him inside her.

Good grief. She hadn't even considered safe sex. Not

good. Especially since both of them had already dealt with unplanned pregnancies.

He reached across to the nightstand, fumbled around in the drawer and came out with a condom. Brennan kissed her while he put it on, and he kept kissing her while he pushed inside her.

Finally!

All the years of wanting him. All that heat. All that need. Finally, they were together just as she'd always wanted.

Brennan clearly wanted this, too. Was also clearly good at making the heat and need soar even higher as he began the strokes inside her. Strokes that would, of course, sate this fierce need she had for him, but it would also make things end too soon.

Ruby hung on as long as she could, but she couldn't stop her body from climaxing. The pleasure raced through her, and she anchored herself by clamping her arms around Brennan. *Finally!* she mentally repeated.

Moments later, Brennan got his own "finally" when he followed her over that edge.

CHAPTER SIX

FOR YEARS, BRENNAN HAD fantasized about having sex with Ruby, and he could now say that the real deal had way exceeded any fantasy. Added to that, he'd gotten the bonus of shower sex along with having her stay the night in his bed.

Everything felt right when he opened his eyes and saw her lying next to him. She was naked, with the sheet only partially covering her from the waist down. All in all, a very pleasant sight to start his day.

He mentally groaned, though, when he glanced at the clock and saw that it was already eight o'clock. Not especially late for most, but he was a rancher, and his day usually started two hours earlier. His ranch hands would no doubt be speculating as to why he hadn't already made an appearance to spell out the duties for the day.

Trying not to wake Ruby, Brennan eased out of bed, located his phone in the pocket of his discarded jeans and sent a quick text to his foreman, Danny Monroe, to let him know that he'd be taking the morning off. Since Ruby's car was parked out in front of the house, Danny would no doubt be able to figure out what was going on, but thankfully the man wasn't a gossip.

Gossip, however, would happen. That was just the way it was in a small town. Brennan hoped that Ruby was ready to deal with that, because he wanted a whole lot more nights and mornings like this with her.

"Now, that's a sight to see," he heard her say.

Brennan glanced up from his phone and saw that she was sliding her gaze down the length of his naked body. He smiled because he saw the heat in her cool blue eyes. Heat that caused him to hope there'd be a round of morning sex, followed by some breakfast and then maybe more sex. His body just couldn't seem to get enough of her.

He set aside his phone, got back on the bed and kissed her. Yeah, this was the right way to start the day. The kiss went straight to his groin and clouded his mind enough that he nearly blurted out that he was in love with her. Talk about the absolute wrong time, wrong place. It was too soon.

But it was true.

It had occurred to Brennan sometime shortly after shower sex. That he was not only in love with Ruby but he had been for a very long time. He was hoping they'd get that chance at love they'd never gotten.

She made a sound of pleasure, slid her arms around him and deepened the kiss. His groin definitely approved of that, and he would have kicked this foreplay up a notch if he hadn't heard a sound he hadn't wanted to hear.

"Someone's unlocking the front door," he relayed to Ruby.

Danny had a key, but the foreman wouldn't have just let himself in. But Seth would have, and he definitely had a key.

"Mom?" someone called out. Vivian. "I saw your car outside. Seth and I are here."

Hell. Normally, Brennan would have enjoyed seeing his son, but the timing sucked.

"I'll be right there," Ruby answered as she scrambled off the bed.

The race around the room to find their clothes began. It wasn't easy since garments were scattered everywhere, though they managed to get everything tugged and pulled on. Of course, they still looked as if they'd had a very enjoyable night of sex. Nothing he could do about that. Brennan probably didn't help matters there by taking the time to kiss Ruby. She took the time, too, to savor it a couple of moments before they both sighed and went to face their kids.

The pleasure from that kiss quickly evaporated, though, when Brennan got one look at his son's face. He muttered another *hell*.

"What's wrong?" Ruby and Brennan asked in unison.

Ruby had obviously seen her daughter's tear-reddened eyes. It coordinated with the miserable look in Seth's. Obviously, their kids' night hadn't been as pleasurable as Ruby's and his had been.

"Mom," Vivian said, sliding glances between Brennan and her. "You two are…together."

"What's wrong?" Ruby asked, maybe to dodge the comment, or, like Brennan, she was just anxious to hear what had caused this swift turn of mood in their kids. They'd been happily giddy when they'd left on their honeymoon only thirty-six hours ago.

Seth cleared his throat, and even though he slid his arm around Vivian, he wasn't giving his new bride a lusty, love-filled look. "I got a call from the justice of the peace who did our wedding. He said he'd forgotten to renew his certification, so our marriage isn't legal. We'd need to do it again."

Of all the things Brennan figured could be wrong, that hadn't been on his list. He didn't curse. Didn't cheer, either, because it was obvious the kids were torn up about this. Whatever *this* was.

One glance at Ruby, and Brennan could tell their kids' dismal moods had given her some hope. Brennan had hope as well, because if Seth and Vivian had wanted to be married, they likely wouldn't have come here. They would have just found another justice of the peace to redo the vows.

"Well?" Vivian said like some kind of accusation that she aimed at her mother. "Aren't you going to say something like this is for the best, that we dodged a bullet or some other nonsense?"

Brennan wanted to spring to Ruby's defense, but it was obvious that Vivian was spoiling for a fight. Maybe because she didn't know what to do with all the hurt over Jordy's death and the anger from the screwup by the justice of the peace. In contrast, Seth just looked weary, as if all the fight had gone out of him. And maybe it had. It was possible hearing news of their non-marriage had prompted a discussion and then an argument between Vivian and him.

When Ruby didn't bite on the argument Vivian wanted, the young woman turned to Brennan. "You never wanted us to be married."

"No," Brennan agreed, thinking for a moment what he wanted to say, what he wanted Seth and Vivian to hear. "But that's because I know how hard it is to make a marriage work when you're just eighteen. If you want to do that work, then I'll do whatever I can to help."

Vivian's expression registered outrage. Yep, spoiling for a fight, which clearly no one in the house was going to give her. It would have given her a good springboard to storm out with Seth, creating an "us against them" scenario.

"If you want to find another justice of the peace," Ruby

said, her voice calm, "maybe I can go with you. Maybe Brennan, too. Then we can be there to celebrate with you."

"You don't want that," Vivian insisted. "You *can't* want that." Tears began to spill down her cheeks, and that prompted Seth to pull her into his arms.

"Could you give us a minute?" Seth muttered, and with Vivian in tow, they headed toward his bedroom.

Ruby immediately looked up at Brennan and sighed. "Not exactly the breakfast sex I had planned for us."

Despite everything, Brennan had to smile. Mercy, he'd needed that. He needed to kiss her as well, so that was what he did. He pulled her to him, gave her a thorough kiss and then just held her. The timing wasn't much better than it had been before the kids had arrived with their marriage news, but Brennan went with it anyway.

"I want you to remember saying I was the right man," he threw out there.

That caused her to ease back just a little to look up at him. "You are."

Some of the tightness in his chest went away. "I don't want last night to have been a one-off. Or rather a two-off, since we also had shower sex."

She smiled, and man, it was good to see. Ruby was beautiful, but when she smiled, she was a stunner. "Are you asking me to go steady?"

"I am," he readily admitted. "But I'm asking for more, too. I want you to give us a chance. A chance we should have had eighteen years ago."

Her smile faded, but she kept her gaze locked with his. He could almost hear her trying to work out what he'd just meant. Since Brennan didn't want her to have to guess about this, he just spelled it out.

"I'm in love with you, Ruby, and I want to let go of the past and have a future with you."

She seemed to freeze. Not exactly a "deer in the headlights" look but close. It took her a couple of seconds to open her mouth to speak. However, before she could say anything, Vivian and Seth came back in. Talk about lousy timing, but at least Vivian was no longer crying.

"I'm sorry," Vivian said right off the bat, and she slid her gaze to both Ruby and him. "Everything just balled up inside me, and it all came out because I know you two don't actually want Seth and me to be married right now."

"No, we don't," Ruby admitted. "But we want you both to be happy."

"Happy," Vivian repeated. She looked up at Seth and gave him a subtle nod.

"Vivian and I think we'll wait to redo the wedding," Seth explained. "Maybe in a year or two."

Brennan felt more of his muscles unclench, and the mountain of relief came. He didn't cheer or laugh, but that was exactly what he wanted to do. He was betting Ruby wanted to do the same.

"A year or two sounds good," Brennan settled for saying, hoping that would extend to at least after college graduation.

"We still want to live together, though," Vivian insisted. "We can get an apartment in Austin, and it'll be cheaper than two dorm rooms."

"All right," Ruby agreed, looking up at Brennan, who gave her a quick sound of agreement.

"We can drive up today to look at apartments if you want," Brennan added.

"Thanks. That'd be great," Seth said, but he glanced at Ruby. "Unless you two have plans, that is."

Best not to mention that breakfast sex could wait. But he didn't want to wait on Ruby's answer to what he'd said to her. "I just told Ruby that I'm in love with her," Brennan confessed.

Every trace of anger and anguish disappeared from Vivian's face, and she hurried to her mom to give her a hug. "Good. It was a long time coming."

"Yes, it was," Ruby readily agreed. When she finished hugging her daughter, she looked up at Brennan. "But I think everything is finally right."

Brennan grinned and pulled Ruby into his arms for a long kiss. Everything was, indeed, finally right. The right time, the right place.

And the right woman.

* * * * *

HARLEQUIN
PLUS

Try the best multimedia subscription service for romance readers like you!

Read, Watch and Play.

Experience the easiest way to get the romance content you crave.

Start your **FREE TRIAL** at
<u>www.harlequinplus.com/freetrial</u>.